PRAISE FOR T

'Incredible pace, terrifically intrig
characters and a searing hot settin
A masterclass in crime fiction, I loved it!'

—Andrea Mara, No.1 *Sunday Times* bestselling author of *No One Saw a Thing*

'If ever there was a book written for summer, this is it . . . deliciously addictive, crackling with cattiness, secrets and betrayal.'

—John Marrs, bestselling author of *The One*

'A ripper of a thriller. Studying abroad forever changes eight young lives—in all the wrong ways. *The Outback* is a story about secrets and how they change who we are and who we become, a tale of friendship and betrayal and those exhilarating years when our friends are our universe. It's atmospheric, emotional, and twisty and destined to be one of the best thrillers of the year. Ace!'

—Alex Finlay, bestselling author of *Parents Weekend*

'With plot twist after plot twist, a richly drawn setting, and steeped in nail-biting tension, Sara Ochs's sophomore thriller, *The Outback*, was an absolute ride—I devoured it in one breathless sitting.'

—Ashley Tate, international bestselling author of *Twenty-Seven Minutes*

'A total page-turner. Compelling, immersive and highly entertaining. Destination fiction at its best!'

—Allie Reynolds, author of *The Bay*

www.penguin.co.uk

PRAISE FOR *THE RESORT*

'A deadly, dangerous, beautiful nightmare.'

—Chris Whitaker, *New York Times* bestselling author of *We Begin at the End*

'*The Resort* is a knockout crime thriller. A stunningly written, twisting mystery, which keeps you glued from the first to the last page.'

—Cate Quinn, author of *Black Widows* and *The Clinic*

'A pacy and accomplished murder mystery… *The Beach* for a new generation—a hot contender for best travel thriller.'

—Janice Hallett, international bestselling author of *The Appeal*

'A fast-paced read, jam-packed with suspense. The idyllic setting, untrustworthy cast, and compulsive storyline make it the perfect summer thriller.'

—John Marrs, *USA Today* bestselling author of *The One*

'An escapist, up-all-night thriller that holds you under and doesn't let you surface for air.'

—Lucy Clarke, author of *One of the Girls*

'Propulsive and devilishly twisty ... Demands to be read in one breathless sitting.'

—Catherine Ryan Howard, international bestselling author of *56 Days*

'*The Resort* takes the delicious daydream of moving to a tropical beach resort to start fresh and turns it into a captivating, twisty nightmare. This is a thrilling vacation read that plunges you into another world where changing currents of trust, betrayal, and revenge will surprise you until the very last page.'

—Lisa Brideau, author of *Adrift*

ALSO BY SARA OCHS

The Resort

THE OUTBACK

SARA OCHS

PENGUIN BOOKS

TRANSWORLD PUBLISHERS

UK | USA | Canada | Ireland | Australia
India | New Zealand | South Africa

Transworld is part of the Penguin Random House group of companies whose addresses can be found at global.penguinrandomhouse.com.

Penguin Random House UK, One Embassy Gardens,
8 Viaduct Gardens, London SW11 7BW

penguin.co.uk

Penguin Random House UK

First published in Great Britain in 2025 by Penguin Books
an imprint of Transworld Publishers
Published in North America under the title *This Stays Between Us*

001

Printed and bound in Great Britain by Clays Ltd, Elcograf S.p.A.

The authorized representative in the EEA is Penguin Random House Ireland, Morrison Chambers, 32 Nassau Street, Dublin D02 YH68.

A CIP catalogue record for this book is available from the British Library

ISBN: 9781804991749

Penguin Random House is committed to a sustainable future for our business, our readers and our planet. This book is made from Forest Stewardship Council® certified paper.

MIX
Paper | Supporting responsible forestry
FSC® C018179
FSC
www.fsc.org

For Filip,

My partner in everything

1
CLAIRE

Now

THE MESSAGE SLINKS INTO my phone.

You up?

My eyes swing to the numbers at the top of my screen. 12:04. Just past a socially acceptable time on a Tuesday night to be awake.

I sigh, rolling onto my side, the mattress springs of my double bed shrieking under my weight. I clench my eyes tight, praying for the sleep that I know will evade me. Even so, I can't help but feel the pull back to the phone, those two words drawing me in.

I know exactly what he wants, and I know I'm weak enough to give it to him.

You're better than this, I think. But even I don't believe myself.

The thought unleashes it. The guilt I've become so familiar

with over the years. It creeps up my limbs, securing me in place, crawling into my throat and suffocating me. The regret all I can taste.

The reason I can never be good. The one night that turned me bad forever.

And I feel it begin. My chest tightening, my breath becoming thinner, a pounding in my head growing to match my rapidly increasing heartbeat. And just as my breath catches in my throat, dusty, I'm back there. The endless sky before me pockmarked with stars, the air cold and dry, the darkness of that night washing over me.

But a sound comes, quick and fast, stopping the memory from progressing further.

It takes me a moment to realize it's my phone again. My earlier resolve has shredded to pieces. I'll invite him over, I decide.

But when I check my screen, it's not the booty call I was expecting. The title of the group text shines at me through the darkness.

The Mob.

I suck in a breath, knowing what this is. Another plea from Ellery to get me to join the ten-year reunion she's organized back in Sydney. I've explained to her multiple times that I won't be coming, that I can't put myself through the painful memories that wait for me there. She seemed to have come around, but now that the reunion is only a week away, this must be a last-ditch effort.

My phone chimes again, the same group message. But this time the sender is different. Not Ellery, but Kyan.

I can't deal with this type of peer pressure tonight, not with the memory of that night thick and cloying. I silence the phone and roll back over, knowing even as I do that sleep is futile.

I toss and turn for another few minutes before giving up and pulling out my phone again.

There are now forty-seven more texts from the Mob.

That's a lot. Even for them.

I'm about to open the thread when another message comes in. But this one isn't part of the text chain. It's on Facebook Messenger. A direct message from Ellery Johnson.

Why would she be messaging me separately when she's on the group text?

But as unlikely as it seems, a part of me already knows. The same part that has been waiting years for the truth to come out.

With shaking fingers, I open the message. As soon as I do, a sharp, startled sound escapes from my lips.

Not sure if you've seen the group text, but they've found Phoebe's body.

I read the one-line message over and over, willing it to change.

My mind freezes on her name. *Phoebe.* And it all rushes back. Those turquoise eyes. Her body, so thin. Too thin. Her dark brown curls shaped into a short cut that framed her face and emphasized her sharp features.

The same hair that was wrapped tight in my palm that night ten years ago.

The same eyes that stared up at me, irises swimming with a mix of regret and sadness as I cradled a knife in my hand.

Even when I tried to convince myself this day would never come, I knew the truth was bound to catch up with me sometime.

Because it was me.

I was the one who killed Phoebe.

2
PHOEBE

Then

SYDNEY SUN BLEEDS THROUGH the windows, illuminating the bones of the Hamilton College dorm room that will be my home for the next few nights. Barely bigger than one of the closets at my family's house back in Atlanta, it fits two matching twin beds, each decorated with a scratchy blue blanket, two desks made of what I can only assume is the cheapest wood available in Australia, and a single wardrobe that looks like it has succumbed to a not-so-insignificant ant infestation.

But it may as well be a castle. I drop onto the bed closest to the door, the mattress sagging under my unsubstantial weight, and deposit my carry-on bag next to me.

A month away from real life. To do nothing but party and meet new people. This is exactly what I need.

A chance to start over. To leave what happened—what I did—behind forever.

I'm luxuriating in my fantasies for the next four weeks when a knock sounds at the door.

"Come in," I say, sitting up straight and tucking my short hair behind my ears, the new cut still feeling foreign beneath my fingers.

"Sorry to bother you." The resident advisor who helped me move in no less than twenty minutes ago is back. His lips, nearly lost amid a wave of painful acne across his chin, lift upwards as he sees me. "Your roommate has arrived."

As he heaves a giant suitcase over the threshold, I work to still the flutters in my abdomen. But they come to a standstill when I take in the lanky girl who follows him into the room, wisps of straw-colored hair matted to her damp forehead.

I feel my expectations lower immediately as I look at her slumped shoulders, her sheepish smile. But I force the grin back onto my face. She isn't the fabulous international roommate I was expecting, but I can work with this.

"Welcome," I say, my voice sugary. "Looks like you're stuck with me. I'm Phoebe."

Her skin is pale, and dark circles hang below her eyes. A smattering of freckles is just barely visible across her nose as if desperately waiting for their chance to come alive in the sunshine.

I begin to go in for a hug before I realize that the girl has awkwardly held out her hand. I shrug aside the odd formality and take it in mine.

"I'm Claire," she says in a soft American accent. She wears a weak smile, one that barely touches her eyes, which are so brown they're nearly black, her pupils unidentifiable in the irises.

The moment our fingers make contact, I pull back sharply. A spark of electricity buzzes between us, radiating up through my wrist.

"Oh," she says, a small giggle escaping her mouth.

I stare at her, my hand still stinging. Maybe she's more than I expected, this girl. And suddenly, the flutters erupt back in my gut, my mind spinning, thinking of the possibilities we have ahead of us this month. And just how much our lives could change in the next few weeks.

3

CLAIRE

Now

I HADN'T PLANNED TO go to Australia ten years ago. The life I'd built for myself in Humbolt, Illinois, was quiet and simple, but it fit me. I lived with my mom in the house I'd grown up in, commuting four days a week to the campus of my exceedingly average-ranked liberal arts college to complete my bachelor's degree in nursing within three and a half years. To rush through the "college life" I was supposed to enjoy as quickly as possible. That is, until one day when my mother noticed me throwing away the mail I had crammed into my backpack between classes.

"What's this?" she'd asked, grabbing a colorful brochure that had slipped from the pile of otherwise drab white envelopes I was attempting to discard in the kitchen wastebasket.

"Just the junk that the school always shoves in our mailboxes. I should have thrown it out on campus, but I was in a rush to get to class—"

"This isn't from the school," my mom said, flipping through the pages. "It's from a different university. Hamilton College. It's all about different study abroad options." As I stole a glance at the glossy photos lining the thick expensive-looking pages of the brochure, I realized she was right. Everything from my school's study abroad office looked like it was created using a version of Photoshop from the early 2000s. This was far more professional.

"Claire, you need to see this." When she looked up at me, I was surprised to see a glow in her eyes I hadn't noticed in a while. If I was being honest, she'd been quieter than usual lately, pulling herself away from our nightly television sessions to head to bed even before *American Idol* was over.

"You know I can't study abroad," I chided, feeling as though we'd swapped our roles as mother and daughter. "I can barely squeeze in all the credits I need to graduate early as it is."

"Mm," my mom muttered as she continued to thrum through the pages. "Well, what about this?"

I reluctantly accepted the brochure she handed me. "Adventure Abroad" was emblazoned in bright white at the top under the Hamilton College logo. Beneath that, a kangaroo stared out at me from the glossy cover, which was bathed in brilliant reds and oranges, all stemming from a globe-like sun hovering at the top of the page and illuminating a dusty rust-colored ground. The university certainly wasn't shying away from stereotypes.

I flipped it open to photos of beaches and surfers interrupted by dense strands of text and started to read:

Are you looking for a study abroad experience unlike any other? Well, it's a "g'day" for you! Hamilton College is ready to deliver adventure, education, and excitement with our Adventure Abroad program. For those students unable to dedicate a full semester or year to studying abroad, we've squeezed everything you need into one short month. Travel through Australia and experience all the culture and fun the continent has to offer.

What are you waiting for? Join us this December!

I shot my mother a curious look. Even ignoring the program's cringeworthy depiction, I was not what you would call an "adventurous" person. At that point, the scariest thing I'd ever done was ride the upside-down roller coaster at the local amusement park, and even that prompted a minor panic attack when I was standing in line. The idea of spending a month living across the world with complete strangers—let alone *adventuring* with them—left a dull cramp in my abdomen. But my mother didn't seem to notice.

"You have to do this, pumpkin," she said, wrapping her hands around my shoulder. "It sounds magical. Plus, look, it says you'll earn four credits for the experience. That should help you with early gradua—"

Her statement devolved into a small cough, which she covered with her hand.

"It's nothing," she said, in response to my raised eyebrows, "just the change in weather. So what do you think?"

"It'll cost thousands of dollars. And that's not even considering the airfare." I could feel my mom flinch. Money—or the general lack of it—was a silent presence in our household, one we never really talked about but that lingered in every room like a bad stench. Mom had worked two jobs—an office receptionist by day, a copy editor for academic publications by night—ever since I could remember. My education to date had been financed by a mixture of academic scholarships and student loans I wasn't looking forward to repaying.

My mother took the brochure back from me, flipping through the pages as if hoping the answer would appear in front of her. Until it did.

"Here," she said excitedly, reading from a sentence in small print on the last page. "'Given the nature of the program, the group participating in Adventure Abroad will always be composed of ten students or less. The Australian Government will fully fund one student's participation in the program based on need and qualifications.'"

I rolled my eyes, unsurprised to find my mother had found a workaround to the problem. It's what she did, whether it was creating a magical Christmas morning filled with gifts despite her measly salary or showering me with extra love every year on the anniversary of my father's death from sudden cardiac arrest when I was only four. But despite her best efforts, she wasn't perfect; the cracks showed through on occasion. The day I'd been left waiting for hours later than the other kids for after-school pickup. The time I was left behind while the rest of my fifth-grade class went on a field trip because my mother forgot to sign my permission slip. But those instances were few and far between.

"Okay, you win. I'll check it out, but I'm sure getting that funding is going to be near impossible."

My mother simply patted me on the leg at that, a smile growing on her face.

Even then, I noticed it. A flash of wariness in her eyes, a flicker of emotion across her face that I couldn't identify. I think constantly of how things could have been different if I'd asked her about it, forced her to tell me the truth. I wonder what life would have been like if I hadn't been accepted into the program, if my personal essay hadn't earned me the government funding, if I'd never met the rest of the Mob. If I hadn't done…everything I'd done.

I don't know how long I stare at that message from Ellery. The words blur before my eyes, the past hounding me from all sides. *They've found Phoebe's body.* Before I can recover enough to even rest my thumbs on my phone's keyboard, a second message arrives.

Any chance you'll reconsider the reunion?

No, I tell myself, after staring at Ellery's message for what feels like hours. I will not be returning for the ten-year reunion of our study abroad group. I promised myself years ago that what happened in Australia would stay there. That it wouldn't consume my life. That I would never return.

I've already broken the first two promises, but I've been adamant that I will never, under any circumstances, return. What good could come of it? If anything, I'll get tripped up, share something that I shouldn't. And the others would discover the truth.

Even so, I can't help but think about it. And I spend hours doing just that. At one point in our group conversation, Kyan offers to pay for all our flights and put us up in his house in the Sydney suburbs. It'll be just like being back in the hostels we used to stay in, he texts. Only with slightly better accommodations.

The call comes the next morning. The sun is just beginning to peek above the small sliver of Chicago skyline I can see from my apartment, but my ringtone doesn't wake me. I haven't slept.

The number is marked as *Unknown*. When I answer, a man's voice comes down the line.

"Is this Ms. Whitlock?" he asks stiffly in a once-familiar accent. As though he can hear me nod through the phone, he continues. "This is Leading Senior Constable Arnold Sawkins with the Australian Federal Police. I'm calling with some news that may be difficult for you to hear."

"I know," I say, wincing as my voice cracks. "I heard from a friend. You found Phoebe."

He clears his throat. "Her remains, yes," he clarifies. "Apologies that you didn't hear it from us first. It took a bit of legwork to track you down. Your friend, Ms. Johnson, ultimately gave us your contact information."

I silently curse Ellery as he carries on. "Of course, given the… erm…circumstances in which we found Ms. Barton's remains, we are now conducting an investigation."

The words lodge in my brain as thick saliva blocks my throat.

"Normally, we would request to question you via Zoom. It is not ideal, of course, but it does prove quite convenient for international investigations. However, we heard from Ms. Johnson that she and several others from your study abroad program will be back in Sydney next week. If you will also be here, we would strongly prefer to interview you in person."

Amidst the panic, worries swarm like the ubiquitous flies back in Jagged Rock: all the ways I could trip up on a Zoom interview, how suspicious it would seem to the police if I was the only one of our friend group not to return.

"Ms. Whitlock?" Sawkins prompts down the line. "I'm sure you can understand how important this is. The file indicates you were Ms. Barton's closest friend and roommate during the program. We would really like a chance to speak with you in person about anything you may have remembered over the years."

I run through my potential options for declining before considering the holes Sawkins could poke in each one. Work conflict . . . but what could possibly be so important in my role as a receptionist to take priority over this? The cost . . . but Kyan's already offered to pay. Any excuse I use would only prompt more questions, more suspicion.

And then the memory pricks at me.

The wooden handle of the knife heavy in my hand, the sharp curve of the blade.

I left loose ends, evidence that could implicate me. I know I did. And if someone is smart enough, if they know just where to look, what questions to ask, they'll figure out what I did.

But not if I work this exactly right. If I point them in another direction, away from my guilt. If I prevent them from discovering the truth.

And I can only do that in person.

"Fine," I say to Sawkins, the word escaping my mouth before my brain processes the implications. "I'll come back."

4

PHOEBE

Then

THE SOUND OF KNUCKLES brushing hesitantly against wood comes a moment before the door to my new shared dorm room eases open.

"You don't have to knock," I say, as Claire walks over the threshold, water droplets left from the shower dampening the shoulders of her T-shirt, her wet hair slicked back into a ponytail. "This is your room too."

Her cheeks flush as she busies herself rearranging her suitcase. I've noticed she hasn't unpacked a single object other than the ones she used in the shower, as if cautious not to leave her mark on the room. My eyes flick back to my bed, the week's worth of outfits I've strewn over the scratchy comforter as I tried to settle on the best option for tonight.

"I wasn't sure if you were doing something. I just figured I'd let you know," Claire mumbles down towards the floor. When she looks up at me, her eyes widen, taking in my silhouette in the cheap mirror affixed to our cinder-block wall and the outfit I've carefully curated: a skirt that falls just below my waistline, showing off my protruding hip bones, the white tank top hovering a few inches above it, the Tory Burch sandals strapped to my feet. "Wow," she breathes. "You look amazing."

"Thanks," I say, seeming to shrug off the compliment, but it buries in my heart. I glance over at her, taking in her wet hair, her baggy T-shirt, the flannel pajama pants.

"Uh-uh," I say, "what is this? Why are you dressed for bed?"

"I'm so tired," she says. "I didn't get much sleep on the flight and—"

I wave away her explanation. "Nope, I won't hear it. We're only here for a month. We need to make the most of it. The campus bar is open until ten. I figured we could stop there first."

Claire looks like she's considering protesting, but then changes her mind. "Okay, just give me a minute to get ready," she says, pulling on a pair of baggy jean shorts.

"Wait," I order, tossing her a discarded sundress from my bed. "This will look great on you."

—

Twenty minutes later, we're ready to go. As soon as we throw open the door to our building and emerge into the shared courtyard, the early evening heat descends like a stage curtain. Sweat pricks my underarms, but I relish it, thinking of how early it's been getting dark back in Atlanta.

We stroll through campus; narrow walkways weave around man-made ponds, small purple flowers littering them, dropped from the perfectly landscaped jacaranda trees that seem to be everywhere. It's gorgeous, that's for sure, but it's also…empty. We don't pass another person the entire fifteen-minute walk to the campus center. Exams must be over by now, I realize, the students all returned home for the summer break. Concern bubbles in my stomach. If campus is this empty, I can't imagine the bar will be much better.

The student center is only marginally livelier. Stores line the hallways—a travel agency, a pharmacy, even a salon—until the building opens up into a food court–style cafeteria. Most of the stores are closed, but I spot an "open" sign outside one at the far end of the hallway. It looks like a convenience store from here. I grab Claire's hand and guide her that way.

"Come on, there's something we should do."

Ten minutes later, we exit the store, each equipped with the type of black Motorola flip phone that was in fashion five years ago. In the dozens of pre-trip emails sent from Adventure Abroad, the coordinators advised us to buy new cell phones for our time in Australia, as the ones we used back home wouldn't have service. I had planned to splurge for an iPhone, but upon seeing Claire blanch at the price tag, I decided not to embarrass her.

"God these are ugly," I say. But then I catch myself. "Wait, I've got an idea."

I dig into the oversized purse I've brought with me, fishing around until I find my small makeup bag. Buried at the bottom are two strips of sticky-backed face jewels. I peel a red one off and stick it on the back of my phone, then do the same with a blue one, affixing it to Claire's.

"This'll spice them up a little."

Claire smiles and it brightens up her whole face. Her lashes are darkened with mascara, and the blush I carefully applied to her cheeks back in the dorm before we left glows in the sunlight.

"Oi, ladies!"

The shout comes from up ahead, and I spot long tanned legs and a head of bleach-blond, pink-streaked shoulder-length hair pushing through the door to the student center. The girl jogs towards us, and as she gets closer, I take in her sun-kissed skin, the loose jean shorts, and cropped T-shirt that screams surfer girl chic. I swallow a bite of jealousy.

"I thought I saw you in here as I was walking past. Claire and… Phoebe, right?"

"Yes," I answer cautiously. "Should we be concerned?"

"No," she says with a laugh, turning the two-letter word into multiple syllables, so that it sounds more like *na-ar.* "I memorized the photos of you all. All the Adventure Abroad students," she clarifies when my eyebrows crinkle. "I'm Hari, the teaching assistant for the program. I'm like your student advisor. I'll be traveling with yas."

We exchange greetings, Claire's smile nearly as wide as her whole face. I feel that same pinprick of jealousy again.

"So where ya headed?"

“We’re going to the campus bar. Phoebe suggested it.” Claire shoots me a shy smile.

“Nah, you don’t want to head there. This time of year, it’s dead as.” I wait for her to finish, but she leaves the comparison hanging. “Everyone’s already gone home for break. But hey, you’ve probably not had a chance to meet the others in the program, ’ave ya? Come on.” Hari grabs our arms gently, and I watch Claire’s eyes widen at the unsolicited physical contact as she leads us back in the direction in which we’ve come. “Let’s head back to your dorm. I’ll introduce yas. Then we can all head to a local pub.”

I want to protest, to regain control of the situation, but at the same time, I don’t want to miss out.

“Sure,” I say instead, increasing my pace so that I’m the one leading the way back.

We reach our dorm a few minutes later, Hari chatting the entire way, peppering us with questions. Where we’re from—me, Atlanta; Claire, Illinois—what our majors are—me, marketing (the easiest major offered at my school); Claire, nursing. But Hari barely stops talking long enough to listen to our answers. When we finally walk up to our brick building, a girl is leaning against the front of it, leg propped, staring down at a cell phone.

Her face is so decorated with silver jewelry it’s nearly impossible to make out her features aside from blue-streaked braids that fall to her waist, but as we get closer, I can tell her eyebrows are knitted together. She gives off a tough vibe, but her face transforms when she sees Hari, the hardness melting away, and her chocolate brown eyes turn warm, gentle.

"Hari!" she yells excitedly.

"Girls, this is Ellery. She's…Canadian?" Hari prompts.

Ellery nods. "I'm from Ottawa originally, but I go to school in Toronto." Ellery's voice is higher than I expected, making her upbeat personality even more incongruous with the safety pins dangling from her earlobes. "Majoring in social work. What about you two?"

Hari leaves us to introduce ourselves, ducking inside the building to find the others, just as another girl exits. I inhale sharply as I look at her. She's gorgeous, like model gorgeous—Hari's beauty on steroids. But unlike Hari's surfer-chic style, every inch of this girl is polished, from her perfectly highlighted long blond hair to her glistening cheekbones to the darkened eyelashes framing her steel-gray eyes. Her tanned legs seem to stretch on forever, something she's clearly aware of given her choice of skirt, a denim number that barely reaches past her pubic line.

"Ah, and this is my roommate, Adrien," Ellery says.

Adrien's eyes skirt over the two of us. She dismisses Claire quickly, but her eyes linger on me, scanning my outfit, spotting a threat. Dislike blooms immediately.

I know this girl. Or her type at least. A mean girl, just like the ones back at my university in Atlanta. The ones who ruined my first attempt at a fresh start. It only took one of them to recognize me, and then the rumors started, filtering through my entire dorm and lingering like a bad scent. All about the thing I did, or what they thought I did at least—no one could ever prove it. But my roommate requested a transfer, leaving me alone in a single, and everyone else followed suit.

"Where are you from, Adrien?" Claire asks.

"Cape Town," she answers in a superior tone. "South Africa."

"So, is this an all-female program or something?" The question sounds more bitter than I intended, but I'm desperate to take the attention off this Kate Moss knockoff. As if on cue, Hari leads out a group of four guys from the dorm building.

Heat throbs in my chest as I take them in, the possibilities. My eyes scan quickly over the first one. He's endearingly nerdy looking. His long brown—almost black—hair is parted neatly down the middle and looped behind his ears, and his wide eyes, located just a touch too far apart on his face, are emphasized by a pair of thin, Harry Potter–esque glasses.

"Okay, okay. Time for introductions!" Hari announces. "This is Tomas. From Italy."

Tomas gives us all a small wave, a broad smile reaching from cheek to cheek. "Ciao."

"And this is Josh," Hari points to the guy next to Tomas, who looks like he just stepped out of a frat house. He's wearing a backwards baseball cap over blond hair that reaches below his earlobes, and has round blue eyes.

"Hi. I'm American as y'all can probably tell. I go to school in California." He rattles off the name of a pretentious college that I should probably be impressed by.

"Declan," Hari pushes on, signaling to the skinny Irish-looking one with auburn curls that set off his pale, freckled cheeks. When he speaks, his thick brogue confirms my suspicions. I feel Claire stiffen next to me, and when I steal a glance over at her, her gaze is locked on him.

"And last but not least." The final guy of the four steps towards us, not waiting for Hari's introduction. He has a perfectly manicured face with dark eyes and a thick-lipped mouth filled with teeth as white and perfectly shaped as Chiclets, all topped with jet-black hair gelled into a side part. He's beautiful, that's for sure, with the confidence that comes with someone being told as much his entire life.

"I'm Kyan," he says, in a posh accent. "From Singapore, but I went to school in the UK. Just finished actually, so I'm a bit older than the rest of you. But I couldn't resist one final hoorah before starting real life." He looks at me with that comment, a glint in his eye, and winks. I feel my heart beat faster, heat rise in my cheeks.

"Nice to meet you all." This comes from Adrien, her previously cold tone now replaced with a put-on honey warmth. I bristle as Kyan's attention turns to her and her typical Barbie-like beauty. I think fast, desperate for a way to get his eyes back on me.

"So, are we going out for drinks or what?" I ask.

Hari chuckles. "Right, right. We can head there now. Bar's just a kilometer or so down the road. Figured yous'd be okay with walking."

We take up behind her, and I make sure to sidle up next to Kyan, close enough that his arm brushes against mine, sending a frisson of pleasure along my skin.

"So, yous ready for your first Australian night out?" Hari asks midstep, turning back to take in our expressions.

I decide to play it cool. "I guess, as long as there's alcohol involved."

But my comment is lost among the excitement from the others.

"Of fucking course," Kyan pipes up, at the same time that Tomas shouts, "Absolutely!"

And I realize my mistake. I don't need to play down my excitement—the others aren't. Instead, I notice a strange glance from Josh, a note of judgment for my lack of enthusiasm.

I force a smile onto my face, hoping no one else noticed my brief error.

Thankfully, it doesn't seem like they did. The others are all smiling and talking as we walk. And why wouldn't they? This group is going to become family for the next few weeks as we have ridiculous adventures and experiences.

I try to do the same, but a pinprick of dread lodges in my chest. Because I know how fine a line I'm walking. How easy it would be to become the girl I left behind in Atlanta.

One small misstep could bring everything crashing down.

5
CLAIRE

Now

THE AIR FEELS THE same. That's the first thing I notice as I exit the Sydney airport. Dry, with just the faintest smell of the distant ocean. I inhale deeply, nostalgia washing over me as my ride share pulls up.

"How ya going?" The driver, a twentysomething guy with windswept hair and board shorts, greets me with a smile and a heavy Australian accent, the sound of which floods me with memories. I respond with a "Good, thanks."

"American?" he asks, and I offer a nod. "Traveling quite lightly," he says, letting his eyes rest on my carry-on suitcase and backpack.

"I don't plan to be here for long," I say truthfully. I have a return flight booked for five days from now. Barely enough time to sleep off the jet lag. But if I handle things correctly, it should be all the time I need.

Ten or so minutes later, we exit the highway into an area I never traveled to during my first time here. The roads are windy, increasing in elevation. Eventually, we turn off a main road, onto a narrow street. As I watch out the window, the houses become few and further between, replaced with gates and lush greenery, clearly designed to block the world from the fancy residences that lie beyond them. Through it all, the driver keeps up a steady thrum of questions, undeterred by my monosyllabic answers.

Suddenly, the car takes a sharp right, pulling to the side of the road, and I feel my stomach shift. As the driver eases off the gas, the nerves I've been battling throughout thirty hours of travel return, the wings of my butterflies flapping loudly in my ears.

I'm not ready to see these people again, I realize. They were strangers turned family in little more than hours, the product of those whirlwind relationships that occur only when you're all thrown into the same foreign circumstances. Like lifelong friends from summer camp, only our version was a month-long trip that culminated in death.

We'd kept in touch over the years, but primarily through our group text message chain. Early on in our trip, Phoebe discovered *mob* was the proper term for a group of kangaroos. One of the others had adopted the nickname for our crew, and it stuck. It was fitting, in a way. We were just as close as the Mob—for that one month at least—and equally riddled with secrets and lies.

"Whoa," the driver says, prolonging the vowels with a surfer-like drawl. It takes me a moment to realize what's prompted it.

The building in front of us is an amalgamation of glass and concrete that seems to rise to infinity. It sits back from the road, a winding concrete pathway leading past a black sliding gate that immediately starts to open as we pull up next to it.

Kyan was never shy about flashing his money, and that was back when he "only" had his massive trust fund to rely upon. Since then, he's managed to invest in numerous tech companies throughout Australia, Singapore, and Silicon Valley, and his wealth has multiplied, as he likes to display on social media any chance he gets. His feed is littered with photos from his private jet or with his arm around some model on an unidentifiable island he seems to have rented out for just the two of them.

I exit the car, mouth open, transfixed by the colossal building in front of me, so the quick rush of force against my abdomen comes as a complete surprise.

The wind rushes from my lungs as limbs wrap themselves around my shoulders, squeezing tightly. Seconds later, the person draws back so that I can see their face, a mix of familiar and alien.

"El-Ellery?" I finally manage. The throngs of metal that once lined both earlobes have been replaced by two modest gold hoops. Her face has been cleansed of the heavy dark makeup and piercings from ten years ago, and now sports only mascara-laden lashes and the faintest spread of foundation across her cheeks. Her once blue-streaked hair has returned to its natural dark color, spreading across her shoulders in a blanket of curls.

"The one and only," she says, a huge smile plastered on her face. I'd seen the updated photos of her on Facebook and Instagram, of course, but they never seemed real. All I could see was teenage punk rock Ellery playing dress-up as an adult, masquerading as a businesswoman for an NGO focused on child welfare in conflict zones. But here, standing in front of me, eyes wide and the faintest of lines dancing their way across her forehead, I can see how much she's changed.

"God, I'm so happy to see you," she says, pummeling me with another full-force hug before grabbing my suitcase from the—for once speechless—driver and pulling me up the path to the compound. "Come on, you need to see everyone else."

I try to maintain my breathing as she drags me through the front door and into an enormous foyer. I glance around at the stark white walls, the absurdly high ceilings, and my gaze lands on Adrien.

The long blond hair that used to reach halfway down her back has been chopped into a sleek bob and parted in the middle, but her skin looks just as blemish-free as it did when she was twenty. She's as stylish as ever, wearing a silk tank top tucked into pair of tailored linen trousers, and as she raises her arms to pull me in, I can't help but notice an enormous oval diamond twinkling on her left hand.

"Oh honey, it's so good to see you," Adrien says, her accent tinkling in my ear as she envelops me in a floral-scented hug. I'm taken aback at first. The Adrien I remember wasn't one for affection of any sort, and she certainly wasn't a hugger. She's so thin that I could wrap my arms around her twice, but her muscles are firm as she leans against me. Before I can stop it, Phoebe's voice pops into my head. *Lots of time for Pilates when you're a stay-at-home trophy wife.*

"Bring it in, Whit," Kyan says, appearing by Adrien's side and using the nickname that only he ever used, his accent as clipped and posh as I remember. As I lean into his hard body, I feel small, like I used to around him. He's always been nearly a foot taller than me and twice as broad, his chest a thick sheet of muscle. "We missed you."

I try to return the sentiment, but it sticks in my throat as soon as I see *him,* leaning against a pearl-white couch in the living room off the foyer, hands shoved into jeans pockets, shoulders slightly rounded, peering sheepishly from those dark brown eyes. I inhale sharply, imagining the woodsy scent of his auburn curls from the same shampoo he used all those years ago, feeling his body curled against mine. But that was in the *before.* Before everything went wrong.

"Hi, Claire," Declan says, raising his hand awkwardly in the air. I can feel the others' gaze on us, wondering how we'll react, whether we'll drop the decade of silence and be friendly. Or whether we'll be cold, refuse physical contact.

"Hi," I say softly, opting for the latter.

"Well, come in, come in," Kyan says, depositing my bags by the door and leading me inside.

"This place is unreal," I mumble. It's an understatement. The huge open-plan first floor must span well over a thousand square feet, and the furniture and walls are all gleaming white, reflecting the afternoon sunlight filtering in from the wall of floor-to-ceiling windows. Plants, as lush and green as those that lined the walkway up to the house, decorate every corner, giving a splash of color to the modern Scandinavian design.

"Wait until you see the bedrooms," Adrien adds.

Kyan leads me into the kitchen, a giant slab of marble surrounded by a half circle of empty countertops and littered only occasionally by a near unidentifiable—but no doubt expensive—appliance.

"Well, I think we know the first order of business," Kyan says, pulling a bottle of whiskey from a bar cart in the corner. "What can I get you all?"

We give him our orders, and I watch as he deftly pours and swirls and shakes, a comfortable volley of conversation running among the others. But I can barely pay attention to it.

My eyes dart from one to the other, everyone laughing and smiling. It's like they all forgot the reason we're here. As if they can't sense the presence of the other people who should be in the room with us.

"Let's head out to the patio," he urges after everyone's received their drinks, and I follow them outside, white wine in hand, sucking in my breath at the view. Beyond the patio, which is lined with a full bar and matching white furniture, lies one of the most pristine beaches I've ever laid eyes on. Green grass, as immaculately cut as a golf course, eventually gives way to fresh white sand, spotted at this hour with families and a few beachgoers who have managed to outlast the heat of the afternoon sun. Cobalt blue waves crash against the sand, the water frothing as if trying to hide what's beneath it. Buildings dart up behind the curve of the beach, a reminder that this paradise exists in the middle of the city.

"To being reunited at last." Ellery's voice draws my attention from the view. I turn to see her raising her glass, and we all join her. My eyes catch Declan's and quickly dart away.

I can't help but remember that first day at the Notting Hill Hotel, the local bar near the Hamilton campus. All of us cheers-ing to the month ahead, nearly overflowing with excitement. Could we have stopped things at that point? Or had we already started down a path that was bound to end in death?

We all take a seat on the pristine patio furniture, Ellery complimenting Kyan on the extraordinary life he built.

"Yeah, work's been going well," he says, taking a deep swig from his glass. "The company's really taken off in the last few years. We're poised to break into the Forbes Top 100 Digital Companies list."

The conversation circles, everyone sharing their life updates. Ellery admits that she recently became engaged, which causes us to erupt into a round of cheers and soft yells. Adrien talks halfheartedly about her job as a lawyer in her father's firm, and I think briefly of how ticked off Phoebe would be to find that Adrien is not, in fact, a stay-at-home wife. And Declan gives a bare-bones account of his work as a journalist, although I notice he avoids any mention of his life in New York, the new home he'd traded for Dublin a few years back. He hadn't told me he'd be living in the same country, only a few hours away by plane. I was left to find that out through social media. The thought still burns, a wound that won't heal.

And then the conversation turns to me. I keep it as short as possible.

"Not too much has changed really. I stayed in Illinois, moved to Chicago shortly after I got back from Australia. I work as a receptionist...for a medical insurance company," I add after a second, hoping to lend more gravitas to the temp job that somehow morphed its way into my career. I feel my cheeks grow red at how pathetic it sounds in comparison to everyone's accomplishments. Ellery's forehead wrinkles almost imperceptibly, probably as she remembers how passionate I was about earning my nursing degree back then.

I don't mention that it never happened. That I dropped out of college with a year left to go. But they don't know how my world collapsed when I came back from Australia, as I tried to cope with what I'd done. As the ground gave out beneath me.

Thankfully they're all too kind to point out the obvious. There are no follow-up questions like with the others, for which I'm grateful. Any answers I'd have would be just as depressing.

The conversation lulls then, and Ellery jumps in, never one to outlast an awkward silence.

"Wow, I really can't believe it," she muses. "The Mob back together at last..."

She trails off, and it's clear we're all thinking the same things. Of the others who should be here. Who can't be.

"Could Josh not make it?" Adrien asks.

Ellery latches onto her question, grateful. "He really wanted to, but he said he had a work commitment. We should FaceTime him at some point."

"What about Hari?" I ask.

Kyan looks down at the watch on his wrist, a blue-faced Omega coated with diamonds. "I talked to her earlier. She said she'd come by. She should have arrived by now. I'll text her."

The group falls into an awkward silence. There are two additional people missing: Phoebe and Tomas. Two people who can't share what they've been up to in the past ten years.

Eventually, after a few throat clearings and the silent passing of seconds, the group moves on to another conversation topic. Rather than joining in, I take a moment and look at these people who were once my best friends, my family. People I used to know intimately, who are now strangers in so many ways. Maybe they always were.

I start with Declan. Even with all the hurt, something beckons me to run my fingers through his curls like I used to. To cuddle up beside him. But then I notice the dark circles around his eyes, the slivers of gray hair in his hair. My eyes skirt to his hands, which are grasped tightly—too tightly—around his whiskey glass.

I shift to Adrien, her perfectly botoxed forehead masking any years that have passed. Sensing me looking at her, she flicks her eyes towards mine, her gaze cold and steely. She catches herself almost instantly, the warmth from earlier seeping back into her face.

Kyan's next to her, his face lit up animatedly as he tells some outrageous story. But there's something off about him, something that wasn't there all those years ago. A hardness that seems to lie just beyond the gregarious mask.

And then there's Ellery, whose lips are pursed in something resembling a smile, but which looks more like a grimace.

For the first time, I consider that I may not be the only one uncomfortable here. But why? The others wanted to return even before they heard the news about Phoebe, and none of them seem particularly broken up about her body being found.

Unless they're hiding something too.

6

PHOEBE

Then

WE MAKE THE TREK to the bar, with Hari leading the way. When we're a safe distance from campus, she pulls out a plastic bottle filled with some unidentifiable alcohol, which she passes around the group. As she prattles on, trying to give us all the insider information we need about Hamilton College and its students, I can't help but feel myself softening towards her. Adrien, however, is a different story. Despite my efforts at ensuring I'm always within touching distance of Kyan as we walk, I can tell she's doing the same. Every time I catch his eyes flicker over to her, my hands fold into fists.

When we finally arrive, Hari waltzes through the front door. I look furtively for the bouncer before remembering the lowered drinking age here. A smile flits across my face as we enter the bar, a drab room with sharp overhead lighting that accentuates the sticky floors and a handful of mostly empty tables and booths. I inhale a stale beer smell, briefly wondering why Hari was so eager to bring us here. But she leads us through that first room and into another, with a huge bar staffed with three bartenders and surrounded by groups of college-age drinkers, all of whom are talking or laughing or tossing back pints. Hari raises her arms as a grungy looking guy with tight jean shorts and a lip ring calls her name. She skips over to him, calling back to tell us to grab drinks and a table and that she'll join us shortly.

The rest of us hang back slightly, taking everything in. I wonder briefly if the others feel like I do, as if the rest of the patrons can easily spot us as outsiders. I shake away the feeling and raise my voice over the din of the crowd.

"First round's on me," I shout before sauntering up to the bar. A bartender heads in my direction almost immediately, bypassing the group of guys further down the counter waving to get his attention.

"What can I get ya?" he asks with a smile that accentuates a dimple in his left cheek.

For a second, I freeze. I don't know what drinks to order in an American bar, let alone one in a foreign country. Unsurprisingly, I haven't had many invitations for nights out back in Atlanta. The only drinking I've ever really done has been at the rare family dinner or charity function my parents have dragged me to, where everyone is so rich and negligent that they don't mind—or care—when someone's underaged child decides to partake in the free-flowing champagne. In fact, I usually need at least a few glasses to get through those things.

But this certainly does not feel like a place that serves champagne. My mind flickers to the little I know about Australia.

"Uh, nine Fosters, please."

The bartender looks at me for a moment and then bursts out laughing. "First time in Oz?" he asks once he's regained control.

I feel my cheeks grow hot, but I paint on a smile.

"Okay, scratch that," I say, craning my neck down and looking up at him from beneath my eyelids. "Nine of whatever you recommend."

The bartender winks at me before turning his back and busying himself, returning several minutes later with his hands full.

"Nine pints of VB," he says, as I note the logo on the side of the glasses: *Victorian Bitter.* I hand over the credit card my father had opened for me several years ago, not bothering to look at the total before signing the receipt.

Declan and Claire come over to help me carry the collection of glasses and usher me through a door in the back of the room into a courtyard. In the setting sun, string lights cast a shimmering glow over a collection of several tables, around one of which sit the other Adventure Abroad participants, including Hari.

After we distribute the beers, a silence falls around us. There's so much we don't know about each other that no one's really sure where to start.

"I've got an idea," I volunteer. I take a long drag from my glass in an effort to create suspense, trying not to wince at the bitter taste of the beer. The name of the brand was certainly on point. "Let's play a game. Truth or dare."

I can't think of a better way to get to know each other—to see what each of us will admit and how far we'll go. I can tell instantly it's a good idea. The others shift uncomfortably in their seats, all of them except for Kyan, who cocks an eyebrow in my direction. His message is clear: *challenge accepted.*

With no overt objections, I look around the group, choosing at random, my eyes settling on the nerdy-looking Italian guy Hari had introduced earlier. "Tomas, why don't we start with you? Pick someone for truth or dare."

Tomas's cheeks glow beneath his olive complexion. He looks around, finally settling on the person sitting across from him.

"I choose Declan," he says slowly in his thick accent. "Would you like truth or dare?"

"Uh, yeah, dare," Declan responds, not entirely confidently.

After a moment of pondering, Tomas finally settles on one. "I dare you to take a shot."

I groan, but Declan laughs, clearly relieved. "Sure, but I'm buying a round of them for everyone." And so he does, trotting to the bar and returning to the table a few minutes later with a platter of shot glasses that he doles out to each of us.

"*Slàinte,*" he says as he downs the shot.

I follow suit, the alcohol burning my throat, but as soon as it hits my chest, I feel warm. It's not the slight dizziness like I felt from the glass or two of champagne I'd have at my parents' parties. It's something better, more solid. Like this is how I'm supposed to feel, an unfamiliar comfort in my own skin.

"Okay," I say, once everyone's put down their shot glasses. "Declan, your turn."

"Well, Phoebe," Declan says, his attention turning to me. A hazy sheen drapes over the table, which I can no longer attribute to the lights. "I think we must put you in the hot seat for starting this. Truth or dare?"

"Dare," I answer without a pause.

"Right, but I'm not going to go easy on you like Tomas did," he shoots a smile at Tomas to show he was joking, which Tomas returns good-naturedly. "I dare you to steal a bottle from behind the bar."

My smile slips, but I force myself to maintain eye contact. "Done."

I straighten my spine and start walking back towards the bar, making sure to swish my hips enough for Kyan to notice.

"There's no way she'll do it," I hear Adrien whisper at my back.

Wait and see, bitch.

I sidle back up to the bar in front of the cute bartender who served me the first time. I lean forward, just enough for him to have a clear view of my cleavage.

"Back already?" he asks, dimple flashing.

"Couldn't stay away," I say, taking my voice one octave lower than normal. I clench my hands into fists beneath the counter and thank God the effects of the shot are still going strong.

"Another round of beers?" he asks.

"Actually," I say, "when I was here the last time, I leaned over to try to see the labels on the bottles—a lot of those are foreign to me, after all—and I think my earring may have fallen out behind the bar. I can't find it anywhere."

The bartender gives a quick glance at the floor around him.

"Sorry, but I don't see anything back here."

"I know this is crazy, but would it be possible for me to take a quick look? It's just that these earrings are super sentimental. A gift from my grandmother who died last year. If I lost one, I don't know what I'd do." I make my eyes as big as possible.

"I mean, it's not really policy to allow customers behind the bar." I lean forward a little more, giving the bartender an even better view. "But I suppose I could make an exception. You'll need to be quick though, and you better not let my boss see you. He tends to pop up when we least expect it."

"Thank you so, so much," I say, as he lifts a makeshift door in the counter to let me through.

Once behind the bar, I pretend to scour the floor, waiting for my chance.

"Oi, two pints of Tooheys down here, mate," a voice yells from further down the bar.

Bingo.

As soon as the bartender heads in that direction, I grab the first bottle I see, not bothering to look at the label.

"Found it! Thanks so much," I yell behind me before ducking under the counter and speedwalking back to the table.

When I get back, I hold the bottle above my head, victorious.

"No fucking way." Josh laughs.

"That's incredible," Ellery says open-mouthed.

"Do I even want to know how you did that?" Hari asks. Her arm is already looped around Josh, despite knowing him for all of an hour.

"Better if you don't, I think," I say with a wink.

Only Adrien looks put out. Of course.

I pour the bottle—some type of off-brand rum—into the empty

shot glasses that litter our table, laughing as liquid spills from the sides, and throw mine back with the others, barely feeling the burn this time. I ignore a snide comment from Adrien about the liquor's poor quality. *Is this bitch serious?*

"Okay, my turn." I don't hesitate. I turn to Kyan, seated next to me, his black hair shiny and full, his face somehow even more gorgeous in the soft glow of the lights. "Truth or dare?"

"You needn't even ask, darling. Dare, always."

I watch Josh shoot Kyan an approving glance, as if he would have chosen the same. I can already tell there's a budding bromance happening there.

My tongue pokes through my teeth, my hands itching to touch him. "I dare you to kiss a stranger."

His eyes widen and then his mouth opens in a smile that shows off every one of his straight white teeth. He looks slowly at each one of us, as if pondering who to choose, mockingly stroking his clean-shaven chin. His gaze lands on Josh, and he takes a step forward, prompting Josh to jump back.

"I mean, I like you and all man, but not like that."

Kyan laughs. "Aw, Josh, I don't know if my heart will ever recover."

He returns to looking at us one by one, lingering on Adrien for a second too long. Her anticipation is palpable, and my heart drops. But before the disappointment can set in, I feel Kyan step towards me. Then his hands are on each side of my face, and he's leaning closer until his lips brush mine. They press harder, his tongue entering my mouth, and I feel my body go limp. He tastes like rum and passion and *life.* Everything else around us seems to stop. I don't know how long his lips stay on mine, but when he pulls away, I have to force myself to remain upright and not collapse back into him.

"Wow," I say breathily. And then I remember the others, all staring at me, most of them with impressed grins on their faces. All of them except for one. Adrien glares at me, her gray eyes narrowed and colder than I've seen them. The hatred spills out from them, an emotion so intense it's instantly sobering. I cough slightly, trying to regain my composure. "You really leaned into that, Ky."

"I always do," he says with a wide grin, apparently not noticing the daggers Adrien's eyes are shooting in my direction.

I laugh, but I can still feel Adrien's eyes on me. And I know one thing for certain.

I've already made an enemy. And for once, it feels good.

7
CLAIRE

Now

THE FIVE OF US have been talking for nearly twenty minutes on Kyan's patio by the time the conversation turns to Phoebe. We've covered pretty much everything you'd expect during a ten-year reunion. Life updates, nostalgic memories, the whole bit. Through it all, my mind keeps flicking back to that first night we spent together at the Notting Hill Hotel. It was the first time I felt like I was a part of a big family. And that truth or dare game was innocent at first. Until it evolved into something else. Something we would play on almost all our nights out or when we were bored. Until it got out of hand…

"Strange that Hari still hasn't shown up," Adrien muses. "Wasn't she supposed to be here an hour ago?"

"She's not always the most reliable." Kyan's eyes flash with an emotion I can't recognize as he checks his phone again. Apparently seeing no new messages from Hari, he looks up and abruptly changes the subject. "We should probably talk about tomorrow."

We all know what's coming, and despite the warm evening air, a chill settles on the patio.

"The police want us to come to the station at ten a.m. They said they would question us separately, that it would take about a half hour for each of us. We can go into the station one at a time if you would all like, so that we don't have to sit and wait for everyone to finish."

"No," Ellery says, delicately slipping her hand into mine so that our fingers lace together, and I squeeze back. "We should do this together."

"Agreed," Declan joins. His eyes meet mine before quickly darting away.

"It's settled then," says Kyan.

There's no further discussion. It's as if our minds have finally returned to the reason we're here. Not for a fun reunion, as Ellery had originally planned, but to confront Phoebe's death.

I open my mouth, trying to find the words to fill this new cavernous awkwardness, but Ellery gets there first.

"Does anyone actually remember anything about the night Phoebe went missing? Did anyone see her after she left dinner?"

I feel the sweat grow heavy on my palms as I try to keep my face void of emotion. The silence returns, but thankfully not for long. Adrien is the first to answer.

"No. To be fair, I assumed she'd run away. I mean, she'd pretty much burned all her bridges by that point."

The rest of the group nods along with Adrien's sentiment—as do I; I mean, what other choice do I have?—but as I sneak a glance around the patio, I can't help but notice that no one is making eye contact. Only Adrien seems confident in her statement, staring at each of us as if waiting for someone to challenge her. In the instant her eyes meet mine, I flick my gaze downward, praying she doesn't see the heat rise in my cheeks.

"Same," Declan mumbles after a pause that is several seconds too long. I open my mouth to voice some inane words of agreement, but as I do, an enormous yawn sneaks out.

"Whoa there, tiger," Kyan says with a wink, and I can tell he's relieved for an opportunity to break the tension. "Looks like it's past someone's bedtime."

I feel my face flush as I sneak a glance at the sun, which has only just started its slow descent towards the ocean.

"I'm sorry, I just didn't sleep much on the flight and—"

"You don't need to apologize," Ellery jumps in. "This jet lag is awful. Come on," she says, pulling me up from the couch. "I'll follow you up."

Declan rises too, and for a moment his arms begin to lift, and I think he's going to wrap me in a hug. But he seems to catch himself, lowering them so quickly that I wonder whether I simply imagined it. "Get some sleep, Claire," he says eventually.

I give him a stiff smile, not daring to talk should he sense the emotion stuck in my throat.

It's dark when I wake. Gradually my eyes adjust, taking in the bedroom. It adopts the same minimalistic approach as the living room—white everything, from the walls to the armchair in the corner to the lush duvet draped over the king-size bed—but with sparkling accents of color. An emerald rug lies against the hardwood, matching the large fern tucked against the wall and a large painting above the bed of the ocean, its crashing waves depicted in paint swirls of deep blues and greens.

I check my phone, which tells me it's just past five in the morning. Despite being unconscious for nearly twelve hours, my body feels as though I ran a marathon yesterday. Even so, I know further sleep is impossible.

Five hours until the police station. Five hours until the truth may come out. Until the police might figure out what I've done. Until my friends—once my family—might never be able to look at me again.

I lie there, in the luxuriously comfortable bed, picking apart our group conversation on the patio yesterday. I think of how cagey everyone seemed to get when the topic turned to Phoebe's disappearance, how quickly they all were to agree Phoebe had simply run away. Am I just projecting, or do they know more than they've been letting on this whole time?

Do they know I snuck out of my room that night, followed her? Do they know what happened after? About the knife?

Anxiety shoots through me, a sudden restlessness gnawing at my limbs. I need to get up, to get my mind straight. To calm down before we head to the station.

I'll make coffee, I decide. And suddenly, there's nothing in the world I crave more.

I get up, stopping in the en suite bathroom to brush my teeth and splash some water on my face before pulling on a pair of leggings and a sweatshirt I'd thrown in my suitcase. I open the door to my bedroom, pausing as a small undercurrent of sound hits my ears. It takes me a moment to understand what it is. Whispering.

I take a cautious step forward. The sound is coming from the end of the hallway, the bedroom Ellery pointed out last night as we headed to bed. The room at the end of the hall belongs to Declan. I remember, because I tried not to react when Ellery told me he would be staying in the room next to mine. Even so, she'd shot me a sympathetic look.

"I'm sorry that things are still so weird between the two of you. I'm here if you want to talk about it."

I didn't. I still don't.

I peer into the dark hall now and make out a person in Declan's doorway, speaking rapidly in hushed tones. I step back quickly, aware that if they turn just slightly, they'll see me eavesdropping, backlit from my bedroom light, which I quietly turn off.

I brace myself against the doorframe, attempting to make out any words through the whispers.

"They don't know." Declan's once familiar Irish brogue floats over to me, strong and certain. "I've told you. It was ten years ago, and no one even suspected back then."

"Shh," the other voice comes again. Still too quiet to make out an accent or gender, nothing to give any indication who it might be. "I just need you to promise that you'll keep this between us."

I crane my neck, but I can't make out Declan's response. Instead, I hear the soft padding of footsteps heading towards me.

Quickly, I pull the bedroom door shut, my heart hammering against my chest.

They don't know… No one even suspected.

Questions flood my brain, but I know one thing for certain.

I'm not the only one here with a secret.

8

CLAIRE

Now

"GOOD MORNING."

His voice is soft and sleepy, and for a moment, I anticipate the feel of his arms around me, his palms on my stomach, pulling me into a tight embrace just like he used to do when we would wake up entwined on one of our small twin beds.

But this time, there's nothing but the brush of air as Declan walks past the stool I'm perched on in front of Kyan's massive granite kitchen island.

"Good morning," I say as he pours himself coffee.

"How'd you sleep?" Declan asks, turning around and leaning against the counter. His ease stings the back of my eyes, as if all of this is normal. The two of us waking up in the same house, sharing a cup of coffee in the kitchen before starting our day.

What might have been if we hadn't ruined everything.

"Pretty good." I hesitate, preparing myself to ask a question I haven't quite formulated yet. One that would resolve all the thoughts that have been floating around in my head the last hour, since I heard Declan and the mystery person whispering.

It was ten years ago, and no one even suspected.

It shouldn't be surprising that Declan's been keeping a secret from me. We've barely spoken in a decade, our communication relegated to messages in the group chat (none of which directly responded to the other, of course) and social media stalking (on my end at least). But even so, his secret still comes as a betrayal.

But before I can begin to articulate any of the questions I have for him, I'm interrupted.

"Ah, God, I would marry that bed if I could." Ellery's upbeat voice cuts through the kitchen. She stops and gives me a hug on her way to the coffeemaker, apparently oblivious to the awkward silence in the kitchen.

When she turns around, her cheerful tone and smile are gone. "So, are you guys ready?"

Two hours later, the five of us are squeezed into Kyan's Tesla Model S, weaving through the narrow hills. He whips around the turns, accelerating whenever a straight stretch of road makes it possible, making my unsettled stomach even queasier.

None of us have spoken since getting into the car. The atmosphere in the house this morning was tense to say the least. No one was particularly talkative, Kyan least of all. Hari apparently never showed last night, something that Kyan assured us repeatedly was "normal," but which seemed to have lodged a permanent crease between his eyes.

After several more gut-crunching turns, we're thrown into the bumper-to-bumper traffic of the city center. Moisture pools in my palms as Kyan pulls into a parking area. In front of us looms a massive glass-windowed building, far more modern than the run-down police stations back in Chicago.

I inhale deeply and hear Ellery do the same next to me. I think again of the others' discomfort last night, the whispers this morning. Are they simply dreading having to relive the night Phoebe disappeared or is it something more?

We pile out of the car and head in. In the lobby, Adrien takes the lead, the rest of us following her to the front desk, where she explains who we are to the severe-looking receptionist.

"Take a seat in the corner over there," the brunette says in a clipped accent as she motions to a sterile area that wouldn't look out of place in a hospital waiting room, decorated with hard-cushioned chairs and end tables stacked with outdated magazines. "Leading Senior Constable Sawkins will be with you in a moment."

We each take a seat, the nervous quiet clawing at us. After a few minutes, our eyes collectively dart across the lobby to the elevator as it dings.

Out walks a man who I can only presume is Sawkins. He's tall, lanky enough that his khaki pants and dull blue button-up shirt seem to hang off him. He appears to be in his midthirties—probably only a few years older than we are—but his receding hairline paints him as older.

"Good morning," he says stiffly upon reaching us. "I'm Leading Senior Constable Arnold Sawkins." He flashes a badge. "I'm very grateful that you made the long journey to assist us in the investigation of Ms. Barton, and thank you also to Mr. Quek," he says, nodding towards Kyan, "for providing accommodation."

I sneak a glance at Kyan, who remains uncharacteristically quiet.

"My colleague Inspector Villanueva and I will question you each individually. It should take about thirty minutes per person." I cringe inwardly at the thought of staying here for two and a half more hours. "We do have coffee while you wait." Sawkins gestures to a counter in the corner of the sitting area, laden with an outdated Keurig machine and a handful of single-serve creamers that look far from tempting.

"We'd like to start with Mr. Walsh." Sawkins's eyes flick around our little group before coming to rest upon Declan, who stands. "If you could please come with me." He gestures back towards the elevator, and Declan turns, shooting us a look of mild fear and resolution. Ellery gives him a thumbs-up. All I manage is a weak smile.

Time passes unbearably slowly. The only noises punctuating the uncomfortable silence are the breeze of the automatic door as people enter the lobby and the buzz of the daytime television show from the TV on the other side of the sitting area.

After nearly thirty minutes, Declan returns, Sawkins again by his side.

Adrien is next. She stands, poised as ever, her height allowing her to meet Sawkins's gaze directly, and follows him to the elevator.

"How'd it go?" Ellery asks in a rushed voice. "What kind of questions did they ask you?"

"It was fine," Declan responds. "They just wanted to retrace those last few days we spent in Jagged Rock before Phoebe...went missing. Nothing unexpected."

Ellery nods, returning to her in-depth examination of her cuticles, but my eyes stay on Declan, his faraway gaze, his hands constantly fiddling. I can't help but wonder what it is he's not sharing.

Eventually Adrien returns, and Ellery leaves. Then it's Kyan. None of them talk much or even make more eye contact than necessary when they get back. All the while, anxiety rises in my chest, filling my lungs like a balloon in serious danger of popping at any moment.

I can't help but wonder if this is part of Sawkins's plan, questioning me last. Does he suspect me?

I keep trying to silently reassure myself. *They don't know anything. They can't.* But each time I repeat it in my mind, I believe it less and less.

Finally, it's my turn. I stand abruptly as I hear the elevator ding once again and head towards it before I'm even summoned, ready for whatever is about to happen to be over as quickly as possible. Kyan nudges me as I walk by him. "Good luck," he whispers.

"Ms. Whitlock, right this way," Sawkins says, leading me into the elevator.

As soon as the doors shut, I'm trapped. It's just him and me in this confined space, no attempts at small talk, not even the soft rhythm of Muzak to alleviate the pressure. I feel my heart bang rapidly against my chest.

Finally, the door opens. I step out the elevator first, eager to get out of there, even though I know what's coming next will be much worse.

Sawkins leads me down a nondescript hallway as people walk briskly past us in and out of the offices that line either side. Eventually, he stops before a closed door.

"Right this way," he says as he opens it, gesturing for me to enter.

I take a deep breath.

The room is small, windowless, with painted white brick walls. Even though it's furnished with only a small rectangular table and four plastic chairs, one of which is occupied, it feels cramped. There's no pane of glass like in the movies, no way for someone to be watching from the other side of the wall. Maybe that's only for real suspects. Should I take that as a good sign? But as my eyes sweep the room, I spot a small blinking red light in the far corner—a camera.

"Good morning, Ms. Whitlock." A woman stands up from her seat at the table and extends a petite hand in my direction, which I accept cautiously. She's slight, her thick black hair parted in the middle and slicked back into a neat braid, but despite her size, she exudes a tough confidence. It's instantly clear that she—not Sawkins—is the one in charge here. "I'm Inspector Samia Villanueva," she says in a voice with just a hint of an accent. "Thank you for making the long journey to help us."

"Of course," I say.

"So," she says, sitting back down and gesturing to the seat across from her, suggesting I do the same. Sawkins sits next to her. "As you are already aware, a few days ago, we found Phoebe Barton's remains in Jagged Rock." She says this without any attempt at empathy, simply recognizing a fact. "We understand the two of you were close?"

"Yes," I say. My mouth is dry, my lips sticky. In every crime show I've ever watched, the police always start a questioning by offering the suspect water. I take a quick glance down at the table, but there's nothing so much as a Dixie cup in sight.

"And you remember the night that Ms. Barton went missing? Looks like that would have been..." She flips open a manila envelope in front of her, although I'm sure that after having already asked this question four times now, she knows the date by heart. "December twenty-fifth, 2015."

"Mostly."

"Can you go through everything you remember from that day?"

Flashes return. The knife. Phoebe pleading.

"It was a normal day, as far as I remember," I start, my voice surprisingly steady. "It was supposed to be our last day in Jagged Rock. We were due to head back to Sydney the next morning, so we spent it mostly packing and relaxing."

"Except for dinner."

"Right. We all had dinner that night together at the Raven Inn, where we were staying."

"And did anything happen at that dinner?" Villanueva continues, not missing a beat.

"Nothing memorable, I don't think." I wait for her to follow up, to remind me of the fights that erupted around the table as the night devolved into chaos, but she stays silent. "And after dinner, I read a little bit and then went to bed."

"Mm," Sawkins ponders. "No drinks together, just reading and bed? That seems like quite a tame night. Especially on Christmas."

A note of panic flicks at me, but I breathe it away. I've gotten used to lying after all these years.

"Yeah," I respond with a humorless chuckle. "By that point in the trip, we were all exhausted. And it didn't really feel like the holidays here. We're used to winter weather and all that."

"Let's back up for just a moment," Villanueva says. "You and Ms. Barton shared a room at the Raven Inn, correct?"

My memory hops back to that room, our two twin beds pushed to opposite walls, spread to reveal the once-maroon carpet, turned faded and dusty.

"Yes."

"And you both went to bed at the same time that night?"

Again, scenes flash across my memory. Sneaking out of the Inn through the back door. Chasing after her as the stars sparkled above us.

"She actually wasn't there when I went to bed," I respond, hoping that kernel of truth will help spear the next lie I'm about to tell. "I don't know where she went after dinner. I didn't see her after we ate."

"And she was acting completely normal that day?" This time the question comes from Sawkins.

"Yes, as far as I remember." I blink, forcing my eyelids to wash clean the memory of Phoebe, her knees buried in the red dirt, hands clasped in front of her, eyes pleading. "She didn't do anything that struck me as strange."

Villanueva looks at me for just a second too long before flicking her eyes back to the papers in front of her.

"Do you know if Ms. Barton was seeing anyone romantically at the time of her death?"

I feel my face flush. "There was a lot of..." I pause. "*Intimacy* among the group in the weeks we were together."

Villanueva interjects again with a knowing look. "And a lot of alcohol, I presume."

I nod.

"We've seen this thing before," Sawkins says haughtily. "Students coming over for study abroad programs, shedding the responsibilities they have at home. That's usually when accidents happen."

I feel as if I'm being scolded, but Villanueva shoos away Sawkins's disdain. "Do you remember who in the group Phoebe had relations with?"

"I know that she and Kyan got together at the beginning of the trip."

"Did that end poorly?"

"It was..." I fumble, trying to locate a word that understates the drama that followed. "A bit tense afterwards."

"And who ended it? The tryst, I mean."

"It was mutual," I say automatically and then instantly regret it. They've already talked to Kyan and Adrien, I'm sure they both gave the detectives an earful about what happened.

"Hmm," Villanueva murmurs, giving me a skeptical look. "And that was it? You're not aware of her being romantically involved with anyone besides Mr. Quek?"

I try to force the image away before it comes. The darkness of the Outback draped like a blanket over the land behind the Inn, the stars illuminating Phoebe's hair, her head tilted backward in passion.

"No."

"One last question," Villanueva says, and I feel my first sense of relief since waking this morning. It's almost over. I'm so close to getting through this without giving myself away. "Do you know anyone who would have wished Ms. Barton harm back then?"

"No, of course not," I say quickly. Too quickly.

"No? Not a single person?"

I shake my head, not trusting my voice as my mind ticks through the long list of people who had reason to be mad at Phoebe. Those of us who hated her.

"Maybe people were irritated with her, but I can't imagine anyone would have been angry enough to hurt her."

"I think what my partner is getting at, Ms. Whitlock," Sawkins interjects, "is that Ms. Barton's death was clearly a crime of passion."

"Wh-what?" My head snaps upward, my eyes zeroing in on Villanueva.

"According to the autopsy our office has conducted, Ms. Barton's cause of death was blunt force trauma to the skull."

"Blunt force trauma," I repeat inanely. "Okay, but couldn't she have tripped? And hit her head on a rock or something? Couldn't that have caused it?"

Villanueva looks at me curiously, and I instantly regret my question. But I need to know.

"No." Her response is terse. "The examination conducted on the remains yielded a finding of multiple skull fractures. Whoever killed Ms. Barton struck her with a blunt object over the head repeatedly. We have yet to identify the weapon, but it is very clear that this was a homicide."

My stomach roils and I feel the color in my skin drain. It's immediately replaced with moisture, clinging sickly to my underarms, my palms, my forehead.

Blunt force trauma.

But that's impossible. I never hit Phoebe. And I certainly didn't do anything to fracture her skull.

I don't think I'm prepared for any more surprises until Villanueva drops her final bomb.

"That same person—or, at least, we suspect it was that person—moved Ms. Barton to her final resting place at the entrance to the abandoned mine shaft a kilometer or so from the Raven Inn."

"The mine," I parrot back.

"Yes. We have evidence to suggest that she was still alive at the time her body was deposited there. Scratches and flicks of red paint that we've identified as nail polish on the inside door to the mine indicate that she tried to escape. However, she died from her head injuries before being able to do so."

Suddenly, I can't breathe, picturing Phoebe clawing at the door of the mine, yelling, pleading to be let out.

"I still don't understand how Jagged Rock police failed to search such an obvious place in the days following Phoebe's disappearance," Sawkins says, either not picking up on my distress or choosing to ignore it. Villanueva ignores him, changing the subject back to Phoebe.

"It would be helpful to know if anyone had strong feelings towards Ms. Barton."

My mind is still racing for it all to make sense, so I barely hear Villanueva's request. But then a sudden clarity descends.

It wasn't all my fault.

There's another killer. Someone who hated Phoebe. Someone she drove to murder. Who smashed in her skull and hid her body away in that mine.

"I...I don't know anyone who would...have killed her like that," I fumble.

Villanueva sighs, as if I've disappointed her.

"Look, Ms. Whitlock, I'm going to be direct with you. It is unlikely that Ms. Barton was killed by a stranger or someone she had only met a handful of times. We believe the perpetrator is someone close to her, likely one of the people staying with her at the Raven Inn in the days before her death."

She pauses, waiting for that to sink in. "So, we are focusing our investigation on those of you who participated in the Adventure Abroad program through Hamilton College."

She doesn't need to say anything further. Her intention is clear. She has a handful of suspects, and I'm one of them.

And most of the others are sitting in the waiting room downstairs.

9

CLAIRE

Now

I'M GUILTY. I KNOW that.

Phoebe would still be here if I hadn't lost control that night, grabbed the knife from the Inn's kitchen, and taken off after her.

But someone else is responsible too. That person struck her over the head repeatedly and left her to die in a dark, abandoned mine.

From the shifting glances and awkward silences, it was clear within minutes of returning to the AFP building lobby that Villanueva told everyone the same thing: that we are the prime suspects. And it's equally clear why she did so: to turn us against each other, to inspire someone to start talking to save themselves.

For the first time since arriving in Sydney, I'm grateful I came back. I need to be here to be the first to figure out what happened that night, to identify who really murdered Phoebe, before anyone discovers my role in her death.

And then there's the other thing.

Maybe finding out who that person is will lighten the burden I've carried with me for the past decade. Maybe it's my way of making it up to Phoebe, my penitence for those horrible mistakes I made ten years ago.

The five of us are back at Kyan's, huddled around his kitchen island, despite the massive empty dining room. Even though it's nearly dinnertime, we returned to the house to find an elaborate, catered lunch—perfectly rolled sandwich wraps, large serving trays of various salads, smaller bowls of veggies and dips—which, so far, only Adrien has had the stomach to touch. I scan the others' faces, everyone's expression carrying similar emotions: anguish, shock, grief, disbelief, and something else. Suspicion.

The car ride back passed mostly in silence, and since we've returned, Phoebe's murder has been hovering over all of us as we make inane comments about the weather and how delicious the hummus is.

"The police said someone smashed her skull in." I'm surprised to hear my own voice make this proclamation, at the strangely emotionless words coming from my mouth. But I can't stand not talking about it anymore. "Villanueva thinks it's one of us."

Four sets of eyes skirt away from me.

I know these people—or *knew* them. They couldn't really be capable of murder, could they?

And then I realize, they probably thought the same about me.

"Did the police question Hari?" Adrien asks Kyan.

He shrugs. "I haven't heard from her."

"I still think it's weird that she just never showed," Ellery says. "Wouldn't she have at least sent a text?"

Kyan nods and pulls out his phone. He types something in and then holds it up to his ear. After nearly a minute he puts it down.

"She's not answering her phone."

"Should we be concerned?" Declan asks.

Kyan sighs. "I didn't want to tell you all this, because, honestly, it's not my story to share. But Hari...well, she's had some rough patches since our program ended."

I lean closer. Hari deleted all her social media channels shortly after the program ended, and she never joined our group message chain. I figured it was because she had better things to do, that we didn't make the same impact on her that she did on us.

"I connected with her when I moved back to Sydney. She told me she took what happened on the trip hard. First with Tomas and then with Phoebe. She started partying more, taking things she shouldn't. She got hooked. First on opioids and then it escalated. Heroin."

Hari never cared what anyone thought of her. She was always carefree and just...happy in a way I always envied. I can't correlate my memories of her with this news.

"She got better, back on her feet. She told me she'd relapsed a few times, but she's been clean ever since I've reconnected with her, for the last year or so."

"Wow," Ellery says, clearly as shocked as I am.

"Kyan, you said she was flaky," I say. "Is this normal behavior for her?"

Kyan shakes his head. "She's not great at returning texts. And there was one time she stood me up for dinner—but she was really excited about seeing you all again. We'd talked about it a few times. I figured something came up last night, but now..."

"We should check on her," Declan says.

"I think you're right," Kyan agrees.

Twenty minutes later, we're back in Kyan's car, but this time we aren't heading into the city center.

"I've been to her place a few times," Kyan said back at his house. "When I would pick her up for dinner or coffee. It's not in a great part of town."

He wasn't lying, I realize, as his Tesla travels silently up dense, narrow streets lined with trash-filled sidewalks and run-down buildings. I spot a few people sleeping rough in the doorways of closed storefronts. We turn onto a quieter road and pull up in front of a black fence, behind which sits a brick apartment complex.

"This is it," Kyan announces. And then a second later, in response to our unasked questions: "Hari had a difficult time finding a job after everything. Despite how liberal and open-minded Australians claim to be, no one was jumping at the chance to hire a recovering addict. She's finally got a position as a grocery store cashier."

The information sits there, all of us remembering the potential Hari had. How she'd planned to get her PhD in sociology after she finished her degree at Hamilton. How she dreamed of becoming an academic, eventually a university professor.

I guess my life wasn't the only one that deteriorated once the program ended. I suppose it should be a comforting thought, but as I gaze up at the worn building, it feels anything but.

We all get out of the car, and I take a shaky breath as we stand there for a second, preparing ourselves. Declan is next to me, and despite everything, his presence gives me a slight sense of relief.

"Let's go," I say, forcing myself to take a step towards the building, and the others follow suit.

The gate opens, unlocked, and Adrien reaches the intercom first, a rusted-looking contraption affixed to front of the building. She finds Hari's last name—Masterson—and presses it. It rings loudly for several seconds, but there's no answer. She tries again. No luck. She begins the process of ringing the buttons for the other units until an older female voice that sounds like it's the product of decades of chain-smoking answers.

"What do ya want?"

"We're looking for our friend, Hari. Harriet. We're here to check on her, but she's not—"

The intercom buzzes as the front door lock unlatches. The woman clearly wasn't interested in Adrien's story, but no matter, at least we're in.

The building's foyer is musty, decorated with the odd piece of trash and one wall lined with a set of dejected mailboxes. A small hallway leads to the first-floor units, but according to the list of names on the intercom, Hari lives in unit 204, so we take the rickety stairway up until we reach level two.

A doormat sits in front of unit 204 that reads *Welcome* in looping cursive font with a picture of a palm tree, and I can't help but smile. This place may be completely and utterly depressing, but of course Hari would find a way to brighten it.

Ellery steps forward, knocks lightly on the door. "Hari, it's us." And then realizing how that sounds, she laughs. "I mean, it's Ellery and Claire and Kyan and..." She trails off when it's evident no one is coming towards the door. Then she tries again, rapping her knuckles against the door.

"Hold on," Declan says, grabbing the doorknob. "Let me try."

It opens without protest.

I've had a sinking feeling in my gut the entire drive over, but now my stomach flips. Something isn't right here. I can tell.

The others must too. I feel Ellery bristle next to me. Declan looks back at us as if for permission. Kyan nods, and Declan pushes the door further open, taking a step in.

The living room is sparse, but tastefully decorated. A surfboard rests against one corner, light green pillows line a beige couch, and a small potted cactus sits on the white coffee table.

But it's also empty.

I follow Declan and the others in, and we look around. A small kitchen sits off to one side of the living room—also empty, and neat, aside from two half-filled water glasses on a small wooden dinette table—and to the other side is a hallway that evidently leads to the bedroom.

"Hari?" Declan says, voice just slightly raised.

Kyan gestures in the direction of the bedroom. "Maybe one of you ladies should check. If she's in her bedroom, she might not be too happy with a bloke barging in on her."

I nod and step forward, clenching my fingers into my palms so that the others won't notice my slight tremble. Other than the unlocked front door, nothing seems off about the apartment, but that horrible feeling in my stomach just won't leave.

I finally reach her closed bedroom door.

"Hari, you in there?" I call gently.

I twist the doorknob, edging the door open to take in a cramped carpeted room occupied almost entirely with a dresser and a double bed, on which lies a figure on her side, facing away from me. I take in the faded blond hair, the long tanned legs pulled up to her chest. And I sigh, relief flooding through me.

Hari always could sleep through just about anything.

I get to the bed in two steps, feeling the others behind me in the doorway, and reach out my hand. "Hari, wake up," I say, my voice unnaturally childlike.

She's wearing a cropped T-shirt and a pair of baggy boyfriend jeans. An odd choice of clothing to nap in, but who am I to judge?

I reach for her shoulder, feeling the cotton of her shirt, and give her small shake.

Nothing.

"Hari, come on," I urge, trying again.

I steal a glance back at Ellery, whose wide eyes stare at me curiously.

I shift my hand to touch her bare arm at the same time I say, "Hari, you have to—"

As soon as my fingers make contact with her skin, I jolt back, as if burned.

"Cold," I say to nobody in particular. It's the only word that rings through my mind. "Why is she cold?"

But my touch was enough to send Hari rolling from her side onto her back. And then I see it, that face I knew so well. Her high cheekbones, now even more pronounced, her cheeks cavernous and blue-tinged. Her rosebud lips coated with dried vomit.

But I don't focus on those. All I can see are her green eyes. Open wide and staring into nothingness.

10

PHOEBE

Then

IN RETROSPECT, I SHOULD have gotten up half an hour ago when Claire first tried to wake me. By the time we get to the dorm's rec room for our Adventure Abroad orientation, Claire and I are ten minutes late.

Once we pull open the heavy door, the rumble of air-conditioning floods our ears. The room looks like it hasn't been updated in decades. A projector hangs from one wall, and pool and air hockey tables are squished into a corner. A combination of beat-up couches and an odd pairing of random recliners and fold-up chairs, almost all of which are occupied, decorate the middle of the room. The others look a bit worse for wear, but at least they all managed to show up on time. Ellery's face is slightly green beneath her heavy makeup, Kyan is wearing sunglasses despite the low overhead light, and Hari manages only a small smile as we enter. The only one who looks immaculate is Adrien. Of course.

A voice booms from the man standing next to Hari. "Oi, you're late." He's the largest person in the room by far, both in height and weight, and he's wearing an impressive scowl. A huge, bushy red beard extends from his chin, complemented by shoulder-length ginger hair tied back in a ponytail. An Australian Hagrid, with all the size and none of the kindness.

I suddenly feel trapped beneath his anger and the others' attention, and I feel my flight-or-fight instinct kick in. I settle on the latter option.

"So sorry about that," I say, my voice saccharine. "But I promise you, we're worth the wait."

I glance over at Kyan, who smirks, and I feel a ripple of victory as Claire and I sit in the two fold-up chairs next to the couch where he is. I feel a prickle of irritation that Adrien managed to grab the spot on his other side.

"Well, aren't we lucky," Australian Hagrid says, sarcasm dripping from his rangy accent. "Just the type of humility I appreciate in my students." He clears his throat. "As I was saying before that little *interruption,* my name is Nick Gould. I'm the faculty member at Hamilton College who'll be leading this expedition. And this here is Harriet, my teaching assistant. She'll be accompanying us over the next month."

"Nice to see you all," Hari says primly. Upon sensing Nick's curiosity, she turns to him, her voice softer. "I ran into a few of them last night."

"Entirely sober, I suspect," Nick says with an eye roll. Before Hari can respond, he continues. "As you should all know by now, this program is intended to introduce you to Australia and all the country's adventures." He flicks his eyes across the paper he holds in his massive hand, reading from it verbatim. "'To establish connections with people from all over the world and to understand why nearly twenty-six million people on this planet have chosen to call this magnificent country home.'" He drops the paper with a flourish. "Well, this is bloody rubbish."

Tomas laughs lightly, apparently assuming that was the expected response. Nick's stare fixes on him until the sound dries from Tomas's mouth.

"Okay that's enough of that shite," Nick says, resuming his presentation. "Since we'll be stuck with each other for a month, we may as well get the introductions over with. You know me and Hari already, but this stupid thing," he sneers down at the paper, "says everyone in the group needs to go around and say their name, where they've from and—oh God—a 'fun fact' about themselves." He sighs. "Well, let's get this over with. You start." He points at Declan.

We go painfully around the group, repeating our names and hometowns like we did yesterday, this time adding in our "fun fact," which, as Nick predicted, is definitely not as exciting as its name suggests. Although, some do surprise me. Kyan's family owns a luxury hotel company that operates throughout Southeast Asia; Ellery is fluent in three languages and proficient in two more; Adrien's spent the last few summers volunteering in an orphanage in Lesotho. *God, those poor kids*, I can't help but think. Others are blander. Tomas has dreamed of traveling to the Outback since he was a child; Claire never learned how to ride a bike (an admission she makes ruefully);

Declan's secondary school football team was named one of the best in Ireland. I scour my mind for one that would be equal parts tantalizing and impressive, but my memory lodges on that one night. My hand on the wheel, the shattering of glass.

"Leonardo DiCaprio hit on me at a bar in LA," I say when it's my turn.

Not exactly true, and by not exactly, I mean not at all, but it got the response I expected. That is, from everyone except for Adrien, who I heard mutter "bullshit" under her breath. Funny, I could say the same about her claim of being an off-brand Angelina Jolie.

Through it all, Nick seems nonplussed. It's not clear if he's even listening half the time.

Kyan leans over to me at one point, the feeling of his breath in my ear sending a ripple of pleasure down my spine.

"Should we continue our game from last night?"

It takes me a moment to remember what he's referring to, but then it clicks. Truth or dare.

I turn and whisper, "Dare."

Kyan smiles, shoots a look to make sure Nick isn't paying attention—he's not so furtively checking his phone as Ellery shares her fun fact—and whispers, "I dare you to do something to embarrass Nick."

I raise my eyebrows. "You're on."

"Well, now that that's over, let's run through the agenda for the trip."

"Actually Nick," I say, raising my hand like a schoolgirl. "I have a question first."

Nick doesn't say anything, simply raises his bushy eyebrows.

"How open are Australians to foreigners?"

Nick looks at me like I'm an idiot. "We're pretty welcoming, yeah," he says in a tone that couldn't possibly be more unwelcoming if he tried.

"I mean sexually."

Nick's face turns a shade that can only be described as puce as muffled laughter breaks out through the group. Confidence flows through me upon realizing some of it comes from the seat next to me. That is until Nick takes a step closer to me.

For a moment, I think he's going to come after me. I close my eyes, already imagining the feel of hands on my arm, a voice in my ear. *You are nothing.*

But when I open my eyes, Nick isn't even within touching distance. *He won't hurt you. Not like him*, I tell myself. *You're safe.*

Although based on the rage in Nick's eyes, I'm not sure if that's true.

"That's enough," he says through gritted teeth. "I don't tolerate that shit here."

I think about making another quip, but his expression makes me reconsider.

"Now, back to the agenda." As he speaks, Nick's tension releases slightly, like a balloon deflating. "We'll be starting here in Sydney for the weekend, taking it fairly easy, exploring, heading out to the Blue Mountains for a day before we head out. All in all, we'll be hitting four destinations. I'm not going to run through it all, as I'm sure yous're all familiar with the program's schedule."

In that assumption, he's wrong. I barely bothered to read the program summary in the brochure I snagged from my school's study abroad office. Instead, I made my decision as soon as I clocked Adventure Abroad's location—the furthest of all the programs from my university in Atlanta.

I steal a glance around the room at the others, all of whom seem to be more familiar with the schedule than I am and who are clearly excited about it. Except for Nick Gould.

"Fine, then. No questions. The bus for today's city tour is waiting. We'll start with the botanical gardens, then the opera house, and we'll hit the barracks on the way back to campus."

As Nick grabs a bag he's slung over one of the tables, Josh perks up from where he's draped across a couch. "Any chance we can stop for a Bloody Mary on the way? I could really use some hair of the dog."

I see Nick's spine go rigid, and when he turns, his face is a deep maroon. "Oi. It seems like some of you think this program is a chance for you to get away from school and be loose and loud and do everything you wouldn't get away with at home. But it's not. This is an educational opportunity." He delivers the last phrase with a healthy string of saliva. "You're not at home anymore, no mum or da here to keep an eye on ya. And you better believe Hari and I won't be babysitting yous. You're on your own out here, so ya best start acting like adults."

The speech is so similar to one of my father's scoldings that I can't help but sit up a bit straighter.

"Straya," Nick continues, "is a dangerous place. It's home to more deadly species than any other country in the world." Taking the time to make eye contact with each of us, Nick rolls up his sleeve, baring his forearm for the entire room to see. Even from here, I can make out two red dots amid the bush of ginger arm hair. "King brown snake," he says, using his left hand to point at the scars. "The largest venomous snake in Australia. Had to suck the venom out myself when I was hiking outside Jagged Rock, where we'll be going. Yous need to be vigilant. Careful. Focused on something other than flirting and drinking."

He shoots us another look as if daring one of us to contradict him. "Now head to the bus," he orders.

I begin following the others to the door, but Nick's gruff voice stops me.

"Oi, you." When I turn, he's pointing one of his hot dog-like fingers in my direction. "Stay back a minute."

He waits for everyone else to leave, until it's just the two of us.

Goose bumps prickle my skin as he walks towards me, apparently no longer concerned with keeping the bus waiting.

He doesn't stop until he's close enough that I can smell his breath, his broad shoulders leaning over me. I clock again how much larger he is than me, how easily he could break me. My spine stiffens as I hear that voice again. *I can do whatever I want to you and nobody would care.*

"As I said," Nick says coldly. "I don't tolerate that type of bullshit on my programs, got it?"

"I didn't—"

"You did. I know your sort. Privileged, rich girls used to getting away with anything. Acting like you're better than everyone."

Despite the fear flooding through me, I feel a small ripple of anger. "That isn't me," I say, even though it's not that far from the truth. "And you don't know anything about—"

He grabs my upper arm, tight. I try to gasp, but my breath catches in my throat.

"Listen." Specks of saliva land on my cheek and I cringe. "You do not want to fuck with me."

I stare up at him, too stunned to speak, already feeling the bruises blooming beneath his fingers.

"Now get to the bus."

He releases his hand from my arm and shoves me towards the door.

11
CLAIRE

Now

"ALL SIGNS POINT TO overdose."

The EMT who arrives to take Hari away is a no-nonsense woman in her forties who looks like she's seen enough to last five lifetimes. "There was a syringe on her nightstand and track marks running up her arms. Unfortunate, but fairly standard. We've been seeing them more and more in this neighborhood."

We're standing outside Hari's apartment building, the shock of finding her body only just beginning to fade, the image of her lying prone on her bed still camped decisively behind my eyelids.

The rest of the group is silent, and I watch them as I try to take it in. Hari's death is *fairly standard.* I can't stop picturing her as she was years ago: full of life, always jumping at an opportunity to introduce us to something uniquely Australian. The first one to crack a joke to relieve an awkward moment, always walking around barefoot, however inappropriate that was given the venue. The only person I ever met who could make Nick Gould laugh.

And now she's gone.

There was nothing back then to indicate a fondness for drugs, nothing to suggest her life would eventually take this path. I mean she drank quite a bit, but didn't we all? No matter how hard I try, I can't make it fit, how she ended up here, sticking a needle in her arm, her dreams long forgotten.

"What time did she die?" Declan asks.

"Hard to tell without an autopsy," the EMT muses. "If I had to guess, based on the state of the body, I would say sometime yesterday. Afternoon or evening. But I'm no coroner."

She loads the covered stretcher into the back of the ambulance, its siren and lights dormant. "We'll take her in and alert the next of kin."

"That's it?" Ellery asks. "Shouldn't we wait for the police?"

The EMT shakes her head. "They don't come out for overdoses anymore, especially if there are no suspicious circumstances. We ran the address through our database, and it looks like we came out here for the deceased on several different occasions, all for previous overdoses. Only those times we caught it early enough." She doesn't bother trying to keep the disdain from her tone.

She shuts the door, and the ambulance pulls away, quickly merging into traffic.

"So, that's it, then," Ellery says, her voice breaking.

Declan rests a hand on her shoulder, and I drape an arm around the other side.

"We should go back up there," I say, feeling as though I'm listening to someone else speaking. "Make sure the door is closed and see if there's a way to lock it so no one breaks in."

The others agree, and Kyan insists on having all of us go together. I'm grateful; the last thing I want is to be alone right now.

Moments later, we're back in Hari's apartment.

"It doesn't make sense to me." This comes from Adrien, who's standing in the living room, staring down the hallway towards Hari's bedroom. Despite the stricken look on her face, her tone is analytical. "Why would she have injected herself when she was planning to meet us?"

"For addicts, it doesn't matter what they have planned or what they intend to do," Ellery says from where she's rifling through a kitchen drawer in search of an extra apartment key we can use to lock the door behind us. "They'll get a hit in any circumstances they can."

Declan looks at Ellery inquisitively.

"I used to volunteer at the Veteran Affairs Canada," she explains. "I worked with quite a few addicts."

Kyan shrugs, having taken a seat on the couch. "But I saw her a week ago and she was completely fine. We met for coffee, and she was saying how she had just hit two years clean. And she was really excited to see everyone again. I even texted with her yesterday morning. She was confirming what time she should come over."

I think about this from where I stand in the entryway to the kitchen. It *is* weird, but then again, Ellery has a point. Maybe something happened that made Hari lose her resolve before she left for Kyan's.

"Wow. Guys, look at this." Ellery is holding a printed photo in her hands, which she evidently just pulled out of Hari's junk drawer. "This is a blast from the past."

Ellery hands the photo to Declan, whose eyes widen before passing it to me. I feel a rush when his hand brushes against mine, and I internally scold myself. This is certainly not the place or time for that.

I look at the photo in my hand. Hari stares up at me, her face older than it was the last time I saw her, her hair more neutral, no pink stripes in sight. A man nearly double her size stands next to her, his massive arm looped around her small shoulder. He's not smiling and is instead looking at the camera as if it offended him. I would recognize that look anywhere.

"Nick Gould," I breathe out.

"I had no idea they were still in touch," Kyan says when the photo reaches him. "God, he was quite a character wasn't he? Remember when he totally went off at that worker in the rest area we stopped at on the way to the Outback?"

Kyan continues, the others joining in on the memory, eager to think of anything besides the body of our friend we found one room over. But my mind drifts. Reliving how I entered Hari's bedroom, the moment my skin made contact with hers. The stiff coldness of her flesh.

And then I see them.

I noticed them before, but I didn't have any reason to find them important. But now...they don't fit. I take a step closer to the counter, my mind processing.

"Why does she have two water glasses set out?" I think aloud.

I feel the others' heads turn in my direction before taking in the two glasses set out on the counter. One has a lipstick stain on the rim—the same shade Hari was wearing, a pink that looked garish against her pale skin. But the other is clean.

"You think she had someone over?" Declan asks.

I don't answer, but my mind is already jumping to conclusions.

"The door was unlocked," Ellery says, her voice almost a whisper. "This isn't the type of place where you keep your door open."

"Wait," Kyan says, as if he's catching up. "You don't think that she...that someone... killed her?"

I want to laugh it away, to blame my paranoia on Inspector Villanueva's not-so-veiled threats earlier. I mean, it's Hari. Who would want to kill her?

Declan jumps in. "It fits with what you were saying earlier, Ky. It does seem like quite strange timing for her to fall off the wagon, especially given how excited she was about the reunion."

"But why?" Adrien considers.

Ellery takes this one. "Maybe drugs. A debt she didn't repay or something. Or..." The alternative dangles there between us for a second. "Maybe it has something to do with Phoebe."

My attention snaps towards her at this.

Ellery picks up steam. "I'm just thinking, Villanueva said someone from the Australian Abroad program likely killed Phoebe. And it seems odd that Hari would die from a suspicious overdose on the exact day we were all meant to be getting back together."

"So you think one of us killed her because Hari knew we were Phoebe's murderer?" Adrien says it facetiously, but it rings true. Anxiety rushes through me.

"That's ridiculous," Kyan says. "We were all at my house last night. None of us could have drugged Hari."

"Everyone went to bed fairly early, though," Ellery says tentatively.

"Someone could have snuck out last night and done it," I add, building on Ellery's thought. "Or even gone to her house earlier in the day, before we got to Kyan's, if the EMT is correct about the time Hari died." My memory flicks back to earlier this morning. The whispers I overheard from down the hall.

The others' eyes dart around the room. No one can bring themselves to make eye contact. Am I really standing in this room with a murderer?

Another murderer, a cruel voice in my head reminds me.

"Come on," Kyan says, forcing out a laugh. "None of us killed Hari, obviously. This is just what Villanueva was saying earlier, screwing with our heads. We should go back to the house. I, for one, could use a cocktail."

We mumble our agreement as we trail behind Kyan out of the apartment, Ellery using the key she finally found in Hari's junk drawer to lock the front door.

I breathe in the air when we get outside, thankful to be out of that confined space. Darkness has fallen, and the harsh squeak of bats comes from nearby. Shadows fall across the others' faces, making them look suddenly unfamiliar.

"It could have been someone else in our group," Declan proposes weakly as we reach the street.

Adrien scoffs. "I'm pretty sure neither Tomas nor Phoebe killed Hari."

Declan shakes his head. "That's not what I mean, of course."

"And Josh isn't even here," Kyan says.

"No," Declan concedes, "but there was another person."

I think back to the face staring out at me from the photo I held minutes ago. The sharp line of his mouth, the unexplained anger in his eyes. And despite the night's heat, I shiver as I say his name. "Nick Gould."

"Does this happen to you often? People camping out in front of your gate?" Adrien asks as we pull up in front of Kyan's house. It's the first time any of us have spoken during the ride back from Hari's, everyone lost in their thoughts.

I've considered calling the police, telling Villanueva my suspicions, having them run a fingerprint or DNA test on the second glass in Hari's apartment to find out who it belonged to, but I keep thinking back to the EMT's reaction. *Fairly standard.* Hari was an addict—they won't waste precious public funds on her.

Plus, it's not like Villanueva trusts any of us. She's made that much clear.

Adrien's question jars me back to the present. Kyan doesn't answer, but sure enough, there's someone standing there, waiting by his gate, a suitcase at their feet. In the darkness, it's impossible to tell the person's gender—let alone if we recognize them. Something about it feels wrong, off. Maybe it's the shock still coursing through my veins, but I'm not up for any more surprises tonight.

Kyan slows the car, rolls down the window. "Can I help you?"

"I think you can," the stranger replies.

And then the shoe drops, just as Declan voices my exact thought. "What are *you* doing here?"

I freeze, my muscles locked in the backseat as I see him lean into the window, the light of the dashboard illuminating his round face and sandy hair.

"That's no way to greet an old friend, now, is it?"

"Josh!" Ellery squeals. "You said you weren't coming!"

He rubs his hand over the two-day stubble covering his cleft chin, his expression sheepish. "Ta-da."

"Well get in, get in," Kyan encourages. "It's just a short drive up to the house."

As the three of us contort ourselves to make room for him in the backseat, limbs brushing against limbs, bones jabbing bones, a heavy anxiety settles in my lungs like dust.

Josh smiles at me across the others. I don't return it, hoping he can read the question in my eyes.

"Ellery said you had a work conflict," I say. I don't mention that he told me this himself when we discussed the reunion. How it made me feel better for initially declining Ellery's invitation. The others don't need to know that we still talk. Especially Declan.

"I worked around it. I couldn't turn down a chance to see you all again. Plus, I wanted to help with the investigation."

"Are you going to talk with the police?" Adrien asks.

"Already did. My flight got in earlier this afternoon, and I took an Uber directly from the airport to the AFP office. Figured I would surprise you guys, but I've been sitting here for the better part of an hour. Surprise is on me, I guess." He gives a little chuckle. "Where were you anyway?"

The silence, warmed by Josh's joviality, now ices back over.

"It's a long story," Adrien says from the front seat. "Why don't we wait until we're inside?"

We've settled back on the patio. Kyan's started the electric fireplace—an entirely infeasible fixture for a Sydney balcony overlooking the beach, especially given how hot it is, but in complement with his pristine white furniture, it gives the evening a chic, cozy vibe.

The story the five of us relay to Josh about Hari, however, sits in stark contrast.

"She's really...dead?" Josh's disbelief reflects my own. Hari was always such a presence in our group. The second-in-line leader, the big sister all of us wanted.

"Yeah," Ellery responds solemnly. "But that's not all..."

She recounts to Josh our conversation in Hari's apartment.

"But that's kind of a stretch isn't it?" Josh responds. "I mean it certainly makes more sense that she shot up herself and overdosed. As tragic as that would be."

"Did Villanueva mention to you that she thinks we're the main suspects in Phoebe's death?" I ask.

He pauses for a second. "Yeah, but I think that's ridiculous. I mean there were plenty of locals back in Jagged Rock. Any one of them could have killed Phoebe. For any kind of reason. And Hari's death could just be a horrible coincidence. We know each other, guys."

I want to believe him; I do. But we *don't* know each other, not really. None of them could ever imagine what I did back then.

"It's not just us, though," Ellery chimes in. "Nick Gould was with us back then too. And Hari apparently still talked to him. She had a photo of the two of them in her apartment."

"Wow, Nick Gould," Josh muses. "God, I haven't thought about that guy in years. But yeah, now that I think about it, he really had it in for Phoebe. Ever since that first day at orientation, but especially after Tomas..."

The name hangs in the air, the brief burst of joyful nostalgia curdling back into grief.

"Nick was really angry the night she disappeared." My tone is serious once again.

"He was our teacher," Declan says. "Would he really have killed her just because she was an irritating student? I mean, he taught Kyan, and he lived to tell the tale."

The joke falls flat.

"Does anyone know what happened to him? Does he still work at Hamilton?" Josh asks.

We all shake our heads. It's not like any of us are Facebook friends with him.

Adrien pulls out her phone, and within minutes, she glances up at us, a victorious glean in her eye.

"Found him. Looks like he stopped teaching in 2018. Online property records shows that he's the full owner of a ranch in"—she squints at her screen—"a town called Rollowong."

Kyan raises an eyebrow in her direction. "That was quick."

"I'm a defense attorney. Digging up dirt on people is part of the job," she says with a half smile, but it still sends a shiver down my spine. *What could she find on me?*

"Rollowong," Declan repeats, his brogue making the town sound even more foreign. "I remember that name. Wasn't it close to Jagged Rock?"

Adrien's back on her phone. "Looks like it's just outside it actually."

Nick Gould went back to where Phoebe was killed.

I think of all those crime shows I used to watch with my mother, when the plot was pure entertainment, not something that could actually happen to me. In them, the police were always talking about how perpetrators went back to the scene of the crime, to relive their experience. Is that what Nick has been doing?

"Interesting," Kyan says, "that Hari still kept in touch with him even though he moved so far away."

"Wow," Adrien says, her finger still scrolling on her phone.

"There's this Reddit thread all about him. It says he got fired from Hamilton, that he attacked a student."

Kyan leans closer to Adrien, reads over her shoulder.

"Attacked?" I ask.

Kyan nods. "Says he lost his shit on some kid, hit him so badly that the student ended up in the ICU."

We all sit with that information for a moment. If Nick lost control on a student once, what's stopping him from having done it before?

"Maybe we could go there and talk to him," Josh proposes.

No.

The word skitters around my head.

Apparently, my expression isn't the only one radiating disgust.

"Whoa, okay," Josh says, raising his hand as he looks around the group. I immediately try to fix my face. "It was just a suggestion."

"We should just leave it to the police," Adrien says.

"I don't know," Ellery says slowly, as if warming to the idea. "Josh kind of has a point. I mean, the AFP made it pretty clear that we're their main suspects."

I think back to Villanueva's proclamation. How she's focusing the investigation on those of us who participated in the Adventure Abroad program.

"Did they mention Nick Gould to any of you during our interviews?" I ask, a thought budding.

The others shake their heads.

"This is the Australian Federal Police, though," Declan says. "It's not like we're dealing with the Jagged Rock cops who couldn't solve a crime if the perpetrator break-danced in front of them. The AFP are the real deal. I'm sure they'll investigate Nick too."

But I'm not. Especially if they don't have reason to suspect Hari's overdose wasn't an accident.

And I start reconsidering. Maybe going back to Jagged Rock isn't the worst idea. If Nick really is behind this—if he killed Phoebe *and* Hari—and we can prove it, it will take any suspicion off me once and for all. My name would be cleared.

Apparently I'm not the only one thinking about it.

"It could be nice, actually." Ellery says. "A way to memorialize the reunion. Maybe we could even swing through Jagged Rock. See if the place has changed at all. I didn't plan anything for tomorrow anyway, since I didn't know how long the police interviews would take."

"Yeah, but it's not like we can just hop on over to Rollowong," Kyan says. "It's about a twenty-hour drive from here."

"But there are flights, aren't there?" I say, thinking back to our hazy bus ride into Jagged Rock all those years ago. I distinctly remember passing an airport at some point.

Adrien's on her phone again. "There's an airport a few towns over from Rollowong. Looks like it's a forty-minute drive from Nick's address. But I don't have any particular desire to either see Jagged Rock or talk to Nick, let alone fly halfway across the country to do it."

Unlike Adrien, I'm convinced now. Hope glows in me at the chance of pegging Nick for this crime. Of making it all okay. Of moving on with my life.

"I think we owe it to Phoebe." The words are out of my mouth before I can reconsider. "None of us were very good friends to her back then. And we should have been there for Hari, with everything she's gone through the last few years. Maybe this is our chance to make up for it. Even if Nick didn't...you know...maybe he knows something that can help us. Something we could pass on to the police."

The others don't say anything, the shame for how we all acted back then draping over us like the night's thick humidity. The only one wearing an expression other than guilt is Adrien. Her gray eyes flash but she remains thankfully quiet.

"She's right." The support comes from the last person I'd expect. When I look over, Declan shoots me a warm smile.

"Ugh, fine," Kyan says eventually. "But we'll fly in and out. Make this trip as short as possible so we can be back by happy hour tomorrow. What do you guys say?"

Everyone nods, some more eagerly than others. I take a sip of my wine, but the thought clings to my throat.

We're going back.

12

CLAIRE

Now

I DON'T SLEEP MUCH that night, my sweaty limbs and disturbing memories twisting themselves up in Kyan's soft sheets for hours. I give up at any attempt as my room begins to lighten, the day just about to break through the cracks in the blinds.

I throw on a sweatshirt and head towards the kitchen, pausing slightly at the doorway to my bedroom, breathing only once I've confirmed the absence of the early morning whispers from yesterday. I wait at the coffeemaker until it finally froths out enough hot liquid for the six of us, and I grab a mug and take it out with me to the balcony.

It's been years since I've seen a sunrise like this one, a decade in fact. Pink crawls upwards in the sky, transforming the darkness into something beautiful. Despite the early hour and the chill in the air, the die-hard surfers are already out, black icons against a sea of color. But the beach itself is empty aside from an unmanned lifeguard stand.

I think how much my mother would have loved this. She was always exclaiming over a sunrise or a sunset, insisting we catch every one. *Tomorrow's never certain,* she'd say. *How could you live with yourself if you missed your last-ever sunset?*

The memory of her words pulses in my chest, a painful heartbeat. While she was dying, I was wasting countless sunsets over here.

I found out that first day I got back from Australia, when she met me at O'Hare Airport. I searched for her at the arrival gate, scanning the crowd, looking for her dark, curly hair hovering several inches above everyone else's with her five-foot-nine stature. But she wasn't there. I almost dropped to my knees at that point. The distress of having had it all for such a fleeting time—a best friend, a boyfriend, a family—only to have it all go up in smoke was too much. I wanted my mother. Only she would understand. Only she would make it better.

But when I did spot her, it wasn't the woman I knew. It wasn't my mother. It was a shell. A skinny frame confined to a wheelchair, red fabric wrapped around her head, dark circles beneath her eyes accentuating the hollows of her cheeks.

Pancreatic cancer, stage four. It was inoperable when the doctors found it, and she'd pushed for me to go abroad so I could avoid the worst of it. So I wouldn't be left with memories of the hardest weeks.

I wanted to collapse into her, but she looked so frail I realized I might break her if I did. I knew then that I would never tell her the truth. I could never tell her what I did, who I really was.

So I swallowed it for the few weeks she had left. I swallowed it as I tried to figure out what life looks like for a solitary twenty-year-old without friends, without a family. As I dropped out of college, swapping classes for a minimum wage job to support myself, selling the family home, and moving into a cramped downtown studio apartment. As I moved forward with a life I never wanted, one streaked with guilt and regret.

It formed a boulder in my throat, something I could never recover from. Until now.

"Hey."

The word yanks me from my thoughts, and I swipe the tear from my eye before Josh can see it. As I do, I realize how far the sun has risen in the sky, the pinkish light replaced by a golden glaze drizzled over the beach.

"Good morning," I respond as he sits down next to me. "Did you sleep well?"

I take in his mussed sandy hair and his sleepy eyes, and something throbs in my chest. There's a familiarity with Josh, an easiness. It's why I've never been able to stay away.

"Damn, that bed's amazing," he says, and I laugh.

We sit there for a moment, occasionally raising our respective mugs of coffee to our lips.

"I thought you weren't coming," I say eventually. I try to keep it light, but the accusation slips through in my tone.

"I know. I should have texted you. But to be honest, you were part of the reason I decided to come back."

"Really?"

"Yeah. I know how much you went through the last time. How close you were to Phoebe. I figured if you were strong enough to relive all that, the least I could do was to be here too."

The back of my eyes burn, and I force the tears away.

"Listen," I say. "The others, they can't know. They wouldn't understand."

He nods, but he won't meet my eyes.

"I won't tell them," he says eventually, resigned. "Don't worry."

I think of how similar the conversation is to the whispers I overheard yesterday morning, and I cringe. So many secrets, so many things we don't know about each other. Was it always like this?

"Hey." He turns to me, pulling a hand away from his mug and placing it on my arm. There's concern in his cornflower blue eyes. "This can't be easy for you, being back here. Are you okay?"

A lump instantly forms in my throat. Despite all the questions I've been forced to answer the last few days, no one has asked about me. How I'm holding up, if I'm alright.

The short answer is: I'm not. It's not just the guilt, the paranoia of what the police will find. It's the memories of all of it, of Phoebe, of what happened after. The stories that live in this place, that have come alive as I keep thinking about the last time we were all here.

My body crumples, and suddenly Josh is there to support me, kneeling beside me, his arms wrapped around me. And it's exactly what I need. A friend.

"Hey, hey, hey," he murmurs as he rubs my back, my tears dripping onto his T-shirt, leaving crescent-sized stains in the fabric. "You're okay. I'm here."

I don't know how long we stay there, but eventually we're interrupted by the unlatching of the door lock behind us.

"Oh." Declan's surprise drifts across the balcony, and I snatch my head up, away from Josh's shoulder.

When Declan next speaks, it's with barely concealed bitterness. "I didn't realize I was interrupting."

I want to stop him, to explain. To tell him how I've thought about him every day over the last ten years. The times we spent hand in hand walking on the beach in the Whitsundays, his arms around me as the others looked on, jealousy hard in Phoebe's eyes at our tangled limbs. I want to tell him that I almost reached out, that I wrote out a novel-length email at least five times, one I was never able to send.

But then I think of how I tried to talk to him in Sydney after everything happened, how I sent him messages when I returned home. How those efforts went rebuffed, the messages unanswered. How he let me down when I needed him most.

I let him go back inside without stopping him.

The plane we take to Everly Airport seats sixteen and is easily susceptible to turbulence. While the flight itself is only about ninety minutes, the last half is dominated by views from our small windows of a barren red landscape, dotted occasionally with shrubbery and gum trees. Every second of it brings my mind back to my time in Jagged Rock. To what happened there, to what I did.

The wheels hit the tarmac, and minutes later, we grab our bags from the sole carousel in baggage claim and secure the two rental cars ordered for us in advance by Kyan, who was quick as always to flash his cash. We pile in, Adrien, Kyan, and Josh in one car, Declan, Ellery, and I in the other, and head towards the address for Nick's ranch, which Adrien found online.

The airport feels as if it was dropped in the middle of nowhere. It's surrounded only by dirt and a small parking lot, its asphalt glistening in the midday sun. There's nothing else around, no shops, no businesses, no roads other than a small two-lane street that turns into dirt after about half a mile.

As we drive, my memories travel back to Nick. That very first day at orientation, he and Phoebe got off on the wrong foot, and it got progressively worse from there. Phoebe doing things—showing up late, intentionally trailing behind on our cultural tours—to piss him off, his face always growing a concerning shade of red in response.

For the thousandth time since yesterday, the thought seeps into my brain. *Did Nick really kill her?*

"I think this is it," Ellery says as Kyan's car stops in front us. I look out the window to the right and there lies a massive gate blocking a dirt road, *Gould Farms* wrought in steel above a logo of a sheep.

As soon as I open the car door, I notice the air is dryer, the temperature at least ten degrees hotter out here than back in Sydney. I can already taste the dust that littered my lungs the last time we were here. I think of the handwritten sign I saw in the baggage claim. *Limit Water Use—We are in a Drought!!!*

"I don't see any speaker." Kyan walks up and sticks his head through the gap in the gate. "And there's a chain on here that needs a key to unlock."

"We could climb it," Ellery says.

"Climb it?" Kyan says, clearly eyeing the height of the gate.

"Oh, come on. Where's the adventurous Kyan from ten years ago? What if I dared you?" Ellery jokes, nudging him in the side before grabbing on to the gate, pulling her right leg up.

And then I see him.

"Ellery, stop!" I yell, pointing to the hulking man walking towards us from over a hill beyond the gate. He must have heard our cars pull up.

Ellery's still climbing back down when he gets close enough for me to hear it. A sound I've only heard in movies. A soft, stomach-clenching click. The safety gauge of a gun coming unclasped.

"Get down from there." The words are a familiar growl. Nick Gould looks the same as he did years ago: bulky, intimidating, with fiery red hair. Only this time, he's carrying a rifle.

"Nick, we're just here to talk," Josh says, taking on the tone of a hostage negotiator, hands raised.

Nick's eyes narrow as he comes closer. After a moment, recognition blooms in his eyes.

"The hell are yous doing here?"

He doesn't bother to hide his shock. Thankfully, the surprise seems to have made him forget the rifle, which he now holds limply by his side.

"We came to ask you some questions," I pipe up, fumbling.

"Can we come in?" Ellery adds.

"We can do whatever talking yous want right here."

"Sure," Kyan says, too agreeably. "We know you and Hari were still in touch—"

"What about it?" Nick says gruffly, before Kyan can finish. I note that he doesn't deny it.

"Well, she's dead."

The news seems to wash over Nick in waves. Shock, then grief, then total and utter devastation. A look I've never seen on his—or any grown man's—face. For a startling moment, I think he may weep or crumple to the ground. Or both.

"No," he says instead, clearing his throat and regaining some control. "She can't be."

"It was an overdose," Adrien says.

"You're wrong." Nick's voice is stronger now, and I notice white peeking out from his knuckles as he wraps his fingers tighter around the rifle. "She was clean."

It's the same thing Kyan had said.

"We think it may have been—"

But Adrien doesn't let Declan finish. "When was the last time you saw her?" she asks Nick.

"Er...a couple months ago, I think."

"So, you didn't see her earlier this week?"

His bushy eyebrows form a sharp V as he stares at her. "No."

"You were here, at the ranch, all week?" she continues, her voice cool, as if she's in a courtroom.

"I don't see how that's any of your business." I notice a flash of something unidentifiable in Nick's eyes, before the grief in his expression begins to harden. "Wait a minute. What are you playing at?"

"What about the night Phoebe went missing in Jagged Rock?" Adrien deftly changes the topic. "What exactly were you doing after the dinner that night?"

Nick freezes for a moment and then his eyes widen. "Are you tryin' ta ask if I'm responsible? If I killed her?"

No one rushes to respond, and Nick doesn't wait. Instead, I watch in horror as he reaches again for the gun at his side.

"Hey, hey," Josh says gently.

"You come onto my property and accuse me of things you have no idea about. It's about time yous all leave," Nick growls.

Declan steps forward. "I think if we could just—"

But Nick doesn't listen to Declan's proposal. "Leave," he grunts. "Now."

So we do, rushing back to our respective cars, before Declan and Kyan step on the gas.

As we drive away, I turn back around, watching Nick, the rifle still in his hand, his face like carved concrete.

"Well, that certainly wasn't successful," Ellery says with a laugh that comes out too high.

But I disagree. Because I noticed Nick's caginess in answering Adrien's questions. His refusal to admit where he'd been this past week or what he'd been doing the night of Phoebe's murder. The flash of something in his eye that I'm only just now recognizing.

Panic.

Nick Gould knows something he's not telling us.

And I'm going to find out what.

13
PHOEBE

Then

THE TROPICAL AIR HITS our faces as soon as we step out of the airport. It's a different feeling from Sydney, where the sea was just a note on the horizon. Here, in Cairns, the proclaimed gateway to the Great Barrier Reef, it's the first thing you notice. The air drips with moisture, every breath salt tipped.

Energy buzzes through me, and I grasp Claire's hand in mine. She shoots me an excited smile. The last few days have been magic. We traipsed through Sydney behind Nick Gould and Hari, taking in the opera house, the botanical gardens with their screeching birds, and the downtown barracks that held the British convicts who later came to inhabit the country. Then we spent a full day in the Blue Mountains, hiking, visiting small mountain towns, taking a cable car to the summit. But, despite what Nick said, this wasn't *really* an educational trip. Every night included a stop at either the Nottingham

Hotel, which we made our local bar, or a downtown nightclub. And most of those ended with me stumbling into Kyan's bed.

The only drawback, aside from Nick—who seemed to be avoiding me after our awful confrontation—was the willowy blond South African that no one asked for: Adrien.

She lingered whenever I was around Kyan—which was pretty much all the time—like a bad smell. And the worst part was, Kyan would lap it up.

I'd catch them exchanging looks at something Nick Gould said before devolving into laughter or see Adrien's mouth pressed against Kyan's ear at the nightclub, trying to tell him something over the thrum of the bass.

It had turned into something of a competition that I had no interest in playing. But at the same time, I knew I was winning. It was me he was taking to bed at night, so suck on that, Adrien. But with every victory, the attacks continued. Dirty looks shot at each other, words muttered just out of earshot. A cold war on the brink of explosion.

I don't know if it would bother me so much if Kyan was interested in anyone other than Adrien. But the fact that it's her, with her mean girl energy and her unwavering confidence, brings me right back to my freshman dorm. The girls who talked openly about me as if I wasn't even there. Who wrinkled their nose when I walked by. The overly loud whispers that greeted me whenever I walked into a room.

Did you hear what she did?

I have been trying to ignore Adrien as much as possible,

appreciating instead how close the rest of us have become. It only took a matter of hours really. By the time we left the bar that first night, we were a family, the only dependable thing we could cling to in a country where everything was foreign.

And there isn't anyone I'm closer to than Claire. Ever since that first afternoon back in our Hamilton dorm when we talked as I applied her makeup, we've been inseparable. We're always laughing over something. Despite her meek first impression, it turns out the girl has a sneaky sense of humor.

We were out the other night when a guy offered to buy me a drink. Kyan was in the bathroom, and I made a point to let the guy know I wasn't interested.

"Bitch," he muttered as he walked away.

That word, that one word was all it took. And suddenly I was back there, in front of *him,* his hot breath on my face.

You're just a little bitch. No one will ever want you.

I felt myself crumple, my knees going weak. I moved to grasp the bar next to me to keep upright, but I missed. I was certain I was going to collapse, when at the very last minute, Claire was there next to me, concern strong in her eyes. She grabbed me, held me up, ordered me a water. She didn't ask what had happened. I guess my expression made clear I couldn't talk about it.

Instead, she just said in her soft voice, "It looks like he has a small penis anyway."

And just like that, the memory dissolved into peals of laughter.

"This way," grunts Nick Gould now, leading our group laden with suitcases and excitement in the direction of the shuttle bus he claims will be our second home for the rest of the trip, transporting us between all our future destinations. We leave the airport and head down a highway that wouldn't look out of place back in Atlanta, until we exit onto a boulevard with a distant sighting of the ocean. Just as I think we're headed in that direction, the bus makes a sharp turn down a four-lane road, bisected in the middle by parking spots and a smattering of halfhearted landscaping.

Souvenir shops, tattoo parlors, and kiosks advertising reef diving and jungle adventures line both sides of the street, with a vibe vaguely reminiscent of a childhood vacation to Myrtle Beach. The bus pulls up outside a large open arcade decorated with a cartoonish orange sign labeling the building as *Gilroy's Hostel.*

We leave the bus, grabbing our suitcases as we exit and dragging them through the open arcade, past a vast space that apparently serves as the restaurant and nightclub, the sight of which brings a smile to my face. We continue, drawn by the lure of a crowded pool towards the back of the building, before Nick Gould gestures us into the heavily air-conditioned hostel lobby.

"You'll be sharing two rooms. Guys in one, ladies in the other. Four beds per room. Hari and I will each have our own," Nick orders after he's secured and distributed our room keys. "Now, get ready and meet back down here in twenty."

My head snaps up, and I can tell instantly I'm not the only one disappointed by this news.

"I thought we had the night off from educational events," Josh pipes up. I steal a glance through the lobby window to where dusk is settling on the street, the screech of birds from the fig trees growing more prominent as the sun sneaks closer to the pavement. In the minutes since we arrived, I've already planned out a perfect night: drinks by the hostel pool in the back, followed by barhopping up the boulevard, hopefully culminating with Kyan and me stumbling into bed. Drinking—which had seemed so new and foreign when I first arrived—has now become a regular part of my time here. It's a nightly fixture, a respite after all our cultural activities during the days. And I find myself counting down the minutes until that first sip of liquor settles in my stomach, when the confidence I need to fake during the daylight hours will start to come naturally. The hangovers that arrive the mornings after are a small price to pay.

"You thought wrong," Nick tells Josh. "Twenty minutes. And dress reasonably. No high heels or tight skirts or any of that shit."

"Athletic clothes," Hari clarifies helpfully, with a mischievous wink.

Twenty-five minutes later, after I've deposited my suitcase on one of the creaky bunk beds in our four-person dorm room and rushed to change, we're all back on the shuttle. Twilight has fallen on the city, casting the boulevards in a low glow.

Nick and Hari still haven't told us where we're going, and our earlier disappointment at a wasted night of, well, getting wasted, has lightened, replaced instead with a feeling of suspense that buzzes through the rows of the bus.

Josh, who's sitting with Declan in front of Claire and me, props his elbows on the back of his seat and turns to us.

"I swear, if Nick pulls an evening educational experience out of his ass, I may need to hitch a flight home tonight," he says, softly enough so Nick can't hear.

But Hari, who's a few rows ahead, turns back our way, that same glint in her eye from earlier. "Don't you worry your pretty little head, Josh. I think you're going to like this."

Declan turns, and I catch him share a glance with Claire, who blushes as she usually does any time he turns his attention on her. It's clear there's something there, some chemistry, but neither one has had the courage to make a move, despite my not-so-subtle prompting.

"Maybe it'll be somewhere romantic," I propose. Declan catches the wink I shoot his way and smiles, while the red in Claire's cheeks deepen. God, these kids.

A few minutes later, we've left the city, the evening darkening around us as the pavement and buildings are replaced by lush green. We're entering the jungle.

"What the…?" Claire mutters, reflecting my thoughts.

It's not long until a sign appears, dimly lit among blooming gum trees, beckoning visitors with only two words: *Sky Adventures.*

Nick takes this as his cue, standing as the bus continues to roll up a stark incline.

"You were promised adventure on this trip, and here you have it. This is one of Australia's most popular bungee-jumping destinations."

I instantly feel Claire tense next to me, my own heart rate accelerating to match hers. Sure, bungee jumping sounds cool and adventurous—in theory. But now, as an enormous, multistory stairwell that looks far too unstable to hold actual people looms into view, it seems more than a touch insane.

I can tell we're not the only ones on the bus having second thoughts. The excitement from earlier has devolved into anxious giggles or, in Tomas's case, a white face and pure silence.

There's little conversation as we pile off the bus and run through the required logistics. Signing disclosures, forking over identity cards, getting weighed on a giant scale. And then it's time.

"I don't think I can do this," Claire says quietly as we stand at the foot of the stairs.

"Yes, you can," I whisper back. "You're stronger than you think. And this thing looks sturdy enough. Plus, I dare you." I nudge her side jokingly. "You have no choice but to accept."

I take her hand, squeezing it, and lead her up the steep stairwell. The first set is fine, just like walking up the steps to our old dorm room at Hamilton, I try to tell myself. But by the third story, I don't believe the lie. Wind rocks through the stairwell, shaking the entire structure.

Sturdy, my ass.

Kyan, Josh, and Declan have all run ahead, eager to show off their courageous manliness, but the rest of us dawdle, no one particularly eager to reach the top. At one point, when a cramp lodges under my rib, I pull off to the side to let the others pass. Claire stops too, waiting without me even having to ask.

As Adrien begins to pass me, I hear her comment to Ellery under her breath, just loud enough for me to hear.

"Looks like someone could use a little more time in the gym if they can't even make it up a few flights of stairs."

Before I can think it through or consider the consequences, I stick my foot directly in her line of passage. Adrien trips just as I intended. For a moment, it looks like she might be able to right herself, but then she goes down, her body colliding with the wooden steps, the force of impact shaking the already precarious structure, a thud ringing out in the night.

"Adrien!" Ellery yells. "Oh my goodness, are you okay?" She's instantly on her, pulling her back up to her feet.

"I-I tripped on something," Adrien says once she's back to standing. She's visibly shaken and blood gushes from a slice in her knee. Bet she regrets wearing those short shorts now.

I steal a glance around, but everyone's attention is focused on Adrien. No one saw me trip her.

"We go back down," Tomas proposes. "You do not need to finish. You need a bandage."

"No," Adrien says stonily. "I want to do this." She shoots a look back at me. "And unlike some people, I can actually make it up the stairs, even with an injury."

"You should probably be more careful, though," I sneer. "Watch where you're going. Wouldn't want you to get *really* hurt."

She doesn't respond, just flips her hair and continues walking, Ellery and Tomas in her wake.

"My cramp is gone now," I say. "Should we keep going?"

When I turn to Claire, she's staring at me more intensely than she has since I met her. I know instantly I was wrong. She *did* see me trip Adrien. I wait for her to reprimand me, but she stays quiet.

"Sure," she says finally. She's going to keep my secret, I realize with a flicker of relief.

Together, we climb the remaining steps, my nerves returning more acutely with each one, until finally, we reach the crowded platform. Kyan, Josh, and Declan must have already jumped, and Ellery, Tomas, and Adrien are being prepped by two burly workers. A wooden plank that wouldn't look out of place on an eighteenth-century pirate ship juts out of the platform, hovering over nothing but air and the black waters of a pond below.

Claire and I watch as the others suit up, my heart thudding as each one takes the plunge: Adrien in a dainty ballerina jump, Tomas—with some coaxing—in something resembling a cannonball, and Ellery summoning all her courage into a swan dive.

Until it's just the two of us left.

"We'd like to jump together," I say to one of the workers in a voice so high and tight I barely recognize it as my own. Claire had proposed it as we started up the staircase. At first, I wasn't on board—it sounded a bit weak—but now that we're up here, the height making my knees feel as though they may give out at any minute, it seems like a much better idea.

"We can do that," the worker responds amiably. His head is covered in a mass of blond dreadlocks, the same matted hair sprouting in clumps from his chin. "Hey, hey, hey," he says when he notices Claire trembling. "You're safe; you can trust me. Look, I have a beard!" He points excitedly to his chin. "Who else had a beard? Jesus, Santa…"

"Bin Laden," I mutter drily.

The worker snorts. "Yeah, fair enough, but listen, you lot are going to be fine. Get on up here."

After what feels like a decade, he and his partner have strapped us into harnesses so that Claire and I are facing one another, connected to the structure with a giant pipelike contraption.

"Okay now, I'm going to need you to hold on to each other and inch out onto the board," the worker directs us.

Slowly, we do as he says. Claire is trembling so forcefully, I'm nervous she may topple us over the edge.

Finally, we're there at the end of the board, the warm air slapping at our faces. I steal a glance outward, the night masking what would otherwise be a beautiful view of the surrounding jungle. But all I see is darkness, and when I look down, the blackness of the pond stories below reflects my fear.

"Three," the worker guides.

I look at Claire, expecting to see my own terror reflected in her eyes, but now that we're out here on the edge, she seems to have been replaced by someone different.

"Two."

Her eyes are even darker than usual, steady, like she's resigned herself to what's about to happen.

"One."

As if in direct proportion, my own anxiety skyrockets, heart racing, sweat collecting in crevices. *I don't want to do this anymore.*

I've changed my mind. I want to yell at the workers to stop, but when I open my mouth, no sound comes out.

"Now."

Nothing happens. Time seems to stand still, locking us both in place. *His* words come back to me, slithering through my veins.

You are nothing. You deserve nothing.

They root me in place, freezing my limbs.

And then a momentum propels us, coming, I realize, from Claire, who's jumped, throwing us both from the plank.

And we're falling.

Air rushes towards me faster than I've ever felt, so harsh it seems to be attacking my entire body, so fast it expels from my mind any thought of the words that had been racing through it moments before. I open my mouth once more, but the scream lies dormant.

And just when we've fallen for so long that I expect the bone-crunching contact of the water's surface, the bungee cord immediately retracts, throwing Claire and I back up in the air with it. And that's when I feel her. Solid, stronger than I expected.

After several more gut-wrenching jerks upwards, we come to rest, hanging upside down, Spider-Man style, mere feet away from the water's surface.

A man pulls us, still shaking, into a small canoe-like boat and rows us the ten or so feet to land. Euphoria floods through me, accompanied by an all-consuming affection for Claire. When the boat strikes the hard earth, I'm on a high I've never felt before.

I scan the shore for Kyan, anticipating him to be waiting there for me, hopefully with a shot in hand. And then I see him. But it isn't a shot he's holding, and he isn't looking at me. He isn't looking at anyone. His eyes are closed and his lips…

His lips are squarely on Adrien's.

Rage consumes me, a feeling I haven't felt in years. Red obscures my vision, just as it did that night years ago in the car, and the anger eradicates the adrenaline high I felt only moments before.

Only one thing remains in my mind, an all-consuming, burning need. A desire for something I've only felt to this extent once before.

Revenge.

14

CLAIRE

Now

"SHIT."

Ellery doesn't usually swear. It was something I found so incongruous about her when we first met—her tough exterior, all heavy black eyeliner and facial piercings combined with her sweet, childlike personality. So I can tell now that something's really wrong.

"There are wildfires in Northern New South Wales and the southern part of Queensland. Our flight back to Sydney has been cancelled. And so are the ones for tomorrow. The next one is Friday."

Two days from now. The day I'm supposed to return to Chicago.

"Shit," Declan chimes in. "Are there any other airports around?"

Ellery is already on it. "It looks like there's one in Alice Springs, but that's eight hours away. And"—her fingers dance across her phone's keyboard—"yup, those flights are cancelled until Friday as well."

Declan punches the steering wheel, hard. I jolt back, never having seen anger like that from him before.

"Sorry," he mutters. "It's just really inconvenient."

I don't say anything, but I agree, making a mental note to call the airline later to reschedule my flight.

The news must have reached the rest of our caravan because Kyan lifts his arm out the driver's side window, signaling for us to pull over. Once we stop behind him, the others are out of their rental and next to our windows within seconds.

Adrien doesn't bother asking if we've heard.

"I've already checked the contract for the rental cars. They don't allow drop-offs more than ten hours away from the originating destination." She sighs. "And there aren't any hotels in Rollowong. The closest one is in Jagged Rock."

"Where?" I ask softly. But I already know what she's going to say. The twist of fate lodges like a knife between my ribs.

"The Inn."

We stop on the way at a grocery store right outside of town, grabbing wilted premade salads for lunch and stocking up on supplies that are mostly alcoholic in nature. We try to ignore the sideways glances and cold remarks from the teenage cashier, evidently the sole employee in the shop, before filing back into our cars.

The asphalt sizzles as we enter Jagged Rock. I'm instantly transported back in time—not to a decade ago when we were last here, but even further. Everything about this place seems like it's stuck in the wrong century. Squat one- and two-story buildings line the road, mostly in neutral colors, aside from one large building with a wraparound porch that's painted a faded salmon pink. A clock tower lies at the far end of the street, and the omnipresent red dirt skitters across the road. I feel a pinch in my heart as I take in the number of boarded-up buildings. Graffiti patterns the various shuttered businesses, which outnumber their open counterparts nearly three to one.

I'm expecting it, prepared for it after all, but even so, my breath catches in my throat as it comes into view at the very end of Main Street. The Inn itself is largely unimpressive, a nondescript two-level building. But it's the mountain that rises up behind it, its tip ascending into the sky like a spindly finger, that brings everything crashing back.

That's what surprised me most when I first came out here. My mind always associated the desert with vast expanses of sandy flats. But the Outback is a different animal entirely. The bush covers everything, worn down in spots by pathways and eroded by wind, but thriving and dense in others, with no apparent rhyme or reason to its patterns. And just when you think bushland is the only thing the eye can see, the rocky brunt of a hill that the locals refer to as "Big Beulah" bursts out of the ground without warning, dominating everything surrounding it.

"He would have loved it here," Ellery says quietly from the front seat.

I don't need to ask who she's referring to. I know. Tomas.

"He would have," Declan says lightly, resting his hand on hers.

I picture him then, his smile so big it took over the whole lower half of his face, chocolate brown eyes always eager behind his glasses. So curious, so innocent.

A sadness lodges deep in my stomach, mixed with the longing for what we had back then, back before it all went so wrong.

The car jolts as Declan turns onto the path that leads to the Inn's parking lot, transitioning from smooth pavement to unpaved dirt. And within moments, we're back. Kyan pulls in next to us, and we empty out of the cars, all of us unusually quiet, taking it in. The memories.

The life that ended here.

"Want to take bets if Randy's still here?" Kyan asks, cracking a smile and propelling us towards the building.

No one answers. I completely wiped Randy, the Inn's owner, from my memories. But I know the bet's a solid one. Jagged Rock isn't a place most people leave.

Phoebe included. My mind leaps to the thought before I can stop it.

A bell chimes above our head as I follow Adrien into the Inn's lobby, and the smell hits me instantly. A mix of dust, of rooms that desperately need to be aired out, and an underlying sourness. A scent that involuntarily lifts my nostril.

"Hmm," I hear Josh murmur. "No Randy, no anyone."

I look around, taking in the faded carpet, the peeling wallpaper, nothing apparently changed in the ten years we've been gone. My gaze lands on the front desk, the top a mess of peeling wood, the rickety computer chair behind it unoccupied.

"Maybe it's no longer in business," Declan poses. It's not an unreasonable thought. It doesn't look like this place has welcomed a single guest in the decade since we left.

I take in the wall behind the desk, the various cubbyholes, each of which is filled with a key—one per room. I scan the twenty cubbyholes before stopping on the middle row. One cubby sits empty, its key nowhere to be found.

I clear my throat. "Well, it looks…"

Slam.

The noise explodes like a gunshot through the small enclosed space and we all jump in unison, the thought lodging in my throat.

We turn towards the source of the sound. A door just steps away from the front desk—one I don't remember having noticed all those years ago—ricochets against the wall, and in its wake stands a familiar lanky man, his dark hair slicked back from his face into a low ponytail that hangs to his shoulders.

"Well, looky here. Most business this place has seen in years." And then his smile slips. "Wait. I remember you."

"Hi, Randy," Kyan says. "We stayed with you a few years back, the group from Hamilton College?"

"Couldn't stay away, I reckon?"

"We, uh, we've found ourselves back in Jagged Rock, and we would love to stay here for two nights if you have rooms available." Kyan's eyes flick obviously to the cubbyhole chock-full of keys. A lack of vacancy doesn't seem to be a problem.

I see something flash in Randy's eyes that I can't quite identify. There was always something about him that made me squeamish.

The way his eyes would track us from his stoop behind the front desk, or how he always seemed to be hovering on the outskirts of our conversations, listening.

"Well," he says resignedly, as if he has no other option. "Let's get yous sorted, then."

We do the whole song and dance of surrendering our passports and Kyan's credit card—he's again insisted on paying—while Randy fiddles with the desktop computer. After what feels like an eternity, it's time for him to divvy up the rooms.

He starts with me.

"I figured you'd like to be in the same one you were last time," he says, handing me a key, his crepey skin brushing mine.

How could he possibly remember the room I stayed in ten years ago? But before I can ask, he's already moved on, talking to Josh.

I barely wait for the others to collect their keys before heading towards the staircase, gripping mine so tightly my knuckles turn white. I'd forgotten how heavy it was—a single silver key looped onto a wooden engraving of a hand-carved raven, overly large and ostentatious, so it would be more difficult for a guest to lose.

My body moves of its own volition, following the pathway I took so many times without thinking. I turn right at the top of the staircase, barely stopping to take in the hallway and its faded green carpets and peeling flowered wallpaper—a mix between what you would find in a funeral home and a crime scene—and pause in front of the third door on the left.

A brass *13* stares back at me from the center of the red framed door, tarnish breaking through the metal's dull sheen.

I pause, bracing myself for the memories that will rush back as soon as I open the door. I take a deep breath and blow it out slowly. And then I shove the key into the lock and turn.

What a dump.

The memory of Phoebe's words hits me like a slap in the face as I push open the door. Her bed is the first thing I see. It's in the same position it was back then: the headboard shoved against the wall, diagonal from the other twin bed in the room, leaving nothing but a small dresser and a wide expanse of faded carpet between them.

And then I see her. Phoebe's impossibly thin body spread out on the twin-sized mattress, her head resting on her hand, staring over at me.

I shake my head, and the image disappears. I sit down on her bed, trying to ignore the puff of dust that escapes from beneath me as I do, and take another look around the room. My eyes scan the maroon-colored walls, the door that leads into the small bathroom, the painting of a raven done in glossy colors so that its feathers appear greasy, its beady eyes staring from its perch on a bending tree branch. A shiver runs through me; something about that painting always creeped me out, but now it's as if I'm drawn to it. I get up off the bed and walk until I'm right in front of it. My brain seems to register something off, but I can't determine what. I reach a cautious hand out towards it and—

A vibration pulses against my leg, and I jump back before realizing it's my phone. I pull it out, the screen lighting up with a number that looks too long by American standards.

"Good evening. Am I speaking with Ms. Whitlock?"

I recognize the voice instantly, and my spine goes rigid. I manage to squeak out a noise of affirmation.

"Ms. Whitlock, this is Inspector Villanueva from the Australian Federal Police. I'm calling to see whether you could come back into our office tomorrow morning?"

The dampness in my palms comes so suddenly that I almost fumble the phone. *They've found out.*

"Ms. Whitlock?"

When I force the words out, they're tight, strained. "I…I'm not in Sydney."

"Oh," Villanueva says, her surprise evident. "May I ask where exactly you are?"

I look through the small chest-height window that faces the back of the Inn. Land stretches, marked with sun-bleached bushes and the odd half-dead eucalyptus tree, until it seemingly erupts out of the ground into the dominating mold that is Beulah.

Villanueva would be furious if she knew we'd come back here. In fact, she'd told each of us to stay local until the AFP had finished their investigation.

"I'm visiting an old friend out of town," I say after a second-too-long pause. "We'd organized it before our…conversation yesterday."

Despite the bile rising in my throat, I manage for the lie to sound somewhat truthful. I guess I've had enough practice over the years.

"Hmm." I can hear the skepticism in her voice. I'm afraid she's about to press me further, and my mind races, eager to remember the name of any Australian towns I can use to support my fake trip.

"Well, I didn't want to do this over the phone." Villanueva sighs.

"But we received more information from the coroner's office this afternoon on Ms. Barton's case."

"Oh?" I ask. Anxiety swirls in my chest.

"The tests are far from conclusive. Given the state of the remains, the coroner can't be certain. But..."

The possibilities dangle in front of me as she trails off. Saliva pools in my mouth and I swallow hard, fear rising in time with the bile in my throat.

"Ms. Barton was likely pregnant at the time of her death."

15

CLAIRE

Now

"PREGNANT?" I CHOKE THE word out.

"It would have been very early on," Villanueva explains. "Only a few weeks along, really. And again, it's far from certain, but the coroner noted a slight deviation in her pelvic bones that is generally associated with the early stages of pregnancy."

But I barely hear her.

"Ms. Whitlock, are you still there?"

"Yes," I answer rapidly.

"Did you have any idea that Ms. Barton was pregnant? Did she ever mention anything to you? Or, looking back, was there anything that may have indicated as much?"

The image comes back to me like a slap to the face. Phoebe's head thrown back, her shiny dark hair collecting the light from the stars like a disco ball of rays.

"I don't think so." I shut my eyes tight against the memory.

"You mentioned that she was intimate with Mr. Quek. Are you aware of anyone else with whom she had sexual relations?"

"No," I say quickly. Too quickly. "And I'm sure she and Kyan used protection."

"Okay, well, if you think of anything, you have my number." I can tell she's getting ready to end the call, but then: "Actually, there's one more thing, Ms. Whitlock." My fingers tighten around the phone. "I'm sharing this information with you because, by all accounts, you were Ms. Barton's closest friend during her time in Australia. I would appreciate if you do not share this with the others, especially the men in your group."

I nod until the pause grows stale and I remember to speak. "Sure."

She ends the call, but I don't hang up right away, the phone still glued to my ear as the implication of her request sinks in.

It should make me feel better, the fact that Villanueva's suspicion has turned away from me. But it doesn't. The news of Phoebe's pregnancy leaves me hollow.

What I did that night didn't just lead to the end of Phoebe's life. It ruined that of her unborn child too.

A knock at my door breaks through the swarm of thoughts in my head.

It's Josh.

"We're all out back. Kyan is grilling some of the sausages we bought at the store. You know, for old times' sake and all that. You coming?"

I look at him blankly for a minute from inside the doorway, before processing an answer. "No, no. I'm not hungry. I'm actually not feeling too well after all that excitement earlier. I think I'm just going to call it an early night."

I can't handle the thought of facing all of them knowing what I know now. Knowing what I did.

"Okay," Josh acquiesces. "But hey, are you sure you're alright?"

He places his hand on my arm, and there it is again: that comfort. I want to sink into him, to tell him everything. And it would be easy, to have someone to share it all with.

But I stop myself.

I focus my eyes back on him, force a small smile. "Yeah, I'm fine, really. Don't worry about me. Go have fun with the others."

He shoots me a small smile before leaving, and I let him go, sinking back into my thoughts. I try to force the grief away as much as possible, focusing instead on what Villanueva's truth bomb could mean for me. For the investigation. Only hours ago, I suspected Nick Gould was the one who killed Phoebe, but this news changes everything. It gives the father of her unborn child a clear motive for her murder: ending the pregnancy he never wanted.

And I can't picture Phoebe having sex with Nick. Not with the open disdain she had for him or his constant scolding of her.

A thought flashes across my brain unbidden, before imprinting itself.

Unless it wasn't consensual.

But then there's Kyan. He was the most likely to have gotten Phoebe pregnant. And what about the other two? Declan and Josh. As much as I'd like to, I can't rule them out either.

And there are still so many other things that don't line up. So many secrets, lies. The whispers I overheard at Kyan's the other morning between Declan and the mystery person. And the incessant feeling I can't shake since I returned, that everyone seems just slightly off. Like they're playing the part that's expected of them.

I think of Villanueva's request. *Do not share this with the others.*

It was one of those whirlwind relationships, where emotions ran high and attachments clicked in seconds. It felt like we'd lived years together, but we were barely together thirty tumultuous days. Not long enough to really understand each other. To know the others' secrets, their motivations. To know what makes them tick.

How well did any of us really know each other, after all?

—

I don't realize I've fallen asleep until I hear the scream.

My eyes snap open, and I'm shocked to see early morning light filtering in through the window. Somehow I slept through the night.

The sound comes again, long and pained. And I realize it's not a scream, but a throaty caw.

I stumble up and over to the window, pulling aside the curtain to reveal a glistening black raven, perched on a tree branch a short distance from the Inn.

Crows bring bad luck, my mother always used to warn me.

I don't know what the protocol is for a raven, but I can only guess the same, if not worse.

I pull the curtain shut, but the bird's call still rings in my ears. As my heart rate calms, I check the time on my phone. It's still early, too early for the others to get up, but there's no chance I'll get back to sleep. And while I'm here, there's something I need to do.

I need to go to the mine, Phoebe's last resting place. I tell myself it's to pay my respects, especially after what I did to help lead her there. But there's a small voice in the back of my head telling me there's another reason.

To make sure there isn't evidence I left behind.

My mind flashes to the knife, its blade glinting in the starlight, my hand clenched so tightly around the shaft it left blisters.

The police would never be able to find it, I tell myself. But I can't be entirely positive.

I swiftly pull on my clothes from yesterday and take the stairs two by two. Despite the early hour, Randy is hunched over the front desk. He opens his mouth to say something, but before he can strike up a conversation, I blurt out that I'm taking a walk and dip out the lobby's back door.

The Outback stretches before me, more uninterrupted land than I've ever seen in one place in my entire life. I'd forgotten how beautiful it is, how untouched by human life. The dirt is everywhere. Loose and pebbled in certain places, tight and compact in others, but it stretches as far as the eye can see, the stark light of the sun absorbed entirely in the red clay, all of it situated around Beulah, the craggy red mountain.

I swipe at the flies that seem to glue themselves to me as soon as I step outside and head in the direction of the mine, the route burned into my memory. I don't remember exactly where I left the knife that night, halfheartedly buried under red dirt I clawed at with my fingertips, specks of it clinging under my nails for days. I was in such a frazzled state, and I didn't dare mark where I'd buried it, assuming that doing so would make it easier for the police to find. But still, I scan the ground as I go, tracing the dirt for any sign of sun glinting off metal.

The chill from the night hasn't yet faded, and I pull down the sleeves of my sweatshirt, glad I decided to wear it even though the peak of the afternoon promises to be at least thirty degrees warmer. My skin feels dry, as if the air is so in need of water that it will absorb moisture from anywhere that has it. I take note of the crispy bushes, the dead twigs that crunch beneath my feet. I realize I haven't seen anything remotely green since we arrived yesterday.

I walk for nearly twenty minutes, until a sound in the distance roots me in place, a loud bang slicing through the quiet morning air.

I startle, my head snapping up from where my eyes have been glued to the dirt. Was that…a gunshot?

I scan the distance but see nothing.

For the first time I think of how dangerous this is. If whoever killed Phoebe really did murder Hari to keep her silent about what she knows, then what's to stop them from doing the same to me? To stop me from sniffing around?

I consider turning back, but I stop myself. I don't know when else

I'll get this opportunity. And I need to see the mine for myself, to confront what I did head-on.

Finally, after several more minutes of walking, I look up and see it.

Memories rush back. The "field trip" Nick Gould took us on one of our first afternoons in Jagged Rock, leading us through the unbearable heat, every one of us growing sulkier as we longed for the cool tropical breeze of the Whitsunday Islands we'd left days before, grief already clinging to us over what happened to Tomas. Until we reached it: the bushland stopped abruptly, giving way to bare ground strewn with discarded rusted metal beams. The only structure aboveground was a tall copper-colored tower that stretched up to the sun.

But as we got closer, I saw something else. A small door, hardly noticeable astride the tower and tall enough for a person to get through only if they hunched over.

Nick explained it as the entrance to the mine, the heart of Jagged Rock, a city that had forged a living in silver, until even that dried up. Nick stood in front of the small door that looked like something out of *Alice in Wonderland* and recounted the city's history. The hope that had surrounded the mine, the locals putting everything they had into building a city that never had a future.

"This here door leads to nearly three kilometers of winding underground mine shafts, none of which are safe to go into. Not that they were back in the late 1800s either. Nearly a hundred miners died down there, from suffocation or collapsed shafts. Some got lost, and no one found 'em til too late. After they died from lack of water."

I don't know if it was the dark history or the blasé way Nick recounted it, but I wasn't able to pull my eyes from that mine door. Glancing over at Phoebe, I saw her doing the same. Her eyes wide, her face a mural of pain. As if she could somehow foresee what was coming.

Today, the mine is different. The tower still sits next to the warped metal door, which sticks up out of the ground like the head of a snake. But it's all wrong. Rather than the flat land from ten years ago, unassuming aside from the entrance, the entire area is cratered, like the remnants of a bomb site. The once hidden mine shafts—at least the shallowest of them—have been dug up, exposed to the world like metallic entrails. A lethal-looking maze.

I suck in a breath at the sight of it, heavy and ominous, and pause until my eyes take in the signs of human life. The piles of dirt stacked in random locations among the shafts, as though whatever construction company was working here abandoned their project as soon as they unearthed Phoebe's remains; a string of discarded caution tape tied around a branch of the singular tree that seems to have escaped construction.

Seeing everything already torn up, for as far as the eye can see, I know any chance is gone of finding the knife around this area. The realization carves a hollow feeling in my gut.

But I don't leave. Instead, I inch closer towards the mine as though I'm drawn to it. Ignoring the sign at the lip of the crater declaring the land a construction site and unsafe for entry, I scoot down until I'm seated, legs hanging, and drop the few feet, landing hard.

I wipe the dirt off on my jeans and head towards the tower, keeping the entrance to the mine in my sight. It's deathly quiet here, no sound other than the occasional caw of a raven from somewhere nearby. Despite the earlier chill, the sun is rising steadily, and I feel a drop of sweat sneak down my spine as I walk.

And suddenly, I'm in front of it. The metal door rests on its hinges, until all at once it slams shut, a gust of wind sending it crashing against its frame. That must have been the noise I heard earlier, not a gunshot after all. I take a deep breath and yank the door open. I'm instantly hit with the darkness of it, and the subterranean scent invades my nostrils.

My feet instinctively move backwards, but I force myself to walk. One step in, two.

I look around as I go, the metal walls caked in red dirt, the stairs hard and unyielding. The last sights Phoebe ever saw.

I picture her here, injured, screaming for someone to help her. While I was outside, free. The guilt returns then, eradicating everything else in my body like lava.

Until I feel something else. A presence a few feet in front of me.

I blink hard and squint my eyes, but the sunlight doesn't reach this far into the mine. Everything is cloaked in darkness, so all I can make out is a form. Someone or something bigger, taller than me. And then I hear it. The soft short breaths of someone trying to be silent.

In the time it takes me to realize I'm in danger, a force slams into my abdomen, knocking me down. The air shoots from my lungs as my spine connects with the stairs. The pain is blinding.

Still, I feel the figure step over me, squeezing by in the narrow stairway.

I force my eyes open, but it's futile. All I see is a blur. I reach my hand out to make contact, but they're already gone.

I try to force myself up, but before I can, I hear a *whoosh*.

My body recognizes it before my mind does, blood pulsing in my ears.

The door to the mine shaft.

Instantly, what little light the outside world afforded is snuffed out. The darkness is smothering.

I throw myself up the few steps, but as I do, I hear a sound that stops me cold.

The door latching.

I'm trapped in here.

16

PHOEBE

Then

"HOW ARE THINGS GOING with Dec?" I ask Claire.

The others are all off skydiving today, which Nick and Hari said was an optional activity. When I found out what the alternative was—sleeping in and having the day to do absolutely nothing—I jumped at it, no pun intended. It's already early afternoon and Claire—the only other person who declined to skydive, which I'm pretty sure is due to the extra cost for the activity—and I only just traipsed down the street to an overpriced café for breakfast.

I take a sip of my Bloody Mary, hoping it will cure my raging hangover. I lost track of the number of tequila shots I took at the bar last night following the bungee jump. Unfortunately, it turns out no amount of alcohol in the world could erase from my brain the image of Kyan and Adrien sucking face.

Claire's smile beams at me from across the table.

"We talked for a while last night. He held my hand on our walk home from the bar." Her signature red cheeks are flaming. I don't tell her that I pulled him aside the other night and unsubtly hinted that Claire was interested.

"God, when is one of you going to get some balls and make a move?"

I intend for it to come out joking, lighthearted, but I hear a snarl in my tone. Claire flinches, her smile dropping, and I regret it instantly. Hurting Claire is like kicking a puppy who wants nothing more than to please you.

"I'm sorry. I'm just in my head about last night," I admit.

Claire nods. "How are you feeling? I can't believe Adrien and Kyan had the nerve to make out like that in front of everyone."

After we left, we all went to the nightclub we'd passed on our way into the hostel. Adrien and Kyan were the first on the dance floor, arms flung around each other. Kyan never bothered to look over at me, but Adrien couldn't seem to tear her eyes away, shooting me victorious looks every chance she got. The alcohol was the only thing that stopped me from running onto the dance floor and pouring a drink over her head.

"I'm not thrilled about it."

"I understand," Claire says. "That was totally uncalled for. I mean, for him to just ditch you like that..."

She keeps talking, but I barely hear her. Her comment brings me back to that house. To *him*. To the voice I can't seem to shake, the one that always hovers directly next to my ear.

He ditched you because you are worthless. Look at that girl, Adrien. How could you ever think you could compete with that?

"Phoebs?" Claire nudges, and it's clear it's not the first time she's tried to get my attention.

"Yeah, sorry," I mutter.

"I was just saying, Kyan seems a bit, I don't know, superficial? Like he's only interested in looks, and once someone prettier comes along..."

Her face flames again as she catches herself.

She's right. He would never be into you. Especially if he knew what you were really *like.*

"I'm sorry, Phoebs. That came out wrong."

"It's fine," I shake it away. Because honestly, her comment gave me an idea. Kyan *is* superficial. And suddenly, I know how to get back at Adrien.

And I remember what I did to silence that voice the first time.

"Can I ask you a question?" Claire asks, her tone suddenly sheepish.

You just did, I want to say, but swallow it down. That's a lame dad joke, not one that this version of Phoebe would make. "Shoot," I say instead.

"Why did you choose this trip?" I don't answer right away, and Claire rushes to fill the pause. "It's just, neither one of us is really that into extreme adventures. I mean, we're the only ones who chose Bloody Marys over skydiving today."

I consider my response. My first instinct is to lie, but something stops me. "It was the furthest place from Atlanta. And I needed to get away. To start over."

Claire leans forward, rests her chin on her hands. "Get away from what?"

I sigh. Am I really doing this?

Claire's dark eyes are filled with concern. And I realize she's the only person who cares about me—*really* cares about me. And as pathetic as it sounds, maybe she's the only person that ever has.

I sigh, preparing myself to finally release the words that have lain stagnant in my chest for years. "I had a...rough childhood, I guess. There was someone who didn't treat me well. He used to say things to me. Horrible things. He did things as well, things I don't want to talk about." I focus my gaze on the drink in front of me, unable to look her in the face as I confess. If I see the compassion in her eyes, I won't make it through. "So I did something to stop it."

I hear her inhale sharply. "What did you do?"

The question is quiet, hesitant.

"I—"

"You ladies all set here?" The waitress's bubbly voice makes me jump. I was so absorbed in my confession, I didn't even notice her approach our table.

"We're fine, thank you."

As Claire answers, I look at her. The innocence, the goodness she wears like a shield. She would never understand. If I told her the truth, she'd never look at me the same again. And how could she? She'd become just like everyone else, all those people who jumped so quickly to judgment, never able to understand. She'd think I'm a monster.

And in that second, I decide.

"So, what did you do?" she asks tentatively once the waitress has left.

"He'd sent me a naked photo. I printed it out and hung it up all over the lockers at our high school." The lie rushes from my lips.

After a second, she laughs. "Well, it sounds like he deserved it."

I force myself to laugh as well, propelling air through the tightness in my chest.

"He did."

17

CLAIRE

Now

I TRY TO SCREAM, but I hear nothing. I can't tell if it lodged in my throat or if the dull blackness of the mine has swallowed it up.

Fear like nothing I've ever experienced courses through me. But beneath that there's a flicker of understanding. I deserve this. To die the same way Phoebe did, buried alive in this discarded mine.

I can't ignore this dark logic, but then I think of what Villanueva mentioned the other day: the scratches and nail polish remnants the police had found on the inner door to the mine.

Phoebe didn't give up without a fight, and I won't either.

I scramble up the steps with my hands out, the fear eradicating the pain I should feel in every bone of my body from my earlier topple down the stairs.

My breath comes quick, shallow. I imagine the lack of oxygen, the chemicals from decades of disuse that must be lodging in my lungs.

Everything feels claustrophobic, the already narrow walls crowding in on me even further.

Until my hands hit something hard, solid. The door.

The metal is heavy beneath my hands, and I brace my body for impact, prepare myself to throw my full force against it.

But the door gives way beneath my palms, and the next thing I know, I'm stumbling outside, my knees dropping into the dirt, chest heaving.

Whoever pushed me down hadn't bothered to lock the door behind them.

I was only in there for a few seconds, but tears stream down my face as I think of what could have been. How close I'd come to Phoebe's fate.

I blink hard, the sunlight burning my corneas after the darkness of the mine. And that's when I see it.

A figure, barely visible over the ridge of the construction area in the direction of the Inn. His back is towards me, that much I can tell, but I squint, trying to make out any defining characteristics.

I inhale sharply. There's no mistaking who it is. The burly shoulders, the bright red hair glinting in the sun.

Nick Gould.

"You're sure it was him?"

The others stare at me over the Inn's version of a continental breakfast—dry Weetabix cereal and untoasted bread with a jar of Vegemite.

"There's no question," I answer Ellery.

"But why would he do that?" Josh asks around a mouthful of bread.

It's the question I asked myself the entire walk back to the Inn, once I waited for Nick Gould to disappear from my view. My mindset may have been far from calm, but I was at least of sound enough mind not to confront him on my own.

"I think I must have intruded on him," I say, presenting the most logical theory I've come up with. "Maybe visiting the mine is some sick way for him to relive what he did to Phoebe all those years ago."

I can tell the others aren't buying it. They still don't seem sold on the fact that Nick killed Phoebe. Kyan's eyes narrow and Adrien's lips twist upward in something like a grimace. But thankfully—likely given my apparent fragile state—no one contests it.

"Well, we should probably report this to the AFP," Declan proposes. "I mean, what's to say he's not going to try to hurt you or one of us again?"

"No."

Josh's response is adamant. His face appears calm, but there's a sharp line running between his brows.

"I mean," he says, appearing to catch himself, "does Detective What's His Name know that we're back here?"

"No, but if we're in serious danger, I'm sure they wouldn't be hung up on the fact we left Sydney," Ellery pipes up. "Especially if it would help their investigation."

"I just think we should give this some time." Josh again. "Making an accusation like this could really fuck up a guy's life. Even if it is Nick Gould."

I shoot Josh a curious glance. He's never seemed too concerned about Nick's well-being before. But I don't challenge it. The fact is, I'd rather not share my suspicions with Villanueva either. Not only would it mean her catching me in a lie, but I need to buy more time. I need concrete evidence to get the police to stop investigating.

Thankfully, the topic of conversation changes before anyone else can disagree.

Josh's phone dings with a news alert, his eyebrows immediately scrunching.

"Shit, have y'all seen this? The wildfires?"

"Yes, Josh," Adrien says, pedantically. "That's the whole reason we couldn't fly back yesterday, remember?"

"No, I mean, I know. But this says they're evacuating the area around Cullamonjoo, the national park we went to. Where Tomas…" He trails off, covering the rest of his unspoken sentence with a cough. "That's only a few hours from here."

Ellery's eyes widen. "Should we be concerned?"

Her question is met with a throaty scoff emanating from the front desk. I shouldn't be surprised. Back when we were first here, Randy had a habit of eavesdropping on our private conversations. I guess nothing has changed.

"Something you want to say, mate?" Kyan asks. The question is casual, but there's a streak of hostility in his tone.

"I wouldn't right consider myself your mate, *mate.*" Randy's voice takes Kyan's hostility and raises it ten levels. It also carries a slight slur. I check my watch. Barely nine. Looks like Randy starts on the bottle early these days. "But it figures yous'd be worried about wildfires. You aren't cut out for a place like this. I don't know why yous bothered coming back. Did you want to gloat at the rest of us? Check that we're still where we belong?"

"I'm sorry," Adrien says, her tone making clear she's anything but. "Have we done something to offend you?"

This elicits another scoff and a mumble of something unintelligible.

"We just found out our friend was murdered," Ellery says. "That's why we're back."

"Ah yes, that slut bitch of yours who—"

"Whoa, whoa, whoa, that's enough," Declan says standing up. But Kyan's beat him to it, knocking his chair over in his haste to get to the front desk. Within steps he's face-to-face with Randy, and for a moment it seems like he's going to punch him.

"You can say what you want about us," Kyan says, his fingers balled into his palms. "But have some respect for the dead."

Randy sneers. "You didn't know the first thing about her, *mate.* You think you were the only one she was screwing back then?"

Kyan lunges forward. Somehow Josh jumps up quick enough to pull him back, but not fast enough to hide the momentary panic that alights Randy's face.

"Yeah, get your bitch under control," he says as Josh shoves Kyan towards the door, telling him to cool off. But the embarrassed flush on Randy's face is evident before he retreats to the stairway.

"Fucking loser," Kyan mumbles, before shouting at Randy's back. "Might want to lay off the hard stuff before noon. One of these days it might get you in trouble, *Randy*." He says his name like a swear word before slamming the back door behind him. Adrien and Declan rush after him.

"Well, that was...something." Ellery gives a humorless chuckle as we sit back down at the table.

"Yeah, it really was," I say inanely, still processing everything that's happened in the last hour.

"I guess we're all a little on edge," Josh considers.

"Well I'm going to go take a shower before any more brawls break out," Ellery says, cleaning up the leftovers from breakfast and dropping them in the lobby trash can before heading upstairs.

"Never a dull moment in Jagged Rock apparently," Josh says when it's just the two of us.

I'm supposed to laugh at his attempt at a joke, but the easy comfort that usually lies between us is absent. My mind keeps snagging on something he said earlier when he was shooting down Declan's proposal to report Nick Gould to the AFP. *Does Detective What's His Name know that we're back here?*

Sawkins must have been the one to call him, just like he did me, but Villanueva was the one leading everyone's interviews; that much was confirmed by the others when we debriefed yesterday. And she was the one who told us not to leave the city.

"How was your interview yesterday?" I aim for a casual tone, but Josh's wrinkled brow confirms it falls short.

"Wow, okay, giving me whiplash with that change of topic."

He chuckles. "It was fine, I guess. Detective Sawkins is a piece of work."

I nod. I should let it go, but something pricks at me. A suspicion I can't shake.

"Yeah, he was. What did you think of the other guy? His partner. Detective Anderson?" I try, wondering whether Josh will take the bait.

Josh's tone is breezy when he answers. "I mean, he seemed a little more down to earth. I feel confident he's got the investigation under control."

No flick of his eyes to the left, no wringing of his hands. Nothing to indicate Josh is telling anything but the truth.

"Yeah," I say, my mouth dry.

"Ellery had a good idea," he says, standing. "I need to clean myself off after yesterday. Hopefully the water heater in this place can handle two of us showering at the same time. I'll catch you down here in a few."

He leaves, but I stay where I am, alone in the lobby. Thinking of everything he just gave away.

He never went to the AFP when he arrived in Australia like he told us yesterday.

Josh is lying.

But why?

18

CLAIRE

Now

I HAD NEVER PLANNED to sleep with Josh.

He wasn't even on my radar during the program. I was so all consumed with Declan that I couldn't fathom being attracted to anyone else. And if I was being honest with myself, Josh was entirely out of my league. Much better suited for someone like Phoebe or Adrien. Someone beautiful and self-assured.

Like the rest of the group, Josh and I mostly lost touch after the program ended, aside from the group message chain. Until one night in Chicago a few years ago.

It was an after-work happy hour, one of the only times my coworkers succeeded at getting me to come out. The other receptionists at the medical insurance company were all around five years younger than me, most of them using the job to pay their way through college. It was Christmastime, the anniversary of the day

Phoebe went missing was quickly approaching, and I knew the only thing that awaited me back in my apartment was guilt and another sleepless night replaying the memories in my head.

I was ordering at the bar, tacky Christmas lights twinkling above my head, when I spotted him, decked out in a slim-fitting suit that showed off his toned physique and expensive-looking haircut. As soon as he recognized me, he sprinted over and wrapped me in a big hug.

I could hear my coworkers tittering off to the side, probably wondering why such a good-looking guy was interested in me, the office hermit.

He explained that his architectural firm in San Francisco had transferred him to the Chicago office, and I deftly avoided his questions of what I'd been up to in the years since the program. Instead, we fell into reliving the memories—the good ones, only—of our time in Australia, the scenes overlaid with a nostalgic sheen. And for the first time in years, I felt like the person I was before *that* night.

As we ordered more rounds of margaritas, the alcohol and attention warming my cheeks, I realized that Josh made me feel seen, important. Something that no man had ever done aside from Declan. That night, we stumbled back to my apartment, falling into bed together. And it kept happening, even beyond when I knew it shouldn't.

Neither of us was interested in a long-term relationship. Too much baggage, too much history unspoken. We were friends, first and foremost, who just happened to be attracted to each other. I should have ended it when it first started, and I promised myself

I would every time after. It wasn't fair to Josh, since I didn't have feelings for him. And somewhere deeper, I also recognized it wasn't fair to me. This friends-with-benefits thing with Josh could theoretically stop me from meeting someone I really connected with. *Someone like Declan*, my mind screamed at me. But I knew the chances of that were slim, as I rarely left the apartment aside from work and the weekly grocery shop.

But even without that emotional connection, it just felt so good to be with someone who knew me in *the before*. It made me feel like I was that person again, the twenty-year old, straddling youth and adulthood, with a life of possibilities spread out before her. One she hadn't yet ruined.

But did I really know him?

Aside from that first night, our encounters usually didn't involve all that much talking, certainly not about our lives since the program. Which was more than fine with me, as I wasn't aching to disclose how I had wasted the last ten years in a haze of grief and regret. Josh had told me a little about his upbringing as an only child raised by parents who were more interested in their work than their son. One night, when he came to my apartment directly from some office party, his breath reeking of whiskey, he became emotional talking about a friend from high school, someone who was like a brother to him, who died unexpectedly in a car accident. But he seemed embarrassed the next time we met, and we never talked about his childhood again.

There's nothing I can think of that would explain why he would have lied about talking to the police. Or why he would have come all the way back to Australia and not agreed to the AFP interview. I'm still lost in thought when I hear a throat clearing behind me.

When I turn, Declan is standing inside the door to the Inn's lobby.

"We were thinking about walking downtown, if you want to join," he says, his hands awkwardly in his pockets.

I hate it, the effect he still has on me. I feel my breath catch as I remember that night in Cairns, after the group had come back from skydiving. We'd traipsed to a local bar, the alcohol flowing freely as it always did. Everyone was happy, adrenaline still coursing through them—except for Phoebe, of course, who was still reeling from seeing Adrien and Kyan get together. The night was muggy, humidity cloaking the street like a blanket, but Declan asked me to wait outside as the others filed into the air-conditioned bar.

"There's something I've been meaning to do," he said. And then it happened, what I had spent weeks aching for. His hands were on my cheeks, his lips on mine, the scent of his sandalwood cologne dizzying. And everything finally felt right.

When we separated, he kept his eyes on mine. "I've been wanting to do that for so long," he whispered.

My response got stuck in my throat then, buried under the weight of affection. But we both knew what I wanted to say. *Me too.*

We meet back in the Inn's lobby an hour later. Kyan's back to his calm, charismatic self, and there's no evidence of the earlier incident other than an open chair behind the front desk. Randy is clearly making himself sparse.

When we step outside, the air is dense and arid, and much hotter than earlier this morning. It feels like something's stirring. The flies seem to feel the same, buzzing erratically around us. I try to force the wildfire warning from earlier from my mind.

We walk in the direction of the clock tower, the center of town. The full main street is about a mile in length, and back when we were first here, about a quarter of that was taken up with shops, restaurants, and businesses. Now, it's far less. By the time we reach the clock tower, our conversation dominated by the weird events of the morning, I can count on one hand the number of buildings we've seen in use.

"Well, that was anticlimactic," Ellery says. Her tone is sarcastic, with a hint of our shared disappointment.

"Is it too early for a drink?" Kyan proposes.

"Randy certainly didn't think so," Josh quips, prompting a few laughs.

"And he *is* an ideal role model if I ever saw one," Ellery joins in. "It looked like there was a small café open a few buildings back. Should we try that?"

We all agree, heading back to the squat building we passed moments before. It's clear as soon as we take in the smeared display cases housing stale-looking pastries that we're out of luck in the drinks department, but we take a seat anyway, grateful for a break from the heat, assuming this is the only establishment that serves lunch in this town. We order bland sandwiches and coffee from an unimpressed waiter who does little more than grunt in our direction.

"If you had told twenty-year old me that I'd come back to this place willingly, I would have said you were full of shit," Josh says, a small smile playing on his face.

"We really hated it here," Declan says with a laugh.

"Phoebe more than any of us," I say. My voice cracks on her name, and I try to cover it by taking a sip of my coffee, which tastes just a touch sour. They all laugh, and I try to join in, but the irony isn't lost on me. Phoebe is the one who's been stuck here the last ten years.

My eyes land on Josh from across the table. Other than a grimace after drinking from his coffee mug, he looks perfectly relaxed.

"So," Adrien says, "I spent some time looking up ways to get back to Sydney today, and I found a regional airport that's just under ten hours away by car. They haven't cancelled flights yet, and it looks like there's one tomorrow late afternoon. I say we leave super early tomorrow morning and head there."

Tomorrow morning. Something curdles in my gut. I need more time than that to figure out how Nick is involved in Phoebe's death. And there's something pulling at me here in Jagged Rock, as if the answer is right in front of me.

I consider trying to come up with a reason for us to stay longer, but I know it's useless. No one wants to be here any longer than necessary. In their minds, we've already confronted Nick Gould, that was all we owed Phoebe. And any attempt to prolong our trip is only going to raise suspicion, which I can't afford.

I need to make the most of the time I have left here in Jagged Rock to dig up whatever information I can.

"I'm actually not that hungry," I announce, pushing away my barely touched sandwich. "I'm feeling a bit…off. I'm going to head back to the Inn."

"Feel better," Josh says with a smile. "We'll see you in a bit."

I catch Declan throw him a sharp glance before I leave.

Back outside, the air hanging heavy around me, I start walking back in the direction we came, formulating a rough plan. I'll start by talking to the locals, asking about Nick Gould, about the night Phoebe went missing. Maybe I can find something the AFP missed. I'm so lost in my plan that I barely register the sound of an engine sputtering behind me, the crunch of tires on the pavement.

A car pulls up alongside me. A "ute," the locals call it, basically a squashed-down version of a truck. I keep walking, looking straight ahead, avoiding awkward eye contact with the driver.

I wait for it to continue past me, but it continues to roll, matching my speed. And slowly, the passenger side window begins to roll down.

Something doesn't feel right. Who would be stopping to talk to me all the way out here? I twist my head to take in both sides of the street. It's completely empty. Only a few cars passed us the entire time we were walking this morning.

I look back at the café and realize how far I've gone in a short time. Too far for the others to hear me if I yell.

The car's window descends slowly, until I can make out the top of the driver's head.

Red. A color so distinct it can only belong to one person.

Nick Gould.

I start to run.

19

CLAIRE

Now

"CLAIRE!" NICK GOULD YELLS through the window, his car keeping perfect pace with me as I try to flee. "I just want to talk."

I refuse to turn. Instead, I swing my arms harder. Sweat forms at my hairline and my breath burns in my lungs.

"I didn't kill Phoebe...or Hari. But I made mistakes. And I regret them every day."

I don't know if it's the words or the grief-stricken tone, but something makes me stop.

I'm panting, one hand on my knee, the other wiping the sweat from my forehead, when I finally make eye contact with him.

"There's no way I'm getting in that car with you," I say.

He gives me a small sad smile, just enough for his moustache to twitch. "No need."

—

A bell dings as we enter, Nick graciously holding the door open for me, as if that will undo what he's done. I agreed to hear his explanation so long as we talked somewhere public. As I looked at the building he'd proposed, a flush of nostalgia washed through me.

It's still the tallest building on the street. Situated on a corner and spanning nearly a block in width, it takes up three full stories, the second of which is bordered by a lattice-fenced terrace. But its age is evident from the exterior. Segments of the terrace have worn away over the years, leaving portions of the ledge exposed; its once bright salmon-pink paint is chipped and peeling; and a single sign—once vibrant gold but now faded into a dusty yellow—hangs over the doorway, labeling the building as *The Royal Hotel & Bar*.

Despite Nick's reassurances, the place seems empty, the front desk unattended, the shabby couch and set of armchairs that reside in the lobby sad and alone. Blood pumps in my ears, and I consider that this could be a trap, until a lighthearted voice echoes through the tiled lobby.

"Come on in. You two look like you're ready for a drink."

I perk up at the sound of another voice. The man it belongs to is tall, bulky, with sharp creases at the sides of his eyes that only deepen as he smiles. He appears to be in his fifties, but he has an impressive head of dark hair, and there's a pleasant youthfulness about him.

He's standing in the entryway to a large room, and as I move closer, I take in the smattering of tables, the stools perched in front of a bar holding dusty bottles of liquor, and the empty stage in the corner. And suddenly, I'm reliving that night ten years ago. Our group went out for karaoke, the only form of entertainment Jagged Rock appeared to offer after 8:00 p.m. I remember the surprisingly packed room, the vibrant lights, the gorgeous drag queen crooning a Shania Twain song into the microphone as she dominated the stage in her pink boa and short jean shorts.

"You alright, love?"

"Sorry," I stammer. "Yeah, a drink would be nice."

The man leads us to the bar. Nick orders a Coke—which catches me a bit by surprise; I had pegged him for a beer guy—and the man grabs an old-fashioned-looking bottle from a hidden cooler. I know I should keep my wits about me, but after everything that's happened today, I can't help but crave a way to blur the fear, the grief, the confusion. To dull everything.

"Rum and Coke, please," I say as I take a seat, the ripped plastic of the stool biting through my jeans.

Once the man deposits it in front of me, he lingers for a second, evidently picking up on the weird energy between Nick and me.

"I'll be over there doing some cleaning up if you need me," he says eventually, giving me a long look before heading to the corner of the room, in clear sight. I smile over at him as he picks up a broom to sweep the immaculate floor, and gratitude floods through me.

"So," Nick says with an awkward clearing of his throat. "Yous all think I killed them. Hari and Phoebe."

The statement is a harsh slap of reality, and for a moment, I find myself speechless.

"I didn't." His voice is hard, obstinate, and I regain some composure.

"Well, you certainly have a funny way of proving that. Threatening us with a loaded rifle and then trapping me in the mine."

I expect him to explain it away, but Nick's eyes grow wide.

"I didn't trap you in the mine," he says, voice clear.

"Okay." I force a harsh laugh. "What would you call it then?"

"I've been trying to talk to you alone since you left my ranch yesterday. That's why I came to the Inn this morning. I asked Randy at the front desk where you went—which was an altogether unpleasant experience I got no interest in repeating—and he said you'd gone out for a walk. So I went out back, tried to find ya. Almost made it all the way out to the mine, but I never saw hide nor hair of ya, so I turned back and went home. Figured I'd try again later, and here we are. I don't know nothing about you being trapped in that mine. You shouldn't be playing around out there though, it ain't safe."

Suspicion swirls in my gut. Why should I trust this man, after everything?

"Why did you want to talk to me and not the others?"

He sighs, and his shoulders slump. "I know how close you and Phoebe were, at least at the beginning of the program. You two did everything together those first few weeks."

His words let loose an unsolicited flurry of memories. Phoebe doing my makeup that first day in Sydney, the two of us sitting on her bed after a night out, drunkenly giggling about Kyan and Declan, Phoebe grabbing my hand and pulling me down the main boulevard in Cairns, running so fast that the wind slapped against our faces.

But I also hear his unspoken implication. How far apart we drifted in those final two weeks.

"I thought of anyone in the group, she might have told you what I did to her."

I think back to my conversation with Villanueva. Phoebe's pregnancy.

"You raped her," I say coldly.

And it all makes sense. Maybe she threatened to tell, to expose him for who he really is, and that's why he killed her. And now he's been trying to pick off the rest of us to keep his secrets, starting with Hari. I feel my blood run cold as the puzzle pieces fit together, and I begin to stand, but his hand reaches out, grabbing for my arm.

Nick coughs, puts his hand down. "God, sorry," he says. "But *rape*?" He whispers the word, looking around as if someone may overhear, and indeed, the worker is looking straight at us, no longer trying to hide his eavesdropping. "I didn't *rape* Phoebe. I'd never do that. I'm not that type of person."

"Then what did you do to her?"

"I... Let me back up to the beginning; this is all coming out wrong." He sighs deeply, stretching out his hands as if he's settling in to tell a long storied tale. "I wasn't in a great headspace during that program. I was...in recovery."

"For?" I prompt.

"Alcohol and opiates. I thought I had it in check for the most part, but one day I showed up to teach a class still high and drunk from the night before. Some students reported me to Hamilton administration. They couldn't prove it, but it was the wake-up call I needed. I started AA and NA meetings, but I needed more than that. Individualized therapy. Alcoholism runs in my veins—my father and pretty much every generation of my family before him was glued to the bottle. I vowed to kick it, end the cycle and all that.

"But treatment ain't always cheap. Australia does a good job with helping addicts, but the state doesn't cover everything. I needed money, so I signed up to lead the Adventure Abroad program. In hindsight, it probably wasn't the best idea to be leading a group of kids through a month of boozing, but at the time I didn't really have any other options. I knew it was going to be hard, so that's why I brought along Hari. I taught her in my Australian history class. She was one of my best students.

"Everything was fine at first. I mean yous all were a handful, of course. I tried to leave ya alone as much as possible, especially when the bottles came out. That's where Hari took over."

Thinking back, I realize Nick was never around when we were drinking. And whenever we would wake up hungover—which in all honesty, was pretty much every day—he would greet us with an annoyed remark.

"I was on edge from the very beginning. I knew it was a mistake as soon as I walked up to that first day at orientation. And when Phoebe asked that question, that...sexual one, it just set me off. I had her stay after, and I just lit into her. When she tried to give it back, I lost control, grabbed her. Hard. I got no excuse," he rushes, seeing my reaction. "I was just... I was struggling."

Emotion breaks through his last few words, and he lowers his head so I can't see his eyes. For the first time ever, I find myself sympathizing with this giant of a man.

"She didn't tell you?" he asks.

I shake my head. All she said about being late to the bus that first day was that there was some administration error, something missing from her paperwork that she had to fix with Nick. What else didn't she tell me?

"I was so ashamed that I avoided her for most of the trip," he says after a pause. "But Lord, she had a way of getting under my skin."

I stare at him.

"I didn't kill her. I wouldn't. But I can understand how she could have driven someone to murder."

The memory flicks through my brain like a warped film reel. The sight of Phoebe, the Outback stars illuminating her like a spotlight, head tipped back, mouth in a lascivious circle. And it floods back, the rage that injected every inch of my body as I watched her. A pure hatred I had never felt before.

"But what about the rest of it?" I say, forcing the memory from my mind. "Adrien said you were fired from Hamilton because of a confrontation with a student."

Nick looks down at the glass soda bottle in his hands.

"I carried around a lot of guilt after that trip. I was the teacher, the guide. It was my responsibility to keep yous safe. Maybe if I'd done something different... None of that is an excuse, but when I got back to Hamilton, things just seemed wrong. By some grace of God, the school still didn't fire me, but they put me on probation, and everyone knew what'd happened on that trip. Everyone had thoughts, opinions, judgments. Hari tried to help me the best she could, but I...I relapsed. And the worst part was that I took Hari down with me.

"She started using and we...well, we enabled each other. Things got dark, and I lost my grip on reality. The students could tell something was going on, of course. One day, a kid got pissed off. I can't blame him, I wasn't teaching him anything; class had turned into a waste of time. But he made some offhand comment about Tomas. And I just... I lost it. Just like with Phoebe after orientation, but this time I couldn't stop myself. I punched him over and over. Didn't stop until a group 'a students pulled me off.

"That was the last straw for Hamilton, as it should have been. In fact, they should have cut the cord years before that. That was my rock bottom. I realized I had to change.

"I left Sydney, moved back to my family's farm in Rollowong. My dad was long dead by then, and Mum was sick. I took care 'a her, got back to my roots, left all temptation behind. I tried to convince Hari to come with me, to get clean and start over, but she refused. We still talked, but I should'a stayed. I should'a done more."

He bows his head again.

"When yous showed up at the ranch, I was in shock. It was like my past had caught up with me. When I heard about Hari, I..." Emotion breaks into his voice, and he stops for a moment. "And then the implication that I killed her and Phoebe. I just... It was too much.

"I spent last night tryin' to process it all. I called my sponsor.

Our program is all about forgiveness—forgivin' ourselves, seeking forgiveness from those we hurt. So I knew what I had to do. I figured since you were closest to Phoebe, you were the one I needed to explain things to, to apologize."

"So you didn't trap me in the mine?"

I need to hear him confirm it, one more time.

"No. I wouldn't do that. Plus, what the hell would I have had to gain from it?"

"Did you see anyone around? Someone was in there, in the shaft. I went in to take a look and they ran out, shoved me down the stairs, and slammed the door."

Nick shakes his head. "With the mine all dug up now, there are a million different hiding places out there. Whoever did it could have been anywhere."

I sigh, disappointment settling in my chest.

"Listen, Claire, as you may have noticed, your group isn't all that well-liked here in Jagged Rock. After the accident with Tomas, the college put the Adventure Abroad program on hiatus. I got the news our last day here. They've never operated it again since. The money that we brought in during the few days our program spent here may not have seemed like a lot for us, but for some of the businesses here, it kept the doors open."

He looks around at the dust clinging to the bottles behind the bar and the empty tables that line the room.

"Things were supposed to change. A big hotel company was gonna build a five-star resort out here. Y'know, one where city folk could feel like they were roughing it with Egyptian cotton sheets and spas and all that crap. They started excavating already; that's why the mine's all dug up. Was supposed to be on the land owned by Randy's family. But when they discovered Phoebe's remains last week, they pulled out. Bad publicity, they said."

My mind flashes back to the rage in Randy's eyes earlier this morning.

"Look," Nick says, pushing himself to a standing position so that he towers over me. "I'm sorry for all of this, and everything you had to go through. I hope you find what you're looking for. But there are people out here who aren't going to take kindly to you trying to dredge everything back up."

He throws a wad of cash down on the counter to cover our drinks.

"Just be careful, Claire."

The warning rings loudly in my ears even after Nick has exited the hotel.

20

CLAIRE

Now

BE CAREFUL.

If my gut is right, Nick wasn't the person who killed Phoebe. Or Hari. Nor did he trap me in the mine.

Which means the person who did all those things is still in Jagged Rock, and they've made very clear what they're willing to do to stop me from discovering the truth.

The thud of a glass on the counter shakes me back to the present.

"Thought you could use another," the kind worker says as he plunks down a fresh rum and Coke in front of me. "That looked intense."

"Thank you," I say, realizing I've somehow drained my first glass already. "It kind of was. And I appreciate you looking out for me over there."

"Can never be too safe." He pulls a beer from the cooler behind him and takes a long pull from it. "What's your name?"

"Claire," I say, taking a sip of the strong cocktail.

"So, I'm guessing you're here because of the body they found up by the Inn?"

I swallow. I'm afraid to admit it after Nick just explained how we helped ruin this town.

"She was my friend," I say, carefully. "Phoebe. We were on a study abroad program here the year she went—" I catch myself. "The year she died."

"Oh, I know it. That was the last year they did that program. The hotel used to make good money off you lot, this being the only bar where you can get loose in the whole town."

The guilt slices at me, and I clear my throat. "Did you work here back then?"

"Honey, I've been working here since I was born. This son of a bitch is a family business," he says, holding his arms out to gesture around him. "I use that term *business* quite loosely, of course." He chuckles. "My great-great-great grandfather built it back when the mine was still in business. But we shut down the hotel portion a few years back. Now it's just the bar and restaurant. Our clientele is mostly locals and some folks like you who are passing through."

I don't know if it's the *honey,* or the sass with which the man talks, but it jiggles something loose in my memory.

"Wait, you said you worked here when Phoebe went missing. You weren't... I mean... the karaoke you used to have here, did you...?"

"Oh, did I ever. You, love, are looking at none other than Miss Daisy Dukes herself."

He does the signature pose of the drag queen I so vividly

remember—hip popped, elbow cocked, hand propping up his chin—and I picture him back up on that stage, decked out in a waist-length bleach-blond wig and those shorts I swear he painted on.

"No way."

"Mmhmm, I know, I know. How the mighty have fallen, right?"

"No, that wasn't what I..." But my eyes catch again on the dust draping heavily on the liquor bottles. "I'm so sorry," I say, and I am. If I had done something different that day, not only might Phoebe still be alive, but this poor guy could have a thriving business.

"It's not your fault that I've turned into a gay Ms. Havisham, honey," he says, and despite the depressing subject matter, there's a twinkle in his voice.

I want to believe him, but he doesn't know the truth. Instead, I settle on another question. "Can I ask why you've stayed here so long?"

"I inherited this place from my grandma. I owe that woman everything. She raised me after my parents cut and run to Melbourne. She wanted a safe space for me to grow up. A place I would feel at home, where I could be myself. Drag karaoke was her idea."

"She sounds like a great woman," I add.

"That she was. Even after everything started drying up, I couldn't bring myself to let this place go. I owe it to her. I know our days are limited, but if the bank or this town wants this place, they're going to have to pry it away from me. Although, I'd be lying if I said they didn't try."

I look at him curiously, silently begging him to continue.

"When the hotel stopped bringing in money, the locals turned against me a bit. They weren't totally on board with having a 'queer' in their midst," he says, throwing up air quotes as if it's a swear word, "but they could at least look the other way when this place was supporting the town's economy. Once that stopped, they didn't hesitate to make their feelings known. Let's just say, there's been a few times now I've had to get these here windows repaired." He gestures to the large rounded glass windows behind him that face out onto Main Street. "But if they think some graffiti and broken glass is going to stop me, they don't know the half of it."

"Wow," I say. "I don't know if I would have the strength to stick it out after all that."

"Sometimes you don't know what you're capable of until you're tested," he says with a wink.

If he only knew.

"So, what is it you all are planning to accomplish by coming out here?" he asks.

"Well, uh…Daisy, that's actually what all this was just now," I say, gesturing back to the door that Nick walked out of minutes earlier.

"Oh Lordy, just call me Luke, darling. I haven't been Daisy Dukes in quite some time now."

I nod. "Luke. I came back to try to find out who killed my friend." I feel my cheeks flush at the admission, skirting over my role in Phoebe's death. I rush to continue, before Luke can notice. "I was actually wondering if you remembered anything about her. The whole group came in here a few days before…she died."

Scenes of that night snap through my head. Daisy Dukes crooning at the microphone as I spun around on the dance floor.

I fumble in my pocket for my phone, pulling up a photo of me and Phoebe in Cairns, the night of the bungee jump. Happier times. I divert my eyes from it, unable to bear the pain it elicits as I hand the phone over to Luke.

He shakes his head, disappointed. "I remember the night the whole group of yous came in. It was one of the last times we were that busy. But no, I can't recall seeing her."

"I get it; it was a long time ago, after all," I say, but my shoulders slump in defeat. "Thank you for all this, but I should be going," I say, realizing how much I still need to uncover if I'm going to figure out what really happened. I move to pull my wallet from my bag, but Luke reaches his hand out to stop me.

"It's on the house, hun."

The kindness pricks at my eyes.

"Listen," he says, placing his hand on mine, "you're staying over at the Inn, right? Randy's place?" I nod. "Are you sure you all are safe there?"

I open my mouth to answer, to assure him we'll be fine, but I can't. It looks like Luke is about to say something, but he seems to shrug it off. "This is just me being paranoid. I'm sure you'll be fine, but in case you need it, here's my number."

He hands me a faded business card with *The Royal Hotel* inscribed in dusty pink letters at the top and a jumble of numbers and email addresses below it.

"Thank you," I say, more grateful than he can know.

I'm almost out the door when he calls after me. "Claire, just... That guy was right before. You all should be careful."

My mind is buzzing by the time I return to the Inn, likely from a combination of the two drinks and everything I've just found out over the last hour. I feign something resembling a smile, expecting Randy to be at his usual post, but the front desk is empty. Instead, there's a piece of computer paper taped to it, proclaiming in prickly handwriting that he will be *Back by 17:00*.

I breathe a small sigh and start heading to my room. I'll use the restroom and then head out, look again for the knife. But a movement outside catches my eye. The others are draped over chairs, beers in hand, talking excitedly. I must have been so caught up in my conversation with Nick that I never saw them walk by the Royal on their way back to the Inn.

I consider joining them, telling them about my conversation with Nick. But then I remember the caginess I've picked up on since I arrived at Kyan's the other day. Josh's lies about interviewing with the AFP. And Villanueva's veiled warning against sharing the news of Phoebe's pregnancy.

The thought stings me.

I can't trust them.

I head up to my room instead. As I start up the stairs, I realize how quiet it is. I've never experienced the Inn like this during working hours. The last time we were here, someone was always around, slamming doors or running up or down the stairs, talking excitedly about something or other. Our group, though small, filled almost all the rooms. But now it's desolate, quiet enough that I can hear the dull thrum of flies and conversation outside.

Once back in my room, I lie down, the prongs of the mattress sticking into my back. I take a deep breath and think, replaying everything I've learned the last few days. As I try to work through it all, I let my eyes roam the room before they land on that painting of the raven. Again, something about it just seems off.

I stand up and walk towards it, until it's only inches from my eyes. I raise my hand, my fingertips tracing the canvas, the thick black paint on the bird's wings. It's not a print, like I expected, but an original.

A sudden thud from the door startles me, jarring my arm and knocking the painting from the wall, sending it spiraling to the floor with a loud crash. The noise comes again, breaking through the pounding blood in my ears.

"Claire?" The familiar voice filters through the wall. "You back?"

Shakily, I open the door, finding Josh once again standing in the doorway. He's wearing a small smile, and despite everything, I can't ignore how handsome he looks. He hasn't bothered shaving since he arrived and the scruff on his chin lends his boyish face a more manly quality.

"Hey," he says. "I tried you when we got back, but you weren't here. I was wondering if I could talk to you."

I think of his lie this morning and consider whether I should avoid being alone with him. But then I look at his sheepish grin and remember all the times he's been in my bed back home. I open the door wider, beckoning him in, and we both take a seat on the bed.

"Have a bit of an accident?" Josh asks, nodding towards the fallen painting.

"Yeah," I say with a shrug, leaving it at that.

"Listen, I have something to tell you. It's been eating me up since our conversation this morning."

I don't respond, leaving him to fill in the silence.

"I lied to you about going to the AFP office when I first got into Sydney the other day. I should have just told you the truth."

"Which is?" I prompt.

Josh sighs. "I've never been a huge fan of the cops. You remember that friend I told you about, a while back? The one who was like a brother to me?"

I think of that emotional story he'd shared when he'd come over to my place, drunk. About the friend who'd died in a car accident. I nod.

"Well, I always suspected there was something off about his accident. Things just didn't add up to me. I told the police my suspicions, how I thought there'd been some foul play or something like that. They just shrugged me off, acted like I was a stupid kid. Never even bothered to investigate. And then, the cops here were completely useless after Phoebe went missing..." Josh trails off. "I don't trust them, the police. I know that may be unfair, but I didn't want to spend what little time I had back here talking to the AFP, just for them to get it wrong like they always do."

I think about this for a second. "So why did you come back at all?"

"I missed this." He gestures around.

"Jagged Rock?"

He laughs. "No, definitely not. I mean having this close group of friends. It's pretty much the closest I've had to a real family. The more I thought about it, the more I wanted to come back and experience that again, even despite the horrible circumstances. So I cancelled that work conference I had at the last minute and flew over. I didn't really want to get into all the reasons why I wasn't planning on talking to the police or listen to why I should—you know how Ellery can get—so I just lied when Adrien asked if I'd already talked to them. Truth was, I got into the airport around three in the afternoon and went straight to Kyan's."

I nod, thinking it through. It makes sense and somehow I feel even guiltier, something I didn't think was possible. This was Josh after all. Did I really think he was capable of killing Phoebe?

"I'm sorry," I say.

"Why are you apologizing?" He laughs. "I'm the one who lied. Listen, we're all outside, reliving some of our wilder times from back then. Why don't you come down and grab a beer?"

"Maybe. I'm a little tired. I might take a nap. After I hang this up, of course." I gesture to the painting sprawled on the floor.

Josh offers to help, but I shrug it off. And then I'm alone.

God, I really am losing it. All this suspicion is really screwing with my head.

I stoop to pick up the painting. As I do, I notice a wire sticking out from the frame. From the bed, I assumed it was something to help affix it to the wall, but upon looking closer, it appears to poke through the canvas. I flip the painting over until I'm staring directly into the raven's dark eye. And that's when I see it. A small, spherical, almost imperceptible object. I trace my fingers over it. It's cold to the touch, like a marble.

I suck in a deep breath, understanding washing over me as I recognize it for what it is.

A small camera. Someone has been filming me.

21
PHOEBE

Then

I LOOK OUT FROM where I stand on the deck of the yacht, hands placed solidly on the metal railing in front of me. Cerulean water stretches in every direction, without a single piece of land in sight. The Great Barrier Reef is just as beautiful as everyone said it would be—from the surface at least—but I can barely acknowledge it. Instead, I can't help but focus my attention on trying not to vomit from the sight of Kyan and Adrien splayed out on the sunbathing area of the deck, hands intertwined.

It's the day after I skipped out on skydiving, choosing instead to lounge by the hostel pool with Claire all afternoon before once again hitting a bar with the rest of the crew, only to be subjected to another showing of Kyan and Adrien's soft-core porno on the dance floor. Enough is enough. Today I put my plan in motion.

I take a sip from my can of Coke, and grimace at the sharp sting of rum. When he found out the yacht bar was open, Nick had a conniption—he usually gets weird when we talk about drinking, always disappearing whenever it's time for us to head to a bar or when bottles emerge after an activity, but this was next-level. He forbade any of us from ordering alcohol before snorkeling, claiming it was a liability risk for the program, but I bribed the bartender with a twenty to throw a shot of Bacardi into a Coke can without Nick noticing. With everything that's been going on, I need that confidence that only comes with a shot or two of liquor. Especially today.

"It is so beautiful," Tomas says, appearing next to me at the railing and gazing out, awestruck. "We have nothing like this back in Italy."

I can't help but smile. Of all of us—even Claire—Tomas is the most innocent. He stares around at everything, eyes wide behind his glasses. And God love him, but he won't shut up about how excited he is to see the damn Outback. Everything about him is just so endearing.

"It's gorgeous," I agree, bending over the railing and letting the breeze whip my hair back. Out of the corner of my eye I notice a flash of red. Adrien is sitting up, her head in her hands.

"Sorry, Tomas, I have to use the restroom," I say, leaving him staring out to the horizon.

It's time.

Adrien has been complaining to anyone who will listen about how seasick she gets on boats. Which is funny. Given her haughtiness, I would have figured she grew up sailing on yachts. Ellery offered to lend her ginger tablets she'd brought with her, but Adrien declined, said she came equipped with her own specially prescribed pills.

Which is what gave me the idea for this plan.

I head down to the bottom level of the boat, which houses the bar, a handful of tables and benches, and racks of life vests. Thankfully, most people are on the deck, enjoying the ride out to the reef. On my way to the stairs, I spot Claire and Declan sitting towards the front of the boat, their heads close together, laughing. She collapsed onto my bunk bed last night, giddy as a schoolgirl as she recounted how Declan had finally made his move. Declan pulled me aside this morning too, before we got on the boat, to thank me for pushing him to man up.

I haven't told Claire about the plan. Despite not saying anything when she saw me trip Adrien at the bungee jump, I know she wouldn't approve of this. And I didn't want to pop her newly loved-up bubble.

The only person downstairs is Nick Gould, hunched over his laptop. He raises one bushy eyebrow in my direction as he watches me descend the stairs.

"Seasick," I say. "I brought pills with me."

Nick grunts, and I return my attention to my mission. I grab my backpack from where I stowed it under one of the benches. Before anyone can notice, I move it to the next table, where I saw Adrien place her bag earlier. Glancing over my shoulder to make sure I'm alone, I grab the monogrammed Louis Vuitton tote and immediately position my body to block it from view before digging through it.

The pills are in the second pouch I check. An orange bottle with a white cap. There's only one catch. They look different from mine. Where mine are small, round, and white, Adrien's are blue oblong capsules. Shit. The only thing I can hope for is that she hasn't taken them before, or that she's so sick she doesn't notice.

I get to work, pouring the bottle of blue pills onto my palm before unscrewing my own bottle. I'm transferring the white pills into Adrien's bottle when I feel a tap on my back.

I turn, abruptly enough that one of the pills goes skidding across the floor.

"Where did you find the restroom? I do not see—"

Tomas stops as he takes in the pill rolling on the floor, the two bottles in my hand, Adrien's signature bag. His eyes widen, his mouth forming a perfect O.

"What are you doing?"

His tone is more serious than I've ever heard it, and I flinch as though he's struck me.

"It isn't what it looks like." I mean, it is, in fact, but hopefully Tomas is just as naïve as he appears.

No such luck.

"You should not be doing that," he says coldly.

"I'm just...I couldn't find my motion sickness pills, and I remember Adrien talking about how she had some. I know she'd never loan them to me if I asked, so I figured I would just take one from her bag. Please don't tell her."

It's not great, but it's the best excuse I can fumble through on such short notice.

Tomas stares at me, and for a moment I think he's going to call me out, brand me a liar. But then he gives me a wary smile, one that almost sends me to my knees in relief.

"Okay. But where is…"

"Oh yeah, the bathroom. It's over there," I say pointing to the back of the boat.

Tomas nods and heads in that direction. I steal a glance at Nick, but he doesn't seem to notice—or care—what we were talking about.

I take a deep breath and twist the cap on Adrien's bottle before stuffing it back into her bag.

It's a good plan if I do say so myself. Replacing Adrien's seasickness pills with the extra-strength laxatives my physician had prescribed me before the trip in case of tummy issues. I really can't imagine anything more wonderful than flawless, always put-together Adrien, shitting herself on a fancy yacht in the middle of the ocean in front of everyone. I came up with it during my conversation with Claire the other day. Kyan only likes perfect things, those that sparkle. And once he sees Princess Adrien dethroned, he'll want nothing to do with her. Plus, it has the added bonus of embarrassing the shit out of her—pun very much intended—in front of everyone.

Twenty minutes after I successfully switch the pills, we're all back on the lower level, huddled around the tables as Nick drones on about the safety precautions we need to follow while we're out snorkeling. But I'm barely listening.

Instead, I'm watching Adrien. She's sitting a few tables over from me with her eyes pressed tightly closed, her skin gradually turning greener. She winces every time the boat shifts.

Finally, Nick stops talking. I watch Adrien reach for her bag, her hands rummaging until she pulls out something. The orange prescription bottle.

This is it.

My heart is pounding, my hands nearly trembling with anticipation. Will she notice the difference in the pills?

Slowly, she unscrews the top of the bottle and pours two into her open palm. Blood pounds in my ears as she pauses, looking down at them.

And then she reaches for her water.

I release an enormous breath, a smile rippling across my face as she raises her palm to her mouth.

And at the very last second, just as she's about to place the pills in her mouth, Tomas is by her side, his hand on her arm.

He says something to her that I can't hear over the others' conversation, and she lowers her hand.

And then they both look over at me.

I'm caught.

22
CLAIRE

Now

I DROP THE CAMERA as if it's burned me. Once it's crashed to the floor, I notice a red light blinking from the back of it.

There's only one person who could be behind this.

Randy.

I shouldn't be surprised. I think about the way his eyes seemed to follow the girls in our group anytime we'd walk past the front desk, or the dirty looks I'd see him shoot at the guys behind their backs. But this is a new low.

How long has this been here? He had no idea we were coming back. Hell, even *we* didn't know we were coming.

Which means Randy didn't just install these for our return.

He's used these cameras for previous guests. And maybe, just maybe, he's had them for quite a while. In which case, they may have captured something that can help me figure out who killed Phoebe.

—

I should wait, at least until it's dark, until Randy's gone for the night. But I can't just sit here and let it be.

I reposition the camera back on the picture frame, just in case Randy's still watching, take a deep breath, and head out of the room.

I tiptoe downstairs, but I needn't have worried. The sign is still at the front desk. I check my watch: 4:06 p.m. That gives me almost an hour until he comes back.

I duck behind the desk, unclear at first what it is I'm looking for. Wouldn't these cameras record to a computer of sorts? The only thing back here is the rusty PC that looks like it's incapable of loading anything other than WordPerfect, let alone storing videos.

Even so, I turn it on. As it loads, I direct my attention to the mess of papers littering the desk. Ten years of paperwork lies before me. Unopened envelopes from the Bank of Queensland sit among discarded spreadsheets and ripped-out loose-leaf papers covered in Randy's spindly handwriting. I shuffle the papers, and they part to reveal a small blue notebook. I open it, the first page nothing more than doodles. I flip through a few more, until I reach one that contains only two lines.

R.Campbell_82

Collingwood123!

It's clearly a username and password. I smile. So much for high security at the Raven Inn. The thought gives me an idea, and I look around for a CCTV camera in the lobby. While I'm at it, it may be worth trying to find old footage from that as well—I can only assume the Jagged Rock police never requested it. But a quick glance around doesn't reveal anything of the sort. Apparently, Randy's only into cameras of the hidden variety.

The computer dings, notifying me that it's fully booted up. The sound ricochets throughout the silent lobby, and my head immediately jerks around to see if anyone has noticed.

All clear. The Inn is still silent, the others still chatting and drinking outside. No one has even bothered to turn in this direction.

But strangely enough, the computer opens directly onto the desktop, not a lock screen. So what was the username and password in Randy's journal for?

I don't waste any time trying to come up with an answer. God only knows why Randy does anything he does. Instead, I start with the home page, scanning the folders he's saved to his desktop. My heart catches when I stumble upon one labeled as "Personal," but when it loads, it reveals only a dozen or so documents that appear to be bills or bank statements, most of which are covered in bold red-colored font.

I switch to the internet icon and wait as the page loads mercilessly slowly, before navigating to the history tab and scanning the list of web pages Randy last visited. By their URLs, most appear to be porn sites, and I cringe at the thought of Randy down here looking at them. But there is one website that I recognize as a big hotel corporation. That must be the company Nick had mentioned was planning to buy up the surrounding land. Despite everything, I still feel a sharp pang in my chest when I think of how close Randy came to getting out, to starting over.

I scan more of his internet history but realize within a few minutes there's nothing helpful. I sigh, leaning back in the chair, defeated. Where else could he possibly be storing these videos?

My eyes roam the lobby. The makeshift breakfast table with a decades-old coffee machine in the corner, some threadbare couches and chairs, the door out to the back, and then...

The other door. The one to the room we saw Randy come out of when we first arrived at the Inn, which I thought was a bathroom.

I'm there within seconds, the notebook from the front desk clasped tightly in my hands. Part of me expects the door to be locked, to meet yet another obstacle, but the knob turns easily under my hand. Inside, I'm met with darkness.

I trace the side of the wall with my fingers, but there's no light switch. So I take another step forward and nearly scream as something brushes against my cheek.

My hands fly frantically to my face, but as my fingertips touch the foreign object, I breathe out and pull down on it sharply.

The cord ignites the light above it, and I realize with a jolt that I'm not in a bathroom, as I'd assumed, but a small closet, its walls crowded with stuff. Or junk, from the looks of it.

I close the door behind me in case Randy or any others happen to walk by. As my eyes adjust to the dim light, I make out the shape of discarded fold-up chairs, a few broken umbrellas, stacks of old boxes, and a large shapeless item over which a blanket has been thrown.

I grip the edge of the blanket, yanking it free to reveal exactly what I expect.

Another desktop and computer monitor, this one much more

modern than the one at the front desk. I hold my breath as it boots up and the screen comes to life.

A password request. Unlike the computer on the front desk, this one has something worth hiding. I barely finish inputting the exclamation point in "Collingwood123!" when the desktop comes to life. I don't have to search long. There's only one folder saved to the desktop aside from those automatically loaded from the computer, and it's conspicuously marked "Private."

I click on it, and the screen floods with icons. Small pixelated images, all with the same background. The once-maroon carpet, the faded green walls. The Inn's guest rooms.

I steal a glance at the bottom left-hand side of the corner. Seven hundred and sixty-two files.

I roll my shoulders and click on the first one.

The first minute or so captures nothing but the walls and the two beds, and despite the similarities between each of the rooms, I recognize the backdrop immediately. The chip in the wallpaper where the walls join, my shoulder bag propped in the corner. Room 13.

My room.

I fast forward impatiently until a body fills the screen. Despite how much I prepare, I still jump when I see myself wandering out of the bathroom, wrapped in nothing but a towel.

It's from earlier this morning, I realize with a start, when I thought I was entirely alone.

The skin on my arms prickles, and a shudder runs through me. I yank at the sleeves of my T-shirt as if that will help ease how violated I feel. I quickly close out of the video, knowing what comes next. I can't bear to see myself dropping the towel, standing naked, completely vulnerable for a moment before pulling back on the one pair of underwear I have with me on this trip.

Instead, I scroll down, choose another video at random. It reveals a man and a woman, both middle-aged, rummaging in their suitcases, and I quickly close out. Another attempt reveals a man in his twenties watching TV on his laptop while lying on the room's single bed.

I scroll even further, clicking again and again, finding nothing helpful.

Eventually, after several more attempts, I toggle the folder options to show the date each video was uploaded. And then I scroll immediately to the day I'm looking for: December 25, 2015. I click on one whose file number starts with 13, which by now I've realized indicates the room.

The image of my room as it was ten years ago fills the screen. It sits empty as the seconds of the red time stamp tick slowly upwards. I skip ahead on the video, pausing when a figure comes into view.

I can tell immediately that it's Phoebe. The sight of her takes my breath away. Her eyes are red, her short hair wild. She's thin, painfully so. She moves frantically, arms flying as she throws her belongings into the black designer backpack she used to carry.

My hands tremble as I watch Phoebe's frenzied motions. And then, suddenly, she stops. She breathes slowly, as if to compose herself, and then turns. Her eyes lock with the camera, like she knew it was there. I fumble to pause the video, and Phoebe stares back at me. Her face gaunt, eyes panicked. There's an aura to her as well. One I don't remember from that night.

Fear.

I don't know how long I stare back at her, my heart silently breaking as I consider all the things I could have done differently. Everything I *should* have done.

Eventually, I check the time stamp: 9:34 p.m.

I think back, trying to situate the video in my memory of that night's timeline. And I know what's going to come next. Phoebe will leave, flee the Inn. I'll come back to this room, anger radiating off me as I realize she's already gone. And then I'll take off, eager to find her.

But not before first stopping downstairs in the small room that served as the Inn's kitchen. Nothing more than a few drawers, a stove top, and a refrigerator that barely worked. I'll pull out one of those drawers, grab the biggest knife I can find. And I'll go out to look for her.

Before I can watch the rest of the video, a sound breaks into the room. A soft thud, followed by another. Footsteps.

Someone's in the lobby.

I think of Nick's story earlier, about how Randy's life was ruined when the construction company found Phoebe's remains. And then I remember Randy's anger from this morning, how he seemed ready to rip Kyan's throat out.

What will he do if he finds me in here?

Hackles raised, I hold my breath, trying to be as quiet as possible. The footsteps slow gradually, before coming to a stop. I can feel a presence hovering just on the other side of the door. I squeeze my eyes shut, try to will him away.

But I flick them back open when I hear another sound. One too familiar, one that signifies I can't escape.

The slow creaking of the doorknob turning.

23

CLAIRE

Now

"WHAT ARE YOU DOING in here?"

I've been caught red-handed, my neck craned towards the computer, Phoebe frozen on the screen.

"I could ask you the same thing," I say to the figure barricading the doorway.

"I came in here to check on you," Declan says, one eyebrow raised. "Josh said you'd gotten back. I was hoping we could…talk. I checked your room first, of course, but it's empty. Then I thought I heard a sound coming from in here, and well, here you are watching videos of…" He trails off as he realizes what—who—I'm watching, and I see his spine straighten.

He opens his mouth as if to say something more, but his jaw goes slack with shock.

"It was Randy," I start, before rushing out the full explanation.

Randy's weird comment about remembering what room I had stayed in, finding the camera, sneaking into this closet.

As I talk, Declan grows more and more tense, his fingers inching up into his palms, so that by the time I'm done with my explanation, his hands are fists, a red flush staining his cheeks.

"That fecking eejit," he manages after a moment. "I should have let Kyan take him when he had the chance."

"I know, it's revolting. But this may be good for us. There may be something on one of these videos that can help us figure out what really happened to Phoebe," I say, gesturing to the screen.

Am I imagining it, or does a flash of panic cross his face? But before I can question it, it's gone, and Declan's pulling another chair away from the wall. I scoot over to make room for him in front of the computer. It's tight when we finally manage to fit the two chairs together. My arm rubs against his as we sit, and despite starting the video, for a few moments I can't seem to focus on anything but his skin against mine.

I think about before. First in Cairns and then the Whitsundays. The almost obscene beauty of both places lost on me, as all I could focus on was him. The two of us together. The days passed laughing and talking, the nights cuddled up next to each other on his twin-size bed.

Before we arrived in Jagged Rock and everything was ruined.

I force myself to sit there next to him as the video plays, unfolding just the way I remember. The fury radiating off me as I enter the room, violently twisting my head in all directions, as if expecting to find Phoebe hiding, before running out of the room.

Declan doesn't say anything, doesn't bother asking why I was so angry.

And suddenly I can't take it anymore. I quickly stop the video. "Looks like that's it from that one."

I check my watch: 4:42 p.m. Randy will be back in eighteen minutes.

"We don't have much time," I explain to Declan. "Just enough for a few more."

Declan nods. "Maybe we should go in order? Try the next video?"

I nod, buzzing inside, in awe of how good it feels to finally have a partner in this. To no longer be in it alone.

I recognize the room in the next video immediately, Adrien's Louis Vuitton suitcase discarded in the corner. The camera is trained on the bed where two figures meld together, writhing in unison, blankets discarded on the floor.

Declan clears his throat next to me and I snatch the mouse to jump forward a few minutes, until they've finished and Adrien has pulled the blanket up to cover her chest and Kyan's waist.

Like all the other videos, it's silent, the camera not equipped to pick up sound. I watch Kyan grab his phone on the nightstand as Adrien lies next to him, breathless and content, judging from the small smile decorating her lips.

Even all these years later, I can't help but feel a jolt of pain for Phoebe, thinking how much she would have hated this. I've never fully forgiven Kyan for how easily he discarded her. It seemed as though he was using her to make Adrien jealous, to prompt her into making a move.

Suddenly on-screen, Kyan jerks in the bed, sitting upright, his gaze glued to his phone. Adrien sits up next to him, resting her hand on his back, peering over his shoulder, her face distorting into anger.

In an instant, they're both out of the bed, ripping their clothes from the floor and yanking them on.

Adrien yells something at Kyan, who snaps back at her.

The exchange volleys back and forth. I lean closer to the screen, as if the proximity will render the video audible, and I feel Declan do the same.

We both suck in a breath at the same time. Even without sound, the video is clear enough to capture Kyan's face, to pick up on the outline of his lips as he talks. He spits one word, his lips first puckered then stretched, baring his teeth.

Phoebe.

Without stopping to wait for Adrien, he charges towards the door, the camera capturing his face as he leaves. It's a mask of rage, a shade of anger I've seen Kyan wear only once before: this morning, when he almost fought Randy. Adrien follows closely behind him, her usual cold expression now warped into something that can only be described as pure hatred.

And then the video ends, plunging the screen into blackness. Declan and I sit in the dark for a moment, neither of us moving.

"Did you know?" I ask softly. "How upset they were with Phoebe?"

He shakes his head.

I rewind ten seconds before the video ends, freezing it on the image of Kyan's face. My eyes clock the time stamp: 10:42 p.m.

Phoebe would have still been out there when Kyan and Adrien

fled the room. She would have been wandering in the vast backyard of the Outback, not realizing she only had a short time left to live.

And Kyan and Adrien went after her, furious.

I open my mouth, but the words are barely audible, a whisper on wind. "Declan, does this mean—"

But before I can finish the thought, I'm interrupted by a sound. The latch of a door.

"Shite," Declan whispers. "Randy must be back."

Declan holds his finger to his lips before taking one large step forward and pulling the string to the overhead light.

We're plunged into darkness, just as I hear footsteps trail closer to the door.

Declan and I back up against the wall, our arms rubbing against each other. After a moment, I feel his fingers slip into mine.

The footsteps continue closer until they veer towards the left, followed by a steady thud against the stairs. Not one set, but several.

I slowly exhale but keep my fingers entwined with Declan's. It's just the others coming in from outside.

I turn to Declan just as he does the same, our faces so close I can feel his breath warm against my cheek. As my eyes adjust to the dim light sneaking beneath the crack in the door, I can feel his gaze lock on mine. And suddenly it's ten years ago again, my world narrowed into nothing but him. His face moves slowly towards mine and I draw even closer. My eyes brush closed as I anticipate the feeling of his lips on mine, one that I never thought I would experience again. And then…

The noise erupts through the closet. So abrupt that I skirt backwards, my spine connecting with the wall.

Declan's wide eyes confirm my suspicions.

"That was a scream."

24
CLAIRE

Now

"IT CAME FROM THE parking lot," Declan says, as we fly through the closet door, no longer caring if Randy sees us. I follow him in that direction. The first thing I notice when I reach it is our rental cars, the only two vehicles in the parking lot aside from Randy's old pickup truck. My sight lands upon the tires, limp and useless. It's clear, even from where I stand in the doorway, that they've been slashed. Randy's truck, however, remains in its usual substandard condition.

"Kyan!"

Declan's shout cuts through my thoughts, and I look at what he's running towards. When I see it, my breath lodges in my throat. Kyan is lying face down on the gravel, legs splayed, unmoving. A sheath of red flows outwards from his body. And then I notice the slash in the back of his shirt, the perfect size for a blade to puncture.

Footsteps erupt behind me, but I can't tear my eyes from Kyan's prone form on the ground.

"Oh my god, what happened?" Ellery yells.

When I finally turn around, I see the others have all joined. Josh, Adrien, and Ellery, with Randy slinking through the door behind them.

"Call an ambulance!" Declan yells from where he's knelt beside Kyan, his hands pressed against his wound. I fumble for my phone, but Adrien's already holding hers to her ear, her hands shaking.

Through the chaos, one thought emerges. A suspicion I hadn't dared to truly indulge before now.

Someone is picking us off one by one.

25

PHOEBE

Then

"THE HOSTEL IS PUTTING on an ABC party tonight." Claire chatters as we dig through our suitcases, yanking out swimsuits and towels. "Anything but Clothes."

It's the day after the total shitshow on the boat in Cairns. After Tomas alerted Adrien about my plan to swap her pills with mine, she lost it on me, yelling her head off about how I was trying to drug her. It turned into a whole thing. Nick got involved, told me if I ever pull shit like that again, he's putting me on the first flight home.

No one could meet my eyes after it all went down. Hari shot me disapproving looks from across the boat. Kyan and Adrien talked nonstop about how crazy I was loudly enough for everyone to hear for the rest of the day. Even Claire has been acting strange towards me since then. In fact, this current conversation may be the most she's said to me in twenty-four hours.

Once that god-awful boat ride was over and we were back on shore in Cairns, we all changed and piled back onto our bus—which had already begun to take on the distinct smell of stale liquor and unwashed bodies—and drove overnight to Airlie Beach, a quirky coastal town, where we caught an early morning ferry out to the Whitsundays.

"They're a group of islands off the coast, with some of the most vibrant marine life outside the Great Barrier Reef," Nick had explained as our bus had pulled into Airlie Beach. "We'll take a speedboat out one day, do some hiking another, snorkel, the works."

"And after this we go to the Outback, yes?"

A groan rose up through the seats. "Tomas, you and your fascination with the Outback. Good lord, man," Josh teased.

"Yes," Nick said gruffly. "The next stop is the Outback. So enjoy the water while you can."

Excitement seemed to flood through the bus as we pulled into the ferry port, crystal clear waters on all sides. I, on the other hand, was too distracted by how royally I'd managed to fuck everything up. Seriously, what was I thinking going after Adrien like that?

The thought played on repeat in my head as the ferry trundled through the turquoise water, coral-crusted islands popping up around us. But even so, I couldn't help but take in the beauty. White sand morphed seamlessly into lush green forests. I had thought the Great Barrier Reef was stunning, but this part of the country seemed to outshine even that.

But despite the scenery, I couldn't swallow away the anxiety that rose in my chest, seemed to block my trachea. I fucked up bad. And

I wasn't sure how I was going to come back from that. I couldn't ignore the glances I would catch Adrien shoot at me across the bus or the ferry, always followed by whispers to Kyan. Something was brewing, I could feel it.

"It's called Lindholmen Island," Nick had informed us as we pulled up to our destination, his voice even louder than usual to compete with the wind. "It's small, only a few miles in diameter, and the hostel we'll be staying at owns the entire island. No other businesses or residents. So it'll just be us and the other hostel guests."

I could feel the freedom the others were reveling in. But all I could think was that I was stuck alone with Adrien and any plans of revenge she may have, far away from everything and everyone else.

As we deboarded the ferry, white sand erupted in front of us from the turquoise waters, dotted here and there by the odd palm tree. Behind that lay a one-story building flanked by swimming pools, and to the left, a long narrow structure that housed the rooms. Beyond, a singular lush hill dominated the entire island, decorated with so many green trees it looked impenetrable. It was the closest thing to paradise I've ever seen.

"It's a hostel," Nick explained, breaking into my thoughts. "So don't be expecting a five-star resort." He shot a look at Kyan specifically, who was never shy about giving his feedback on the accommodations.

Now that we're in our rooms, it's clear Nick wasn't lying. Ours is furnished with rock-hard beds topped with starchy sheets and an air-conditioning unit that doesn't even attempt to masquerade its futility. I can practically hear Kyan complaining from here. At least

Claire and I are back to having our own shared room, although I'm guessing I'm happier about that than she is. Adrien and Ellery are next door, and the guys are split into two rooms back further from the shore, up near where the island morphs from beach to dense rainforest.

"Anything but Clothes, huh?" I respond to Claire. "Should be fun."

But I can't shake the feeling I'm wrong.

—

Despite the weird tension, I still laugh as Claire and I drape random objects over ourselves, trying to figure out a way to cover the parts of us that the law requires while still looking somewhat stylish. The hostel had distributed orange and blue plastic bags for those who haven't come equipped to fashion an outfit out of everyday items, and Claire has made something that looks like a one-piece bathing suit covered by a hula skirt, while I've gone more scandalous in a plastic two-piece, although my bottom half looks more like a blue plastic diaper.

We squeak over to Kyan and Josh's room a few doors down, and Josh opens the door, clad only in a speedo covered by an inflated pool float.

"Come in, come in."

I wrinkle my nose at the smell of college boy that strikes me from the doorway, but ignore it upon seeing the stash the guys have acquired. Three boxes of wine—which Hari informed us the locals call "goon"—a bottle of some pink sparkling thing, the label of which reads *Passion Pop*, and a fifth of vodka. I add the small bottle of rum I picked up at a liquor store back in Cairns to the collection.

I'm more relieved by the alcohol than I should be, I know that. But I can't think of a better way to shake off the weird feelings I've had since Cairns. Plus, if there's any chance of me acting like the carefree, confident Phoebe everyone expects tonight, I'll need it. And lots of it.

The others pile in as Josh pours us glasses of room temperature white wine. I take in their outfits, all of which display varying degrees of effort. Declan's pale white chest nearly glows beneath an orange life vest, Adrien's fashioned two pillowcases and a belt into a dress that I must begrudgingly admit looks kind of good, and the rest of us have all made do with the plastic bags distributed by the hostel.

"Seems like as good a time as any to introduce you to the official Aussie pastime," Hari announces to the rest of us. "Slap the bag."

One-handed, she pulls the wine bag from its box, lifts it over her head, and with the other hand pours a healthy dose of wine into her mouth before slapping it. "That's all there is to it. Who's next?"

Josh raises his hand eagerly and Hari walks over to him, tells him to lie back, and pours the wine into his throat, handing it over to him to slap before instructing him to do the same to Claire. And so it goes, the volume of our voices and laughter increasing with each round. But I can't tear my eyes away from Adrien and Kyan. She sneers when she catches me staring, and I consider trying to broker a peace deal. Anything to make the anxiety stop. But the game keeps going and the wine bag keeps circling.

When the bag is finally depleted and we're all a bit unsteady on our feet, we traipse across the island to the hostel's bar and restaurant. The others ate earlier, but the idea of sausages in stale bread for the eighth day in a row wasn't too appetizing, so I'd skipped dinner, an idea I regret as the wine sloshes in my empty stomach. Darkness has settled on the island, the enormous full moon illuminating the footpath as we walk. The night has taken on a gauzy quality, everything shimmering, lines blurring, and colors more vibrant than I know they should be. When we arrive, the party is already in full swing, tables pushed apart to form a dance floor, house music pumping from massive speakers, and flashing neon lights illuminating a few dozen or so other people already taking advantage of it.

I see a group of Danish backpackers we'd met on the beach earlier, two Indian girls on their gap year, and a bunch of other strangers. Nick Gould is notably absent, as he usually is whenever there's fun to be had.

We start with shots, all of us together, and as the liquor courses through my veins, it starts to feel like it did at the beginning. When relationships were just beginning to form and anything felt possible.

"To the Mob," Ellery yells as we hold our plastic neon shot glasses up towards each other. "To family!"

We all mimic her words, some of us more enthusiastically than others, as we throw them back.

"Let's dance!" Tomas grabs my hand and leads me onto the dance floor. I accept it for what it is—an olive branch. I know he feels bad for ratting me out to Adrien. So I force my resentment aside and follow him.

The beat pulses through my body, my limbs loose. Someone hands me another drink—vodka and pineapple juice, not my preference, but I still down it in a few sips. Claire and Declan are dancing together a few feet away, her hips grinding into his in a way that even makes me blush. *Get it, girl.* And then I find myself dancing in between Ellery and Tomas, and a wave of affection for them overcomes me. The two little siblings of the trip, as I've come to see them. Always together, heads close, whispering or laughing to some inside joke.

The tempo changes, the beat transitioning from the up-tempo rhythm I recognize as the Two Door Cinema Club song Kyan and Declan haven't stopped playing since the trip started, into something more mellow and less recognizable.

"I need to pee!" I announce before forcing my way through a mass of grinding bodies to the restroom. It's empty, aside from one person examining her face in the mirror, swiping lip gloss over her perfect cupid's bow lips.

Adrien.

The euphoria of the night seems to flood out of me at the sight of her, replaced by the anxiety from earlier. I need to end this before it gets out of hand. Before she does something to get even. Something I can't come back from.

This is your last chance to start over, I remind myself.

"Adrien," I say, a noticeable slur in my words, and she turns to me, one eyebrow raised. "We got off on the wrong foot. Let's call it a truce, okay?"

She stares at me for a moment, her eyes blank. She seems sober, much more than I am.

"I don't think so," she says after a minute.

The room tilts, solids becoming less concrete, the world itself fuzzier and less tangible.

"Seriously?" I manage.

"You tried to drug me, Phoebe. That's not something I'm quick to forget."

"It was a joke," I say, dragging out the last word. "Get over yourself."

"No, I don't think I will. I don't need any more friends. Especially someone like you." She trails her eyes up and down the length of my body, contorts her lips in noticeable disgust. "Now, if you'll move out of my way, I'd like to enjoy the rest of my night without dealing with your usual bullshit."

Anger washes over me, her words eradicating any thoughts of reconciliation. And I'm back in my childhood bedroom, *his* voice in my ear. *You're disgusting.*

He's in front of me, stepping forward, about to put his hands on me.

I'm the only one who will ever want you.

You should be grateful.

Poor Phoebe. No friends, too disgusting to ever love.

"Stop!" I reach my hands out and shove him, hard.

No, not him. Her. Adrien.

Her back strikes the water-stained mirror, which wobbles precariously against the wall.

"Oh." The sound from my mouth is like a balloon deflating. "Adrien, I didn't mean—"

She stares at me, dumbfounded. An expression I've never seen from her before. "You…you…"

"I'm sorry, it wasn't— I—"

Wordlessly, she pushes her way past me, her elbow striking me in the shoulder before she throws open the bathroom door.

I rest my hands on the sink and look into the mirror, frosted over with fingerprints. My reflection—wild red eyes, stark cheekbones—swims in front of me. Despite everything I've done the last few months before this trip—the new haircut, the weight loss, the upgraded wardrobe—to become the type of person I wanted to see in the mirror, all I see is the girl I was. The overweight, self-conscious outcast.

I can never escape her.

I don't know how long I stand there. Minutes, hours? Long enough for a revolving door of girls to push past me, shove me aside to fix their makeup, stare at me as if I'm crazy.

I barely notice them. I'm stuck in my memories. Of everything I did.

Everything I ruined.

And suddenly, it's all too much. I need to get out of here. I need air. I push out of the bathroom and elbow my way back across the dance floor, through the claustrophobic heat. The music is now too loud, screeching in my ears. The flashing lights too disorienting.

Limbs brush against mine. The closeness of other people feels sinister, like nails clawing at me, threatening to rip me to shreds.

My breath comes more and more shallow, and my temperature skyrockets. I need to get out of here.

I push and shove until I finally make it through the doors, gagging down gulps of hot evening air as I fall outside.

"Phoebe, you alright?"

The voice is familiar and a wave of emotion floods over me. "Hari?"

She's standing next to a tall guy covered in tattoos, a cigarette dangling cooly from her fingers. "Phoebs, you're not looking so good. I think we should get you back to your room."

But suddenly, that's the last thing I want. To be alone with my thoughts.

You're disgusting.

"No. Where are they, the others?"

Hari takes a moment, tries to interpret my slurring. "I lost track of them. Why don't you let me walk you back?"

"I'm going to..." I don't bother finishing the sentiment. Instead, I stumble away, ignoring Hari's pleas and narrowly avoiding the edge of the hostel's pool.

The music from the bar slaps at my back as I continue towards what I think to be the beach. With every step, the party recedes, the dull thud of waves on sand replacing the rhythm of the speakers.

I stumble down a set of three wooden steps that transition the halfhearted landscaping of the hostel grounds into the beach, until my feet sink in the sand, grit already clinging to my toes. I walk until the water kisses them, my flesh massaged by the sea. And then an overwhelming exhaustion settles in my bones, so heavy and all-consuming that I drop to the ground, sand coating the plastic shrouding my body.

I close my eyes, and then I hear it.

My brother's voice, again. As usual. And this time I know he's right. I clamp my hands around my ears, but still it comes.

You thought you could fool them, make them love you. But it only took them a few weeks to see who you really are.

I put my hands over my ears, but his words still come, slippery and cruel.

You can't just start over.

I throw myself upwards, running in what I think is the direction of the rooms. I want to collapse, to throw myself onto my mattress, stab my headphones in my ears and turn up my music as loud as it will go. Anything to drown him out.

As I run, my feet sliding over the silky sand, the voice comes back.

Why would any of them ever want to be around you? Even Claire is too good for you now.

And I know he's right. I tried to convince them that I was this cool, take-no-shit woman. Someone who the guys wanted and the girls wanted to be like.

Little did they know.

The sob erupts out of me from somewhere deep and primal, stopping me in my tracks and bringing me to my knees. Dirt clings to my legs, and as I look around, I realize I have no idea where I am. I'm no longer on the beach, and judging by the silence, marked only by the soft call of a bird somewhere deep in the trees, I'm nowhere close to either the rooms or the party.

Panic floods through me, every thought and image coming in jagged pieces. I'm alone. And lost.

Until I hear it. The soft whisper of my name. *Phoebe.*

"You!" I yell, taking the person in. And I've never been happier to see someone in my life. I run straight towards them, wrapping my arms around them tightly. Because I know I'm safe.

"Come with me," they say. "I'll help you."

So I do. And it's not long before I realize I've made the worst mistake of my life.

26

CLAIRE

Now

THE NEXT HOUR IS chaos. Everything seems to happen too fast, too out of control to be real. The ambulance arrives first, a model that looks like it would be better suited for the 1980s. A skinny paramedic who barely looks old enough to have graduated high school loads the stretcher holding Kyan's unconscious body into the ambulance before closing the doors against Adrien and her demands to accompany him to the hospital.

"No one unrelated to the victim can ride with us. You will have to meet him there," the paramedic keeps repeating with all the empathy of a robocaller.

That word, *victim*, sticks in my throat, dusty and thick like the air hanging heavy around us. It's the same word they used to describe Phoebe. And Hari.

Which one of us is next?

The question plays in my head, but I refuse to ask it aloud.

I don't know how much time has passed when the police finally arrive, an ancient sedan gliding leisurely up to the Inn's parking lot in a cloud of dust.

Out of the driver's side steps a heavyset man who looks to be in his sixties. I recognize him instantly. It's the detective—or the closest thing to in Jagged Rock—who had run the "investigation" into Phoebe's disappearance. He's aged, just like everything in this town. Gray hairs stick out among the brown in his half-grown beard, which is riddled with holes. He's wearing dark sunglasses and carrying a solid twenty pounds around his waist that weren't present a decade ago, and he's clothed in a pair of threadbare jeans and a khaki shirt with a neckline already rimmed with sweat. I figured his name would come back to me immediately, but it's as though my brain has blacked it out.

"Detective Allen," Declan says coldly. I look over at him, his white T-shirt smeared with Kyan's blood, faint traces of it on his cheek. He looks like he's gone through battle. The others' faces are tear streaked, their eyes blank and heavy. Randy is nowhere to be seen, having scampered inside as soon as Adrien called the ambulance.

Allen, of course, I think as the detective approaches, trailed by another tall gawky officer wearing a variation on the same outfit.

"We met a long time ago," Declan explains. "We were part of the cohort of students Hamilton College sent back in 2015."

"Yeah, I'd heard yous'd come back," Allen drawls. "Figured it was a joke. What good reason could you possibly have to visit us again?"

I stand frozen before him, the memories from the morning

after Phoebe went missing gluing me to the spot. Allen arrived at the Inn around two in the afternoon, hours after I reported to Nick Gould that Phoebe hadn't been in her bed when I'd woken up.

"Sounds like a classic runaway to me," Allen said then, stroking his thin facial hair, pulling an absurdly long one around his dark-rimmed fingernail.

"It's not like her," I said. "She wouldn't just leave."

Allen leaned towards me at that point, close enough that I could smell the coffee on his breath, stale and acidic.

"Why are you so worried?" he asked. "You do something to her?"

That shut me up.

"What exactly happened here?" he asks now, his voice just as apathetic as it was all those years ago.

Josh steps forward. "Our friend, Kyan Quek, he was stabbed. We had—"

"That the oriental one?" Allen interrupts.

I'm disgusted—but not surprised—by the casual racism. I remember the harsh glances our group would conjure as we walked down the main street of Jagged Rock. The whispers, aimed just loudly enough for Ellery to hear, about the "unnatural" color of her mixed-race skin, or the "go back where you came from" comments muttered as we'd sit in the town's café.

"Uh, he's Singaporean," Josh says, clearly also taken aback.

"Right," Allen says.

"The four of us—Kyan, Ellery, Adrien, and me," Josh continues, "we'd been hanging out around back. Ellery, Adrien, and I headed inside, but Kyan stayed out, said he was going to take a call. A few minutes after we went in, we heard Kyan scream."

So no one was around, I think to myself. Or that's what they claim. But what was to stop any of them from sneaking back downstairs and stabbing Kyan?

"And where were the rest of yous?" Allen's deep-set eyes focus on me and Declan.

I stand there, trying to come up with a lie, but my mind freezes.

"We were both napping. Separately. It's been a pretty eventful few days." The lie slips from Declan's lips easily.

"Okay then," Allen says, clearly disinterested in anything we have to say. "Officer Cain"—he gestures to his silent, gangly sidekick—"and I will be looking into this. We'll be in touch."

"That's it?"

The question escapes my lips before I can stop it, the hostile undercurrent certainly not lost on Allen, judging by his disgusted expression.

"Yes, that it is for now, *ma'am*." His emphasis on the last word is accompanied with a spit, saliva hitting the dusty ground heavily.

"What about the tires on our rental cars? They're slashed."

The duo glances lazily over at the cars. Allen tries to mask his surprise with boredom.

"Guess someone didn't want yous to leave."

His sidekick gives a single wet laugh.

"Now if you'll excuse us, we'll be having a word with Mr. Campbell," Allen announces, heading towards the Inn, apparently referring to Randy.

"Oh," he says, stopping a few steps short of the doorway. "There is one more thing. This place is now an active crime scene." The irony of his statement in light of his complete negligence would be laughable in any other situation. "You'll need to find somewhere else to spend the night."

"But our cars," Ellery says, her arm looped tightly around Adrien's shoulders, as if she's keeping her upright. "We can't drive anywhere, and there aren't any other hotels in town."

Allen shrugs. "Guess yous'll have to figure something out."

He turns before anyone can respond, the door shutting out his sidekick's chuckle.

27

CLAIRE

Now

"LIKE I TOLD MISS Claire, we stopped operating this place as a hotel several years back. There just wasn't the demand for it. But we still have the rooms and furniture. They're livable, but definitely not five-star accommodations," Luke says in apology as he leads us into the lobby of the Royal.

As we stood in the Inn's parking lot, trying to figure out our next move, I remembered the business card in my pocket from the drinks I'd had with Nick earlier. I'd called the number listed below The Royal Hotel & Bar logo, and Luke picked up on the first ring. When I told him our predicament, he didn't hesitate to offer up the hotel for us to spend the night, even picked us up in his beat-up hatchback.

"I think you're forgetting that we just came from the Raven Inn," Josh says, with a smile that I find nearly unimaginable at this point.

"As long as you don't go assaulting any of us, I'm pretty confident you'll exceed our expectations."

Luke laughs, a shimmery sound incongruous with the events of the last hour. "Well, we only have three rooms, so you'll have to bunk up." He distributes a key to Ellery, who wraps her arm around Adrien, another to Josh to share with Declan, and one to me. "I would offer to help you with your bags, but it looks like you all travel pretty light." He gestures to our lack of luggage.

"We didn't plan on coming back here," I begin to explain, but I'm stopped by Adrien's steely voice.

"We *shouldn't* have come back. We should never have gone to Rollowong to see Nick. That was a stupid idea."

I'm surprised to see the cold rage burning in Adrien's eyes beneath her swollen lids. Before this afternoon, I've never seen this side of her. She's always been poised, collected, but now it's like something's snapped. She seems one push away from losing control. I don't plan to respond, not wanting to be the person that pushes her over the edge, but she keeps going.

"This is your fault," she spits, pointing at me. "You wanted to come find Nick, to dredge up everything that happened a decade ago. So we could help *Phoebe*, of all people." She says her name as if I suggested trying to help a terrorist. "She was the last person who deserved our help."

"That's not fair," I say as calmly as possible, but even I can hear the slight waver in my voice. "Phoebe was a good friend to us." I turn back to Luke, as if he'll understand.

Adrien coughs out a bitter laugh. "That's hilarious."

This ignites something in me. What would Adrien know? The only time she spent around Phoebe was when she was trying to draw Kyan's attention away from her. "She was a good friend if you treated her like she was an actual person. If you hadn't—"

"Shut. Up." Adrien growls. "You have no idea what you're talking about."

"Then tell me!" My voice arches.

"She ruined my life." Adrien's tone is calm now, measured, rendering my sudden outburst all the more hysterical. I flinch, realizing how I must look. "And she ruined Kyan's life."

"Oh come on," I say. "She tried to give you a laxative, not ruin your life."

Adrien shakes her head, her voice poisonous. "You were always so blind. So goddamn naïve. It was right under your nose."

I think of the rage I saw in her and Kyan in the video I'd watched of them earlier this afternoon. Phoebe had done something awful to them, beyond her ridiculous prank in Cairns and shoving Adrien in the bathroom in the Whitsundays. Was it awful enough to push Adrien over the edge?

"Where were you the morning we realized Phoebe was gone?"

"Where was I?" Adrien's forehead crinkles as if I'm asking something completely ridiculous, but I notice a flash in her eye. "At the Inn, I guess. I don't remember. It was ten years ago."

"You weren't. You weren't there that morning. Neither was Kyan. You didn't get there until the afternoon."

I remember that morning vividly. I didn't sleep once I got back to the Inn the night before. Shock and desperation flooded through my veins. And more than anything: shame.

I could still feel that knife in my hand, the anger boiling just under my skin. I could feel my fingers grasped around Phoebe's hair. I lay there, in our two-person room that was now too big for one, and I thought through how I'd ruined everything. How nothing would ever be the same again. I lay there until the sun poked through my window, illuminating the empty bed across from me, where Phoebe should have been.

I kept waiting for a knock on the door, for someone to shout accusations at me, for the police to swarm in and collect me.

They never came.

Eventually, I forced myself up, made my way downstairs, bracing for the pandemonium I was about to encounter.

But everything was normal. Everyone just assumed Phoebe was still asleep in our room.

The dichotomy was unbelievable. I had just done the worst thing I'd ever done in my life, and the rest of the world didn't even notice.

It wasn't until later, once I reported to Nick Gould that Phoebe hadn't come home the previous night, that anything seemed to change.

We started a search. Casual at first. Just me, Nick, Ellery, Declan, Hari, and Josh. More like a walkabout through the Inn's sprawling grounds. We didn't find anything of course.

It wasn't until we got back to the Inn that afternoon, after Nick called the Jagged Rock Police to report a missing person, that Kyan and Adrien returned to the Inn.

I remember spotting them from the window of the lobby, strolling hand in hand up the walkway, as if they had no concern whatsoever for Phoebe, and of course they didn't. But more than anything, I remember the smile on Adrien's face. It wasn't her typical smile. It carried a hint of something that I'm just now identifying. Victory.

She fumbles now. "We *were* there. You must be misremembering."

I'm about to retort, but Josh beats me to it.

"Actually, Claire is right. You *weren't* there that morning," he says slowly, as if it just dawned on him. "You both didn't get back until after we'd already gone out looking for Phoebe."

A flush appears along Adrien's refined cheekbones, and I can't tell whether it's from frustration or embarrassment at being caught in her lie.

"I mean, like I said, it was ten years ago. I don't know about the rest of you, but I don't keep a diary of exactly where I was on every day in every decade. We were probably out for a walk or out to breakfast or something. We certainly weren't killing Phoebe if that's what you're implying."

She grabs the key from Ellery. "Now if you'll excuse me, I'm going to go find a way that we can get to the hospital. At least one of us is interested in making sure Kyan survives." She doesn't stick around for a response, storming up the stairs that jut off the lobby.

"Well, that was something," Josh says, apparently trying to lighten the mood.

No one responds. Instead, Ellery jogs up the stairs after Adrien.

"Come on," Luke says, "I'll show you all where your rooms are." He steals a glance back at the bar. "Unless you'd prefer to grab a drink first. Feel free to help yourselves. God knows you could probably use it."

"I'm going to go upstairs and call the hospital. See if there's any way they'll give us an update on Kyan's condition," Josh says.

Declan and I exchange a look. This is perfect. It will give us a chance to talk through everything that's come to light in the last few hours.

"What did Phoebe do that ruined Adrien and Kyan's lives?" I muse, staring into the amber liquid Declan's poured in the glasses in front of us.

"I have no idea," he responds. "But whatever it was, I bet it happened the night she went missing, given how angry the two of them looked in that video."

"I think they may have killed her," I whisper, barely loud enough for myself to hear, let alone Declan. But it's as if he can tell what I'm thinking, just like he used to.

"No. There's no way. They couldn't have. Plus, Nick…"

"I'm not so sure anymore that Nick was responsible. He wasn't the person that trapped me in the mine."

Declan raises his eyebrows. I give him a brief summary of our earlier conversation.

"Wow," Declan says, once I've finished. "And you believed him?"

"I did, surprisingly," I say. "And I think you would have too. He was genuinely remorseful."

Declan gives a slight laugh. "Well, who would have thought."

"But you saw Kyan and Adrien on that video," I say turning back to my first point. "If they had found her that night in the state they were in, they may have been angry enough to hit her, to use something and smash it over her head."

"But maybe they didn't," Declan protests. "Find her, I mean. Maybe someone else got to her first."

Declan's gaze is fixed squarely on the glass in front of him. I take in the boyish freckles that still dot his face, the long chestnut curls that seem incapable of being tamed. I want to trust him completely, I do. I want to tell him everything, but something holds me back.

My mind flits back to our first time here in Jagged Rock. Up until then, I had been living on cloud nine. Declan and I had fallen easily into a relationship. We spent virtually every waking minute together, and all the others too, sleeping curled tightly in his arms on his hostel bed while Tomas was kind enough to bunk with Ellery.

It was everything I had ever wanted in a relationship, yet something I never even hoped for. Back home, guys didn't even seem to notice me. And why would they? I was a quiet, introverted college student who lived with her mother and never went out. But here, in Australia, I was someone different. I channeled the confidence Phoebe had in those first few weeks, until it felt almost vampiric, as if I was draining her of her charm and extroversion as she retreated inward.

I wasn't the best friend to her in those days. I know that.

Once Declan and I finally got together, our relationship pretty much consumed me. All the time, attention, and affection I once had for Phoebe I now directed at him. And then on top of it, she kept doing all that strange stuff to Adrien. First, that attempt at switching her pills, and then shoving Adrien in the bathroom in the Whitsundays in a drunken haze, the account of which Adrien repeated constantly to all of us.

I should have known then that there was something wrong, but instead of asking Phoebe about it, making sure she was okay, I distanced myself. I didn't want the others—especially Declan—to associate me with her erratic behavior. I didn't want to be blamed for her mistakes. It was selfish, and the thought of it now twists my stomach.

"You two doing okay?"

Luke's voice startles me from my memories.

"Grand," Declan says, raising his glass. "Care to join us?"

"I never turn down a drink," Luke says, pulling up a stool as Declan pours another glass of whiskey and hands it to him.

"So, how are you two holding up after everything that happened?"

I notice my glass trembles slightly as I raise it to my lips. "A little shaken, but as good as can be expected I guess."

"Who do you think did it?"

Luke's question hits me with full force. Who, indeed? If I'm right, and whoever killed Phoebe is picking the rest of us off one by one, then my hypothesis that Kyan and Adrien were behind her death wouldn't make sense. But who else could it be? And why?

Declan answers first. "No bloody idea."

Luke sighs, takes another sip. "Can I ask you something?" He pauses as we nod. "What did Adrien mean about your friend, the one who died? She said she was a horrible person. What did she do?"

Where to even begin?

Declan looks over at me, a question in his eyes. Are we really going to tell him?

But I think of everything Luke has done for us, welcoming us into his hotel, letting us stay for free.

He deserves to know.

I take a deep breath, force myself to say the words, to revisit that night.

"She thinks Phoebe killed our other friend. Tomas."

28

PHOEBE

Then

THE REST OF OUR time in the Whitsundays passes in a flurry of beach days, sunsets, and rowdy nights, all layered with the steady intoxication provided by countless goon boxes and bottles of whatever liquor the hostel bar has on hand. We take speedboats to private coves where we snorkel and sunbathe, hike the lush rainforest trails on our island.

It should be perfect. But it's far from. Adrien's told everyone who will listen about our little altercation. From the way she'd recounted it, you would have thought it was a brutal attack rather than a drunken shove. She even had the nerve to report it to Nick, which prompted yet another scolding in which Nick's head turned so red I thought it may be in danger of spontaneously combusting. Another threat that this time was *actually* my last warning.

And the others have pulled themselves even further away. Claire barely meets my eye anymore, choosing to spend every night in Declan's room, as if to minimize her exposure to me. I'm constantly the odd one out, the only one left sunbathing on the beach while the others party in the water, the one staying in when the others spend yet another night getting wasted.

There's only one person who wants anything to do with me. And it's only ever at night, in private. No one can know, they say. They don't want to be publicly associated with the outcast.

It's pathetic, degrading, all of the above. But they're the only person I have left. And apparently, the effects of loneliness are stronger than my remaining dignity.

I'm right back to being the girl I always was. The outsider, alone, unwanted.

The sliver into my old life that emerged in that bathroom when I shoved Adrien has opened into a crevasse. The regret, the shame, the disgust I've worked so hard at keeping buried during our time in Sydney and Cairns has now metastasized, destroying the easygoing, confident persona I've been creating this entire trip.

By the time we leave the island, I'm clinging to anything that will remind me of the Phoebe the others think I am.

None of us are eager to leave, especially given our checkout time at the ass crack of dawn to grab the ferry and then pile back into our stale, smelly bus for endless hours to head to the barren tundra of the Outback. None of us, that is, except for Tomas.

"Dude, what is it with you and the Outback?" Josh asks as our bus drives away from Airlie Beach, heading west.

"My father showed me *Mad Max* when I was a kid. It became

our favorite film. We would watch it once a year, at least." Tomas's smile falls. "He became sick a few years ago. He did not make it. But I promised him before he died that I would go there."

"Shit man, I'm sorry," Josh says.

Tomas smiles at him, and Ellery loops her arm around his shoulder.

"Alright, listen up," Nick announces hours later, after we've been driving for what feels like eternity. "Our next stop is Cullamonjoo National Park. We're officially in the Outback. We'll be spending the night there, camping. It's a cultural experience so I expect yous all to be respectful." He shoots us a stern look, taking the time to make brief eye contact with each of us—his eyes lingering on mine.

"I wish we could have just stayed in the Whitsundays for the rest of the trip," Kyan moans once Nick has taken his seat.

"It's beautiful in its own way; don't worry," Hari says, turning in her seat. "Plus, we're going to have a campout under the stars. You're going to love it, I promise."

The view from the bus window stays the same for hours. Red dirt, barren land, sporadic termite mounds. No one seems particularly interested in the stagnant scenery, except for Tomas, who sits glued to his window for the full length of the trip. Finally, the bus tumbles over a speed bump next to a sign that identifies it as the entrance to the national park. As we follow a road that leads us past a small building with a single man sitting outside it, I realize Hari was right; this place isn't like anything I've ever seen before. The compact red dirt gives way to featherweight cream-colored sand as dunes the size of small mountains erupt out of the ground and roll as far as the eye can see. The light breeze grabs on to it, spinning it in the air.

We're in the desert, but not the type I've seen in films and books. This is beautiful. Soft, sparkling.

Apparently I'm not the only one mesmerized. It takes Nick Gould several attempts to regain our attention.

"For God's sake, listen up, will ya? We're going to get off here and meet the tour guide, who'll lead us through the park."

When we exit the bus, I see a bare-chested man seated to the right of the building, blowing into a long tubelike instrument that sends an eerie sound echoing throughout the desert around us. A didgeridoo, I remember, plucking the word from somewhere in the recesses of my mind. He's dressed only in loose-fitting black pants and a red band that circles his forehead. The gray hair that sprouts from his dark chest matches the thick moustache above his lips, which twitches with each blow into the instrument.

We listen patiently to a solemn song that sinks into the hollowness of my gut and clap hesitantly when he finishes.

"Welcome to Cullamonjoo National Park," he says in an Australian accent that sounds different from the one we've been immersed in for the last few weeks. "I am Birrani, and it is my pleasure to welcome you to this beautiful place in the heart of the country belonging to the Wangkangurru and Yarluyandi people."

Nick had told us about this throughout our travels—the colonization of the country by white settlers that systemically destroyed much of the population of the Aboriginal peoples who had made this place their home—but seeing this man, his passion for his culture, makes it more real than ever.

Birrani speaks to us for several minutes about the land's history and his people's struggles, before he leads us around the side of the building, where a line of dune buggies sits waiting for us. Nick divides us up into groups of two—I'm paired with Claire as usual, who looks less than enthused not to be partnered with Declan—and gives us a long rundown of all the instructions and things we are not allowed—I repeat, *not allowed*—to do on the buggy.

"We're hours away from civilization out here," Nick warns. "If something goes wrong, we're on our own. No one's coming to help us."

And then we're off. I let Claire drive first, which may have been a mistake, as our trip towards the dunes is composed of short bursts of acceleration punctuated by sharp slams on the brakes. Eventually though, she seems to get into it, and soon, we're climbing the dunes, tires struggling to grip the loose sand beneath our seat. We get going so fast that the tires arc upwards as we graze the dune's summit, and for a moment we're weightless. The seat belt digs into my chest, but I barely notice it as I raise my hands above my head and unleash a wild, almost savage yell, one that releases the pent-up emotions that have threatened to flood out of me the last few days.

We connect back to the ground with a bone-jarring jolt, and I steal a glance over at Claire, expecting her to be shocked. But it's my turn to be surprised. There's a devilish glint in her eye and her smile is almost manic, something I've never seen in her expression before. Then she tilts her head back, joining me in another wild shout.

—

After an hour or so of playing in the dunes, and just as the sun begins to descend, Birrani leads our caravan of buggies away to flatter land. The view changes from sand as far as the eye can see back to the red dirt, groupings of bushes eventually morphing into larger trees, until we enter what looks to be a forest in the middle of the desert. But that isn't all, I realize. Further ahead, I spot lights sparkling against water.

The red dirt drops off suddenly, merging with the dark blue waters. A lake, I realize, in the middle of all this arid land.

"We'll camp here for the night," Birrani announces once we've pulled to a stop. "Miraka Lake. It is beautiful, yeah, but don't be fooled. It's dangerous. That water holds some of Australia's most deadly species. We should be fine to stay up here away from the shore, so long as we make sure our tents are zipped before sleep. But none of you best go anywhere near the water." Birrani shoots us a sharp glance, fortified by Nick's glare from where he stands behind him.

On Birrani's instructions, we grab the tents and other supplies from the backs of our buggies and try to set them up. Or Claire does at least. I wait until Birrani comes over to help us. Eventually, we're settled, sleeping bags laid out in our two-person tents, darkness polluting the sky. Birrani prepares a fire for us in the middle of our tent circle, and Nick pulls out sausages—of course—for us to grill.

An hour or so later, with all of us fed, Nick and Birrani head to their respective tents. Perfect timing for Kyan to pull out a bottle he's been holding on to since Airlie Beach. I feel my heart rate speed up at the sight of it. The effects of my ride with Claire have worn off, and I'm desperately in need of another source of adrenaline to act normal. Kyan passes it around the circle, the fire painting an odd glow against his face, and when it reaches me, I take a deep swig, the now familiar fire of the whiskey burning the lining of my throat.

There's a warmth hovering over us, light flickering from the fire. But even so, a familiar longing blooms in my chest. A feeling of wanting more, like my basic needs aren't satisfied.

I take another swig from the bottle before passing it to Declan. I close my eyes, feeling the liquor course through my chest, eradicating the gaping hole that's ballooned there.

"So," Ellery says at one point, "I suppose this whole camping experience doesn't come with public bathrooms?"

"I think you're looking at 'em, El," Josh says, gesturing around.

Ellery rolls her eyes. "That's what I was afraid of."

"I will go with you," Tomas says. "To keep watch."

The two of them head off, and a brief lull falls over the rest of us.

"Truth or dare?" Adrien proposes, a twinkle in her eye. "We haven't played in a while."

A faint chill blows up my arms, the desert temperature falling rapidly.

"So, how about it?' Adrien asks. "Claire, truth or dare?"

Claire's head darts up from where it's been resting on Declan's shoulder.

"Oh, uh, truth."

Of course, she always chooses truth.

"Fuck, marry, kill. Out of our group."

"What?" Claire asks, eyes wide.

Adrien laughs. "You need to choose one person you'd like to sleep with, one you'd like to marry, and one you'd like to kill."

Claire's face turns redder than I've ever seen it, which is saying something.

"Um okay. Well, marry Declan, I guess."

Declan winks at everyone else, and a few people—Hari and Ellery, specifically—laugh.

"Sleep with Josh." Claire ducks her head, and Josh lifts up his fist.

"Better watch your girl, Dec," he says jokingly, and I notice something—jealousy maybe?—flicker across Declan's face. But I'm too distracted to dwell on it, too busy wondering who Claire is going to choose to kill. Adrien, hopefully. Or maybe Tomas? It didn't seem like they ever really connected.

"And kill...Phoebe."

My name out of her mouth strikes me like a bullet.

A few hours ago I would have said it was a possibility...maybe. But after the time we just spent out in the dunes? We reconnected, or so I thought.

"Good choice," Adrien says proudly.

Claire refuses to meet my eye. Disappointment curdles in my throat, hardening into anger.

Smart girl, the voice says.

I try to contort my face into something resembling apathy, but based on Declan and Josh's embarrassed reaction, I can tell I've failed. The bottle reaches me again. Not a moment too soon.

They hate you.

The idea comes to me as soon as the whiskey hits my throat. A way to change everyone's minds. To remind them of who I am—or who they should think I am. A way to get back to the Phoebe I was at the beginning of this trip.

"I've got a dare," I say once I swallow.

"Isn't it Claire's turn?" Hari asks.

"I don't mind," Claire says sheepishly. "You can take this one, Phoebe. I don't have any ideas anyway."

I know this is her attempt to try to smooth things over, but I ignore her, scanning the group to determine who to pick. I would choose Adrien, but I can't run the risk that she would accept and upstage me. God, that's the last thing I need. No, I need to pick someone much less risk averse. Someone with nothing to prove.

At that precise moment, Ellery and Tomas return, giggling about something, before dropping cross-legged next to Claire. Perfect.

"I choose Tomas."

He raises his head towards me, his pupils big in the glow from the fire.

"I dare you to go skinny-dipping in the lake."

"Oh, come on Phoebe, that's not even funny," Adrien chides. "You heard Birrani."

"I'll go with you," I say.

"No one's going in the water," Josh proclaims.

"I will go," says Tomas.

I feel my jaw drop. No. That is not the plan. Tomas wasn't

supposed to accept. But what am I supposed to do now? I can't change my mind once I've thrown down the gauntlet.

"I don't think—" Ellery starts

"It will be fun," Tomas says, his voice higher than usual. "Like *Mad Max.*"

I pull up next to him, lower my voice so only he can hear. "Tomas, it was a joke; you don't need to—"

"I want to," he responds with a big smile.

And before I have a chance to protest, he's stripping off his pants, pulling his shirt over his head. I join, discarding my clothes near the fire, and stand there in my bra and underwear. I see Claire divert her eyes, but the others'—including Kyan's, I notice with relish—stay glued on my body.

And then we're off, my hand laced in Tomas's, our feet sinking in the red dirt, running until the lukewarm water skirts our toes. We rush in fast, droplets spraying everywhere, until the water reaches our waists, shoulders, necks.

The lake is deeper than I expected. After a few steps, my feet no longer touch the bottom, my toes only brushing silt. As the water rushes over my head, my hand still locked in Tomas's, I feel a sense of relief, of freedom. And a silence.

For once, I don't hear *his* voice, the insults he levels at me. Just quiet.

Until I feel something slimy brush my foot.

With a jolt, I surface, pulling Tomas with me. I release his hand as I start back towards the shore, running from whatever I felt below the water. But even so, a smile spreads across my face, the freedom from that moment lodging in my bones.

I collapse into the dirt, not minding the red mud clinging to my hands and knees, and someone—Claire?—throws me my clothes. It's only once I start pulling them on over my wet skin that I hear it.

"Where is he?" Ellery's voice is loud, panicked. "Where's Tomas?"

And then the sound comes, inhuman and piercing. A scream that shakes the world around us.

29

CLAIRE

Now

"IT WAS A SNAKEBITE," Declan says. "An eastern brown snake."

Luke inhales sharply. "That's one of the most venomous snakes in the world."

I close my eyes tightly against the memory. Tomas stumbling out of the water, pale faced and naked. Someone screaming, Ellery maybe? Blood dripping from his leg as we hurried to throw clothes on him.

Birrani and Nick emerged from their tents instantly. As soon as he learned what happened, Birrani administered the antivenom he carried with him, but it didn't matter. Eastern brown snake bites require multiple rounds, and Birrani didn't have enough.

"It is okay," Tomas said over and over as the world rushed around him, Birrani loading him into his dune buggy to drive back to the main office where he would radio for a helicopter to get him to the nearest hospital. "I feel fine."

It was the last thing he said to us as Birrani pulled away. But Tomas was wrong.

He didn't even make the trip back to the office. The snake venom paralyzed his heart, striking him dead in the middle of the Outback, the place he had longed to visit his entire life.

I feel a tear sneak down my cheek at the memory, and Luke places his hand on my shoulder.

"It sounds like he was a good friend," he says comfortingly.

"Phoebe wasn't the same after that," I say once I've regained my composure. "She knew she was to blame. Tomas never would have gone in that water if she hadn't dared him. And some of us—Adrien in particular—were pretty eager to remind her of that."

Once we've finished our drinks, Declan and I go upstairs, retreating to our respective rooms. It's certainly not the Raven Inn, that much is clear as soon as I enter mine. A faux fur rug lies flat on the beat-up hardwood floor, and dark maroon wallpaper interspersed with framed photos of various sex symbols decorate the walls. Pamela Anderson blows a kiss from above a desk, while Marilyn Monroe's skirt flies up over a sewage grate directly above the double bed. I understand Luke's reluctance to rent them out. The floor warps in places, the wallpaper peels, and a thin sheen of dust covers everything in sight.

I collapse onto the bed, which is significantly more comfortable than the one I slept in last night. Despite the darkness seeping in from the windows, not one part of me craves sleep. Instead, my mind whirs. Recounting the story of Tomas's death has brought me back to ten years ago. The resentment that filled the cracks in our group. The once happy family turned broken. The grief that festered into blame, all of it leveled at Phoebe.

Is that what led someone to kill her?

All of us have secrets; that much is true. I think of Adrien's claim that Phoebe ruined her life, of Josh's lies, of the secret whispers I overheard between Declan and someone else the other morning. *No one even suspected.* I recall the rage on Adrien's face in the video I watched of her and Kyan the night Phoebe went missing, and I replay our conversation from earlier. *She ruined my life.*

Why won't she just admit what happened? Why all this caginess? Can't anyone just be honest for once?

Anger curls around my skin like wisteria, threatening to strangle me. This is enough. We all need to come clean.

I throw myself off the bed and walk decisively back out to the hallway. I knock on the door to Ellery and Adrien's room loudly, and Ellery answers a moment later.

"Hey," she says, "I've just been on the phone with the mechanic. He'll be out here tomorrow morning at nine. Luke offered Adrien his car to drive to the hospital, but he said there's pretty much no way that thing is going to hold up for the hundred miles it takes to—"

"Where is she?" I interrupt. "Adrien."

Ellery looks startled. "She went downstairs to try to get better cell service."

I'm halfway down the stairs when the din of voices coming from the lobby stops me short.

"Thank you," Adrien's voice filters up to me. "For everything. Back then and now."

I cling to the banister, hanging onto Adrien's every word. I'm shocked by the voice that responds. The gruff Australian accent, softened for the occasion.

"Of course, honey."

Luke.

Adrien knew Luke back then, somehow. The taste of betrayal sits heavy on my tongue, coppery and metallic like blood.

I knew enough not to fully trust the others, but this hurts too much to process. Sweet, kind Luke, who tried to protect me earlier from Nick Gould. This patient stranger who I immediately developed a fondness for.

I want to run back upstairs, to throw myself onto the bed and rip the covers up and over me. But I'm not hiding anymore. It's time to confront the truth.

"What exactly did Luke do for you back then?"

My tone is cold, unrecognizable as I step from the stairs into the lobby. Adrien and Luke's eyes dart up at me, guilt plastered on their faces. Two children caught red-handed.

"Seems like now is a good time as any to come clean." My words turn into a snarl.

I expect Adrien to protest, to strike out once she realizes she's backed into a corner, so I'm surprised to see her shoulders drop slightly, the fight leaving her.

"Fine, it's about time anyway. Grab the others; I don't want to do this more than once."

30
PHOEBE

Then

THE PROGRAM SHOULD HAVE ended after Tomas's accident. Any self-respecting company would have called it quits then, refunded our money. But not Hamilton College. It's not enough that one of us died a horrible death while the rest of us watched. No, they had to make sure we pushed through. God forbid they lose a cent.

So on we trundled, our bus pulling away from Cullamonjoo National Park and on to our next destination. The scenery stayed the same outside our window for hours, the red of the dirt reminding me of the blood dripping from Tomas's leg. And any time I closed my eyes, trying to block out the wasteland around us, I saw his dark eyes, his kind smile, the freckle above his lip that winked whenever he talked.

Sweet, decent Tomas. My friend.

"This is your fault!" Adrien had shouted on the bank of the lake as Birrani drove off with Tomas in the buggy. "You were angry with him for telling me about your juvenile plan back in Cairns. And this was your revenge. To get him in that water, to get him killed!"

What could I say? She wasn't wrong. It was my fault.

And maybe, just maybe there was a part of me that was bitter towards him for ratting me out back on the yacht. Is that why I did it? Am I really as horrible as they say?

Yes, you are.

There was no stopping the voice now. It had become my internal soundtrack, constantly blaring in my ears. And I could no longer argue with it.

I wake up to light filtering through the window of my room, illuminating Claire's empty bed. We arrived at the Raven Inn late last night, a dump in the middle of nowhere that makes me long for the tents we used in the national park. No question, we had a lesser chance of catching bedbugs in those.

I wipe sleep from my eyes, the dreams from my fitful night still clinging to me. Unidentifiable screams mixed with the feeling of being underwater, the brush of something slimy against my skin. I shiver and look over at Claire's bed. Empty. She must have slept with Declan last night. Unsurprising, given that she's made no effort to say more than two words to me since Tomas's accident. I didn't think our relationship could get any chillier after her admission during the truth and dare game, but now it's downright frozen.

I pull the threadbare blanket up to my neck, freezing. Odd, since this doesn't seem like the place that would waste money by blasting the air-conditioning, even though the daytime temperatures are topping a hundred degrees. My eyes fall on the sole painting hanging on the wall opposite my bed, one I didn't notice when we checked in last night. A slick black raven with beady eyes stares out from inside the frame, and I can't fight the feeling that it's watching me, judging me along with everyone else. I hear a loud gurgle in my stomach and heave myself from the bed, making it to the bathroom just in time to get sick in the toilet.

I don't know how long I'm in there, but at some point, I hear Claire return.

"We're going to be late," she yells through the bathroom door, her voice colder than usual. "We're supposed to meet downstairs in two minutes to visit that mine."

"I'm not going to make it," I yell back. "Tell Nick I'm sick."

"Sure," she says, and I hear the latching of our door. I know what the others will think: that I'm too ashamed to show my face after what happened. But I know the truth.

Later that afternoon, when the others are supposed to be off riding camels—an Outback attraction, who the fuck would have thought?—I leave the Inn and walk towards town. The shopping options are severely limited, but eventually I find what I need. A small, locally owned pharmacy.

I don't make eye contact with the middle-aged female cashier as I fork over the box I found on one of the sparsely stocked shelves. Its cheerful pink lettering shouts up at both of us from the counter as she rings it in. *Results 6 days sooner!*

When I get back to the Inn, plastic bag in hand, I'm relieved to find the front desk empty of the creepy ass receptionist who checked us in last night. Randy, I heard Nick call him. As I took my key, his eyes cut through my clothing. I watched him do the same thing to Adrien, and when she shot him a look, he muttered something unintelligible under his breath. Like most men, he appears to have two approaches to women—disgust and pleasure—and he erratically oscillates between the two.

But as I head towards the stairs, a door next to the desk flies open, nearly striking me in the side.

"Jesus," I say, jumping back as Randy exits, a strange smirk on his face. In the flurry of activity, I drop the plastic bag in my hand, the box tumbling onto the carpet in full view of me and—

Randy reaches for the pregnancy test before I can, making no effort to hide his glee.

"Give me that," I say, grabbing for it.

His lips contort into a disturbing smirk. "Someone's been having fun."

I ignore him, my face on fire as I shove the test back into the bag.

"Who was it though? Those little boys didn't seem like they were much interested in ya. Maybe that curly-haired fucker. The Irish one. Or..." His eyes light up with disturbing excitement. "Maybe it was that big bulky leader of yours. I can see 'im givin' it to ya."

Anger pulses through me. "You're disgusting." I should stop there, I know, but all the emotions that have been coursing through me over the last few days—the grief, the anxiety, the never-ending guilt—turn explosive. I turn so that I'm facing Randy head-on. "You sit down here all day, every day with your dick in your hand and watch guests come in and out, living their lives. While you stay here, in this dump. You're nothing. No, you're less than nothing. A pile of worthless shit."

Randy's jaw slackens and he looks like he's been struck. I don't wait around for his response. Instead, I spin, taking the stairs two at a time. It's only once I'm back in my room that I realize why those words sounded so familiar, why they came so easy.

They were the same things my brother used to say to me.

And then a second thought strikes me.

Randy doesn't seem like someone who lets things lie. And he certainly isn't the kind of guy who lets a woman talk to him like that.

What will Randy do to get his revenge?

31

CLAIRE

Now

BY THE TIME I get back downstairs, Ellery, Declan, and Josh trailing behind me, Luke has turned the bar area from empty to cozy. Two tables have been shoved together, a jug of water and several bottles of wine placed alongside individual glasses for each of us, and candles flicker from the edges of the room, dousing everything in a pleasant light that contrasts the quickly darkening sky outside. But I barely notice any of it. Anxiety sits heavy in my chest at what Adrien's about to confess.

The six of us gather around the table, Kyan noticeably absent.

"What is all this?" Josh asks. "I feel like I'm at an intervention."

"Well," Adrien says, "I know that some of us"—she shoots a sharp glance in my direction—"have become a bit obsessed with knowing every little thing that happened during our first trip here. And there's something I never shared with you all."

Luke busies himself pouring glasses of wine and water for each of us, ignoring my stare.

"I knew I was in love with Kyan the moment I met him."

This is certainly not how I expected Adrien to begin her confession. I've rarely seen her express any emotion that wasn't fully calculated. The surprise must be evident on my face because she sighs, rolls her eyes.

"I know you all thought it was some fling, a silly vacation romance. And I know some of you"—she narrows her eyes at me—"feel like I 'stole' him from Phoebe. But he was the first guy I ever loved.

"Neither one of us made a move at first. You know Kyan, how big of a flirt he is. I couldn't be sure he felt the same way, and I refused to be the one who initiated things. But eventually, we both admitted how we really felt.

"We tried to keep it under wraps for a bit. It wasn't my finest moment, sneaking around with him while Phoebe thought they were basically in a relationship. I see that now. And, of course, she found out eventually—I mean, we weren't exactly subtle. At first, she basically just stared after Kyan everywhere he went like a lost puppy. But after a while, things...changed. It was like a switch flipped, and she became mean, vengeful, acting like I had stolen Kyan from her."

I breathe in deeply.

"It was little things at first. Stupid mean-girl things. And I know, I know." Adrien cuts another glare at me. "I wasn't exactly innocent myself. But the night she went missing, we found out just how far she was willing to go."

Adrien sips her wine as if fueling herself for the rest of the story.

"That night, Kyan and I had been…together." My mind skids to Randy's video, Adrien and Kyan lost in passion, and I try to blink it away. "Afterwards, he checked his phone. We had both been tagged in a Facebook video posted by some anonymous profile—one of those ones with no information and no friends. It was…" She coughs, as if to cover the emotions rising in her voice. "It was a video of me and Kyan. A private video. One we had no idea had been taken. I don't know how Phoebe managed it; she must have left her phone recording in my room at some point. We searched everywhere for it after, but it was nowhere to be found. The video was filmed the night before, so she must have found a way to sneak it out after that."

"A sex tape?" I ask.

Adrien shoots me a glare and nods. "And she tagged all our relatives as well—basically anyone with whom we were friends on Facebook who shared our last names. And it had been a while since she shared it. You know how sketchy service was at the Inn back then. We only tried to log on to Facebook a few times a day. That was probably why none of you saw it. But by the time Kyan found it, our entire families had seen. It was…humiliating."

I imagine the shame that must have flooded over Kyan and Adrien in that moment, their postcoital bliss devastated by the worst invasion of their privacy. I remember the fury that flashed across Kyan's face in Randy's video, and for the first time, I understand.

"Kyan wanted to find her. To confront her," Adrien continues. "I mean, I did too. We were so angry. He nearly pounded down the door to her room, but neither of you were there." Her steely gaze is once again on me. Heat flushes the apples of my cheeks, remembering where I must have been in that moment, but Adrien doesn't seem to notice. "So, we went outside looking for her. We knew it was a lost cause immediately—I mean, you know how open it is behind the Inn—but Kyan didn't want to give up."

She sighs again. "Finally, I stopped him. I took his face in my hands, and I told him that none of it mattered. We had each other. That was enough. We agreed to leave the Inn for the night. We couldn't stay there after what happened. So we came here."

She raises her hands gesturing around us.

"You came to the Royal Hotel?" I confirm.

Adrien nods. "The rooms were still open back then. We were just going to spend the night, have a bit of a getaway, but we noticed the bar was still open, so we decided to have a couple drinks.

"I guess we got a bit tipsy, and one thing led to another, and Kyan, well…he proposed."

My jaw drops.

Luke chimes in. "We popped champagne to celebrate. But it's been so long, I didn't recognize Adrien until she just reminded me."

"It was impulsive and ridiculous. I mean we were barely twenty; we didn't know anything. But even so, it was so special," Adrien says wistfully. "We spent the night together and then made a morning of it. Breakfast in bed, the whole bit. It was nearly noon by the time we decided to head back to the Inn, and we walked straight into a shitstorm. It didn't seem right to share our happy news when Phoebe had just gone missing."

"But why didn't you say anything about the sex tape?" I ask. "Why didn't you tell us?"

"We weren't super eager to share that information with anyone, as you can probably understand," Adrien says. "It was a blessing enough that you all hadn't seen it. Really the only time I'd ever been grateful for the horrible internet connection in this town."

She was embarrassed, I realize, surprised. It's an emotion I've never seen Adrien wear.

"So, what happened?" Declan asks it as kindly as he can. "Did you and Kyan get married without us knowing?"

I look pointedly at the huge diamond on her finger, the one Instagram informed me was given to her by her tall handsome husband back in South Africa who bears absolutely no resemblance to Kyan.

Adrien wraps both hands around her glass, staring into it as if something therein may provide her with a different answer.

"Even with everything that happened with Phoebe, things were magical between Kyan and me for a few days. We turned off our phones and tried to escape reality, to enjoy the last of the trip together. We felt pretty invincible, like nothing could touch us. When we left Australia, we agreed we would tell our families as soon as we got home and try to work out visas so that we could come back. We'd both fallen in love with Sydney and decided that was where we wanted to stay and get married. I was going to transfer to Hamilton to finish my degree, and Kyan was planning to begin working on a start-up there.

"But we were naïve. As soon as we got home, everything came

crashing down. Our families were furious, of course; not only had we embarrassed them with the leaked sex tape, but both of our parents had a clear plan of how our lives were meant to go. And marrying a foreigner after a whirlwind relationship when we were only twenty or so years old was not in the cards. Even so, Kyan said he was ready to leave his family and all the money that came with it, vowed that he would give up his inheritance for us to be together. But..."

She trails off, and when she resumes, her voice is thick with emotion. "But when my father found out about the engagement, there was no reasoning with him. He didn't understand—or care—that we were in love. He told me I had brought shame to the whole family." She sniffs.

"Why didn't you just leave? Do like Kyan did and give it all up? I mean, if you loved him so much and all," I ask, not trying to keep the bitterness out of my voice.

"You don't know my father," Adrien snaps. "He's not the type of person you say no to." She pulls up the sleeve of her shirt, and I inhale sharply at the mottled skin coating her forearm. "I ran away when I was little. He had grounded me, and I was stubborn and acted out. When he found me, he dragged me home and held my arm over a lit flame until I promised never to do it again."

I have nothing to say.

"That was for running away as a child," Adrien says. "Imagine what he was willing to do when he found out I was planning to elope."

The statement fades into silence. I know the others are thinking the same thing I am. Adrien was always the perfect one. Rich, beautiful, poised, never a hair out of place. We all just assumed the reality of her life back in South Africa matched her glittering veneer.

The thought strikes me again. *None of us really know each other.*

"My father gave me an order," Adrien continues. "To end the engagement and go back to the plan he'd made for my life. Graduating with my law degree, working at his firm, which I would one day take over, marrying a powerful man just like him. He didn't have to tell me what would happen if I didn't. So, I did what he wanted.

"Kyan and I lost touch, mostly, other than the group text and the occasional message on Instagram. It was too painful for us to stay connected, even though I thought about him constantly." My eyes dart to Declan, catch him looking at me, before I turn away. "Kyan did end up moving back to Sydney, and I lived the life my dad wanted me to live in South Africa.

"When I got here and saw Kyan, it all came rushing back. All those feelings." Her eyes gloss over with a sentimentality I didn't know she was capable of. "I made a huge mistake. I should have done more to get away from my father, to make our relationship work. And now, it might be too late..."

I watch as a tear drops from her cheek, landing on the table's wooden surface. Ellery wraps Adrien in a hug, and I feel the familiar pang of guilt. This time for wrongfully accusing Adrien, without having any idea what she and Kyan went through back then.

I open my mouth to apologize, but before I can, a sharp, screeching sound erupts next to me, causing everyone to jump in unison.

My phone, vibrating against the table, where I'd placed it when I first sat down.

Confusion blurs my mind as I wonder who could be calling me. It isn't until I see the familiar, overly long number on the screen that the confusion turns to panic.

It's Inspector Villanueva.

32

PHOEBE

Then

I STARE AT THEM for what feels like hours. Two lines that change everything. That cleave my life in two.

I think of how it happened. I do the math, count the days back to our time in the Whitsundays. And then I think about my options.

I'm still on the bathroom floor when I hear the door to the room open. Quickly, I shove the test in the trash under some used tissues so Claire won't stumble across it.

"Phoebe, you still sick?" she asks through the closed door.

Taking a deep breath, I open it to see Claire, a slight sunburn across her cheeks.

"I'm feeling a bit better," I say. It's partially true. My nausea—or morning sickness, I now realize—has gone, only to be replaced with a soul-crushing anxiety.

"That's good," she says. I'm about to ask how her day was, more out of politeness than curiosity, but she beats me to it. "We're planning on going out tonight. There's a place down the street that apparently does drag karaoke. In the middle of Jagged Rock, can you imagine?"

"You can't be serious."

If Claire can tell that I'm referring to the olive branch she's extending me, rather than the existence of a drag bar in the middle of the Outback, she doesn't show it.

"It's what Tomas would have wanted," she says.

And there it is. The blame that laces through her words, twisting in my gut. *This is your fault.*

I'm pretty sure Tomas would *not* have wanted to be lying in a morgue in the middle of Australia somewhere while his friends partied in his name, but I force myself to stay quiet.

"Please say you'll come," she pleads.

I stare at her for a moment. Days ago, she was volunteering me as tribute for her fuck, marry, kill game. Up until now she's barely looked at me, let alone spoken. Why the sudden about-face? I'm trying to articulate that in a way that doesn't sound completely bitchy, but she beats me to it.

"Something's going on with Declan."

And there it is.

"He's been so distant. And I can't seem to reach him. It's like he doesn't want me around."

I know she wants me to tell her she's wrong, that Declan is just as head over heels for her as he's always been. But I can't. I'm exhausted, too drained to protest.

"Fine. I'll come."

I immediately regret my outfit choice—jeans and a tank top—when we get down to the Inn's lobby. The others are all dolled up, Adrien in a sequined dress, the guys in button-up shirts. Even Ellery is wearing a nice red top in lieu of her usual ripped band T-shirt.

It's then that I remember. It's Christmas Eve.

We've seen a smattering of decorations—lights strung up through the boulevards of Cairns, a blow-up Santa outside our Whitsundays hostel—but it's been so difficult to reconcile the holiday with the ninety-plus-degree weather we've been experiencing.

Thankfully, our group agreed to forgo gifts, but I listen as they all regale the others with talk of their calls home, how much their family misses them. I didn't even bother calling my parents. I haven't received so much as an email from them since I started the program.

Music floods out of the front door of the Royal Hotel as we walk up, Mariah Carey's "All I Want for Christmas is You" reaching our ears before we even come into sight of the enormous pink building, which is wrapped in lights. When we get past the bouncer, wristbands biting into our skin, the others head straight for the bar.

I meander onto the dance floor, feet away from the stage where the drag queen is crooning into the microphone, a red and green boa around her neck complimenting her barely-there shorts. Someone grabs my shoulder, and I flinch, but it's only Claire, pulling me towards the bar.

"We're doing shots," she yells over the music. I want to yell back, to tell her I don't want to join, that I have a human growing inside me who probably wouldn't enjoy the taste of alcohol, but I don't. I let her lead me back to the group, take the shot glass she shoves in my hand, and stand in a circle with the others, ignoring the hatred sparking from Adrien's eyes, the disdain from Kyan's. Ellery is the only one who makes eye contact as we clink our glasses together, shooting me a small sad smile. When the others throw back their shots, I dump mine on the floor.

Soon enough, everyone's made it back to the dance floor, but I resist Claire's drunken pleas—evidently now that she doesn't have Declan, I'm back in her good graces. Instead, I hang back by the bar, watching from afar. The song changes from something upbeat to far more romantic.

"This one's for the lovers," the drag queen croons, and I flinch. God, now of all nights, I could use a drink.

Josh grabs Claire's hand, and she follows him out to the dance floor, shooting a look back at Declan, who avoids her eyes. I watch them for a moment, jealousy swirling in my gut. Claire's miserable, clearly. But from where I stand, she has everything.

"Not having fun?"

I turn to see Declan with a glass of amber liquid in his hands, elbows propped against the bar.

"Not really feeling it tonight," I say to him. "You either?"

He shrugs. I look out onto the dance floor, and my gaze falls on

Adrien, her head tipped back, Kyan's hands resting territorially on her hips, and before I can stop it, the burn behind my eyes becomes solid, tears welling.

Hormones, I think, trying to push the emotion away. But I know it's more than that.

"You alright?"

I try to hide the emotion on my face but it's useless. Declan's already noticed. His eyes are laced with concern, but I note how tightly he's holding his glass, his knuckles gleaming white.

"I think I just need some air," I say lamely.

"I'll join you," he says, finishing his drink in one gulp.

We walk far enough down the street so that the music doesn't weigh down our words. I take in deep gulps of the night air, nausea once again brewing in my stomach.

"I wanted to ask you before," Declan says, his eyes avoiding mine. "Have you been okay? Really, I mean. I can only imagine how hard it's been with everything that's...happened."

I start to prepare a shallow joke in response, something that'll make light of the situation, that'll bring us back to safer, more comfortable conversational ground. But to my utter shock, my throat constricts, the throwaway comment lodging itself in my windpipe. And I realize Declan is the only person who's asked me this since Tomas's accident. The only person who's cared.

The emotion that has been leaking out of me in drips and

drabs—mostly in private, thankfully—suddenly erupts. Through sobs, I try to explain how it was an accident, how I loved Tomas and would never want to hurt him, but how no one will ever believe me. Not even Claire.

Declan listens wordlessly to my tearful monologue. When I finish, my shoulders hunched and my breath coming in rapid puffs, he rubs my back thoughtfully, and I want to melt into him.

"I've made mistakes too," he says eventually, so softly I can barely hear him. I expect him to leave it at that, but he continues, his eyes glued on the street in front of us. "I grew up with a younger brother, Malachy. When I was about thirteen, Mal was only five. My mum asked me to watch him one weekend, but I'd already agreed to play in this community football match. I'd had it planned for ages, but Mum had to go out of town to visit her sister at the last minute and Da was doing God knows what.

"So, I told Mum I'd look after Mal, and I also told my mates I'd be at the match. Thought I'd rigged the system. I'd leave Mal on the sidelines, he'd entertain himself, and I'd get to play. And it all went well, at the beginning at least. But once the match was over, I couldn't find him. I looked everywhere. At first, I was angry. It was just like Mal to wander off, but as the hours passed, I got more and more nervous. Eventually, we had to call in the Gardaí."

I swallow hard, waiting for him to finish.

"They found him the next morning." Declan's face is drawn, his skin bleached of color. "He'd wandered onto a nearby farm at some point during the match. He must have been so excited, seeing all the machinery. He loved trucks and tractors and all those things…" His voice breaks, and he shakes his head.

"He found an old dried-up well on the property. He must have leaned over too far and…the fall broke his neck.

"If I had just done what my Ma had asked, he would still be alive. But I was fecking selfish. I couldn't bear to take a day off to do her a favor, to look after my little brother. My own family. It was all my fault that he died."

He balls his hands into fists, and I delicately rest my hand on his shoulder.

"It's why I decided to come here. Even after I moved away from Sligo, started university in Dublin, I couldn't get away from what I'd done. I needed to get out of Ireland, as far away as possible. I figured Australia was about as far as you could go to get away." He smiles, but it's one of sadness, and it doesn't reach his eyes.

I think of how similar we are, how we had nearly the same motivation for going on this trip. I look at him, really look for the first time. Ever since day one of the program, he was always Claire's, nothing more than a guy for her to lust after. But there are so many different layers to him, so many things for us to connect over that Claire could never appreciate.

"Does Claire know?" I ask after a moment.

He shakes his head slowly. "I don't think she'd look at me the same if she did. And it's been difficult to talk to her after what happened to Tomas. It feels like she was so quick to move on, whereas I can't stop thinking about him. She's never been close to death before so she doesn't know how to feel, and I can't be the one to help her through that."

I take a deep breath. I know what he means. I pause, considering. The words I've kept locked up for years strain to get out, the admission I've refused to share with anyone.

And then I decide. If Declan was brave enough to tell me his story, then I can at least return the favor.

"I had a…rough childhood," I start, slowly. "My brother was the golden child. Jimmy was straight out of a teen movie from the nineties. He was handsome, got good grades, was the quarterback of the school's football team. He could do no wrong. But that was in public. Behind closed doors he was someone else entirely. It was like he flipped a switch as soon as we were alone. Any time my parents left the house, he became someone else. A monster.

"He'd say horrible things to me. Tell me I was nothing, that I had no friends, that I didn't deserve love. I don't know where it came from, this apparent hatred he had for me. But what he said stuck." I remember his words lodging like a knife between my ribs, worming their way through my flesh, until they infiltrated my bloodstream, becoming a part of me. "I became incredibly shy; I removed myself from all the public situations I could. I was an outcast in school. All because of him."

I clock Declan's shocked face, and a small part of me takes pride in the fact that I was able to bury that version of myself deeply enough that no one would ever suspect. But I look away, not wanting to see his reaction to what's coming next.

"Apparently that wasn't enough for him. When I was about

thirteen, it started turning physical. Jimmy would sneak into my room at night, long after my parents were asleep. And he would do…things. And the entire time, he would whisper in my ear, 'You are nothing, you are a disgrace.'"

I hear Declan inhale sharply.

"There was no way I could stop him," I continue. "No way anyone would believe me. He was the perfect one, and I was the weird, nerdy little sister. They would have said I was desperate for attention. That it was a sick way for me to get back at him. I remember I asked my parents to put a lock on my bedroom door. I told them I'd been having nightmares. They laughed in my face.

"When I got to high school, it started happening more and more." I squeeze my eyes shut as if to force out the memories. The sounds of his footsteps in the hallway outside my bedroom door, the way my muscles would lock up when I would hear him turn the doorknob. "I knew I had to do something. That if I didn't find a way to end it, I wasn't going to survive.

"And then, one night, I went to a birthday party. It was for a girl in my grade who had a massive crush on Jimmy. She had no interest in me whatsoever. It was just a way for her to get closer to him, by befriending his social disgrace of a sister. I hadn't planned to go, but she must have mentioned something to him, and he brought it up to my parents, who were over the moon. Being invited to parties wasn't a regular occurrence for me, if you hadn't already guessed. They thought this was my chance to start being more 'normal.'

"So, they forced me to go, and it was terrible. A group of us huddled in this girl's basement. Everyone ignored me at first, until someone pulled out a bottle they'd stolen from their parents' liquor cabinet. Peach schnapps or something like that. Someone passed it to me, and I declined. And that's when the fun started. All the comments Jimmy used to make to me were suddenly coming from those girls. And they were just as relentless as he was.

"The party was supposed to be a sleepover, but I couldn't stand to be there a single minute more. Even the idea of going home, to risk a run-in with my brother during the night, was more appealing than staying and being their punching bag. So, I called my parents, asked them to pick me up. They were out, some fundraising gala or something, and Jimmy answered the phone. He agreed to get me.

"He picked me up with a big smile and a heartfelt apology to the girl and her parents." God, I can still remember her swooning as he appeared in her front doorway. "But as soon as we got in the car, it started. His hand on my leg, steadily working its way up my thigh as he said disgusting things."

Even now, I cringe as I hear his words in my head. *You are pathetic; even those girls think so.* The feel of his skin on mine.

"Before I knew what I was doing, I grabbed the wheel. He only had one hand on it, and between that and the shock, it turned easily. We swerved directly into this big old oak tree. He would have been fine if it was just the collision. In fact, after the shock wore off, he started screaming, grabbing at me. Blood was rushing from his head, but he would have made it if…"

My mouth grows dry, and I struggle to swallow.

"The tree came down." It was sick, I learned later, one that the owner planned to have cut down just a few days later. "It split from the force of the collision, and it crashed down on the car, directly onto the roof over the driver seat. He died instantly."

I leave the story hanging between us, not daring to speak, to move, to breathe.

Until I feel Declan's hand crawling into mine, his fingers wrapping around my knuckles.

"You did what you had to do to save yourself," he whispers.

I thought coming to Australia was the escape I needed, but that clearly didn't work. And now it's almost time to go home, back to that house in Atlanta where my parents pretend not to know me. The police never formally charged me with causing the crash, there wasn't any clear evidence to do so. But they also didn't believe that Jimmy swerved to avoid a deer in the road, like I'd told them. Neither did my parents.

And word got around, as it always did. Not only did I become even more of a social outcast—something I hadn't imagined was even possible—but I was now the girl who killed her brother. The star quarterback, the charming high school senior that everyone loved.

I had become the monster.

Declan's words ring in my head long after we go back inside the bar, and I still hear them replaying as our group stumbles back to the Inn hours later.

You did what you had to do to save yourself.

I did it once; I can do it again. And it's not just me who needs saving now. This little baby growing inside me does too.

And as I lie there, in my uncomfortable twin bed back at the Inn, the threads of a plan start to weave together.

A way to save us both.

33

CLAIRE

Now

I EXCUSE MYSELF AND walk outside to take Villanueva's call. A claustrophobic darkness hangs over Main Street, the only light from the blinking sign for the Royal Hotel. The smell of woodsmoke lingers in the air. I watch something move down the street, back towards the Inn—an animal maybe?—but from here it looks sinister, almost supernatural.

"Claire," Villanueva says as soon as I'm standing outside. "You lied to me."

I freeze.

"I know you're in Jagged Rock."

Detective Allen must have chosen this as the one time to do his job. He must have contacted Villanueva after what happened to Kyan, figured he'd get in the AFP's good graces and screw us over at the same time.

"You are not visiting friends as you told me. So would you mind sharing exactly what it is you are doing there?"

The words rush out as I try to hobble together an explanation. "We came to talk to…to someone. The leader of our program back then. Nick Gould. And then our flight was cancelled because of the wildfires, and we were stuck, and then Kyan was stabbed…"

I know I'm talking gibberish. She's silent for a moment, and it strikes me, this odd yearning for her approval, just like I once had with Phoebe. The more I think about it, there's quite a lot that the two women share. The dark hair, the clear eyes, the bold confidence.

Villanueva sighs, and when she speaks it's with a cold, professional tone. "I believe I was quite clear. We are in the midst of a murder investigation. Figuring out what happened to Ms. Barton is our responsibility, not yours."

I'm quiet, Villanueva's scolding sending waves of shame flooding through me.

"But that's not all I wanted to talk with you about." Villanueva clears her throat, and I perk up, hope lighting in my stomach.

"I had mentioned that we were running some additional tests," she says, and the flame of hope grows brighter. "One of those tests was on a knife that we had found within a kilometer of the scene."

Instantly, the flame goes out. The wind picks up around me, throwing specks of dirt into my face with a speed that renders them as sharp as shards of glass. I close my eyes tight, leaning into the darkness.

The knife. The piece of evidence I left behind.

Villanueva's voice suddenly sounds far away.

"It had been buried just beneath ground level. Our canine unit discovered it. It was rusted and old, so it needed to be handed carefully, but it was largely preserved by spending the last decade in the dirt. That's why the tests took so long. But the results came back today. And they were quite surprising."

I refuse to open my eyes, refuse to accept this news as true, to acknowledge that I put myself in this position.

"Claire, we found a partial fingerprint on the handle. From what we can tell, based on the fingerprints you submitted prior to the Adventure Abroad program, it belonged to you."

My world stops.

"And on the blade, we found blood. Blood that belonged to Phoebe Barton."

Immediately, I'm back there. On that night. The insides of my eyelids replaying the scenes like a film unfolding. The knife in my hand, the rage in my stomach. Holding out the blade towards Phoebe. Wanting nothing more than to make her pay for what she did, how she hurt me.

"As you should understand, that alone is probable cause for arrest. We're sending an officer down to Jagged Rock. I'm telling you this both as a courtesy and a caution. I have been notified that you are currently staying at the Royal Hotel. You are under strict orders not to leave your accommodations until the officer arrives tomorrow morning. At that point, he will arrest you and transport you back to Sydney, where you will be formally charged with Ms. Barton's murder."

My legs give out immediately, my knees grinding against the

harsh dirt scattered across the pavement, the denim of my jeans staining a dark red.

The same color as Phoebe's blood on the night I made the worst mistake of my life.

34

PHOEBE

Then

IT'S CHRISTMAS.

Our last night in Jagged Rock. Tomorrow, we'll drive to the closest airport and fly back to Sydney, where we'll spend two more nights before returning home.

It's time to implement the plan I came up with the other night after talking with Declan.

My reflection watches me from the dirty bathroom mirror, as unfamiliar as a stranger. Dark circles hang below my eyes, my cheeks concave. I've lost so much weight since I arrived here, since things began to crumble. My eyes, while always big, now look massive, staring back at me blankly.

I thought if I could convince the others I was the person I wanted to be—confident, brash Phoebe—I would somehow turn into her. But all I did was cause more problems, hurt more people. And now I'm back at square one.

The quiet, beaten-down outcast.

This is what you deserve, my brother's voice whispers in my ear.

I shake my head violently. I need to start over, for real, to make it stick this time. For the sake of the baby growing inside of me. And the only way to do that is to get away. From the others, from Jagged Rock.

"Oh," Claire says as she opens the bathroom door. "Sorry, I didn't realize you were in here. You were so...quiet."

She's tried a few times to get my advice on Declan, why he's withdrawn from her. She even slept in our room last night for the first time in weeks.

All I can tell her is that he's grieving Tomas. He'll come around. It doesn't satisfy her, but I'm not really her friend after all, am I? I'm only something of convenience, a person she turns to when she doesn't have anyone else.

And I don't want to be that person anymore.

"Are you going to the dinner tonight?" she asks.

I wish I could say no—that I could leave the others, and especially the person who put me in this situation, without so much as a goodbye—but it's part of the plan.

So here I am, sitting at a long table filled with people who won't catch my eye.

We're in the room off the Inn's lobby. The one equipped with a subpar kitchen and a wide expanse of space.

I snag a seat across from Declan, who shoots me a small smile. The others pretend not to notice when I sit down. A quiet buzz of conversation traverses the table, gliding directly past me. It's like I'm back in high school. The one no one dares to acknowledge, let alone talk to.

A few bottles of wine sit together in the middle of the table. Two are empty, having already made the rounds. And there's a static in the air, a looseness, as everyone leans into the intoxication.

Something rumbles in my stomach. Not from hunger, but something else. Anxiety. An ominous tension bubbles in my gut as the minutes tick by.

Out of nowhere, raised voices break through the wall from the lobby next to us, sending a hushed silence over the table. Without warning, Nick Gould's massive form shoves through the door as he emerges into the room red-faced and seething.

Despite myself, I flinch. He yanks the chair at the head of the table away, but before he can sit down, Randy comes rushing in after him.

"You can't do this," Randy says, his greasy hair standing on end, his eyes wild.

"Do. Not. Tell me what I can or cannot do." Nick's voice fills the entire room, and Randy flinches.

"But I was dependent on that money. Those bookings. I'd made plans."

"Enough," Nick booms.

And that is that. Randy looks as if there are a million more things he wants to say, but Nick is done, his body turned away from him, facing the rest of us.

Nick holds up his water glass, which looks miniature in his hand. "Merry Christmas," he snarls towards the rest of us as Randy slinks off back to the front desk.

None of us have any idea what's happened, what we've just witnessed. But on autopilot, we raise our glasses anyway—mine filled with water, like Nick's, everyone else's with wine—terrified of what his reaction will be if we don't follow suit.

Moments later, as if on cue, two people walk in, hands laden with food. Locals the program apparently hired to cook for us. They deposit the food on the table, not sausages for once, but plates stacked high with reddened beef, bowls of roasted vegetables, a side of fried potatoes.

I feel my stomach flip. I know I need to eat, but I don't think I can force any of this down. In contrast, the others at the table eagerly pass the plates and dig in, ravenous. Crowns of broccoli and burnt edges of meat tip over from the bowls with their tipsy handoffs.

"I'd like to make a toast." Nick's gruff voice once again cuts through the conversation, and we all halt. "I know this wasn't the experience some of yous had hoped for. And I know we're still upset about Tomas. What happened was a horrible accident, but I hope that—"

A loud, upbeat tune blasts through the room as Nick scrambles for his phone. "Goddammit," he says, although I can tell he's relieved to be spared the rest of his speech. "This is the school. I've got to take this."

As Nick hurries out into the backyard, an excited hum returns to the table.

"What do you think that was?" Ellery asks.

"I heard Tomas's mother is suing Hamilton. That the college is cancelling the Adventure Abroad program," Josh says.

All eyes shift to Hari, her fork raised halfway to her mouth.

"I can neither confirm nor deny."

Josh continues. "Based on that showdown we just witnessed, I'm guessing Randy wasn't too happy about the news."

"It's not right." The comment comes from two seats down on my side of the table. Adrien, her words sluggish. Clearly, she's hit the wine hard already. "Randy shouldn't be punished for what happened to Tomas. The only person at fault is her."

She extends her long manicured finger in my direction in front of Claire, and I resist the urge to grab it and snap it back.

"It was an accident, though," Ellery says. I would be grateful, but she says it halfheartedly, as if convincing herself. Adrien acts as if she doesn't hear her.

Keep it together, Phoebe, I say to myself. *Just let it slide*. But Adrien's finger doesn't move, and every second it remains pointed in my direction, my rage grows.

"Get your fucking finger out of my face." The words come out like a growl.

Adrien finally lowers her hand, but before I can feel any relief, her mouth is open again. "He would never have gone in that water if it wasn't for you. And all for what? Because he tattled on you? Because you were jealous of me and Kyan? Because—"

"Oh, honey, you flatter yourself. As if I could ever be jealous of you and *this.*" I let my eyes graze over Kyan.

The remark escapes my mouth before I can think better of it, and within seconds, chaos erupts. Kyan shouting, Ellery trying to calm everyone down.

Adrien, hand wrapped tightly around her glass of red wine, stands up so abruptly that her chair falls backward. The noise must alert Randy, who flies through the door of the room, curiosity clearly piqued.

"Whoa," he yells, which startles Adrien, who spins around quickly. Too quickly. The wine flies out of her hand and directly into Randy's chest, dousing his white shirt—one of those horrid pieces you get from souvenir shops that reads *FBI: Female Body Inspector*—in red. It looks like he's been shot.

And suddenly, everything falls silent.

"Get out!" Randy's yell alights the room, his face the same shade as Nick's mere minutes ago. "Ya fucking bitch, get out!" For a second, I think he's going to lunge towards Adrien.

"Don't you dare talk to her like that," Kyan says, his voice cold, inching towards Randy.

Randy instinctively takes a step away from Kyan, which I can tell makes him even angrier. "Get out. Get the fuck out of here. You privileged pieces of shite."

And then he's gone, leaving us standing there.

Adrien's eyes turn once again to mine, but before she can say anything more, I take Randy's advice and leave the room.

I run, past Nick who's absorbed in his phone call and oblivious to this latest drama, and I keep going, until the sounds coming from the Inn are only whispers.

When I finally stop, I look up, taking in the stars glittering in the night sky. I play Adrien's words back in my head.

He would never have gone in that water if it wasn't for you.

And suddenly, I picture Tomas's face. His round tan cheeks pursed in a smile, his dark eyes wide behind his glasses.

A beautiful, generous man. One whose life I ripped away from him.

And I start to cry. A tear or two at first, until it avalanches into a torrent of emotions, so strong that it drives me to my knees.

"Phoebe?"

There's a part of me that wants it to be Claire, giving me one last chance to make things right. To get our relationship back to where it once was. To give me a friend again.

But it's not.

"Are you okay?" Declan asks, his face illuminated by the stars. And then, when he sees my face, "Oh, Phoebe, no. You didn't deserve that."

"I *do* deserve it. All of this was my fault."

"Hey," he murmurs, pulling me into him so that my nose is buried in the wool of his sweater, a shield against the evening chill. I inhale deeply, the woodiness of his scent hitting me like aromatherapy.

And then I pull away, bringing my face up to meet his.

There's a part of me that knows this is wrong. So wrong. He's with Claire. Even if we're not close anymore, I can't do this to her.

But the thought flees as soon as his lips touch mine.

35

CLAIRE

Now

I DON'T KNOW HOW much time passes as I kneel on the sidewalk, like a victim preparing for execution.

"Hey, you've been gone a while; everything okay?" Declan asks, pushing open the front door to the Royal, but as soon as he takes in the sight of me, his casual tone turns serious. "What's happening?"

I try to speak, but dust clogs my throat. A manifestation of the guilt that's festered within me for the last decade.

"Come on, let's get you inside," Declan says as he helps me up to my feet. I steal a glance in his direction, but looking at him directly, at what could have been if everything was different, is too much.

Once inside, he starts to lead me back toward the bar, where the group remains sitting, their voices blurring into indecipherable conversation. But I stop him.

"No," I say as quietly as I can. "Upstairs." I'm not ready to confess to them what I did. Especially not when I've just spent the afternoon accusing some of them of lying.

Declan leads me up the stairs, but it all feels so unreal. I've dreaded this moment for years, always knowing that one day my lies would catch up with me. But now that it's happening, it feels just like it always has—a possibility, not the real thing.

Once in my room, Declan and I settle on the bed. I take several deep breaths, trying to calm myself, but each one stays trapped in my trachea.

"Claire, what is it? Let's just tell each other the truth. No more secrets."

I look at Declan, force myself to really look at him. I take in the glint of his hazel eyes, realizing this is likely the last time he will look at me with affection.

I still don't know if I can trust him, but I have no choice. I need help, and he's the one person who can provide it. But only if I confess.

I take a deep breath and begin.

"I saw you."

Declan looks at me, confusion etched in the fine lines of his face that have appeared and deepened in the last ten years.

"That night with Phoebe. The night she went missing."

"Claire." The confusion crystallizes into something stronger, more real. Fear. "It wasn't what you think."

"It was," I say, my voice oddly clear. I thought when I finally admitted to him what I'd witnessed, I would be more upset. Emotions frayed, the hysteria I felt that night returning to me multifold. But it feels as though my admission has cleared the dust that has been welling up inside me, whisking away the emotion with it.

"You had sex with Phoebe," I say, so as to leave no doubt, nothing unspoken. It's one of the scenes from that night that I can never unsee, never unknow. Phoebe straddling him on the ground in the vast backyard of the Inn. Her head thrown back in passion, his eyes closed tightly. Neither of them even trying to hide.

"I had come out to look for you. You ran out so quickly after Phoebe. I wanted to check on her too. To make sure she was okay after Adrien went after her at dinner like that. I looked for ages and then I heard..."

Phoebe's moans still ring in my ear from that night, cutting through the darkness.

"I'm sorry," Declan says, his face crumpling. "I'm so, so sorry. You'll never know how sorry I am for that. It was only that one time, and it was a mistake. My feelings for you scared me. I sabotaged what we had, just like I always do when people get too close. And then Phoebe and I connected and then she came on to me and... none of that matters. I regretted it even as it was happening, and I've regretted it every day since. I've regretted losing you."

The emotion that dried up in me earlier now comes rolling back. I want to believe him, but something stops me.

"But you never reached out. Afterward," I say through tears. "You let me leave Australia without ever talking about it, without even officially ending our relationship. And you've been living in New York all these years, and you never even called."

I considered reaching out myself, but I couldn't bring myself to do it. The fact was, I couldn't face the truth. Couldn't listen to him admit how he had chosen Phoebe over me. And another part of me was scared that I would give in and admit to him what I'd done that night. And I wasn't ready to do that.

Declan looks down, shame splayed across his face. "It was my penitence," he says quietly. "I knew you didn't deserve me after what I did. I didn't want you to think that you should take me back and settle for a man that would treat you like that." He inhales, and his breath vibrates with emotion. "A few years after the program, once I'd graduated and started working in Dublin, I received a job offer from my current paper in New York. You were the first person I thought of, the only one I wanted to share the news with. And I couldn't get out of my head that we would meet somewhere on the streets of New York, just like in one of those romantic comedies. And we could start over. I wouldn't have to break my rule against contacting you; it would just happen naturally. Like fate." He lets out a sad chuckle. "It was stupid."

"No," I say. "It wasn't. But I don't understand. Why would you do all that for me, put yourself through that?"

"Isn't it obvious? I love you, Claire. I've always loved you."

For a second, I feel like I did after Villanueva's phone call, blood pumping in my ears, an unidentifiable ringing underlying its steady beat.

I shake my head, but he grabs my hands. Before I can stop them, tears well up in my eyes, crashing down on the carpet one at a time.

He moves to pull me in, but I stop him.

"No," I say, pulling away. "You can't love me. You don't know what I'm capable of. What I've done."

"So tell me."

"You'll never look at me the same way," I say.

"Try me." His gaze is steady like his tone, and it bolsters me slightly.

I take a deep breath and remember. Behind the Inn. The stars glinting down at me, taunting. Rage pulsing in my stomach.

"I walked for a while that night, after I saw you. I was angry—so angry. And I was trying to calm myself down…" I squeeze my eyes shut as if that will block out the image that has tattooed my brain for a decade. "Eventually, I went back to my room. I wanted to confront Phoebe, but she wasn't there. Her backpack was missing, and I could tell she'd left. And that made me even angrier. Having the nerve to do what she did—to betray me like that." I watch as Declan's eyes dart away. "And then to just run away."

Even now, my hand is trembling.

"I don't think I've ever been that mad. I wanted her to look in my eyes and see what she'd done to me.

"So, I went after her. I figured she was out back behind the Inn somewhere. I knew she liked to wander out there to clear her mind. I passed the kitchen on my way out and…I don't even know why I did it. I was so damn angry, and my emotions were all over the place…" I trail off. You would think after ten years of reliving this night I would have a clearer story. But the words stick in the far back of my throat, refusing to escape.

"Claire," Declan prompts gently.

"I grabbed a knife from the kitchen—one of the big steak knives. And I went after her."

36

PHOEBE

Then

I KNOW, EVEN AS Declan and I recover, dirt entwined in my hair and both of us breathing heavily, that there's no going back. I have no choice now. It's time to set the plan in motion.

"Phoebe," Declan says gently as his breathing normalizes.

"Stop." I can't listen to his explanation, his clichéd excuses. Telling me it was a mistake, urging me not to say anything to Claire. I can't bear any of it.

So, I stand, yanking my pants up, avoiding his eyes. "There's nothing more to say, Dec." His name squeaks out of my mouth as I force myself to regain control. "Goodbye."

I don't bother to turn around once I start walking. I know what I'd see. Declan, sitting in the dirt, confusion on his face and hurt in his eyes.

Instead, I take off at a steady pace back to the Inn. There's one more thing to do.

Thankfully, Claire's left the door to our room unlocked. I hold my breath as I throw it open, overcome with relief when I see she's not there.

I grab my backpack, packing it full of essentials, including the box of hair dye I picked up from the town's convenience store earlier today, and stuff my phone in my pocket. It's too outdated to have any sort of tracking.

I'm out of the room in seconds, pausing only to glance at that hideous painting of a raven that hangs on the far wall. It looks even more ominous than usual.

"I can do this," I say out loud to myself.

My brother's voice claws at the edges of my brain, but I refuse to let it in. I refuse to listen to him anymore.

This is finally my chance. To start over for real. To leave Phoebe behind forever. To begin again as someone entirely different, with this baby growing inside of me. To build the life that this child deserves. The one my parents never gave me.

I rush out of the room, taking the stairs so quickly I nearly fall. But soon enough, I'm outside, the night air cool against my cheeks, my lungs finally expanding.

One day last week when Randy was out on a break, I fired up the old desktop in the Inn's lobby, using Google Maps to pull up directions. Fifteen miles, the directions said. Far on foot, but not impossible. People run that for sport. The map showed me a shortcut—rather than cutting through the town of Jagged Rock,

I could head west, out through the vast expanse of land that lies behind the Inn and into the neighboring town. Then, I'll just need to make it one more town over until I reach Rollowong.

I'll still be close to Jagged Rock, sure, but who would ever think to look for me there?

I take a deep breath, hitch the backpack up on my back and start walking. I've made it about half a mile, or at least that's what I estimate, when I hear the sound.

A yell that reverberates through the dark silence of the night.

"Phoebe!"

My name is garbled in her voice, strung with anger and betrayal. As it should be.

My spine goes ramrod straight and I consider running. But I know Claire would catch up with me in a matter of seconds.

So I turn.

"How dare you?" Her eyes are wild, hair sticking up from her head like flames. "How could you do this to me?"

I don't pretend not to know what she's talking about. It's too late for that.

"I'm sorry, Claire. You didn't deserve this. I—"

But the sentence withers in my throat as I see what's in her hand, starlight refracting off a piece of silver. A knife.

"Claire," I say again, this time more cautiously, as I take a step back. I've been this person before. I've been Claire. Hurt beyond what anyone should take, with no other choice than to hurt someone else, to make them feel the same.

It happens in a blink. Claire raises her hand as I cower, arms in front of my face, as if that will be any defense against the sharp blade of the knife.

And then I wait. One second, two.

When I dare to open my eyes, I could cry.

Claire stands there, her eyes glued not on me, but on the knife in her hand like it's the first time she's seeing it. She releases her fingers as if she's been burned, and I watch the knife tumble down silently, the dirt around it erupting as it connects with the earth.

"I don't know what the fuck I'm doing," Claire says, dropping to her knees.

And then it strikes me. How different she is from me. When backed into a corner, with no hope, I do one of two things. Lash out or run. But Claire is different. She confronts her problems head-on.

Within seconds, I've joined her on the ground. With the knife discarded several feet away, I wrap my arms around her protectively.

"You didn't deserve this, Claire. You didn't deserve any of this," I murmur as she sobs. After a few minutes, she lifts her head, her eyes glazed and cloudy.

And I decide in that moment to tell her.

About my brother, what he did to me. And how that impacted how I've acted this entire trip.

I don't tell her *everything* of course. I don't tell her how I got my revenge on him. And I leave out some of my more pathetic moments. What I did in secret during our time in the Whitsundays, the life growing inside me as a result. I can't bear her reaction to that on top of everything else. And I don't tell her how much she hurt me by pulling away after Cairns. How she was the best friend I ever had. Until she wasn't.

I don't need to lay that on her on top of everything else.

"After what happened at dinner tonight, I felt so alone," I say, emotion thick in my throat. "And Declan was just there, and he knew what I'd done, who I am…"

I stop as she pulls back in pain. "You trusted him more than me?"

"I was wrong," I admit. And I know that's the truth. I was hurt, so I chose to confide in the one person she was closer to than me. "It was never you. It was never your fault."

Claire is silent for a few moments.

"So where are you going now?" she finally asks.

I take another deep breath, thinking through the best way to explain this to her.

"I'm getting out," I say. "I'm going to try to start over again. As someone else."

"What?" Claire asks sharply. "What are you talking about?"

"I have hair dye and this fantastic Aussie accent," I say, impersonating the omnipresent dialect we've been hearing for the last few weeks. "I can basically be anyone."

Claire doesn't return my smile.

"But h-how?"

"I'm going to walk to a women's center a few towns over. One of those places where people with violent partners can go to escape. They don't ask questions."

I watch her eyes grow wide.

"I'll stay there a couple days. Until I can work things out, figure out where to go next. Until I can secure a new identity."

"But..." Claire fumbles as if trying to understand. "We only have a few more nights in Australia, and then you can go home, forget any of this ever happened."

"You don't understand," I say, more forcefully than I intend. "I don't have a home. I'm not sure I ever have. This is my only option."

She stares at me, disbelieving, and I know she's trying to think up further questions to deter me. I stop her before she can.

"It's the only way."

"But I can't just let you go," she says, emotion clouding her voice. "I can't let you walk however many miles out here in the dark. It's not safe."

"I'll be fine."

"At least take this," she says, shoving the knife in my direction. "I don't know why I took it. My anger went to my head. Use it to protect yourself."

"Actually," I say, thoughts thundering in my head as I look down at the knife. "There is something you can do with that... You're going to think this is crazy, but—"

Without warning, I wrap my hand around her fist, yanking her arm towards me so that the knife brushes against the skin of my forearm. A scream of pain buries in my flesh, and I watch in awe as teardrops of blood break through the new slit.

"What the— Phoebe, what the hell!" Claire yells. Her vision darts between her hand, still clasping the knife, and the blood seeping from my arm. I turn my arm over, allowing the blood to drop down onto the dirt.

"If the police do search for me," I say calmly, my adrenaline whisking away the pain, "they'll find evidence that I was hurt. They'll be looking for someone abducted or murdered. Not a girl using a false identity at the nearby women's center. But there's one more thing."

Claire barely seems to hear me, still fixated on the knife in her hand.

"Can you cut a lock of my hair?"

"No. No," she stammers.

"Claire, please. I'll never ask anything of you ever again."

That seems to do it, the reality of what's coming. The fact that—if everything goes to plan—she'll never see me again.

Without any words of agreement, she raises the knife as I bend towards her. Gently, so gently, I feel her fingers entwine themselves in my hair as she drags the knife across. There's something about the feeling that's nurturing, maternal even.

When she pulls away, a lock of my dark curls is laced around her index finger.

"Thank you," I say softly, taking the hair from her and tying it around a nearby dehydrated bush. "Now, if you search tomorrow and can lead them here, that should be everything I need to point them in the wrong direction. If you feel like it, you can wipe the knife for prints and bury it somewhere out here. No one will ever find it."

Claire nods, her face bleached white in the darkness, grief staining her eyes.

"But how will I know you made it safe?" she asks finally.

"I'll find a way to get a message to you. On Facebook or with a burner phone. You'll hear from me, I promise."

It's one I intend to keep.

I take her free hand in mine. "You were a great friend, Claire. The best."

She nods, and I can tell she's fighting tears. There's still so much to say between us. So many things that will forever remain unsaid.

"Goodbye, Phoebe," she finally manages.

"Goodbye," I whisper, already turning back into the darkness.

37

CLAIRE

Now

"I DID WHAT SHE asked. That next day, when we were looking for her, I led us to the spot we'd been the night before, but it was no use. There were heavy winds earlier that morning. They must have covered her blood with dirt and blown the lock of hair away."

I've sat here and explained all of it to Declan. I keep waiting for him to turn away in disgust, to run and never look back, to leave me in the mess I've created for myself. But he's stayed, listening intently to the entire story, even taking my hand when I described how Phoebe had grabbed my arm, dragged the knife blade against her skin.

"I remember how quiet you were that day," he says now. "I could tell there was something wrong, but I figured it was the shock of Phoebe going missing."

There was so much wrong, where would I have even begun?

"I waited for her to contact me after that," I continue. "When I didn't hear from her after a few days, I knew something wasn't right. Phoebe did a lot of screwed up things, but she would have made right on her promise. She would have found a way to contact me."

I think back to those days, the unknown sitting heavy around me, wrapping around my neck like fingers.

And there was no one I could talk to. No one who would understand what I had done. How I'd just let her go, shedding her identity. I'd been an accomplice in the murder of Phoebe Barton. In name at least.

"It was my fault," I say now. "If I had stopped her, if I had tried to talk sense into her, I could have made her turn around that night. We could have gone back to the Inn. She would still be alive. But I was so…stupid. She was basically a child. And I just let her go all alone into the middle of the Outback. I knew it wasn't safe and I let her go anyway. I—I killed her."

"You didn't," Declan says, shifting closer to me on the bed.

"You don't understand, Dec. She was pregnant. That's what Villanueva said."

Declan jerks back like he's been punched, and something unidentifiable flashes across his face before he manages to compose himself. "Who was the father?"

I shake my head. "I don't know, but I can't stop thinking that's it connected to her murder somehow. And how did I not know? I was rooming with her for God's sakes. Was I that completely oblivious?"

"You're not to blame," he says, taking my hand in his. "You were a child yourself. You did what you thought was best. And

Phoebe was strong-willed. When she made up her mind, there wasn't any stopping her. Her murder had nothing to do with you. Nothing."

Declan's so sure, but it doesn't assuage the guilt that has built up over the years, like a parasite eating me from the inside out.

"I also feel like I need to say this. So you don't have to ask. What happened between Phoebe and me was a one-time thing. It hadn't happened before. I wasn't the father of her child."

"I know," I say gently.

"So what happened with the knife?" he asks after a moment.

"I did what Phoebe suggested. I wiped the handle off on my T-shirt and dug a small hole on the way back to the Inn. I thought I was safe. Randy never reported it missing, and it wasn't like the Jagged Rock police ever searched for it.

"My mind was a mess back then though. I must not have done a great job of making sure the handle was completely clean of my fingerprints. And after all the years of wind and erosion, the knife must not have been too difficult for the AFP to find after Phoebe's remains were reported."

I take a deep breath, which rattles in my lungs, and tell him what they found.

"You can tell them the truth," Declan urges, ever the optimist. "You can explain."

"No, Dec," I say, my patience thinning. How does he not understand? "I had motive, a weapon, opportunity. Isn't that the trifecta for proving any murder case?"

"Wait." I can see the cogs whirring behind his eyes. "You had a weapon, but not *the* murder weapon. The police said themselves that Phoebe wasn't stabbed, that someone fractured her skull."

I nod, thinking of Villanueva's blunt delivery back in the AFP offices in Sydney.

"That weapon was never found," Declan continues.

"Maybe they think I used the handle of the knife?" I muse.

"And what, held on to the blade when you beat her?" I flinch at the image, but Declan continues. "Then it would certainly have cut your palm. And they didn't find any of your blood on it. No, it had to be something else."

"I mean it could have been anything. A rock or a bottle. Something heavy enough to break bone..."

"But there aren't really rocks out there."

Declan's right. There's dirt for as far as the eye can see behind the Inn, but it isn't very rocky. Sure, there are larger rocks out towards the mine, where the land has been dug up, but otherwise it's mostly just compact dirt and pebbles. Someone would have to really search for a rock big enough to kill someone. So whoever killed Phoebe likely brought the weapon outside with them.

"Whatever weapon they used had to be strong enough to endure repeated hits. Something like a bottle would have broken; we would have seen shards of glass out there when we searched." I cringe at Declan's analytical approach, but then I realize, this must be how he approaches his stories as a journalist.

We sit in silence for a few moments, thinking. Declan shifts on the bed.

"Ow."

I look at him curiously.

"Something just poked me in the leg," he says, reaching for something in his pocket. He pulls out his room key from the Inn. "Shite, I forgot to return it to Randy before we left."

I look at it. The wood carved roughly into the shape of a raven. It's almost obscenely heavy for a room key. I take the key from him, holding it in my hand.

"You don't think..." Declan says, his eyes glued on the object.

I wrap my fingers around it and imagine raising it over my head and plummeting it back down.

"I mean, this would definitely be heavy enough to crack bone," Declan says, taking it back. "It's a possibility."

My mind jumps back to yesterday afternoon.

"When we checked in, I noticed there was a key missing from the cubbies behind the front desk. And we were the only people staying there. It's a reach, but maybe..."

"Did you see what room the key was missing from?"

"Room eleven," I answer quickly, the image of that empty cubby and the number beneath it burning bright in my memory.

"Right. Is there any way for us to figure out who was staying in that room back then?"

"I can't think of..." But then I stop, remembering.

I rush to my tote bag, flinging out items until I find what I'm looking for: the notebook I stole from the Inn's front desk when I was searching for the computer connected to the hidden camera. I forgot about it amid everything that happened.

I throw it open on the bed. Declan hovers behind me, peering over my shoulders as I flip through the pages. The first few are filled with lines of numbers, which I surmise must be finance related. But as I continue to thumb through it, those fade away, leaving only blank pages or those decorated with scribbles and doodles of half-naked women.

"There's nothing here," I mutter, disappointment sinking low in my heart.

I wait for him to comfort me, to reassure me that things will be alright, even though there's no way they can be. But he's silent, and when I turn to face him, he's staring down at the notebook, having flipped back to a page I'd previously ignored, discarding it as nothing more than doodles.

"This is a list," he says finally.

My eyes follow where he's pointing, and I realize that in between the inexpertly crafted cartoons are numbers and names. And then I notice a set of numbers on the upper-right corner of the page: *17-11-2012*. A date, in the flipped day-month-year format that Australians use.

Declan is already flipping the pages, and it doesn't take long until he reaches the date we're looking for: *22-12-2015*. December 22, the day we checked in.

It's all there, a list of 1 through 20, which I assume must be the Inn's rooms, and a hyphen and name or two to go along with each number, depending on whether the room was a single or a double. A quick scan reveals all our names—the students plus Hari and Nick. I start with the most familiar number—*13*—and look at its accompanying names: *Phoebe Barton and Claire Whitlock*. I hold my breath as my eyes move up two lines to room 11, the one with the missing key.

I drag my eyes along the line, to the name of the person who was staying in that room.

Ellery Johnson.

We both stare at Randy's spindly handwriting, the silence growing stagnant between us. Morphing into something darker, more real.

Ellery stayed in that room. She had access to the missing key.

"That doesn't mean anything, though," I say, my voice shaky. "We still have nothing to suggest the key was the murder weapon. Ellery or anyone else who stayed in room 11 after her could have lost it."

Declan nods. "You're right. But there's something else too."

I feel the blood crash in my ears. "What?" I ask urgently.

"If Ellery *did* do it, if she killed Phoebe, then I think I know why."

38

CLAIRE

Now

BEFORE DECLAN CAN EXPLAIN further, a sharp knock sounds at the door.

His eyes shoot to me, and I force myself to breathe, to go to the door and open it like nothing's wrong.

"Hey. Luke made us all dinner. It's ready downstairs." Ellery seems relaxed, her voice almost inappropriately chipper for the occasion.

"Thanks," Declan says from behind me, saving me from my struggle to form words. "We'll be down in a minute. Need to change my clothes right quick."

But Ellery doesn't move. "Oh, don't bother; it's not fancy. Plus, Luke's already put the food out on the table. You don't want it to get cold."

Declan and I exchange a look. Whatever information he was about to share is going to have to wait.

"Luke, this is divine." Ellery pops a piece of penne in her mouth and rolls her eyes up into her head. I know she means it as a compliment, but now, with my suspicions at full force, it looks terrifying.

"It's delicious. So kind of you to do all of this for us," Josh says, spearing a floret of broccoli on his fork.

"It's the least I could do after everything you all have been through," Luke says.

I nod along silently. The pasta primavera Luke has made *is* delicious, but I can't bring myself to eat. Every time I try to swallow, the food seems to crumble into dust between my molars, one image seared behind my eyelids: Ellery standing over Phoebe, bringing her room key crashing down on Phoebe's skull.

I watch her now from across the table. Her lips are moving, saying something to Luke, apparently, but the noise doesn't reach my ears.

Ellery and Tomas were close, extremely so. Instantaneous best friends. So it would make sense if Ellery blamed Phoebe for his death and wanted to get revenge. But what doesn't click is that after Tomas's death, Ellery never seemed particularly angry with Phoebe. Unlike Adrien, I never once heard Ellery blame Phoebe for what happened. In fact, she even seemed to defend her during that last dinner.

So, what could have sparked in always patient, calm Ellery that would have caused her to lose control?

I can't help but remember the few times I'd catch Ellery shooting a glance at Phoebe across the bus or the dinner table at the Inn when she thought no one would notice. An expression was painted on her face, naked and vulnerable. I was never able to identify it back then.

Was it hatred?

"Claire?"

The sound of my name breaks through the cloud of jumbled thoughts, and when I look around, I find the entire table's attention on me. It's clear this isn't the first time I've been asked the question.

"I was asking if the food's okay," Luke says, wearing a generous smile. "You've barely touched your pasta."

I look down at my plate, where Luke has rested his eyes to find a mess of shredded pasta and vegetables.

"Of course, it's delicious," I force myself to say. I aim for a kind tone, but my voice comes out flat and faraway. "I'm just not feeling that well. It must be everything catching up with me." I know I've overused that excuse the last few days, but I push my chair away from the table before anyone can protest. "I think I'm actually going to lie down."

I move to clear my plate from the table amid a round of empathetic murmurs, but Luke reaches out a hand from where he sits several seats away, as if to stop me. "Leave it, honey. I'll handle the dishes. You just get some rest."

I give him a small smile and stand. As I walk past Declan, he reaches out behind the chair so that his hand brushes mine.

Walking up the staircase that leads to the rooms, I steal a glance back at the table. Adrien's shoulders are hunched over her plate, her eyes glassy and faraway, and Ellery, Luke, Josh, and Declan seem to have pushed their efforts into overdrive to keep the conversation going.

Just as I'm about to look away, Ellery looks up at me. Her face is blank, but her eyebrow is slightly raised. After the briefest of moments, she seems to catch herself, replacing her expression with her standard soft smile.

I don't return it.

When I get to the top of the stairs, I make a beeline for Ellery and Adrien's room.

I can't waste this opportunity with all of them downstairs. Hope blooms in my chest again, dangerous and deceptive. There's still a chance I can avoid what I once thought was my inevitable arrest tomorrow. I just need to find *something*. Some evidence I can show to Villanueva.

I twist the handle and push forward, breathing a sigh of relief when the door shifts beneath my hand. Like at the Inn, the doors are not self-locking—that level of technology hasn't yet made it to Jagged Rock—and Adrien and Ellery hadn't bothered to lock theirs.

The room is similar to mine, equally worn down, but a tad more subdued. The walls are covered in chipped navy paint, and a chandelier with several burnt-out lights hangs over the double bed.

I ignore the quilted YSL handbag strewn across the bed, the one Adrien has had delicately looped across her body since we arrived, and head for the canvas tote that sits on a threadbare velvet recliner in the corner of the room.

The bag bears a logo for the charity that Ellery works for, the letters *WCDD* printed in intertwining font, short for *What Children*

Don't Deserve. And I find myself questioning all of this. Ellery is a saint; she's devoted her life to helping children in war zones. Could she really be behind this?

But I shake my head. This isn't the time for doubts.

I rifle through the tote, disappointed to find its contents are nearly identical to those in my own day bag: a wallet, some ChapStick, a Kindle. I step back, resigned, and as I do, a splash of blue in the corner of the room catches my eye.

I recognize it instantly. The sweatshirt Ellery has been wearing off and on the last few days. I discard the tote bag and head there directly. When I lift it up, I know for certain that I've hit gold. It's much heavier than its thin fabric would suggest, and when I reach into the pocket, my hand brushes cold metal.

I pull out her iPhone, igniting the screen with a push of the side button and illuminating a lock-screen photo of Ellery with her arm wrapped around a woman. The woman's hand is outstretched, a small diamond glittering on her finger.

Her social media is devoted almost exclusively to her work; the only personal posts she shares are usually of her dog, an old husky named Oscar. This is the first photo I've seen of Ellery's fiancé.

I take in the woman's pixie cut, the dark curls, the wide eyes, and—

Aside from some very small distinctions—the roundness of her face, the mole sitting just above her lip, brown eyes instead of turquoise—this woman could be Phoebe's twin.

I try to think what this could mean. Why is Ellery engaged to someone who looks just like Phoebe?

A laugh filters through the floorboards. I don't have much time. They'll be finished with dinner soon, and Ellery will come looking for her phone.

I turn my attention back to the next obstacle. The passcode.

Birthday, I think. I know it's not likely, but it isn't like I have anything better. I rack my brain trying to remember Ellery's birthday, but it comes back to me more easily than I expected. After spending ten years reliving nearly every single day of that month in Australia, I can pretty much recite the calendar by heart. And Ellery's birthday was one of the first nights we went out in Sydney.

December 3.

I plug *1203* into her phone before remembering the Canadian date format and shifting it to *0312*.

Incorrect PIN entered

"Shit," I mutter under my breath, my palm clutching more tightly around the phone.

Ellery's passcode could be pretty much anything. There's so much I don't know about her. So many things that would signify an important series of numbers.

Then, an idea sparks in the back of my mind. Another date that could be important to Ellery. It's a long shot, but it's not like I have any better options.

1912.

December 19. The day Tomas died.

To my complete surprise, as soon as I type the date in, the phone clicks, the screen erupting into a series of different icons. My eyes widen at my luck, but I force myself to continue, promising to dissect the passcode's significance later.

I start with her gallery, scanning her recent photos. They're all images of Ellery and the same Phoebe-like woman from her lock screen, of the elderly-looking husky, of Ellery surrounded by families, shaking their hands.

I navigate to the photo album labeled as "Favorites." I expect it to be more of the same, but as I open it, my muscles freeze in shock. These are all grainy photos, clearly older than those in her recent gallery, but I recognize them instantly. Every photo in here is from our time in Australia. And most of them are photos of Ellery with Tomas or Phoebe.

Why would she keep all of these? Especially given the memories they hold. And why save them as her favorites?

Another sound erupts from downstairs. The creak of a chair sliding against the floor. I'm almost out of time.

Desperately, I shift gears, heading to Ellery's text messages. Nothing appears out of the ordinary at first—an ongoing message chain to someone named Grace, who I can only guess is her fiancé, one to Mom—and then my eyes alight on the fifth name in the list. A message chain with a contact marked by only one letter. P.

The sight of it burns my eyes. P? As in Phoebe?

I shrug the idea away. Phoebe's been dead for years. Ellery hasn't been talking with her. But still, hope alights like a fire in me, one that demolishes everything in its path.

I think of how I left Phoebe that night. The words she said to me as the tears dripped from my cheeks onto the earth, deepening the redness of the dirt. *I'm getting out.*

Maybe she did. Maybe Phoebe really did make a new life for herself. Maybe the remains the police found belonged to someone else. Someone no one even thought was missing.

And then I hear the sound I've been dreading. The soft fall of footsteps on the staircase.

I need to move, to get out of here before Ellery or Adrien come back, but I'm frozen, my eyes still locked on that one letter hovering above the text chain: *P.* My body so consumed with clinging to this string of hope that it can't engage in any other function. One thought revolves around my mind like a loop, the words repeating, over and over.

Phoebe could still be alive.

39

PHOEBE

Then

AS SOON AS CLAIRE turns back to the Inn, I trudge onwards, using an old compass I picked up at one of the side-of-the-road tourist shops we stopped at during our drive to Jagged Rock to make sure I'm heading in the right direction. Ten miles north, five miles west. I've pretty much engrained the Google Maps directions into my memory.

I think of what Claire said as I walk. *I can't just let you go.* But she did, and it really didn't take much convincing.

Suddenly, I feel more alone than I have in all the months I've been out here. Even when I thought I didn't have Claire, she was always there, on the periphery. And I had Declan. I even had Ellery. And now all of them are gone.

A crack in the ground sends my sneaker twisting, and a shriek of pain explodes from my ankle.

"Shit!" The word echoes through the night, and for the first time I realize just how silent it is in the darkness.

But as I listen, waiting for the pain in my ankle to subside, I realize I was wrong. It's not silent out here. Sounds begin to hit me from every direction. A rustle in the brush on my left, the scampering of light paws on the ground further ahead, a slight hiss from the right that has me lifting my feet just an inch higher as I walk.

You're imagining it, I try to tell myself. But it's too late.

I turn back in the direction I came, but I've walked so far that the Inn is no longer visible. I'm disoriented.

I force myself to take a breath, to look once again at where my compass is guiding me, to ignore the sounds of the Outback like I had minutes ago, even though they now seem to be screaming in my ears. I take a tentative step forward, testing out my ankle.

It holds, and I take another, but something else hits me. The surge of panic deteriorates into an almost all-consuming fatigue.

I haven't had a good night's sleep in days. And I've been so consumed with this plan that I've barely eaten. The only thing I had today was a bowl of cereal at breakfast.

As if on cue, my stomach growls, a low, dull roar. I clasp my arms over it, trying to prevent it from drawing the attention of whatever animals are out here.

God, how freaking stupid could I be? I've eaten, what, a total of four hundred calories today? And I never even thought to throw snacks in my backpack. There's no way my legs are going to carry me one mile, let alone fifteen, and I'm sure as hell not going to lie down and nap with God knows what insects and reptiles are out here.

This whole idea has been ridiculous.

The only person I've told about my plan is Claire. She'll understand if I change my mind. In fact, I almost laugh imagining the sheer relief on her face when I enter our room.

And suddenly I want nothing more than to be back there. To have a friend who can look past all the hurt I've caused.

I turn, before I can rethink it, heading back the way I came. As I walk, I allow my hands to caress my abdomen.

"We'll make this work, little one," I mumble softly. "Somehow we'll make it work."

I'll go back to the United States and be the mother to this baby that I never had. It'll be hard, that much is certain, but I'll have help. I'll have Claire. Maybe I can even move, join her in Illinois.

For the first time since I've arrived in Jagged Rock, the future once again feels bearable, if not—dare I say—bright.

Until I hear one word that shakes me to my core.

"Stop."

I recognize the voice immediately, and my spine stiffens.

And that one word, enough for a chill to race up my neck, is all it takes to snuff out any hope for the future.

40
CLAIRE

Now

THE FOOTSTEPS KEEP COMING. Any second now someone will be outside the door, pulling it open to find me here with Ellery's phone in my hands.

I shut my eyes tight, as if that will ward off the inevitable.

And I wait.

The seconds tick by and I crane my ears to hear, but the footsteps have stopped.

This is my chance. I need to get out. I scramble up, trying to be as quiet as possible and tiptoe rapidly to the door, Ellery's phone still clenched in my hand.

This is a risk, I know. Someone could still be standing in the hallway. If I leave now, they'll see me. But I have no choice.

I put my free hand on the door handle, ready to push. And then the door suddenly vibrates, accompanied by the short, rapid sound of a knock.

The shock of the sound propels me backward, and I manage to catch myself before stumbling over my feet.

"Claire?" Declan's voice, so soft it's nearly a whisper, filters through the door. "Are you in there?"

I breathe a deep sigh of relief and throw open the door.

"We need to go," Declan says, "They're about to come up."

I obey wordlessly, letting him lead me quickly down the hall, closing the door behind me just as I hear another set of footsteps on the stairs.

Once we're back in my room, I eagerly pull out Ellery's phone, navigating once again to that mysterious string of messages.

"What is that?" Declan asks.

"Ellery," I say offhand, barely aware of the words I'm stringing together as I open the message chain. "She was…"

I don't finish the thought. Because I'm finally reading the message chain between Ellery and "P." It's entirely one-sided. All outgoing messages, no responses. The first one to catch my eye is the most recent, from yesterday.

I can't believe we're here without you. It doesn't seem real.

I feel my forehead scrunch, my eyes narrow. I scroll upwards, skimming as I go.

We checked into the Inn today. So many memories.

I wish you were here.

The words blur by until my eyes land on one from a little over a week ago. A date that feels like another lifetime entirely. The day the police contacted us about finding Phoebe's remains.

> I am so sorry, Phoebe. I am filled with so much regret. So much guilt, every day. And nothing I do or say will ever make up for what I've done.

"Claire," Declan prompts.

But just as I open my mouth to tell him what I've found, a heavy knock lands on the door, louder and more severe than Declan's moments earlier.

We exchange a wide-eyed look. Whoever's on the other side of that door knows we're in here.

I shove the phone in my back pocket, pulling my T-shirt over my jeans to cover it, just as Declan opens the door. It's Ellery.

"Hi," he says.

"Hey...uh, you two," she says, clearly curious as to why this is the second time she's found us together in my room, but thankfully she skirts over that. "This is weird, but have you guys been in my room?"

"No," I say, joining Declan at the door, trying to form my face in an expression of innocence and confusion. "Why?"

She pauses, her eyes narrowed. "I can't find my phone, and my tote bag seems to be in a different place than where I'd left it."

Shit.

"You don't think," Declan says, his voice cautious, "that someone got in here while we were eating, do you?"

It's an impressive lie, but something about the ease with which the suggestion slides off his tongue unsettles me. Ellery seems to buy it. Her eyes, which were narrow with suspicion at my response, widen with a burst of fear.

"But who—" she stutters, "who would do that?"

"I'm sure it wasn't anyone," Declan says, resting his hand reassuringly on her shoulder. "It was a stupid idea. How would they have even gotten by us when we were downstairs? Your phone will turn up somewhere. And maybe Adrien moved your bag, or maybe you left it that way and just forgot. We *have* been under a lot of stress."

Ellery nods. "You're right. It's just, everything that happened today...you know." Her eyes dart away from us, and I notice a flash of panic in her expression.

I don't blame her. She must know how bad her strange texts to Phoebe look.

"I'll go check the room again. I'm sure my phone is in there somewhere. See you guys later," she says, leaving me and Declan alone, finally.

As soon as Ellery's footsteps trail down the hall, I rush to tell Declan what I found.

"She must have been texting Phoebe out of guilt," I whisper after I've brought him up to speed. "For killing her. This must be her way of apologizing to Phoebe. Phoebe's phone was never found, after all. Ellery probably thought no one would ever see the messages."

Declan sits down quietly on the bed, his brow furrowed. I sink down next to him, lost in thought.

"It must be because of Tomas," I muse. "Killing Phoebe must have been her way of getting revenge for his death."

I think of Ellery's passcode, of the array of photos of her and Tomas saved in her Favorites album. It makes sense. Tomas and Ellery were closer than any of us. Maybe even than me and Phoebe at the beginning of the trip.

"Claire," Declan says softly. "I don't think it's as simple as that."

In all the chaos of the last few minutes, I'd forgotten what he'd said earlier, before dinner. *If Ellery did do it, if she killed Phoebe, then I think I know why.*

"The day after Tomas died, I heard Phoebe and Ellery talking," Declan continues. "We were on the bus to Jagged Rock, and everyone else was sleeping. Phoebe and Ellery had taken the seats in the far back, and they were whispering. I was sitting in the row in front of them and had just woken up. I didn't mean to eavesdrop, but they sounded so serious, I couldn't help it."

"What did Ellery say?" I ask, my voice tight.

He sighed. "She said she killed Tomas."

If I hadn't been sitting down on the bed, I would have needed to grab something to stay upright.

"What?" I ask incredulously. "We were there; we—"

"I know, I know." He sighs again. "Remember that truth or dare game we used to play?"

I nod. It's why Tomas went into that lake in the first place. Nothing good came of that game.

"Well, one night in Cairns, the three of us were hanging out, and

Ellery hit Tomas with a dare. She'd been drinking and she was half kidding, but he took it seriously."

I pause, waiting for him to go on.

"She dared him to buy drugs off these seedy German backpackers who were staying in our hostel, and well, Tomas did."

"Really?" I ask. Aside from me, Ellery and Tomas were the two most innocent people on the trip. I can't picture either of them doing drugs.

"Yeah. I think it was MDMA. Apparently, their original plan was to buy some for everyone to take together, but the lads they bought it from didn't have enough. So Ellery and Tomas decided to do it themselves—"

"During the camping trip," I finish for him. I remember Tomas following Ellery away from the fire under the pretense of needing the restroom, Ellery's odd body movements when they returned, how I kept catching Tomas staring off into nothing. I figured it was just from the whiskey Kyan had been passing around, but I was wrong.

"Ellery and I talked about it after Tomas's...accident," Declan continues. "She said he would never have agreed to Phoebe's dare that night if he hadn't been tripping. She was convinced his death was her fault, not Phoebe's."

I think of the guilt I've carried all these years. My constant obsession over how blame should be allocated. The array of circumstances—of choices—that can ultimately lead to someone's death. Where do we draw the line at who's guilty?

I picture once again the expressions I would catch on Ellery's face when she'd look at Phoebe in Jagged Rock. Was it guilt? And then something else clicks into place, like a fire lighting a blaze. The whispers I overheard the other morning at Kyan's. *It was ten years ago, and no one even suspected back then.*

"I overheard you two whispering at Kyan's the other morning," I say bluntly. I want him to clear up why he's hidden this from me, yet another breach of trust.

"I didn't realize you heard that." Declan sighs, looking down at his hands. "I didn't feel like it was Ellery's fault, I mean it *was* an accident. But she was adamant I never tell anyone else about the drugs. And that morning at Kyan's, she wanted to make sure that I was going to keep my promise, that I wouldn't say anything to the police or the rest of us. Although, I suppose I just broke that."

"Maybe something happened," I say after a moment, struggling to fit all the pieces into a neat puzzle. "Maybe Ellery changed her mind, realized Phoebe was really to blame. Or maybe she confessed to Phoebe about the drugs and Phoebe threatened to tell the others," I say, spiraling. "Maybe Ellery killed her to make sure Phoebe kept her mouth shut."

"But, I mean, it's Ellery," Declan says. "Good Samaritan, dedicating her whole life to making the world a better place, Ellery. Do you really think she could have...?"

"Yes, I do." Despite the threadbare assumptions, I believe she is the one who killed Phoebe. I don't know whether the certainty comes from a need to save myself or a desire to make this all make sense. To finally have an answer. "We need to go back," I say in the same breath.

"Back where?" Declan looks at me with confusion, a second before clarity seeps into his eyes. "You can't mean the Inn, surely?"

"There were other videos from Randy's hidden cameras that we didn't get a chance to watch. We didn't even see any videos of Ellery's room. There could be something on them."

"But you heard Detective Allen, it's a crime scene."

Before I can stop myself, I wrap my palms around his forearms, pleading. "I need this, Dec. I either find a way to show that Ellery killed Phoebe, or the police are going to arrest me tomorrow as a murderer."

And suddenly, I realize how desperate I am. A few days ago, there was nothing in my life that felt worth living for. But things have changed so much since then. For the first time in ten years, I can see a future. A way to move forward, if not guilt-free, then at least capable of enjoying the life around me.

And just as I'm close to getting it, it's about to be torn away.

"The only way the police won't arrest me is if I prove that someone else murdered Phoebe," I urge. "And to do that, I need to go back to the Inn. Tonight."

41

CLAIRE

Now

"I'M COMING WITH YOU," Declan insists after a brief pause. "But how will we get inside? Randy must have closed it up after this morning."

"Maybe he hid a spare key somewhere. If not, then I'll break a window. I'm about to be arrested for murder; I think the police are going to be a bit too preoccupied to be concerned with a vandalism charge."

My answer reflects a confidence I don't quite feel.

It takes a while, Declan considering other infeasible options that don't involve breaking and entering, but eventually we come up with a rough plan. Get inside; watch the remaining videos, focusing on the ones that feature room 11, Ellery's room; get the evidence; get out.

We wait until the sounds from the other rooms have fizzled out and silence has covered the Royal Hotel like a blanket. When the clock finally ticks over to midnight, we tiptoe out of the room, down the stairs, and through the front door of the hotel, barely daring to exhale.

And then we're out in the night, the air immediately smelling like danger. I glance upwards, prepared for the glittering show the night sky usually puts on, but tonight the stars are hidden behind a rolling curtain. The faint smell of smoke from earlier seems stronger, and I remember the wildfire warnings. They must be getting closer. But the realization doesn't ignite fear. If anything, it's motivating. I pick up the pace as we head to the Inn. I need to get to those videos before it's too late.

At one point, Declan slips his hand into mine, my fingers coming alive at his touch. Neither of us acknowledge it. We just continue walking, fingers laced. Even in the face of everything, the lies, the truths, the history, this feels good. Right.

But any warm feelings fade as we approach the Inn.

I don't know what I was expecting, but it looks like an entirely different place than it was this morning. Police tape is looped around the parking area where Randy's crappy pick-up truck and our useless rental cars still sit, forgotten like some never-visited monuments. The front of the building looks even more run-down, more desolate than it does in the daytime.

I stop and take it in, the reality of what we're about to do finally hitting me. Declan squeezes my hand in his, and when I look over, his eyes are clear, reassuring. It's enough to propel me forward.

As we approach the door, I pull my hand from Declan's and begin searching around the building for either a spare key or something large enough to crash through one of the windows.

"Wait," he whispers, going instead to the door. He places his hand softly on the handle, and it turns easily under his palm, the door opening without resistance.

"Well, that was easier than expected," I say with a slight chuckle, and I wait to feel relief, but realization strikes me instead. Randy wouldn't simply leave the building unlocked. That would be too easy.

I hear a small noise from somewhere nearby. An unidentifiable sound filtering through the night. There's something off about all of this; I just can't tell what it is.

"Randy must not have locked up after the police left." Declan shrugs, and I nod as if I believe him, but I notice the white crease in his forehead that tells me he shares my hesitation. I remember from last time we were here that Randy has an apartment in town. It's where he spends his nights.

We tiptoe in, neither of us daring to turn on the lights, reaching our hands out straight ahead as our eyes adjust, feeling as we go to avoid colliding with anything. An eerie darkness drapes over the lobby.

After a few steps, my eyes begin to adjust. I take in the front desk, the small table and chairs, and I find myself aching for a time when our full group would sit together each morning for breakfast, before losing Tomas, and Phoebe, and then Hari, and now possibly Kyan. Before everything went so drastically wrong.

Finally, we reach the door to the closet where Randy keeps the computer. I pull it open, preparing to step forward. But I stop short.

The chairs we sat in earlier are folded up neatly against the wall, the stacks of boxes still in place.

But the computer is gone.

"No." My voice is loud, too loud.

"Maybe the police found it," Declan says, but it's clear he doesn't believe that. He seems like he's about to say something more, but before he can, a noise hits my eardrums. Loud and savage. A grunt.

My spine stiffens, every muscle in my body tensing. Someone's here.

The sound comes again, followed by another pause.

Declan and I freeze.

It's coming from out back, and I walk from the closet to the rear door, noticing a light through the window that wasn't there when we walked in.

I move towards it to peer out, but as I do, a figure fills the window.

"Claire!" Declan whispers urgently. But it's as if my muscles are frozen, my feet glued to the floor. I feel his fingers wrap around my wrist as he yanks me away from the door just as it flies open, inches from me.

We manage to make it a few steps away so that we're standing at the bottom of the staircase, our backs flattened against the wall, by the time the door ricochets right where I'd been standing seconds ago.

The figure that comes into the lobby is breathing hard, anger radiating off him. I force myself even further into the wall.

He's so close that his smell wafts into my nostrils. A musty, familiar scent.

Randy.

He doesn't turn on the lobby light, and I send up a silent prayer of gratitude. If he did, he would surely see us. Instead, he moves forward to the closet, and I realize, with a stab of regret, that we never shut its door. He grunts again, muttering something under his breath, and slams it shut.

I wait for him to turn, knowing that when he does, we will be entirely and utterly exposed. For the second time tonight, I feel Declan's hand snake silently into mine, and I squeeze back.

Randy stands in front of the closet door for a moment, his spindly limbs suddenly looking larger, more formidable.

I don't dare to move an inch, to even inhale.

And as if my prayer has been answered, he turns in the opposite direction, walking away from us. He stops for a second as he looks to the right, taking in the backyard, and there's something sad in his gesture.

And then he continues onwards, through the front door without pausing. Seconds later comes the telltale click of the lock in the door, but still, I don't dare to move. I don't know how long I wait there, long after I hear the engine of Randy's truck roar to life, his tires crunching on the dirt parking lot as he pulls out, until Declan nudges me.

His touch sparks me back to life.

I rush to the back door, throwing it open and racing outside, although I already know what I'm going to see.

A fire roars in the pit, flagrantly violating all the wildfire warnings. An unidentifiable metallic smell emanates from its source.

"The computer," I say flatly, watching the flames lick the dark sky. Even with the warmth from the fire, I'm cold. It's an unbearable, bone tickling cold that invades my skin from every which way. I begin to shiver, slightly at first, then uncontrollably.

Because I realize what this means.

There's nothing left to connect Ellery or anybody other than me to Phoebe's murder. Nothing to even show that Randy had been filming us.

The AFP are coming in a few hours to arrest me. With the proof they have, I'll no doubt be convicted, sentenced to rot in some Australian prison. Forced to spend the rest of my life in this country.

Just like Phoebe.

Suddenly, I feel movement behind me, and Declan is there. I fall into him, my legs giving out, tears pooling in my eyes.

"Hey, hey," he says, pulling me up to face him. "It's going to be okay."

But I can't bring myself to meet his eye.

He brushes back the hair from my forehead so delicately that it makes the tears come faster.

"I'm going to do everything I can to protect you from this. I'll stay with you in Australia for as long as it takes."

Slowly, I lift my chin to meet his gaze. Those hazel eyes that I used to know so well stare back at me. And the meaning of what he's saying slowly trickles through the shock of the last few minutes.

I'm not alone.

They're the words I've longed to hear all this time. Since I returned to Australia without Phoebe. Since I lost my mother. Since I forged a life based in solitude and isolation and guilt.

Before I can stop myself, I lean forward, pressing my lips against his. I know this isn't the time and it's certainly not the place, but I can't help myself.

His lips are tentative at first, fleeting, as though he wants to resist. But he must reach the same conclusion that I do. That another time may never come.

And then he's kissing me back, hard. He lifts me up, and I wrap my legs tightly around his waist.

Effortlessly, he carries me back to the Inn, where I shove the door open behind me, my lips never straying from his. He leads me up the stairs, and as if on autopilot, he guides me to the room he was staying in, using the key he still has to open the door, and we tumble inside.

He lays me down gently on his twin-size bed, his lips exploring every part of my skin, and it's only a moment before I lose myself to him entirely.

42

CLAIRE

Now

WHEN MY EYES OPEN, I'm met with that startling feeling of having no idea where I am or how I got here. Seconds later, it hits me.

I jerk upwards. We never intended to fall asleep. If Randy figures out we're here, he'll kill us. And then there's the fact that the police will be coming soon to arrest me for murder. I glance out the window. No light has begun to creep in, so it must not yet be dawn.

Despite everything, I slept soundly, shuffling only once when I heard Declan get up, I suppose to use the restroom. I know we should leave, but when I turn over and see Declan, hands tucked under his head, his breath gently moving in and out, I realize it's the calmest I've seen him this entire trip. Affection surges in my chest for this man I've been completely and totally in love with for the last decade. The one I pretended to be with whenever I was with

Josh. I'll let him sleep, just a few more minutes, while I get ready, I tell myself.

I gently stand from the side of the bed, planning to creep as silently as possible to the bathroom, in case Randy came back sometime in the night, but as I start tiptoeing in that direction, the pad of my foot steps on something, and it digs into my flesh. I stumble, sending the object skidding across the floor.

I swear under my breath, a pain throbbing in my foot. Looking down, I realize I stepped on Declan's jeans. There must have been something hard in his pocket. Curiosity gets the better of me, and I grab the pants in my hand as I enter the bathroom, closing the door softly behind me. Before turning on the faucet, I dip my hand in the denim pocket, feeling something cold. It's only when I turn on the overhead light that I know what I'm holding.

I stare in shock at the black phone in my hand. One of those old flip-phone models that we all purchased when we first moved to Australia because they were cheaper than buying a new SIM card.

But it's not the phone itself that makes my blood run cold. It's the small red jewel on its upper backside. I've only seen two phones like this in my life, and the one that belonged to me is somewhere at the bottom of discarded boxes in my apartment's storage unit. I think back to that first day in Sydney ten years ago. Phoebe and I walking through the empty Hamilton student center, purchasing the phones. Phoebe affixing a blue jewel to mine, a red one to hers.

This'll spice them up a little.

Declan has Phoebe's phone. The one that's been hidden for ten years, the one that no one has been able to find since she went missing.

No more secrets.

His voice from last night runs through my brain unbidden, and I want to scream, to run back into the room, to tear at his skin.

But I make myself stand there, my eyes flicking everywhere besides the dusty mirror in front of me. I'm not able to look at my reflection right now. To see how gullible I've been this whole time.

I knew better than to trust him, after the shit he did back then. Pulling away just as he knew I was falling for him, then sleeping with my best friend out in the open, like he was begging me to catch them. God, how stupid could I be? And he's been feeding me these lines, trying to get me to trust him again, casting suspicion on the others.

Could Declan really have killed Phoebe?

My brain feels slow, like a television show where the actors' mouths can't quite match up with the dialogue. I have so many questions. Why would Declan keep the phone after all these years? And what did he have had to gain by killing Phoebe?

But that last question isn't very difficult to answer. The image comes back as it always does, with the force of a fist against my cheekbone. Phoebe's legs wrapped around his waist.

He promised me last night that it happened only once, that it was a mistake. But clearly I can't believe anything he's said.

I think of Villanueva's call the other day, about Phoebe's pregnancy. Maybe Declan was the father. Maybe they'd been fooling around behind my back for weeks. Maybe Phoebe told him she was pregnant…

I hold my breath as I push my finger against the power button, willing the pixelated intro image to awaken the screen. But it doesn't. The phone is dead.

Bile courses up my throat, and for a fleeting second, I'm certain I'm about to be sick. Eventually, I manage to swallow it, one thought overcoming the nausea.

I'm not safe.

I need to get out of here.

I inch open the bathroom door. When I hear Declan's soft breathing, I pad to the side of the bed, Phoebe's phone clutched tightly in my hand, and gather up my discarded clothes as quietly as I can. As I'm pulling on my jeans, the sound of movement behind me sends my spine ramrod straight.

"Claire?"

His sleepy voice hits my back, and my heart feels like it's trapped within a fist. Phoebe's phone is still in my hand; there's no hiding it. I turn slowly, bracing myself.

Declan's eyes are closed again, his breath once more coming in slow waves.

I don't allow myself to feel any relief. Instead, I rapidly gather up the rest of my stuff, not bothering to throw a shirt on over my bra or to pull on my shoes, stuffing them all under my arm instead, and I silently bolt towards the door. As soon as I'm through, pulling it shut as quietly as possible behind me, my body sinks against the hallway wall.

My heartbeat is erratic, my breath coming in panicked bursts. I need to take a moment to figure out what to do. I close my eyes tightly and try to make sense of what I just found, but everything seems jumbled, none of the pieces connecting, all my suspicions swarming.

Am I overreacting?

Maybe, but if Declan *did* do this and he knows I've found Phoebe's phone, what's stopping him from killing me?

I need to get as far away from Declan as I can.

But where do I go?

If I go back to the Royal, the police will be there to meet me. And I have no evidence to prove I didn't kill Phoebe. They'll simply think that I've been holding onto the phone this whole time. And it's not like the others will support me, especially after I've accused most of them of the same crime. And Declan, well, he'll undoubtedly throw me under the bus to save his own ass.

I think of the rental cars downstairs in the parking lot, their rubber tires slashed. The mechanic that Adrien talked to won't be here to fix them until later this morning, which will be too late.

I consider Phoebe's plan all those years ago. To walk fifteen or so miles to the next town. To use it as a chance to start over as someone new. But she had money, a backpack of belongings at least. I have nothing.

Still, it's my best bet.

I take off down the hallway, pulling my shirt over my head as I go, a fierce determination lighting in my stomach.

My head pokes through the fabric just as I'm about to turn onto the stairs, but something—someone—walking up the staircase stops me short.

The shock of it causes me to drop everything in my hands, and for a moment, my mind stops.

Randy, I think immediately. But when my eyes focus on the figure on the stairs, nothing makes sense.

"What are *you* doing here?"

43

CLAIRE

Now

"I FEEL LIKE I'VE heard that before on this trip," he says with a joking smile. "It's enough to give a guy a complex."

"Shh," I say fiercely. "Randy could be here and—"

"Relax, he wasn't at the front desk."

Josh looks at me pointedly, and I feel my cheeks flush.

"I'm assuming Declan's up there?"

I don't know how to answer, so I don't bother. Instead, I brush past him, pulling at his arm to follow me down the stairs. "Come on, let's talk outside."

The sky is foreshadowing its first sign of sunrise as Josh and I enter the parking lot. As soon as the Inn door closes behind us, I feel a rush of relief, but it's quickly replaced with curiosity.

"So, what *are* you doing here?" I ask again. "You should be asleep."

He rubs his hand over his face. "I was, earlier. I woke up and realized Dec never came back to the room. After what happened with Kyan, I got nervous. I went to your room. I've noticed how close you two have been getting." My cheeks flare again. "But no one answered. Everyone else was asleep, so I started looking around, couldn't find y'all anywhere. Thought maybe you came back here for something. It's dumb luck that I ran into you when I did."

"Oh wow, that was really nice of you," I say, feeling a pulse of affection towards him.

"Yeah," he says, looking down at his shoes sheepishly. "There was actually another reason too."

"Okay," I say skeptically.

"This, uh, this trip, it really got me thinking," he starts awkwardly, and now it's his turn to look embarrassed. "I know we agreed to keep things back at home pretty casual. But seeing you and Declan getting closer, it's made me feel a certain type of way."

"What kind of way?" I ask curiously.

"I think we have something here, Claire. I think we could really be something."

It's the last thing I expect him to say, and in my shock, I take a small step backwards. Josh quickly closes the gap.

"You deserve better than Declan, Claire." Now it's my turn to look embarrassed. I mentioned to Josh offhand one night how I'd caught Declan and Phoebe, but he didn't have much of a reaction then. He's never brought it up again, and I figured he had forgotten. But apparently not.

Josh gives me his signature lopsided smile, reaches his hand out for mine. After everything that's happened with Declan, feeling so used and manipulated, here's this kind, funny guy telling me he has feelings for me. I know I should feel something more for him—love or at least something close to it—but I can still only see him as a friend. I've used him, I realize. All these years, I've kept him close, not because I wanted to pursue a relationship, but to feel better about myself. To be that twenty-year-old again, the girl who had yet to ruin her life. It wasn't fair. And I don't deserve him now.

"I know it's a lot," Josh says, dropping my hand in the wake of my silence.

"No, no, it's not that. There's just…so much you don't know." I try to think of a way to explain everything I haven't told him, but it seems impossible. "I just—I need to get out of here."

Josh nods eagerly. "You want to go back to the hotel?"

"No." My response is sharp. I could tell him about the police coming, but there's too much to explain and not enough time. And to be honest, after pouring my soul out to Declan last night, I'm not sure I'm ready to repeat that again. "I need to get out of Jagged Rock. Just…somewhere else."

Josh's eyes go wide. I feel my chin drop, a terrible burning sensation forming behind my eyes.

"We'll go," he says finally, and my head darts up, clinging to that one word. *We.* "We'll get out of here. Drive to another town and figure out our next steps."

"I appreciate the thought, but we can't. We don't even have a car."

"Actually," he says, reaching into his back pocket. "We do."

I stare in awe at the keys in his hand. "Where did you get those?"

"Turns out Luke has been calling all his friends trying to see if anyone has a car we could borrow to visit Kyan in the hospital. One of them finally came through after the girls went to bed, so Luke handed these over. I drove it here actually, parked down the street."

I should tell him, I know I should. I should admit I don't share the feelings he has for me, and I need to tell him the rest of it: the knife, the impending arrest. It's not fair to let him try to save me when he doesn't realize how much I've ruined everything. What if the police pull us over? I would be evading arrest, and wouldn't that make Josh an accomplice?

But what choice do I have?

I think of what Phoebe would do. The answer is easy: whatever it takes to protect herself.

"Okay," I say, so quietly I'm not sure if he hears me at first.

But he smiles, grabs my hand, and leads me away from the Inn towards the car, a dust-covered four-door SUV parked at the edge of the street. I smile back, trying to ignore the lump in my throat that I can't swallow away.

As we walk, I turn back once more to the Inn, and that's when I see it, a figure filling one of the window frames on the second floor.

Declan stares down at me, his eyes wide.

And suddenly I'm angry. The betrayal, the hurt rises over me like a wave. I watch with clenched fingers as Declan mouths something to me through the window.

But I ignore him. Instead, I turn back around and follow Josh into the car.

44
CLAIRE

Now

THE SCENERY CHANGES QUICKLY, the rustic, dying main street of Jagged Rock giving way to dry land that stretches as far as the eye can see, intercepted by a single two-lane road. As we drive, the sun breaks above the horizon, dousing everything in a gentle pink. It should be reassuring, but the beauty does nothing to calm my racing heart.

"Wildfires rip across rural Queensland as firefighters struggle to douse the blaze. The monthslong drought continues to present arid conditions that are prime for spreading fires. Evacuation orders have begun to be issued for Everly and—"

The name Everly sounds familiar, but before I can remember why, Josh flicks off the radio. I'm sure he expects me to tell him the full story, but I still can't bring myself to relive it all. He seems to understand, leaving me alone with my thoughts, for which I'm grateful.

The entire time, Phoebe's phone sits in my pocket, pulling me downwards into the seat like a deadweight. I need to know what's on it. I need to know if there's any evidence that proves Declan murdered Phoebe. And why.

I need to know if I can use it to help prove my innocence.

Again, I consider telling Josh about it, but I resist. Maybe it's the lingering hangover of betrayal that I feel from Declan, but I'm not ready to fully trust anyone just yet.

When we've been driving for a solid thirty minutes, I notice a sign far off in the distance. As we inch closer, an ancient filling station comes into view, complete with two pumps, rusty nozzles dangling from the consoles. And behind them, a one-story square building, yellow paint chipping from its wooden sides and gabled roof. A white hand-painted sign labeled with *Ariah Springs Servo* and a red arrow sticks out of the ground a few hundred yards before the turnoff.

"Hey." I turn to Josh. "Do you mind if we stop here?"

He looks at me, and for a moment, I think he's going to say no, but at the last second he spins the wheel, swerving the car into the station.

"Might not be a bad idea to fill up. God only knows how far away the next gas station is."

My adrenaline spikes as the possibility of finding out what's on Phoebe's phone draws nearer. I know I should tell Josh my plan, but once again something stops me. It'll be easier if I can get in and get the phone charged for a few minutes without him knowing. That's all the time I'll need to see if there's any evidence on it to definitively prove that Declan killed Phoebe. And then I'll explain everything to Josh.

Josh opens his door and begins to walk around to the pump.

"I'm going to use the bathroom," I say. "I'll grab us some snacks too."

"Great, mind grabbing me a water?" His attention is already mostly absorbed by figuring out how to work the decades-old pump.

I nod and head inside.

A bell chimes as I shove the door open, and I'm immediately met with the now familiar smell of must, as if this place hasn't seen customers in years. It's a thought that doesn't seem so shocking as I take in the one other person in the shop: a gnarled old man with a tall forehead and beady eyes.

"G'day," he says to me, running a hand through his thinning, greasy hair, in a tone that suggests he wishes me anything but.

"Hi," I say, speaking quickly and pulling Phoebe's phone from my pocket. "This is a strange request, but do you happen to have a charger for this phone?"

He looks at me skeptically for a minute, pausing long enough for my frustration to rise, for a scream to bubble in my chest. But just as I'm about to let loose, he raises a spindly finger topped off with a long feminine fingernail that's stained just a touch of yellow, and extends it to the corner of the shop.

Following his gaze, I take in a dusty rack of electronics, a mix of headphones, old phones, and—thankfully—chargers, all of which are individually wrapped in Ziploc bags. It's clear they're second-hand, most likely stolen from previous customers and resold. I thank him, wrapping my fingers tightly around Phoebe's phone, and head to the rack, flipping through the products until I find a familiar-looking charger.

I hurry back to the checkout, handing the plastic-shrouded charger to the cashier. Up close, he's younger than I first expected. Likely only in his forties, but his mottled skin and the dark, painful bags hanging beneath his eyes indicate he's felt every year of his age.

"Surprised to see anyone in here," he says. "Figured everyone was leaving town."

"Why's that?" I ask, half paying attention, still lost in my thoughts.

"Evacuation order, course. Them wildfires. What, you been living under a rock or something?" A smile erupts on his lips, revealing a haphazard set of teeth, some crooked, some yellowing, some missing entirely. The sight sends a ripple of discomfort through me.

"I, uh, yeah something like that." I think of the others back in town. Do they know about the evacuation order? I consider calling them, but when I glance through the station window, I see Josh already removing the gas nozzle from the car.

"Thirty-five dollars," grunts the gnarled cashier, the disturbing smile still lingering on his face.

I know what this is. There's no way this charger should cost *five* Australian dollars, let alone seven times that amount. But I don't have the patience or the time to contest it.

"Do you have a place where I can plug it in?" I ask as I dig through my wallet for cash, thankful that I decided to exchange currency back at the Sydney airport when I first arrived.

The cashier once again points that spindly finger towards a rusty outlet squeezed between a cooler of soft drinks and a rack of chips in the opposite corner of the shop.

"But it'll be ten extra dollars to use it," he says, his eyes glowing now. "Electricity bills run high out here."

I don't bother protesting and throw a crumpled stack of bills on the counter, not waiting for him to count them before I grab the charger and head to the back of the store.

I work as quickly as I can, unfurling the charging cord, plugging it first into the phone and then into the wall.

And then I wait.

Nothing happens at first. The screen remains frozen in its dead black state. And then, after several interminable seconds, an image pops up. I feel my heart sputter until I recognize the symbol. An empty battery.

"Shit," I mutter.

I look out the window again at Josh, who's finished fueling and is now resting against the SUV, his sunglasses on, head alternating from the road to the shop window.

I only have a minute or two, at most.

And then the phone comes alive, the battery symbol replaced with Phoebe's home screen. I sigh in relief, remembering how the phones were so old and cheap that most of us didn't bother using passcodes back then.

I start with the photo album. I know I don't have time to read through Phoebe's texts, but I may have just enough to scan her photos for anything out of the ordinary.

I steal another glance out the window, just as Josh steps away from the car and towards the store.

I scan the screen, which is now filled with thumbnail images, most of which I recognize. A landscape shot of the Inn's backyard, the wild outback sprawling in front of the camera. A photo of the Mob all huddled together after our bungee-jumping adventure in Cairns, another of our group at a Sydney nightclub. And then one of Phoebe and me on our first night together. I swallow a burst of emotion.

But the most recent image is unfamiliar. It's a close-up of Phoebe, clearly taken at night, her face fuzzy against a coal black background. As I look closer, I realize it's a video, not a static photo as I first thought, and I click on it eagerly.

When the image fills the screen, I instantly see what hadn't been visible in the thumbnail. Phoebe's face is covered in scratches, a harsh bruise blooming on her cheekbone. And her eyes are two giant moons, fear imprinted on her features.

I check the time stamp: 11:14 p.m. on December 25, 2015. Over an hour after I left her.

And undoubtedly shortly before she died.

My breath catches. Despite everything I've done to get here, there's a part of me that still isn't ready to know exactly what happened to Phoebe. That isn't ready for the truth.

But it's now or never.

I press the play button.

Her words are quiet but rushed, as if she was hurrying to get them out before someone stopped her.

"I'm leaving you this video, Claire." The sound of my name hits me with a shock, momentarily freezing my rapid heartbeat. "Because

I want you to know what happened. To explain. But more than any of that, to warn you."

Despite the musty heat of the shop, a shiver runs through me.

Suddenly, her head jerks to look behind her, as if she's heard something. When she turns back to the camera, her eyes are more frantic, her words coming even faster than before.

"The people we're friends with, they're not who you think they are. One of them is a bad person. A really bad person. And I don't want you to get mixed up with him like I did."

I hear the bell chime above the door. Josh is coming in, but there's one second left in the video, and I can't bring myself to turn it off. Instead, I turn around so my back is facing the door, as if I'm focused on picking out a soft drink. Phoebe's voice continues to talk at me.

"Claire, you need to stay away from Josh McBride."

45
PHOEBE

Then

"STOP."

I spin around, taking in the source of the command that froze the blood in my veins.

"What are you doing?" I ask, irritated to hear the tremble in my voice.

"What does it look like? Looking for you."

He approaches me from the side—not the front as he would have done if he'd been heading directly from the Inn. How long has he been out here searching for me?

"Josh." His name is a whisper on my lips.

I didn't recognize him at first, not in the first few weeks of the program.

Not until that night in the Whitsundays.

The relief I felt when I saw him—after stumbling around Lindholmen Island drunk and on the verge of a panic attack—was unparalleled. I collapsed into his arms, allowed him to lead me blindly back through the dense trees to the row of rooms our group shared.

I never once questioned how he found me, what he'd been doing wandering in the wooded area behind our hostel like I had been.

I should have.

And then, we were back in my room. I started it, I'll admit that much. He tried to leave me in the doorway, to drop me off for the night, but the alcohol, the sadness, the regret, all of it mixed into a lethal combination, and in that moment, I wanted nothing more than a connection, for someone to want me back. I threw myself at him, my lips landing messily on his.

"You're drunk," he mumbled into my neck halfheartedly, but I ignored him, leading him to the bed instead.

He was gone when I woke up the next morning.

I figured that would be it, a one and done, but to my surprise—and not total disgust—it happened again the next night, and the next. There was something about the fact that he'd seen me at my lowest point and still accepted me that kept me coming back. We kept it secret. I didn't care about the others finding out. In fact, I would have loved to see the jealousy on Kyan's face when he learned I'd been sleeping with his "best mate," but Josh had some excuse about not wanting the others gossiping about his private business.

I didn't care, to tell the truth. Until the last night in the Whitsundays. I was drunk, as usual, and Adrien had made some comment that set me off earlier in the night. I'd been talking to one of the Swedish backpackers staying at our hostel, and when he walked away, I overheard her whisper something intentionally loud enough for me to hear about how I could never *seal the deal*.

"I'm going to tell her about us," I said, as Josh and I lay in his bed, Kyan sleeping over in Adrien's room as usual. "That will shut her up."

"No."

Josh's response was so firm that I shrank back. Keeping our relationship—or whatever it was—on the down-low was one thing, but why was Josh so intent on keeping it a secret from everyone?

"Okay, what is this? Are you embarrassed to be hooking up with me or what?"

"You don't even know who I am, do you?" he asked.

"What do you mean?"

He laughed, a hard sound that seemed to echo against the walls. "I was on your brother's football team when I was freshman. He was a senior. I was in your grade, and you still don't even recognize me?"

The upbeat, joking expression he always wore was replaced by a mask—cold eyes and a thin line for his lips—and I felt something crack inside me, as if my chest was cleaving in two.

I thought of those high school years, how I walked through a perpetual fog, barely noticing anyone or anything around me, always counting the minutes until my brother made his next move.

"You said you're from California," I said, my voice a barely audible squeak.

"No, I said I go to school in California. I grew up in Atlanta."

I felt a coldness enter my veins. How could I have been so blind? How could I have not recognized him?

"Your brother, Jimmy, was my idol," Josh continued. "I was an only child; my dad was barely in the picture. More concerned with fucking his secretary and any other woman who smiled at him than staying home and raising his own son. But Jimmy, he was like the older brother I never had. He'd stay late after practice, helping me with drills, giving me advice about girls and college and... I mean, I loved him."

I sat there, still shocked that this was happening. His words didn't seem to fit together right in my head.

"He was like my role model. And then, well, you know what happened to him."

I felt my hand back on the wheel of the car all those years ago. The headlights twisting as we swerved, the crash of glass as it fractured around us.

"I'd driven with Jimmy before, to parties and things. He was a good driver, knew how to handle himself even after a few beers. It didn't take long for people to start talking, for the rumors to start about his weird fat sister who was in the car with him that night. How she had something to do with it."

I flinched. *Weird. Fat.* The labels I'd spent years trying to drop.

I'd come all this way to leave that girl behind. To try to start over, to make the others believe I was someone different.

But she followed me.

"I barely recognized you at orientation, I'll give you that," he continued. "You did a good job trying to become someone different. The hair, the diet." His eyes skirted over my naked body appreciatively. "But the name gave it away. Barton. Jimmy's last name wasn't that common, and when I looked closely, I could see it. The family resemblance, in the chin."

I felt my hand rise instinctively to cover my mouth, to hide anything that could ever connect me to Jimmy.

"This whole trip, I've been trying to work up the nerve to ask you what really happened that night, but there's no real way to gently broach the question of whether someone killed their brother. But now I know. I knew it as soon as I mentioned his name. I could tell from your reaction—that deer-in-headlights look. You murdered him. Your own brother."

My intoxication from earlier dissipated, leaving me stone cold sober.

"You didn't know him—really know him." I caught myself. "He wasn't the person you thought he was. He was a monster, he—"

But Josh held up a hand, clearly unimpressed with my explanation. "No, *you* are the monster. God, I can't believe I fucked you. I can't even tell you how much shit I would get from my high school friends if they knew I hooked up with *Phoebe Barton*." He laughed again, a cruel sound, and I felt myself wither. It was just like looking at my brother. The same derision, the same twisted smiles.

"You better not tell anyone about this," Josh warned. It was the same thing Jimmy used to say back then. And I had no choice but to nod, to take it.

"Good, because if you do, I'll tell everyone what you did. That you killed Jimmy. I'll tell them what you are. Oh, and if it's not clear enough, this…thing we have going on here. It's over."

I stayed frozen to the bed. And just as Josh was about to walk out the door, to leave me to gather up my life after this bomb he'd dropped, he turned back to me, the lights from outside casting a glow across his face that made his features look twisted.

"If either of you deserved to die, it was you."

That parting shot stayed with me. I didn't sleep that night, and the next morning, we were on the road to Cullamonjoo, where I drank too much. Where I lashed out, dared Tomas to do something so stupid, so reckless. To prove what? That I was a new version of myself. That I wasn't that poor lonely girl I was in high school?

And look how that turned out.

Since that final night together, Josh has barely looked at me. Until now.

He stands in front of me, his face twisted in disgust. The Outback sprawls behind him, with no one and nothing around us.

"What the hell is this?" he says, shoving a looseleaf sheet of paper with handwriting scribbled on it in my face.

"Looks like a note."

"Don't be smart. We both know you aren't."

I swallow. I know exactly what it is, of course. The note I slid under the door to his room at the Inn before I left.

I'm pregnant. And I'm keeping it.

I shouldn't have done it. There was no reason for him to know. But I couldn't resist one final parting shot.

"Is this true or are you fucking with me?"

I don't owe him an answer, certainly not one that he can put together himself. So, I sidestep him, choosing instead to continue my walk back to the Inn.

That was the wrong decision. Without warning, his arm grasps my shoulder, twisting me backward so forcefully that a small "oh" escapes my mouth.

"I asked you a fucking question."

I stare at him, shocked. And then I feel his knuckles connect with my cheek. It's the first time I've ever been punched—let alone by a guy nearly double my size. It's nothing like the movies, when the victim immediately jumps up and recovers. My vision flickers at the seams as I drop to my knees. My teeth feel loose, and pain radiates through every inch of my body.

I'm too shocked for tears, but I feel blood dripping steadily from my lip as though to make up for it.

I need to get away. The thought cuts through my pain. *This man is insane.*

I can feel him looming above me before I hear him.

"I can't believe you would ever think I would have a baby with *you* of all people. You piece of trash. You *murderer.*"

There it is again. Not only did this person idolize my brother, but he has become him. The thought sends bile rising in my throat.

I force myself up to a standing position. "Listen," I say quietly, my voice shaking.

He leans in, expecting me to finish the statement. And as he does, I press my hands against his chest and shove with all my might.

It shouldn't work. I weigh nothing compared to him, but the movement must catch him off guard, and he steps backwards onto a piece of uneven ground, sending him lilting to the side.

I take my chance and run, throwing my backpack off my arm once I realize it's only slowing me down.

I hear him swear behind me, a rustle against the ground as he gets up. I don't bother turning to look.

I run faster than I ever have in my life.

Ten seconds pass, then fifteen, but he's still not on me. I can't hear anything over the quick rush of my breathing, but I still refuse to turn around. I just need to get to the Inn. Once I'm there, I can get help. I can figure everything out.

But despite my speed, the distance I've traveled, I still don't see the outline of the familiar building, its dark walls rising out of the earth.

Am I going in the right direction? Without the compass, there's no way to tell. And then I see an object ahead. Not big enough to be the Inn, but I recognize it regardless. It's the copse of bushland lining the hike up the huge mountain, Big Beulah. This is the trail-head, the Inn just on the other side of the hill.

I'm so close.

And then I hear movement behind me. The sound of footsteps,

of harsh breathing. Before I can think otherwise, I dart onto the trail and, just as quickly, off it into the brush. Scraggly branches prick my skin, dragging against my face, but I refuse to cry out. Instead, I stop and press my body against the ground, trying to ignore the sharp twigs cutting into my flesh. I don't move. I stay as silent as possible until I hear his footsteps.

And I know, more than I've ever known anything before, that it's over. I'm trapped here. Despite my efforts to hide, my body is easily visible from the trail. He's going to find me.

I could stay silent, hope against all hope that he'll give up, turn around, and go back to living his life. But my brother would never let this go. And I know Josh won't either. He's going to kill me.

My heart breaks. Thoughts of what my life could be—of what the life inside of me could be—cut against me at all sides, digging into my consciousness.

I squeeze my eyes shut. This isn't how I want to spend what could be the last few minutes of my life.

I want to use it to help someone for once. To ensure that no one else is hurt by the evil that is Josh McBride.

So, I force the emotions aside and pull my phone out from where I've kept it in my front pocket. I fumble with shaking fingers to bring up the camera app, stabbing at the keypad to turn it to video mode, and turn it to face me just as I hear the footsteps slow.

"I'm leaving this video for you, Claire," I whisper. I know this isn't the message she expected to receive from me, but she needs to know. I try to make the message as succinct as I can, finishing it with a clear warning.

I manage to save it and attach it as a text message, my fingers fumbling to type Claire's name in the top of the message box. I'm just about to hit send when I sense someone behind me. I turn to look at him. I'm about to open my mouth to tell him exactly what I think of him, or maybe to challenge him. But before the words can come out, I feel something rush through the air towards my head.

And then it makes contact.

46

CLAIRE

Now

"READY TO GO?" JOSH'S question hits my back, a note of impatience in his voice.

The shock of Phoebe's video radiates through me. "Just a minute," I say without turning around, hoping Josh doesn't recognize the spasms of fear in my voice.

I pretend to casually peruse the store's limited beverage options, while fumbling to free Phoebe's phone from the charger. I shove it in my pocket as I bend down, ostensibly to grab a drink from the bottom shelf, and drop the charging cord to the floor, kicking it lightly in the hope that Josh won't see it.

"Got us water and a Coke," I explain, as I finally turn to face him, holding up the bottle and can. "Figured we could share."

I know there's no possible way his features could have changed in the few minutes since I left him in the parking lot, but when I take him in now, he looks like a different person, someone I don't know. Dark circles line his eyes, which seem more narrowed than usual. The fine lines I've barely noticed in all the times our faces have been pressed together are now deep, craven, lending his face a worn, villainous quality. When his lips lift upwards, the result is closer to a grimace than a smile.

"Great. Well, we should probably hit the road," he says. I nod, clenching both hands tightly around the drinks to hide my nerves as I follow him to the front counter.

The cashier looks at me as I place the purchases in front of me, a slight glint in his eyes as if we're sharing an inside joke, and I cringe. If he decides to say anything, to mention the charger, I'll have no explanation for Josh. He'll know instantly what I'm up to. To guess what I know.

And then he'll kill me.

For some reason, this result hasn't yet occurred to me. I've been so absorbed in what Josh has already done, that I haven't considered what he's prepared to do.

I watch as the cashier opens his mouth and I level all my panic towards him in one look, a last-ditch effort to get him to help me. To do something.

Something resembling surprise washes over the cashier's face, and his mouth flops closed, before he hands me back the drinks. "G'day," he mumbles as we turn to leave, no longer willing—or daring—to make eye contact.

I eye the car as we approach, the keys already in the engine, ready to take me somewhere no one will ever find me. And then I scan my surroundings. But everywhere is the same. Red dirt, spotted with the odd bush and eucalyptus tree. Empty flatness for as far as the eye can see.

I won't get far, that's for certain. If I try to run, Josh will be on me in a minute. And even if I do manage to get away, where would I go? There's no one for miles and miles. Hell, we didn't even pass a single car in all the time we've been driving this morning.

I have no choice but to get in the car with him. To play along with this façade he's created.

And hope that I'll somehow be able to escape.

47

CLAIRE

Now

THE VENTS WHIR AS air pulses into the car, but it makes no difference. Sweat pools beneath my legs, clings to my underarms.

Josh hums nonchalantly as he drives. I consider the phone in my pocket, not Phoebe's, but my own. I turned it off when I first left the Raven Inn, concerned that the AFP may have some way to trace it. It seemed like a clever idea at the time, but now I'm kicking myself for not seeing this little jaunt with Josh for what it is—an abduction.

And as I think through it, the signs *were* there. The way he never wanted to talk about our time in Australia—an aversion that I embraced as a welcome relief. The way he changed his mind so abruptly about coming back here without giving me any warning. And how could I be so blind not to recognize the alarm bells blaring when he arrived at the Inn this morning?

I'm disgusted at how wrong I was about everything, how eager

I was to blame Phoebe's murder on the others. First Kyan and Adrien, then Ellery, and then… I can't bear to even think his name.

I still don't understand why Declan had Phoebe's phone, but he clearly didn't kill her.

It was Josh.

I steal a glance over at him, his fingers clenched tightly around the steering wheel, his jaw set. He must feel my gaze on him because he turns, his face contorting into a smile.

He extends one hand, places it on my leg. I try to leave it there, but his touch burns, and I can't help but recoil.

And that's when everything changes.

His smile slips, disappears, and a coldness filters into his face like a brisk wind.

"You know." He returns his gaze to the road. His voice is matter of fact, as if he's recognizing something incontrovertible. Which somehow makes everything all that much worse. "How did you find out?"

I consider bluffing, claiming I have no idea what he's talking about. But I know there's no use.

"Phoebe's phone. She left me a video. She said it was you."

One side of his lip turns upward in something that falls between a smirk and a snarl. "That damn phone. Where was it?"

I sit quietly, unable to speak.

"I can't tell you how long I looked for it that night. It was the one loose end I could never tie up. It's the reason I came back after all."

His admission hits me harder than I would expect. Despite the sweat that's suctioned my T-shirt to my skin, my arms break out in goose bumps, a feverish chill invading the car.

"But why?" I manage. The two words carry so many questions I want to ask but can't seem to formulate.

He barks out a laugh that sends my spine rigid.

"I thought you'd have put it all together by now, running around here playing detective like you've been." A vein in his neck throbs as he stares straight ahead. While his attention is on the road, I sneak a look at the car door.

Just as I expected, it's locked.

"Anyway, you already know. She got pregnant."

Despite everything, the statement slides into my heart like a cold knife. God, Phoebe must have been terrified, pregnant with this horrible person's child inside of her, thousands of miles from home, completely alone.

"You know, I went to school with Phoebe and her brother," Josh says unprompted. "He was a couple grades ahead of me, but we were close, played football together. He was like a hero to me. The whole team was devastated when he died. It was so sudden, so much potential wasted."

I feel my jaw slacken with this news. I remember the way Josh talked about his friend who had died in a car accident. *That* was Phoebe's brother. The one she told me about the last night I ever saw her. The monster who abused her.

But she never told me what happened to him.

"That's why I got with her in the first place," Josh continues. "She intrigued me, the little sister of one of my idols."

I want to cover my ears, to drown out the animosity, the coldness in his voice. But his words are like a drug I can't kick.

"We hooked up a few times in the Whitsundays. I made her promise she wouldn't tell anyone." He lets out a humorless laugh. "One night, I confronted her about her brother's death. He crashed when Phoebe was in the car. The police could never figure out how he'd just run off the road. He wasn't drunk, there wasn't anything on the street that would have blocked their way. Phoebe told them he swerved to avoid a deer, but at that time of year, they aren't all that common. She must have yanked the wheel out from under him as he was driving, ran the car right off the road," Josh says, and instantly, his joking demeanor crystallizes into anger.

"She basically admitted it to me. I wanted to wring her neck right then and there, but I controlled myself. I stayed away from her after that. I didn't trust myself with what I would do if I was around her. And then, that last night in Jagged Rock, I came back to my room and found a note shoved under the door. Just sitting there, half in the hallway so anyone could have seen it. She never had any regard for anyone else, that cunt."

The word catches me off guard, the bitterness of it swelling throughout the car.

"What did it say?" My voice is nearly a whisper.

"Said she was pregnant and keeping it. All the anger I felt for her kind of, like, bubbled up in me, and the world went red. I went off to find her. I was looking everywhere at the Inn, but she wasn't there. So, I went outside. God, I don't know how far I walked, but then I heard her. Walking with a damn smile on her face. Like she was *happy*.

"To be honest, I was just planning on talking to her. Telling her she needed to get rid of the thing. There is no world where I would have a child with her. But she was so fucking obstinate. And then she just took off running, like we were playing a damn game. She was the one who started it, really.

"I looked for her for what felt like hours. And just when I was ready to give up, to wait until the morning to confront her, I heard her whispering."

I think of the video I just saw on Phoebe's phone. The one she must have recorded for me. To protect me. That's what killed her.

The guilt once again sticks in my stomach, sharp as a dagger.

"I followed the sound, and I found her hunched over that phone. I expected her to be scared, dragging me on this cat and mouse game across the entire fucking desert, but when she looked up at me, it was like she was asking for a fight."

I remember the defiant gaze Phoebe could level at someone in an instant. The one I was on the receiving end of so many times, and somewhere deep in my stomach, buried beneath the fear and panic, I feel a bloom of something different. Pride.

"I snapped. I had my room key from the Inn in my pocket. You know how heavy that shit was." I think back to my earlier suspicions. Declan was right, the murder weapon *was* the room key, but it wasn't Ellery's. It belonged to Josh.

And the memory slaps me. Things were quite chaotic as we checked into the Inn. Seven students, plus Hari and Nick Gould, all vying for their preferred rooms. Ellery was assigned to a single, but I remember Kyan striking deals with everyone to rearrange, so that he and Adrien could have a room together, with full privacy, something that irked Phoebe to no end. Somehow, among all the room shuffling, Josh must have ended up in the single room meant for Ellery. Room 11.

"Before I even realized what I was doing," Josh continues, "I brought the thing down on her head. The damn phone must have fallen out of her hands. When I went back there later, I couldn't find it anywhere."

I don't say anything. I can't. My vocal cords are so tight that if I make a sound, they might snap in two.

"But anyway, you know how she was," he continues. "We talked about it, remember?" His eyes dart to me. There's something I've never seen in them before, something crazed, wild. And for a moment I have no idea what he's talking about.

"That first night we reunited in Chicago, remember?" I cringe, remembering what I said after a few margaritas. "You told me that you caught her fucking Declan just totally out in the open. Said how much it hurt you, how selfish she was. Never did trust that guy." He tsks, a sound that grinds my teeth together as shame flashes hot on my face. "Really, I did you a favor getting rid of her. Figured you'd be grateful."

It's the small shrug he gives at the end of that sentence that does it. The carelessness of the gesture that tips my emotions from shock and terror to a fiery rage I haven't felt since the night I stumbled upon Declan and Phoebe with their limbs locked.

"You did me a favor by murdering my friend?" My fingers fold in on themselves, my nails digging deep into the flesh of my palms. "By dumping her in a mine?"

"The mine ended up being a great hiding place, didn't it?" He chuckles, a sound that runs like kerosene through my veins. "Shit, they didn't end up finding her for a decade. In all honesty, it was a split-second decision to shove her in there. That mine has done me a world of favors now that I think about it. Helped me out with you the other day too."

The flashback rocks through the car. The body slamming into me, shoving me down the stairs, the door to the mine slamming shut, the air growing thin around me.

Nick Gould wasn't lying after all. It wasn't him who trapped me in there. It was Josh.

"I went out that morning to see if I could find that goddamn phone. Figured since we were here and all, I'd check out the mine. See if I'd left any other evidence. And then you come along, snooping, nearly scared the shit out of me. I couldn't let you see me. I mean, it wasn't like I had a good reason to be there. Didn't really mean to shove you that hard; I just needed to get out of there. Sorry about that."

His tone is flippant, like he's recalling a casual mistake, not one of the most terrifying moments of my life. I feel removed, like I'm watching the conversation unfold on a television show. One where someone else is the victim.

"You're a psychopath," I finally manage.

A flash of anger sparks in his face at that. "No. I'm not a *psychopath*;

I just do what it takes to survive. You could learn a lesson or two from me, Claire." He spits my name like a curse word.

"So, is that why you came back? To save yourself?"

And just like that, the small smile is back on his face, a gruesome pantomime of authentic feeling. He snaps his fingers. "Bingo. I really did think about sitting it all out, letting the police come to whatever conclusion they felt like. But I couldn't risk the others digging around and uncovering something." I shiver, realizing how similar our motivations were for returning. "And I guess I was right. Look at you; you've been like a dog with a damn bone. Plus, I had another loose end to tie up."

For a moment I have no idea what he means, and then it clicks.

"Hari," I say softly, hoping he'll contradict me, tell me he had nothing to do with her death, that it really was just an accidental overdose.

"Ding ding ding. She saw me leave Phoebe's room in the Whitsundays the night of the Anything but Clothes party. It wasn't a big deal at the time, of course, and then the drugs completely warped her mind."

He sighs. "I liked Hari; I did. We actually stayed in touch off and on throughout the years. I was glad to hear she got clean a few years back. But then she had to go and text me after the AFP told her about Phoebe's remains being discovered. Telling me she remembered that I'd hooked up with Phoebe, asking me straight out if I had anything to do with it. I knew she wouldn't let it go; that wasn't Hari's way. She was kind of like you in that respect. So, I made sure she would keep her mouth shut."

My insides freeze. "But the police said it was an overdose," I stammer.

"God, you really do underestimate me," he says with a sneer. "You were right, though, figuring out that I didn't go to the AFP to talk to them when I landed in Sydney. I could tell you knew something was up that morning at the Inn when we were talking. That's why I 'came clean.'

"I actually landed in Sydney the day before I showed up at Kyan's. I went straight to this hell house called the Wharf, a place Hari used to tell me about. She said you could buy anything there, and I can attest to that. I found some lowlife willing to sell me some heroin and took it straight to Hari's apartment. She was surprised to see me, of course. Thankfully, I caught her right before she was about to head over to Kyan's. I told her I wanted to talk to her before we all got together to tell her what really happened between me and Phoebe. She let me in, poured me water like a damn homemaker. I sprinkled a couple of the sleeping pills my doctor had prescribed for the flight into her glass. It only took her a few minutes before she conked out, and then I dragged her to her bed. Injected the smack. It's just a shame she wasn't conscious to enjoy her last hit."

I look away, disgusted.

"I spent the night at some seedy motel where I could pay in cash and waited around until the next day when I went over to Kyan's. Pretended I had just arrived."

I want to end this, but I know I'm playing for time. It's the only thing currently keeping me alive. I scour my brain thinking of things that still don't fit.

"And Kyan? Why did you stab him?"

He laughs. "That wasn't me. I always liked Kyan. And honestly, he was too dumb to ever suspect I had anything to do with Phoebe. My best guess is Randy. I mean you saw how totally ballistic he went that morning."

I remember the pure rage encapsulated on Randy's face. The hatred he harbored for our group, and for Kyan more than any of us.

"But why slash the tires on our rental cars?" That had to have been Josh. Even if Randy had stabbed Kyan, he'd have no reason to keep the rest of us around longer than we needed to be.

"Well," Josh says, "once we ended up back in Jagged Rock, I couldn't give up the opportunity to find Phoebe's phone. I needed time, and I couldn't have any of you scurrying off before I found it."

I have one question left. One that I don't want to ask, but that I need the answer to more than any other.

"And," I clear my throat, my mouth dry, "what do you plan to do with me?"

To his credit, Josh's careless façade seems to crumble just slightly. But his eyes stay glued to the road, on the single yellow line dragging to the horizon.

"I didn't want to have to do this, you know, but you left me no other choice. I thought our encounter in the mine might have scared you off, but you just wouldn't quit. And I could tell you were getting closer. Even before you found the phone, I knew what I had to do."

His tone turns practical.

"You'll disappear. I managed to find a shovel back at the Inn that I threw in the trunk. There's plenty of places to hide a body out here.

The police will think you pulled a Phoebe—ran away to escape. They'll see it as a sign of your guilt. It will get rid of any suspicion they may have of me. I've already staked out a place in the middle of nowhere, a turnoff where the pavement turns into a dirt road and then to nothing. I'll try to make it quick. Painless."

His fingers tighten on the wheel, and I picture them around my throat, pressing.

"Josh, you don't need to do this," I fumble, grasping on to anything that will save me. "I understand why you did everything else. You were just trying to cover your tracks with Hari, and what happened with Phoebe, that was…a terrible accident—"

But it's the wrong thing to say. Any remorse slips away as his neck tightens, that vein bulging yet again, and his eyes dart towards me.

"It was not an *accident*," he spits. "She deserved it. The things she did to me, to you, to her apparent friends. She deserved it."

I can tell this is the mantra he's adopted in the years since he killed her. A way to justify his actions. If only I can unpack this, to make him see he's wrong.

"She made mistakes," I say slowly, wading in. "She did things she regretted, deeply." My mind touches on the image of her wrapped around Declan, but it's quickly replaced by the scene from later that night: Phoebe, so small against the pitch-black sky as she explained how she had no other choice than to run away. "Jimmy hurt her. She had to—"

"Don't you dare say his name." Josh's words are icy, and he jerks suddenly, the car jumping over the center of the empty road. "You always tried to defend her. Even after everyone else could see what she really was."

And it's that comment that shifts the panic into something else. Something sturdier, more forceful.

Josh's comment is a variation on the same thing I've been told over and over this week. By Adrien, who was so certain that Phoebe's death wasn't worth investigating. From Randy, who could only see Phoebe as a haughty, arrogant teenager. And even from Declan, who so easily deflected his responsibility to Phoebe. *She came on to me.*

No more. I will not let this person, this man, excuse his actions because of something a vulnerable, traumatized girl did years ago. Phoebe was flawed, sure. But she was my friend.

Suddenly, I'm back in our dorm room at Hamilton that very first day. I was terrified, so far from home, and drowning in homesickness. Overcome by the anxiety of having to meet a whole new group of people, I was nearly trembling as we got ready. I remember how astutely Phoebe picked up on it, how she urged me to take a seat on her bed as she softly spread blush across my cheeks and darkened my lips. How she asked me questions the entire time she worked, making me feel not only more beautiful, but more interesting.

Despite everything she did, all the mistakes she made, I loved her. And this man who stripped her of her life has the gall to talk about her like she deserved it.

Anger floods through me, infiltrating my every thought. I think of what Phoebe would have done in this situation. What she *did* do, all those years ago.

In an instant, everything becomes clear. Before I can think better of it, I snatch my hand out, grabbing the steering wheel.

Josh's shock is written clearly on his face, and his fingers momentarily release their clutch. I use that opportunity to yank the wheel as hard as I possibly can, sending the car veering off the road.

It's the weightlessness I feel first, the lack of gravity as the tires leave the ground, as the car flips.

Then comes the sound. The breaking glass, the devastating crunch of metal and bone. The pain flashing through my body like the vibrations of a pulsing speaker.

And everything goes silent.

48

CLAIRE

Now

THE FIRST THING I notice when I come to is the pressure.

My head feels like a balloon. Strobe lights of pain flicker through my vision, complemented by a ringing in my ears.

And then I understand why. The crash comes back to me in flashes. My hand on the wheel, the SUV flipping through the air, the bone-crushing contact as it collided with the ground.

When I force my eyelids open, I take in a blurry view of the windshield, so smashed it's almost unrecognizable. And close, far closer than it should be. Then I feel the pain in my chest, the sharp, digging pressure of something cutting into my heart. The seat belt.

I try to unbuckle, but everything feels wrong, disorienting.

I blink and realize the ground is where the sky should be. I'm hanging upside down. I contort my body, every single bone and muscle screaming, and eventually manage to unbuckle the seat belt with one hand and prop myself against the roof of the car with the other.

I force open the door, which became unlocked at some point during the collision, and collapse with a grunt onto dirt and glass.

Shards dig into my back and legs, and my head feels as though I recently extricated it from a blender, but I force myself to a standing position. I realize with a wince that I can't put any weight on my right leg.

Since I regained consciousness, my thoughts have floated around me like clouds, light and ethereal and just out of reach. But suddenly, the memories break through with sudden clarity.

Josh.

It's then that I hear it. Something between a grunt and a groan filtering through the hazy, disturbed air.

He's awake.

I hear glass crunch as he heaves himself from the vehicle, but I don't bother turning. Instead, I run. Each step is agony, pain screaming through my leg. But I continue to hobble. I don't have a specific destination in mind; I just need to get away.

I try to think how far we must have driven from the gas station. Josh had been weaving his horrible story for what? Ten, fifteen minutes maybe?

Could I get back there before he catches me?

No. The pain in my leg answers the question for me. In this condition, there's no way I'll make it.

But I need to try.

I don't know how far I go, my breath shouting in my ears,

drowning out everything aside from the pain that spasms through my body with every step.

I don't even hear him behind me. Not until it's too late.

And then he's on me, his hands pushing into my back, forcing me onto the ground in one fell swoop. The air rushes from my chest, the pain in my leg temporarily forgotten as my forehead smacks the ground.

Suddenly his hands are around my neck, forcing out whatever air remains. I try to breathe, to tear his hands away, but the pressure is too much. Black dots dance in my peripheral vision, and I wonder if this was what it was like for Phoebe in her last moments.

I wish for someone to save me, but I know it's futile. I've exiled myself, worn my friendships down to razor-thin lines, so threadbare they may never be able to be sewn back together. Just as Phoebe did. I think of Kyan, clinging to life in some remote hospital. Of Ellery, shocked and hurt by me turning my back on her at the first chance. Of Adrien, reeling from my brazen accusations. And finally, of Declan. The man I lost twice.

I can tell I'm near the end. My muscles spasm as if I've lost all control over them. The black dots before my eyes become larger.

I prepare myself for it all to disappear.

And then the feeling is gone. Josh's hands release. I don't have time to question it. I'm too consumed with sucking in oxygen, my lungs burning deliciously as I gasp.

Seconds later I hear the sputtering of an engine, the crush of tires against the earth.

A car door slams, and I turn my head painfully, just in time to see a figure fly out of the driver seat. Taking after Josh, who's already running in the opposite direction, back towards the car.

I blink hard, trying to clear my vision. It barely works, but it's enough to identify the person chasing him.

Luke.

And suddenly I'm surrounded by three figures, all of whom are asking me questions in voices that are far too loud. I blink again as I take them in, their words humming around me like the flies I can never seem to escape out here.

Adrien. Ellery. And...

"Thank God you're okay."

Declan's breathless words break through the haze of trauma and pain.

I move my arm towards him, a pathetic gesture, but one he accepts all the same, dropping down to the dirt, pulling me onto his knee.

But I need to know that Josh won't get away. That after all these years, he'll pay for what he did.

Declan tries to stop me, but I twist my body to follow the two figures running through the Outback, already so far away that they look like caricatures of themselves. I briefly wonder why Josh is heading in that direction, back towards the car. And then his earlier comment breaks through the haziness of my mind. About the shovel he took from the Inn and threw in the trunk.

He's going to use it as a weapon against Luke.

I try to call out, to warn Luke what's coming. But before I can force out the words, the world around me erupts in flames.

49

CLAIRE

Now

"WE HAVE A FEW questions for you."

Villanueva stands in front of my hospital bed, looking even more polished than usual against the aseptic white walls of Tilloborra Hospital.

I take a deep breath. For the last three days, I've been waiting for this moment. In the wake of everything that happened—the car exploding, three ambulances arriving at the scene, speeding nearly an hour away to the closest hospital, the frantic surgery I needed on my fractured femur and the endless tests they had to run for internal bleeding—I didn't receive any word from Villanueva or the AFP. I gave a statement on that first day to an officer with the Queensland Police Service, a middle-aged man with a buzz cut who listened attentively as I explained what happened, from that night ten years ago up through the car crash and its aftermath. But there was nothing to clarify whether I was still the AFP's main suspect in Phoebe's murder.

"Are you planning on arresting me?" I pull the blanket of my hospital bed closer to my neck, suddenly very conscious of the thin gown I'm wearing.

Villanueva sighs deeply. Just as I expect her to answer, she returns my question with one of her own. "Do you mind if I take a seat?"

My head moves forward involuntarily, which Villanueva takes as a nod. It's clear she's not going to let me off easy.

"I thought I was clear when we last spoke," she says once she's seated, one ankle crossed over the other. "I told you not to leave the Royal Hotel."

I feel my cheeks grow hot. "I had no choice," I say, my eyes downcast. "I had to prove it wasn't me who killed Phoebe."

As I say it, I remember all the mistakes I made in trying to do so.

"I couldn't sleep that night after we...well," Declan explained to me a few days earlier, as he sat in the chair he'd pulled up close to my hospital bed, his hands in mine. "I knew I should've woken you and returned to the Royal, but you were so peaceful, and I couldn't bear the thought of disrupting your last night before..." He trails off again. "I decided to look through the Inn since Randy appeared to have left for the night, to see if there was any other evidence besides the videos.

"I went back down to the closet where you found the computer. It was crammed with all sorts of stuff, and I came across what looked like a lost and found box. In it was Phoebe's phone. A guest must have found it and turned it in, and Randy didn't know who it belonged to. I thought it might have been yours from all those years ago—I remember yours used to have a jewel on it; I just couldn't remember the color. I was going to give it to you in the morning, when we woke, but..."

I blushed then, thinking of how different things would have been if I'd simply confronted Declan about the phone that morning.

"I understand where you were the night of Ms. Barton's murder," Villanueva says now, bringing me back to the present. "Mr. Walsh filled us in. I've reviewed the witness statement you provided the Queensland Police, and we've corroborated it with other evidence."

"What other evidence?" I manage to limit myself to only one question, despite the many swirling in my brain.

"Well, first, we enacted a search warrant of Randy Campbell's house."

"Randy." The name tastes sour in my mouth, a combination of surprise and disgust. In everything that's happened, I nearly forgot about him.

"Yes, we wanted to investigate your claims about the hidden cameras. And we found sufficient proof to confirm he has been recording his guests without their permission."

"But...but we saw him at the Inn burning the computer," I stumble, not understanding.

"He had backed up some of the videos to the cloud. We found them on his home computer when we executed the search warrant," Villanueva explains. "He's in custody now, both for the illicit videos and for the assault on your friend, Mr. Quek, which he confessed to."

I feel my shoulders relax for the first time in days. God only knows how many people—how many women—Randy's violated over the years. And Josh was right—Randy *was* the one who stabbed Kyan.

"We watched them as well." I don't understand Villanueva's comment at first. "Your friend, Ms. Viviers, had mentioned that an… intimate video had been posted of her and Mr. Quek during your first time in Jagged Rock. We were able to match that to one of the videos on Mr. Campbell's computer."

Phoebe never posted that video of Adrien and Kyan. She may have made mistakes, done things she regretted, but she wasn't a monster.

I think back to how angry Randy had been at that last dinner when Adrien spilled her wine on him. How that was the same night he'd discovered that Hamilton was pulling the Adventure Abroad program. Releasing the sex tape must have been his way of getting revenge.

"And, of course, we've watched the video on Ms. Barton's phone accusing Mr. McBride of attacking her. On top of that, we have proof that he returned to the country, of course. My partner, Leading Senior Constable Arnold Sawkins, had reached out to him at the time we identified Phoebe's remains—as he did with all of you—and requested that he come to Australia to answer our questions." The ease with which Villanueva transitions to referring to Phoebe by her first name isn't lost on me, a familiarity she never utilizes with the rest of us. "But Mr. McBride refused, said he had work obligations that prevented him from traveling. So, it was a bit odd to discover that he *did* end up making the trip, while never advising us that he was in the country."

I open my mouth, but Villanueva continues, as if reading my mind.

"We also have evidence to connect him to the murder of Harriet Masterson. When we questioned her neighbors, one mentioned having seen an individual matching Mr. McBride's description entering her apartment the afternoon before you reported her overdose.

"It is unfortunate that Mr. McBride is unable to answer our questions." Villanueva at least has the courtesy to divert her eyes downward in a fleeting moment of silence for Josh.

The explosion plays in my head then, just like it has so many times over the last few days. Luke running behind Josh, only to be thrown backwards, his body tossed aside. And Josh nowhere to be seen, the lights searing my eyes as I tried to look. The despair that flooded me, cruel and surprising, as I realized what had happened. The car had a full gas tank—we had just filled up minutes before—and the accident must have damaged the car's wiring. In retrospect, I remembered a hissing sound, the sight of sparks, as I dragged myself from the battered SUV, but in my panicked haze, I hadn't even registered them. We found out later that after weeks of drought and arid weather, the sparks started yet another fire that raced through a large portion of rural Queensland before firefighters were able to extinguish it.

But in the seconds after the explosion, Ellery didn't bother waiting for the scene to clear. She sped forward, directly towards Luke, with Declan close behind her.

"We've not yet been able to corroborate your claim that Mr. McBride attacked Phoebe with his room key from the Raven Inn," Villanueva's voice breaks into my memory of that horrible scene. "But we have reason to believe he may have held on to it after all this time, potentially even transported it back to the United States with him. We've coordinated with the Federal Bureau of Investigation, and they will be executing a search warrant for Mr. McBride's townhome in Chicago.

"So, no," Villanueva concludes. "You are no longer considered a suspect in Phoebe's murder."

Her words fly through me with giddy elation, mixing noxiously with grief and shame. But Villanueva's eyes grow hard once more.

"I do have one more question for you though."

I feel my breath catch.

"The accident. The crash with the car Mr. McBride had stolen." I found out shortly after the explosion that Josh hadn't borrowed the car as he'd claimed but had broken into one of the houses in downtown Jagged Rock and stolen the keys.

"It doesn't seem likely that Mr. McBride just ran off the road," Villanueva continues. "What happened?"

The real question hangs silently between us. *What did you do?*

I can't tell her the truth. That I yanked the wheel, took Josh by surprise, just like Phoebe did to her brother all those years ago. I'm sure they would consider that a crime.

Then I think back to what Josh said about the police's conclusion regarding Phoebe's crash and her brother's death. How Phoebe had told them her brother had swerved to avoid a deer.

"A kangaroo," I say before I can think better of it. "It hopped in front of the car. Josh swerved to avoid it."

"Ah." Villanueva raises an eyebrow, one side of her lip lifted. "Exactly what I thought."

Somehow, somewhere, I feel Phoebe smile.

"Well, that's all I have for you for now. When you're released from hospital, I suggest you return to Sydney for a few days. The wildfires have largely been contained, so you shouldn't have any more issues with your flights. But stick around for a bit until we clear you to leave the country."

I nod, but she's already standing, walking away from the bed. Just as she reaches the door, she turns back, that mischievous smile still on her face.

"Oh and, Claire, I think it's probably best if you don't return to Jagged Rock after this."

I can't help but smile back. "You don't have to worry about that."

I'll never come back here again.

50

CLAIRE

Now

"I CAN'T BELIEVE YOU guys are really leaving," Kyan says as he stands, his arms open as he leans in to give me a hug. We're back in the kitchen of his Sydney house, where we've been staying the last few days, and which seems to look even more grandiose following our accommodations in Jagged Rock. "It's been so nice having you here, even with everything that's happened."

"Come on, Kyan." Adrien walks over, blocking our hug and pressing her hand on his shoulder, lightly pushing him back into his wheelchair. "You know you shouldn't be standing. You'll rip out your stitches."

As fate would have it, Kyan was recovering from his stab wound in the same hospital that I was rushed to following the crash. Or maybe it wasn't fate as much as it was the biggest/only hospital within two hundred miles of Jagged Rock.

It had been touch and go, he explained to us later. He'd lost a lot of blood during the ambulance ride to the hospital and had been rushed into surgery immediately upon arrival. Randy's knife had punctured one of his kidneys, which the doctors had removed before they'd sewn him up. Life would be a bit different, they'd advised him. Less alcohol, healthier food, and more moderate exercise.

But he'd survive.

He recounted the stabbing to the others in the hospital, which Declan then passed onto me. Kyan had gone to the parking lot to take a call when he spotted the slashed tires on our rental cars—the ones Josh was responsible for. Unfortunately, at that same time, Randy had come out for a smoke break. Kyan launched himself on him, accusing him of slashing the tires. One thing led to another, and Randy retaliated, screaming at Kyan about how privileged and arrogant we all were, how we'd ruined his life. And before Kyan knew what was happening, before he had a chance to defend himself, Randy pulled out a pocketknife and shoved it into Kyan's stomach. Randy fled immediately after that, leaving Kyan to bleed out.

Declan also relayed how Luke, Ellery, and Adrien had received the wildfire evacuation notice early on the morning I'd gotten in the car with Josh. With no other choice for transportation, they'd decided to pile into Luke's beat-up hatchback with only a prayer that it would make it to Tilloborra, where they could be in relative safety and visit Kyan in the hospital. Just as they were coming to our rooms to wake us, Declan burst through the doors of the Royal Hotel, explaining how I'd left the Inn with Josh in a car he didn't recognize, heading to God knows where. Declan knew something was wrong, call it intuition or whatever, but it was enough to convince the others.

When Declan told me this part in the story, I couldn't help but tear up, thinking of how they chose to save me even after everything.

There were so many directions Josh and I could have headed in, but they figured we would be heading away from the wildfires, so they scanned the windows for any sign of me or Josh as they drove. They stopped at the same gas station we had to check if there had been any sightings. They spoke to the cashier, who pointed them in the direction we had headed. It only took a few more minutes for them to come across the wrecked car, to spot Josh's hands around my throat.

Thankfully, Luke wasn't burned in the explosion; the force of the blast propelled him away. But he broke his wrist in the fall. A small injury in the scheme of things, but one I'll never be able to fully repay him for.

"Can't you guys stay just a few days longer?" he says now, a plaster cast affixed to his forearm, his signature kind smile adorning his face.

Luke came back to Sydney with us. He is taking everything that happened as a sign. After nearly a century of operations, he realized that it was time to say goodbye to the Royal Hotel. It had run its course, he explained to us, and he'd paid his dues. It was time to stop living just to defy others and time for him to go after what he wanted.

He was going to move to Sydney, use the money from the sale of the hotel to finance the purchase of a small bar in Darlinghurst, where he could revive Daisy Dukes and return to the life he was supposed to be living. After everything he'd done for us, Kyan insisted Luke stay with him as he sorted out his new life.

Although, that would mean that Kyan would now have two houseguests. Adrien has also decided to stay in Sydney. Being back with Kyan made her realize how unhappy she was with her life in South Africa, how trapped and apathetic she'd become with a career and husband she didn't love. She hasn't called her father yet—she is planning on doing so after we all leave—but she knows what she'll tell him. She is an adult, and she has the right to live her own life. To do what she wants, to love whom she wants. She's already spoken to her husband, the divorce papers are en route to him, and she is sending a moving company to pack up her things and bring them to Sydney.

"Sorry, Luke. We would if we could, but some of us have things to get back to," Ellery says with a wink. "Wedding planning and all that. Don't forget to mark your calendars in October for a trip to Canada. Our next reunion."

Ellery had come clean to us about her lingering feelings for Phoebe.

"I'd been head over heels for her," Ellery admitted to all of us over dinner at Kyan's. "It was the first time I'd had feelings like that for a girl and it scared me, honestly. I handled it poorly. Maybe if I did something different, she would still be..."

Ellery didn't finish her thought, but we all knew what she meant. Maybe Phoebe would still be alive. I was struck by how every single one of us had been haunted by what happened in Jagged Rock. How I wasn't the only one scarred by guilt after that trip.

Ellery went on to admit what really happened during our camping trip in Cullamonjoo National Park. How she and Tomas had taken the drugs in secret, and how that was likely the only reason he agreed to Phoebe's dare. Ellery said she'd talked to Phoebe after, confessed her role in the accident. Phoebe promised not to tell anyone and insisted Ellery do the same. Tomas's death was her own fault, Phoebe had told Ellery. She would take full blame.

Phoebe had protected Ellery, and Ellery had been riddled with grief—like me, like all of us—ever since. She'd call Phoebe's phone occasionally, just to hear her voice, and would text when the guilt got to be too much.

Ellery hadn't had any relationships after that, never felt like she was worthy. Until she met her now fiancé at a charity event. She admitted she'd approached her purely because of her physical similarities to Phoebe. But as Ellery learned more and more about her, she realized all the differences too.

"Grace is just as fiercely loyal, but she doesn't have the same hard edges as Phoebe. She's warm, open. Honestly, I don't know if I deserve her."

But I know it. We all deserve goodness. We've spent enough of our lives dwelling in guilt.

"You lot will have to visit New York soon," Declan says, lacing his fingers through mine, and I feel my heart flutter. In the hours that he sat by my side in the hospital, we talked through everything. How stupid we've been these last few years, letting our guilt and regret dictate our lives.

So, we reached a decision. I'll move in with him in New York.

His friend's architectural office needs a receptionist, a part-time job I can easily do as I finish my degree at a local community college. His apartment's big enough for both of us, he promised. I'll return to Chicago, of course, to pack up and quit my job in person, but he'll be with me. And we'll build a life together, trying to make up for the years we let slip away.

We all exchange hugs as Declan's phone flashes with a notification that the Uber's arrived outside.

Tears are shed by everyone—even a few from Adrien—as Ellery, Declan, and I wave from the back window of the SUV. Declan holds my hand as the car winds us through the narrow streets of Bondi, back to the airport. And as flashes of ocean whip by, I think back on how much has changed in the week and a half I've been back here in Australia.

I came with nothing but guilt. And I'm leaving with everything.

I smile, my eyes glued to the window, but Phoebe's voice breaks through it, raspy and cruel.

You don't deserve this.

The guilt clasps at my heart, a familiar affliction, but this time I'm able to force it away, to convince myself I've made up for it. We've all made mistakes. My actions may have led to Phoebe's death, yes, but I wasn't the only one. And I achieved justice for her.

I've done everything I can to make things right. That's all she can ask for.

"You alright?" Declan asks, his brow furrowed in concern.

I smile at him reassuringly. "I am now."

EPILOGUE

CLAIRE

Then

I TRY TO PUT it behind me, I really do.

I lie there for hours after my encounter with Phoebe, staring at a hole in the ceiling in my uncomfortable twin bed, our shared room at the Inn feeling emptier than ever. And I think of Phoebe out there, heading by foot to Rollowong, escaping from it all.

I forgave her in the moment for sleeping with Declan. I always did. Whenever she was selfish or condescending—as she incessantly was—I always let it go. I've been so weak, always letting her get what she wants.

Even now, she barely apologized before using me, taking advantage of my rage to leave traces of herself behind as evidence. And as usual, I let her.

I throw the covers off, the feeling of the starchy cotton against my skin suddenly unbearable. I need to get outside, to walk.

I know Phoebe's already made it way too far for me to ever catch up with her, plus I can't remember the precise direction in which she was headed. So, instead, I walk the route Nick Gould led us on the other day, out to the mine. I plan to let my anxieties run rampant until they wear themselves out.

But it doesn't work.

The farther I walk, the more I replay the conversation with Phoebe in my mind, and the more my anger grows. The ease with which life seems to come to her, the way she skirts away from any responsibility, whether it's turning up late or killing one of our best friends. It's infuriating.

And I decide. I'll report her tomorrow to Nick. I'll let him know she's at that shelter in Rollowong. I'll get my revenge.

By the time I reach the ruins of the mine, I'm confident in my newfound decision. I'm so distracted that I almost don't notice the door to the mine cracked slightly opened. The last time we'd been out here, it'd been tightly shut.

"Hello?" I say hesitantly, a slight waver in my throat. "Is someone there?"

My question is answered by the silence of the night, the galaxies above stretching out before me. I repeat it once more as I take several cautious steps towards the mine door, dread pulsing in my chest.

I can tell something is wrong. But even with everything else that has gone to shit tonight, I could never expect the sight that awaits me as I pull open the door.

The stars provide only a slight sliver of light, but I can just make out a frail form curled up on the stairs leading down to the mineshaft.

I recognize her immediately, short brown curls, arms that I could easily wrap my fingers around, her turquoise eyes tightly closed.

I don't know what happened. It looks like Phoebe's injured, a trace of blood lines the steps leading to her body.

Instinctively, I take a step forward, arms outstretched, ready to carry her back up to steady ground, to haul her the entire way to the Inn if need be.

But the image from hours earlier comes back with the weight of a fist. Phoebe's head thrown back in passion, her body wrapped tightly around Declan's.

My legs move, taking a step backwards, before my mind can catch up.

I remember the conclusion I came to minutes before. Phoebe is never punished for what she does. She needs to realize that her actions have consequences. She needs to pay.

I'll come back for her tomorrow, let her spend the night in here.

The door creaks under my hand as I push it shut. I steal one last glance back in the mine, the moonlight striking the metal in such a way as to illuminate Phoebe's face for a flash of a second.

In the instant before the door slams closed, I think I see her eyes flash open.

My heart is pounding as I process this. It could have been a trick of the light, or just a flicker of my imagination. But if I'm wrong, if she did see me, then she would know that I left her in here. And she wouldn't hesitate to tell the others what I've done.

No, I won't come back tomorrow. I'll convince the others to search and lead them away from here.

I have no choice, I tell myself. *She deserved this.*

I'm still trying to convince myself as I drop the door's heavy metal lock into place.

As I walk away.

READING GROUP GUIDE

1. What were your first impressions of Phoebe? Of Claire? Did you connect with one of them more than the other?

2. Which members of the group did you trust initially, if any? Which were you hesitant about?

3. What do you think the significance is of truth or dare being The Mob's favorite game to play? What are the risks to truth or dare? Have you ever played?

4. What was your reaction to what happened to Tomas? Knowing what you know by the end of the novel, who do you think is really to blame? Why?

5. What do you make of The Mob's friendship? Does it feel

healthy? Genuine? Do you think it will last? Compare and contrast it to your friendships in college and early adulthood.

6. Revenge is a major theme in the novel. Is there ever a time, in this novel or outside of it, that you feel revenge (big or small) is justified?

7. The town of Jagged Rock is almost entirely dependent on money brought in by tourism and, specifically, by the Adventure Abroad program, which makes the relationships between the town's residents and the students in the program quite complicated. How did you feel about the dynamics of these relationships?

8. What did you make of Phoebe and Declan's final night in Australia? If you were Claire, what would your reaction have been?

9. Discuss Phoebe's death and the events that led to it. How does her story connect to larger cultural conversations around believing women and violence against women (especially when speaking out)?

10. What was your reaction to Claire's truth in the epilogue? Did it change your perception of her?

A CONVERSATION WITH THE AUTHOR

What inspired you to write this novel?

Like the characters in *The Outback* I also studied abroad in Australia, but thankfully, my six months in the country involved far less drama and murder! During my time in Melbourne, my friends and I participated in a two-week adventure-based spring break trip—very much like the Adventure Abroad program—that took us all up and down Australia's eastern coast and involved bungee jumping, white water rafting in crocodile-infested waters, scuba diving in the Great Barrier Reef, and skydiving. It was an absolutely incredible experience and one I still think about often more than a decade later. Moreover, even though I only spent two weeks with many of the people in the program, we formed unbelievably close and quick friendships. Writing a fictionalized version of that trip allowed me to relive those travels and friendships in many ways and consider all the things that could have—but thankfully didn't—go wrong!

Why make Phoebe the only narrator of the past?

Primarily, I chose Phoebe to narrate the past as it happened because I wanted to highlight the differences between her experiences and opinions of events and the way Claire remembers them a decade later. I really enjoyed writing that juxtaposition between her views and Claire's.

Do you think The Mob will stay friends after they leave Australia for the second time?

I like to think that they will! But I wonder if Claire will ever share her secret of what really happened the night of Phoebe's death with Declan…

How did the novel change as you were writing it?

No matter how many manuscripts I write, First Draft Sara is always naïve enough to think that the final draft of the book will be virtually the same as the first with only small tweaks. And every time, I couldn't be more wrong! *The Outback* went through numerous rounds of edits (I've lost track how many!), but each round helped flesh out the plot and the characters. One thing that changed substantially was the nature of the Adventure Abroad program. Initially, the program was predominantly set in the Outback and lasted for six months. Ultimately changing this to a month-long program that explored much of Australia's eastern coast opened so many more possibilities for the characters to get into trouble!

Why end the book with Claire's epilogue? How do you think readers will react to it?

I can't resist ending on a twist! One of my favorite things to do in writing thrillers is to wrap everything up nice and neatly only to have one final gut-punch at the very end. More than anything, I hope readers are surprised on that final page. And apologies for any conflicted emotions it may cause!

Any books on your TBR that you want to share?

So many! But as a huge fan of destination thrillers (no surprise there), I am super excited to read Amy McCulloch's forthcoming novel *Runner 13*, a thriller set during an ultramarathon in the Sahara Desert, and Lucy Clarke's *The Surf House*, set in the cliffs of Morocco.

ACKNOWLEDGMENTS

This is my second novel, and the second murder-based thriller that I've based on my personal travels. In reality, my trips are much calmer. Less drama, and—knock on wood—no murders to date (I promise). *The Outback* is based on a spring break trip I took at the ripe age of twenty while I was studying abroad in Australia. Like the characters in this book, I scuba dived the Great Barrier Reef, skydived, and bungy jumped. Did I mention I was much cooler in my twenties?

It's not an exaggeration to say that experience and the six months I spent living and studying in Melbourne changed the trajectory of my life. It opened my eyes to how amazing traveling and living abroad can be and introduced me to some of the most incredible people I've ever met. Marissa, Candice, Wittla, J.P., and M.D., those six months rank among the most fun and ridiculous of my entire life, and this book wouldn't have been possible without each of you.

Kate Burke, I am eternally grateful to have you as an agent. Thank you for always being on the other end of a call or an email thread to answer my thousands of questions or to talk me down about something or other. You made this book happen, and I wouldn't be writing these words if I didn't have your encouragement and ridiculously impressive editing skills. Thank you also to all of Blake Friedmann, especially Julian Friedmann, Sian Ellis-Martin, James Pusey, and Nicole Etherington. I'm so lucky to be part of your team!

Thank you to my excellent editor, Finn Cotton, who knows exactly what each book needs and how to coax it out of me. And thank you to the wider team at Transworld, including Judith Welsh, Katrina Whone, Beci Kelly, Anna Carvanova, Lucy Upton, and Oliver Martin.

Thank you to all the fantastic Instagrammers and book bloggers who post tirelessly and spend their spare time reading books from authors like me. You are amazing. And thank you to all the authors I've been lucky enough to meet throughout this wild journey who are always there to celebrate with me during the good times and lend an ear and a virtual glass of wine during the not-so-good ones.

Mom and Dad, my first readers, my biggest fans, and my most loyal supporters. Thank you for always being there and for making all this possible. To Erin, Cruz, Mason, and Harper, I love you all so much, and your support means the world.

Writing this book saw me through several stages of life: I wrote the first draft while living abroad in Sweden, did my initial edits during my honeymoon, and worked on my substantive edits during night feeds and naptimes in the months following the birth of my son. Filip, you have been there for all of it and more. I am so lucky to have you as my partner in all of this, and I don't want to know what life would be without you—certainly less adventurous, I'm sure. I love you.

My Stellan Boy, thank you for giving me endless creativity, love, and support. Everything I do is for you. Thank you for letting me be your mom.

And once again, thank you, reader, for making this author's dreams come true.

ABOUT THE AUTHOR

Sara Ochs is a law professor and the author of *The Resort*. When she's not writing or teaching, she can usually be found planning her next trip. Born and raised in Upstate New York, Sara now lives in North Carolina with her husband and son.

Read on for an excerpt
from Sara Ochs' debut novel,
The Resort.

'A pacy and accomplished
murder mystery . . . *The Beach*
for a new generation.'
JANICE HALLETT

Prologue

Friday Night

The bass thumps from somewhere behind me, echoing the beat of the blood pulsing in my ears. I look back at the group I've left behind. Bodies painted in flashy greens and sickeningly sweet pinks rub against each other. Cheap beer froths out of gold and green bottles while friends sip collectively from fishbowls filled with noxious blue liquids. Further down, a dancer swirls a hula hoop of fire for the acclaim of an impressed – and extremely intoxicated – crowd.

Everything suddenly seems hazy, like I'm watching it all unfold from outside of my body. A neon cacophony of colour set to music that's become nothing more than one long, blurred note, deep enough and loud enough to shake my chest bones. My muscles are heavy, and I need to remind myself to breathe, like my body has forgotten to engage in its normal functions. Maybe they put something in my drink to make this easier. Or maybe I'm just intoxicated on the knowledge. The awareness that time is running out.

I call back towards the group, pleading for anyone to help me. But it's no use. The raucousness blasting from the party's speakers sweeps down the beach like an avalanche, picking up my voice and carrying it away into the silence.

I thought I could do this myself. That I was smarter than them, that I could figure out the darkness that lives on this island and stop it from hurting anyone else.

But I was wrong.

I made a mistake. I trusted the wrong person. I should have known better after everything that happened.

I feel a palm on my lower back. It's light, and I know what it would look like to any onlooker, even one who decided to walk this far down the beach away from the party. Two partygoers escaping the dancefloor for the romantic seclusion of the moonlight. It's so far from true it almost brings a smile to my lips, a bubbling euphoria that nearly escapes.

But it doesn't.

Because I know what that palm signifies. And I feel what the others down the beach don't. The thin prick of a knife digging into my lower vertebrae.

I hear a voice close to my ear, the tone hard and cold, the music doing little to muffle it.

'Move. Forward.'

I look before me, the ocean stretched out to the horizon, black waves glittering in the light from the moon – as round and full as a pregnant belly. I've looked at this view in awe several times since I arrived here, a beauty like nothing I've ever seen.

I do as I'm told and walk. What choice do I have?

The pulsing bass emanating from the bars' speakers recedes with each step, until I'm far enough away that the music becomes nothing more than a memory. This distance from the party, the beach is bathed in darkness, the shops lining this stretch long since closed. The only light comes from the smattering of stars over my head.

As I feel the water lap against my toes, I take one more

look over my shoulder. The people are only small blurs at this distance, but I can still make out their bodies grinding together, so many aching to make contact any way they can. Despite the sloppiness – the drugs and drink making them flop on to each other in lurid movements – there's a beauty to it.

For so long, I've felt nothing but coldness, even with the heavy humidity of the island cloying at my skin these past few days. People always talk about rage burning, but it sat inside my stomach, as hard as ice, freezing my veins. I couldn't think of anything besides revenge. A need to impose pain that I've never felt before.

But now, as the ocean water grazes my kneecaps and I watch the people down the beach from me dance in the glittering moonlight, so far removed from the rest of the world, it's as if that ice finally melts, the brief giddiness from earlier returning.

I wonder if she felt this way before it happened to her. An appreciation for life that comes only at its end.

Before I can think about it any more, my feet stop moving, and the single palm on my back turns into two, pushing me hard, face-first into the water. I gasp for breath as I fall, my forehead striking one of the rocks that litters the ocean floor. But it's not enough. The hands grip my neck tightly, holding my head under, legs now wrapped around my hips, pinning me down. Even though I fight back, the person barely moves. I lift my arms up, reaching for anything to grab hold of, but it feels as if I'm draped in a weighted blanket. My fingers finally grasp around wrists, and I drag my nails across flesh as hard as I can. But the water turns everything soft, and I barely make a dent.

My eyelids force open against the sting of the salt water. Small fish flick by me, deftly avoiding the bubbles erupting from my lips, seemingly unconcerned with the life seeping from my lungs.

My hands release, floating back downwards as if my muscles have realized the futility of the fight before my brain. And I picture her again, as I have so many times since she left. She's the reason why I'm here. Why I've sacrificed everything.

It's her I'm thinking of when the beauty of the water fades to black.

The Resort is available now.